TRAITORS, CANNIBALS, HIGHLANDERS, AND VIKINGS

Carolyn Jean Nicholson

Somewhat Grumpy Press

TRAITORS, CANNIBALS, HIGHLANDERS, AND VIKINGS

Published by arrangement with Somewhat Grumpy Press Inc. Halifax, Nova Scotia, Canada. The Somewhat Grumpy Press name and Pallas' cat logo are registered trademarks.

ISBN 978-1-7380743-3-4 (paperback)

ISBN 978-1-7380743-4-1 (eBook)

September 2024, v4

CONTENTS

DEDICATION

This book is dedicated to my grandfather, the Reverend John Finlay Mc-Donald, whose ancestors, William and Ann McDonald and their infant son, Finlay, came to Pictou County, Nova Scotia, from the Highlands of Scotland in the early 1800s; and Malcolm Nicolson and Margaret McPhie (my third great-grandparents), and their son, Donald, and four other sons, who came to Prince Edward Island in 1841 from the Isle of Skye, Scotland.

MAPS

Map of Nova Scotia: Early 1800s townships, courtesy Peter Landry, History of Nova Scotia: Book 3, The Road to Being Canada (1815-1867) http://www.blupete.com/Hist/NovaScotiaBk3/Ch01.ht

Map of Prince Edward Island: Early townships (modified), courtesy National Archives, Samuel Holland, Library and Archives Canada, H2/204/1775, NMC 18146, http://central.bac-lac.gc.ca/.redirect?app=fonandcol&id=3705866&lang=eng

Map of Scotland: Selected story locations, by Eric Gaba (Sting – fr:Sting) - Own work; Topography: NASA Shuttle Radar Topography Mission (SRTM3 v.2) data (public domain); Bathymetry: NGDC ETOPO1 data (public domain); Reference used for confirmation for the additional data: ViaMichelin; Locator map: composition of Image: British_Isles_Northern_Ireland.svg, Image:British_Isles_Scotland.svg and Image:British_Isles_Wales.svg (modified) created by Cnbrb under PD., CC BY-SA 4.0, https://commons.wikimedia.org/w/index.php?curid=3216830
Modified as follows: Some locations added. https://commons.wikimedia.org/wiki/File:Scotland_topographic_map-en.jpg

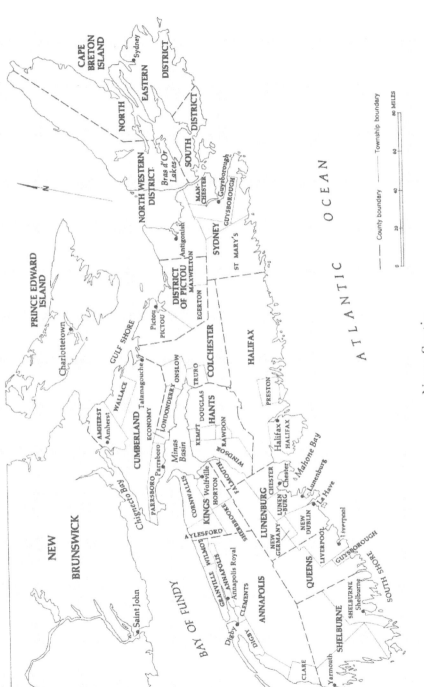

Nova Scotia

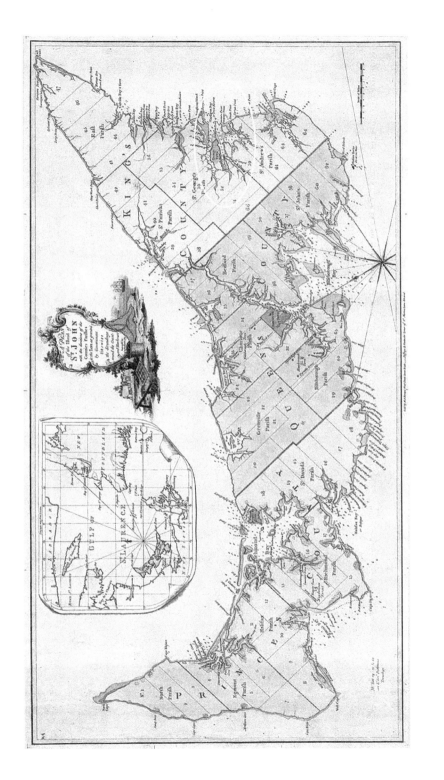

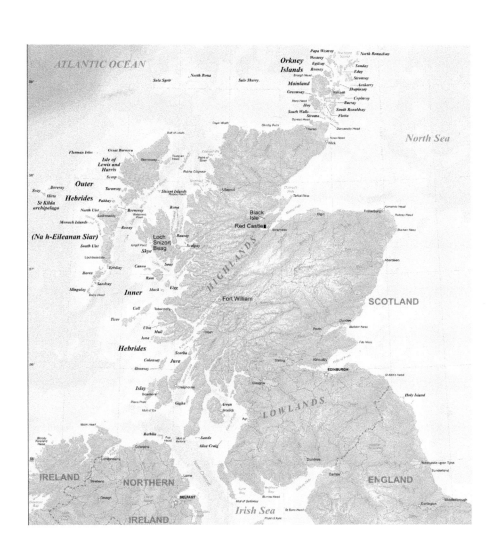

Therefore, since we are surrounded by so great a cloud of witnesses, let us also lay aside every weight, ... and let us run with perseverance the race that is set before us.

Hebrews 12:1

Chapter One

CAROLINE MORTON

Present Day: Halifax, Nova Scotia

The four sisters climbed into Elizabeth's black Volkswagen Jetta and headed out of Halifax. The weather was warm and bright, the leaves a verdant green, the highway not too crowded after they turned east at Truro.

"We're glad you decided to leave your office and have a bit of an adventure," Joan said, looking over her shoulder into the backseat where Caroline was watching the countryside go by and Janice was checking her text messages.

"I don't know why you talked me into this," Caroline said. "I need to be working on my book."

"We were worried about you. You've been working on that book for over a year and, as far as I can tell, not getting past the first chapter. You need to get out, enjoy yourself, maybe get a job and re-connect with some of your old friends or make some new ones. You're only thirty-two, for heaven's sake."

"Still not feeling up to it. It's just too soon, after ...."

"We loved Malcolm, too, Caroline. He was the perfect husband for you, and we all miss him terribly. But he wouldn't want you to hide yourself away in your little condo; he loved you too much for that."

"I know. But I have no energy and my migraines are still almost constant. You'll have to give me a little longer. We both loved our jobs as archivists working for the Nova Scotia Archives and enjoyed our vacations together, but now that's all gone, too."

"Where shall we go first?" Elizabeth asked, wanting to change the subject.

"Let's head down to the Bridgeville Cemetery. It's a lovely drive through the country and once there, we can check on the McDonald graves," Caroline suggested. The others nodded. It was a familiar place.

After half an hour, they turned off at Exit 25 and found the East Side East River Road. As the houses and farms became fewer, Caroline said, "I always enjoy this drive. It feels like we're moving back in time to another era." The others nodded again. She always said that.

"Look," Elizabeth said. "There's the beginning of the road signs in Gaelic. The whole of the East River used to be Gaelic-speaking communities in the 1700s and 1800s. There were general stores, schools, wagon and harness shops, tanneries, and lots and lots of one hundred plus acre farms."

It wasn't that the sisters didn't know this. It was just a reminder of how very different this river was in the present, as they drove through the peaceful, green lushness of the quiet fields and forest that surrounded them.

"I think the end of this farming community began once the Gaelic speakers learned English and after the railways were available to whisk people away to the four winds," Caroline said, "How I wish we could go back and see the East River as it was and speak to the people."

"You always say that," Joan remarked. "There's the sign for Bridgeville. The trees get a little closer to the road each year. Where's the turnoff to the bridge? Oh, there, I see it now."

"Well, the little church has survived another winter. Looks in good shape. And the bridge hasn't moved." Caroline smiled. They crossed the bridge.

"Now here's the intersection with the West Side East River Road," Elizabeth noted. They turned left and headed to the cemetery. "This road sure needs some attention. Besides the lumps and bumps, there's now grass growing up through the cracks. In a few years, there won't be a paved road."

Soon, up ahead, they spied the gates to the old pioneer cemetery, where many of the original settlers in the area were buried.

"We're here. Don't forget to put on your sunhats and let's lock our purses in the trunk," Caroline said.

"Now, Caroline," Joan said, "who exactly do you think is going to steal our purses—the farmer on the hill across the valley or the cows on the other side of the river?"

"I guess you're right—but I still want to lock up my purse. The rest of you do as you please."

The four women strolled over the grassy carpet under the shady trees, pausing often to point out some of the gravestones. It was a small cemetery and many of the stones had fallen over.

"Look, there's Catherine McDonald and her husband, Robert Grant Chisholm, and four of their sons."

"Remind me again. Catherine is our great grandfather's youngest sister?"

"That's right." Caroline softly patted the hard, grey granite. "And her sister, Isabel McDonald Fraser, is over there on her first husband's gravestone. I think Helen McDonald—the oldest sister who was living with Catherine—is buried here as well, but I've never found her grave. Flora married Evan McKinnon of Sunny Brae and she's buried there. Of course, Elspet McDonald McKay—she ended up calling herself Elizabeth—lived in Sydney, Cape Breton."

"I don't know how you manage to keep all those names straight," Janice said.

"Oh, they're not just names to me; they're real people who had real lives right in this area. I can almost see them in my mind's eye."

"Some people might think you're a bit odd," Janice smiled.

"I am a bit odd." Caroline smiled ruefully.

Caroline and Joan walked up the little knoll in the middle of the cemetery that held the oldest of the still standing headstones. Joan examined William McDonald's headstone. She had paid for it to be repaired and resituated on its base.

"Steven did a good job. It's still holding up. How about Mary's stone, as well as her husband's and daughter's?"

"All in good shape now that you've had them cleaned. So is William and Janet's son, John's headstone with all his family members inscribed around the sides."

The visit brought back many warm memories of previous ancestor hunts, and even though it turned out that this William McDonald and his family was not their William McDonald Caroline had so thoroughly researched him that they knew where he came from—Kiltarlity Parish, Scotland—and that in 1801 he came over on the ship Sarah of Liverpool with his wife, Janet, and their five children and bought land in March 1802 from a previous grant holder, Alexander Cameron, in St. Paul on the East Branch of the East River. Inexplicably, their warm feelings toward this William had continued, maybe because they had found out almost nothing about their own ancestors, William and Ann McDonald and their son Finlay, except for the location of their land grant on the West Branch, East River.

Joan had wandered back down the hill and was checking out another stone in the process of tilting over when Caroline said, "Guys, look what I found on William's gravestone."

"Give me a minute to get there. This little knoll gets steeper every year." Joan was puffing a little.

"That's because you eat too many cookies," Janice suggested, as she puffed up the other side.

"Could be, but you're none too swift yourself," Joan retorted.

"Just a little kink in my hip from those ten-kilometre walks," Janice said.

"Right." Joan looked unimpressed with her explanation.

"Okay, we're here. What did you find?" Joan said.

"This little shiny, oval, black stone." Caroline showed them the stone in her palm.

"You called us over for that—that pebble!" Joan was laughing as she stared at Caroline's find.

"No, look, it's got a design on this side." Caroline was totally taken up by the mysterious object.

"Oh, yeah, it looks like the etching of a stylized bird. Could be Celtic, maybe," Joan said.

Elizabeth just arrived at the top of the knoll to hear the smirks and see the rolling eyes of her twin sisters.

"There's some scratching on the back as well," Caroline said. "Can't make it out. But it looks like—but it can't be, I'm sure—runes. You know that ancient kind of Germanic or Scandinavian lettering."

"Whatever." Joan shrugged. "Put it back on the gravestone. Probably someone visited the cemetery and left the stone as a memento of their visit."

"Oh, you mean like when people in times long-ago used to always put a pebble on a gravestone after a visit." Caroline said.

"Yes. Like that. Maybe William McDonald has a living relative in the area," Janice said.

"I think I'll keep it." Caroline polished it on her sleeve and put it in the pocket of her hoodie.

"No, put it back, Caroline. It belongs with the gravestone." Elizabeth would never have said she was superstitious, but, well, it was part of the gravestone, wasn't it?

They visited William and Flora (McMillan) McKenzie's graves in the Elgin Cemetery at the far end of the Elgin Road before the afternoon was over. Their third great-grandparents and their two children, Isabel and John, had arrived from Urquhart Parish on the Black Isle, Scotland, in 1801 on the ship Sarah of Liverpool.

"Their stones look pristine even though they died over one hundred and fifty years ago," Joan said.

They spent some time picking up the twigs and dry grasses around the headstones. They were far out in the country and the air was fresh and clean and the cemetery quiet and peaceful.

"What is it about graveyards?" Joan asked. "I always feel so, so, maybe the word is serene, almost like I had gone away for a while." The others agreed.

"Well, let's go get some supper and check into our hotel in New Glasgow. I'm glad you suggested this trip. I feel better already," Caroline said.

"Ready for another road trip?" Elizabeth asked.

"No, ready to get back to work on my book."

The other three glanced at each other with dismay.

After supper, the sisters went back to the hotel and, after check-in, went to their respective rooms. Unbeknownst to them, Caroline—who had a spare set of keys to Elizabeth's car—slipped out to go back to the cemetery, convinced that the black stone had some special meaning.

It had never been there on any of their previous visits, had it? People who put a pebble on a gravestone didn't put designs or carvings on them, did they? No, I'm sure they did not. Somehow that stone is meant for me, she thought, and then immediately remonstrated with herself. *You must be kidding to believe that! But still ....*

The sun was low in the sky when she arrived. Locking her purse in the car, she retraced her steps to William McDonald's gravestone. The object of her desire was still there. Looking around furtively, she grabbed the stone and put it in her jeans pocket as the sun sank behind the trees that ringed the cemetery.

I'd better get back to the hotel before dark, she thought, and headed for the car.

As she put her hand on the car door handle, she felt the hair on the back of her neck stand on end, and turning, she saw some pale figures against the tree line. With shaky hands, she opened the door and jumped in, locking the door and turning the key.

Slow down, slow down, she told herself, as she tried to drive quickly on the narrow, bumpy road beside the river.

Her focus on the road ahead didn't prevent the words of the wraiths forming in her mind. *"We're all here."* She shook her head, trying to dislodge the words and keep her eyes on the road.

She was still shaky when she arrived back at the hotel. Entering the lobby, she saw Joan pacing back and forth.

"Where've you been?" Joan asked with a scowl.

"Oh, just out for a little drive. What are the rest of you up to?"

"We're going to get together in Elizabeth's room and watch some TV. We've got popcorn."

"I'll get us some drinks from the dispensing machine. See you up there."

The next morning, they started back to Halifax.

"So now that we've pried you out of the house—and you seem to have enjoyed yourself—maybe we can plan a longer trip?"

"I don't think so," Caroline felt a little frustrated with her sisters' continued pressure. "Not this year. Maybe next when I'm finished the book."

"Look, at your pace, that may be in ten years. What would it hurt to take a little break from time to time? It's good for your mental health, you know."

"I'll think about it, okay." Her sisters took the hint and conversation moved onto other topics.

During lulls in the conversation, Caroline reminisced about her childhood. It had been boring for a girl who was interested in travel and adventure—no road trips or flights to interesting destinations. But she had taken a degree in library science due to her migraines. That's where she met Malcolm and her friend, Ruth. After she and Malcolm married, there had been some enjoyable tours to Europe, Turkey, and Morocco, but these weren't really adventures and always carefully planned to minimize the chance of migraines.

Maybe, she thought, *there are no real adventures anymore*. Climbing mountains didn't interest her, and neither did hang gliding off mountains. What was left? It seemed all the new lands had been discovered and explored. The latest craze for those who were, well, crazy, was going to Mars. That seemed like a suicide mission. No, there didn't seem to be much left that one could consider real adventure. She reached into her pocket and rubbed the stone with the rough etching. It felt smooth and warm.

Her reverie was broken when Janice asked, "Do you know why you're so interested in ancestors, Caroline?

"I think so. The first people who crossed the ocean and came to Nova Scotia were true adventurers. For them and for their families, everything was at stake—not just their futures but their very lives."

"Like our McKenzies and McDonalds?" Janice suggested.

"Exactly. Imagine coming to a place with no houses, no stores, no roads, no fields, no nothings and having to build a life from scratch in the middle of a forest. Imagine women being pregnant, giving birth, and raising children where there were no doctors, no hospitals, no baby formula, no baby clothes or children's clothes for that matter, nothing. I can't even imagine."

"But there were people here—the Mi'kmaq," said Joan.

"Oh, certainly. I guess I was just thinking about our own ancestors from the Highlands of Scotland. They were tenant farmers there and here there was no place to build a farm."

"There are hardly any trees in the Highlands, for sure. The Mi'kmaq must have wondered about these people who were completely unsuited for living in the forest as they did," said Caroline.

"Unfortunately for the Mi'kmaq, as soon as the Highlanders got the hang of chopping down trees, they went into the lumber business and cut down every tree in Pictou District," Elilzabeth said.

"It always makes me sad to think about that: the people of the forest who soon had no forest," said Joan.

"I hope things are getting better for them now. If anyone deserves more support and kindly treatment, it's the Mi'kmaq," Caroline said, looking downcast.

The others nodded and they were reflective for a moment.

"So, back to my question about why you're so interested in ancestors," Janice repeated. "Is that why you dig and dig for any little detail that will help you imagine their lives, help you get closer to them, to who they are? To their experience?"

"Yeah, so many of them have been completely forgotten even by their own families. Most didn't even get a gravestone since there weren't any available—and even if there had been, they wouldn't have been able to afford them. And besides, there was no monetary system in the early days."

"But you care about them, don't you?" asked Janice.

"Yes, I do. They are true heroes and adventurers. Why make up fictional heroes when there are real heroes to be found, if only you have the time and patience to search for them?"

The other sisters nodded. It sort of made sense. But, unlike Caroline, they had careers and families to get back to.

"By the way, how are your migraines these days? Elizabeth asked.

"Manageable, if my environment is quiet and orderly. Or the weather isn't too variable."

"Good to hear." The sisters all knew that the migraines were some indication how well Caroline was going to be on any given day. Despite her wish for adventure, she had even chosen her profession based on keeping them under control.

"So hopefully this outing has inspired you," Janice said as they arrived at the door of Caroline's condo building. "Suppose you take the rest of the day to write, and we meet tomorrow to see how it's going?"

"I'm not sure ...."

Joan pitched in. "We'll go somewhere they have good muffins—no, banana chocolate-chip muffins, and excellent coffee. What about Second Cup in the Mall? We can meet in the food court."

"Okay. See you tomorrow." She closed the car door and waved goodbye to her sisters.

Caroline lived in a small condominium apartment furnished with a few precious antiques: a cross-stitched fire screen that had belonged to her great-great grandmother, a one hundred-and-forty-year-old glass-fronted cabinet holding some crystal and good china, and a couple of wing-back chairs. She had a four-poster bed with petal-pink sheets and a homemade quilt in shades of pink, mauve, and blue, with an embroidered picture of a unicorn over it; something she had embroidered herself many years before. Her tiny office contained a desk, lateral file, and a bookshelf, all piled with books and research material. The apartment got the morning sun, and the large balcony, overlooking the Public Gardens, held metal-frame chairs and little metal and glass tables.

Malcolm's picture, with that brilliant smile and his arm around her, was on the desk where she could give him a kiss and say good morning every day. He with the blond hair and she with her curly brown hair and both with bright, blue eyes, both looking out at the happy future before them, before, before ... the diagnosis.

She often thought how lucky she was that Malcolm had left her enough money to buy the apartment outright and live there, if frugally. Tours and cruises were not within her budget, and the years of caring for her husband and the grief and depression that followed had left her unable to work, thus her decision to write a book about her ancestors in order to find a purpose for her life.

I'm never going to be a world-class writer, she told herself, but maybe I can tell some interesting stories that people will appreciate and enjoy.

She set the black stone on her tiny bedside table and crawled beneath the fine Egyptian cotton pink sheets and pulled the quilt up to her shoulders. She enjoyed going to bed and going to sleep, although some nights she had insomnia, not falling asleep until three or four in the morning. Those nights she often entertained herself by thinking through story ideas or trying to see how many of her great-great-grandparents she could name. It worked better than counting sheep.

"Well, Samson, she's sleeping peacefully."

 "Aye. Seems so."

 "What are we going to tell the rest?"

 "That I think she needs our help."

 "And we need to find a way to ...."

 "Still trying to figure that out, Martha. I've called a meeting of the firsts—all of us—and I better have a plan by then."

Caroline woke with the sun. As she got up and tried to run a comb through her curly brown hair, she noticed the black stone seemed to have moved from the spot she had placed it. Picking it up, she rolled it between her fingers, enjoying the satiny smooth finish and the roughness of the little etching. She wasn't looking forward to meeting her sisters, as she had written little yesterday. She wasn't able to add more before it was time to meet them.

"So, what are you going to have besides coffee?" Elizabeth asked, as she took off her sweater and put it over the back of the chair. The mall wasn't too busy, so they had no problem finding a table with four chairs in the food court.

"A chocolate-chip banana muffin, of course," said Caroline. "What are you having?"

"A brownie. That's my favourite," Elizabeth said.

Joan and Janice said they were just having coffee.

After getting their favourite food and drink from the coffee shop, they settled around the table, prepared to listen.

"So, read us the first chapter," Joan said.

"Well, it's still pretty much a sketch rather than a complete chapter."

"Whatever, just read us what you've got so far," Janice said.

Caroline read as much as she had written.

"I guess that's fine as far as it goes, but you're not making much progress. Even after a year, it's just a sketch, as you say," Elizabeth said, enjoying another sip of her coffee.

Caroline nodded in agreement and took a bite of her muffin. *Not enough chocolate chips,* she thought.

"Which of our ancestors are you interested in? I can't tell too much from what you read," Joan said.

"The ones I've got the most material on are Samson and Martha Moore of Truro Township, Nova Scotia. They came to Nova Scotia in 1761 from Londonderry, New Hampshire. Their parents, James and Isabel, were from Londonderry, Ireland. In the early 1600s, King James the Sixth of Scotland and the First of England, decided to colonize northern Ireland with English and Scottish Protestants and push out the native Irish who were Gaelic-speaking Roman Catholics. As you know, that has caused war and bloodshed right down to our day."

"You certainly know your history, but how are you going to make that into a book?" Joan took another sip of her coffee.

"That's just the problem. I'm not sure how to do it, or I would have done it by now."

"How do you choose which ancestors are going to go into your book?" Janice was still waiting for her black coffee to cool enough to drink.

"The most interesting, I suppose, or the most accomplished."

"In a good way, I hope."

"Well, as far as I can tell, all our ancestors were very well-educated, civilized people—and that's why I like to research and write about them."

"What if you found an ancestor that who wasn't educated or civilized?" Elizabeth made air quotes for civilized and smiled.

"Well, I wouldn't want to write about anyone who didn't make our family look good, or, rather, look bad. Why would anyone want to make their family look bad? That doesn't make sense. So, hopefully, none of our ancestors were nasty, uncivilized people."

"Wait a minute, you had your DNA done recently, didn't you? Didn't it say you were four percent Norse? I don't recall the Vikings were civilized!" Joan grinned.

"You can't always go by those tests. It could just be some testing anomaly. Anyway, I'm not interested in anyone who isn't an asset to the family."

After Caroline finished speaking, the twins left the table and shortly came back from Second Cup with brownies. They both looked sheepish, as they had initially foregone any sweets. The coffee break ended with the agreement to meet again in a few days.

"Try to have chapter one finished by then," Elizabeth said.

Caroline nodded, as they all rose from the table and gathered up purses and sweaters before heading to their respective cars.

"She's sleeping soundly again, Samson. So, tell me how many are going to be attending the meeting?"

"Maybe fourteen or so—all the firsts from Pictou, Colchester, and St. John's Island."

"You mean Prince Edward Island."

"Oh, aye."

"Where are we meeting?" Martha asked.

"Tomorrow, here at Caroline's. We've got to find a way to help her write this book."

"Agreed, but that's not going to be easy."

"We'll find a way if we all put our heads together—metaphorically speaking, of course."

"Of course."

The following day, Caroline spent hours before the computer, determined to finish the first chapter. It was so difficult when you couldn't really imagine your ancestor's personalities and circumstances. After much pondering, she thought, maybe I just need another good night's sleep and a little more research. She ate her supper and read for a while before curling up in bed.

"Well, everyone is here? Right! We've gathered to see what we can do to help Caroline write this book," Samson said.

"So far," Martha chimed in, "she's only got a bit of an outline for chapter one, even though she's been doing research and writing for over a year."

"How are we going to help her?" Malcolm Nicolson asked.

"I know," his son Donald said, "let's help her out in her dreams. We're from the Isle of Skye, so dreams, fairies, omens, and portents are our bread and butter."

"I don't see how any of those things are going to get this book written," Samson said.

"But don't you see," interrupted William McDonald, "she can come with us and see for herself."

"Probably scare her to death is what you'll do," David Stewart said.

"Nay," his wife Mary said. "I think she's up for a little adventure."

"A little adventure is not what we're talking about. Did any of you have a 'little adventure'? If so, say 'Aye'. I thought not. We're talking about authentic experience."

The rest were silent for a moment.

"All right," Samson said, "nothing spared—but nothing added either. I'm thinking of you, McDonald. You can be a bit over-the-top at times."

McDonald grinned.

The Moores, Stewarts, Beggs, McDonalds, McKenzies, and Nicolsons all agreed to try out Donald's suggestion. They hoped it would help Caroline.

"Now," Samson said, "I hope we can all agree that at the beginning of the adventure we will introduce ourselves—if she doesn't already know or guess who we are—but after that she will not know what will happen or how the adventure will turn out. The experience needs to be real."

"Will she know any background to the adventure?" Martha asked.

"I think she can know the history leading up to the adventure but, again, not what happens during the adventure," Samson said, looking around the group.

"Agreed?" They all nodded their agreement.

Just before the meeting ended, Janet Begg asked, "What is the book about? We need to know to best be of help."

Samson smiled broadly. "It's about us—the firsts."

"The first of her ancestors to come to Nova Scotia?" Ann McDonald asked.

"To Nova Scotia and Prince Edward Island," Malcolm Nicolson corrected.

"Someone actually remembers us?" William and Flora McKenzie spoke in sync.

"Caroline does, and she wants others to know about us. We're going to be in a book!"

Caroline appreciated that her sisters cared enough to support her in her research and writing. She was thinking of that as she touched the black stone one last time before she went to bed the next night. *But they won't be too impressed that I've gone back to doing research*, she thought as she drifted off to sleep.

"Caroline, would you like to come with us?"

Caroline slowly awoke from the strange dream. Propping herself on her elbows, she wondered what had caused her to wake up. She heard the voice again.

"Caroline, would you like to come with us?"

Caroline fell back on her pillow and pulled the covers over her head. *What was that? I'm hearing things. Oh, my goodness, my mental health must be worse than I even thought.* She stayed, huddled under the covers, until full daylight before she got up, tentatively at first, to start her day.

The following night, she had the same experience. I'm going to stay up all night, she thought, and find out what is happening. Why am I hearing voices? Nothing happened. After three sleepless nights, she finally fell asleep out of sheer exhaustion, forgetting this was the day she was to meet with her sisters.

When Joan arrived to find out why she missed the meeting and why Caroline wasn't responding to her cell phone, she got no response to her knock at the door. She let herself in with her key. Finding Caroline like a lump under the quilt, she shook her shoulder. "Caroline, what's the matter? Are you ill? Wake up! Come on, wake up and tell me what's happening."

Caroline, pale and with dark circles under her eyes, pulled down the quilt so she could peek out at her sister. "Oh, Joanie, I've been having such strange dreams and hearing voices. I've stayed up for three nights to try to figure out what's happening."

Joan noticed the black stone on Caroline's bedside table. "That's the stone from William McDonald's grave!"

Caroline fell back to sleep and Joan left to tell her sisters that Caroline was ... was acting strangely.

The sisters arrived at Caroline's place and found her in a state of agitation. "It wouldn't hurt for you to see your doctor," Janice suggested.

"And just what would I tell her, that I'm hearing voices?!"

"Well," suggested Elizabeth, "that you're having trouble sleeping. Perhaps she could prescribe something just to get you back to your normal sleep pattern."

"I suppose if this keeps up much longer, I'll have to do something. Maybe I'll take an extra amount of melatonin tonight and see if that helps."

"Promise us that you'll make an appointment with your doctor if the melatonin doesn't fix the problem," Joan said.

"I suppose I'll have to. Thanks for your concern. I'm going to try to get some sleep right now."

"Okay. We'll call you soon and see how you're doing," Elizabeth said. "And if you don't answer, we'll drop by again."

Caroline nodded and pulled the covers up to her shoulders. The sisters left, shaking their heads at the situation.

"Well, that didn't work out too well. Any other suggestions?" Samson glanced at the glum-looking firsts.

"I told you this was just going to scare her," David Stewart said.

The others nodded. It was hard to deny the facts.

"What's our next big idea?" Samson seemed determined to arrive at a solution.

"I know," Martha Moore said. "Let me come to her in a dream and just suggest how lovely it would be to have an adventure that could help with her book. Just plant the idea in her mind. You know she's always wanted to have a real adventure, so might this idea appeal to her?"

"We should just grab her and pull her into an adventure. No time to think about it, just find herself in the middle of the action."

McDonald grinned at the effect this would have on an unsuspecting Caroline.

"That's the trouble with you, McDonald. Always leaping before you look. And you don't ever learn your lesson. How many times did you almost get yourself killed for all your illegal stills and sheep stealing?" Samson said.

"Calm down, Samson. You asked for ideas. That was an idea."

"Right." Samson rolled his eyes.

"Any other ideas? Good ideas?"

The rest pondered their options as Samson scowled at them.

"Alright, Martha, it's your turn to convince Caroline that she should come with us."

"What shall I wear?" Martha asked as she looked around the group.

"Wear whatever you would meet her in," her husband suggested.

Caroline gradually woke up from her deep sleep. It was late in the afternoon. But she had caught up on some necessary rest. She made some coffee and ate a cranberry orange muffin. *Stale.*

As she drank her coffee, she tried to imagine what was disturbing her sleep. Hearing the phone ring, she picked it up, only to find a credit card scammer on the other end of the line. It happened so often now she hardly gave it a thought. She picked up the black stone from off her bedside table and enjoyed the smooth surface with the rough etching.

I know, she thought. I'll search for this image on the internet. Google knows everything. I might find out why the stone is so attractive to me. An hour of searching didn't result in any satisfaction, except that the image might be of Norse origin. *Norse,* she thought, *not interested in those blood-thirsty Vikings,* and threw the stone into the drawer of her bedside table.

That night Caroline dreamed about a petite woman in home-spun clothing covered with an apron. She had a linen cap that covered her hair and wooden shoes on her feet. Just to add to the appeal, she brought along her little daughter, and namesake, Martha. Caroline was enjoying the dream until Martha asked, "Would you like to come with us?"

"No," she said out loud. "No. Leave me alone." She was awake for an hour after that, worrying that her mental health was worse than she thought. *What kind of condition caused people to hear voices?* She couldn't recall, but it wasn't a good sign.

A week passed and Caroline began thinking the strange dreams were over. She had assured her sisters she was sleeping better and had agreed to meet them soon to read them what she had written, though she had not written much more. But the dreams were not over.

McDonald showed up in full Scottish regalia and playing the bagpipes to the lovely tune of "Rowan Tree." Caroline loved the bagpipes and was fully enjoying the dream until the piper ended his recital and came right over, reached out his hand towards her and said, "Come with me, lassie!"

Caroline woke up with a start, yelling, "No, leave me alone! Go away!"

"I told you, McDonald, that such a tactic was just going to scare her. Now look what you've done!

"Thought it was worth a try. Your ideas," he scanned the rest of the firsts, "haven't worked either, David Stewart."

"No, but you've really scared her. Now we'll have to work twice as hard to find a solution."

McDonald shrugged. The rest of the firsts looked disapproving.

"Now what?" Martha asked Samson.

"Not sure. Let's all mull it over. Surely, among all of us, there is an answer."

That morning, an idea came to Caroline: exorcism. She looked it up on Google. Maybe a little too extreme, she decided. *I'm really not getting enough sleep.* She spent the day listlessly reading over some old research and trying to imagine what her ancestors were like: big and brave; small and scared? She didn't know.

"This is just not working," Samson sighed.

The rest were silent. Martha cleared her throat to speak, but then changed her mind.

"It's disappointing that she thinks we're demons or something. We're all Presbyterians, aren't we?"

They all nodded. More silence.

"I know," Samson said. "I'll appear to her in our church. She goes to church every Sunday, so that should be a comforting sign."

"Can't hurt to try," McKenzie said. And the rest nodded agreement.

Caroline took ten milligrams of melatonin and climbed into bed. Amid her deep sleep, Samson appeared in a lovely little church surrounded by trees and flowers. The inside of the building was polished wood and there was a little wooden pulpit and a few chairs to one side for the choir. There was a large chair for the minister, made of carved wood with a red cloth cushion seat. Samson was dressed in the weekday linen clothing of a farmer and holding the hand of his youngest daughter, three-year-old Martha.

It was a lovely dream. Everything was sweet and peaceful. Caroline recognized little Martha from a previous dream. The child smiled at her and waved her little hand, lisping to Caroline, "Would you like to come with us, Miss Caroline?"

Maybe it was the peacefulness of the dream or perhaps it was the invitation by the sweet little child she had seen before, or it could have been that she was used to the dreams and found the invitation tempting, even adventurous. Whatever the reason, Caroline said, "Yes."

But Samson and Martha and the rest of the firsts were in for a surprise.

CHAPTER TWO

PURITANS — THE MORTONS

1760: MASSACHUSETTS TO NOVA SCOTIA

I awoke in a strange bed. I knew I was in a strange bed because my feet were sticking out over the edge of the bed and were quite cold as the short blankets were pulled up over my shoulders. The mattress was lumpy and the linens scratchy and there was a faint hint of mustiness. Where on earth was I? If this was a dream, where were little Martha and her family?

The bed was surrounded by linen curtains, so I peeked out and found myself in a small room with a wide plank floor. In the light of the small, glazed window I could see, against the far wall, a washstand with a bowl and pitcher. Closer to the bed was a chair with a valise and clothing on it. I got up, washed, dried with a linen hand towel, and combed my hair with a conveniently placed comb near the bowl, then turned to the clothing. Taking off my pyjamas, I pulled on the petticoats, floor-length blue linen-woollen skirt, linen blouse with a wide, square collar, then a contraption that looked like a bodice and laced up in the front. Everything fit. Pulling on the stockings of unknown construction, and stepping into the buckled shoes, I hoped I had arranged everything in the right order. Leaving the hat, as I didn't know how to put it on, I opened the door and saw a set of stairs.

Holding tightly onto the railing, I went down gingerly, as the steps were steep and narrow. As I descended the stairs, I could see a few small, glazed windows in what seemed like whitewashed wooden walls, the smallness of the windows making the room quite dark. At the foot of the stairs was a large room with a huge fireplace, the embers glowing and occasionally spitting off some sparks, and brightening that corner of the room. Around a trestle table in the centre of the room were benches and a group of adults and children eating something, probably breakfast.

"Caroline, join us for breakfast! Come, sit here. Will you have some bacon and eggs?" the older woman standing near the fireplace asked.

"Eggs and toast," I said hesitantly. "And would you have some tea?"

"Sorry, no tea, but we do have beer to drink."

"Thank you."

"Now, I suppose you're wondering who we are?" the older man said.

"Indeed," I smiled weakly, as I took a sip of beer and tried to decide if I liked the taste. A little watery, I thought.

"I'm Elkanah Morton, and this is my wife Elizabeth Holmes, and you're in Plymouth Colony."

He was a man with a white beard, perhaps in his sixties, dressed in breeches and stockings with buckled shoes and with a linen shirt with very large sleeves, covered with a vest with many buttons, perhaps made of fine wool. His wife may have been a little younger, and she wore much the same costume as I had just put on.

"Oh, Mr. Morton, how pleased I am to meet you and your wife. My sixth great-grandparents, I think."

"Quite so, and this is my son, my only surviving son, Elkanah, and his wife, Rebecca Tupper. And these are their four children. Children, say hello to your cousin, Caroline."

They smiled. I smiled. I understood why they called me cousin. How could you explain to the children that I was a descendant, a descendant specifically of the child, Lemuel?

"Now this biggest boy is Lemuel, born in 1753, his brother, Roland, and sisters, Sarah, and Mary.

"How old are you now, Lemuel?" Elkanah asked.

"Seven years old, Grandfather," Lemuel said, with a faint smile.

The children looked confused as to who I might be. I didn't blame them—I was confused myself. What was going on? How did I get here?

I had read extensively about my Puritan ancestors, but had never expected to meet them, naturally, so I was excited and pleased as well as confused. As we ate, the adults picked up where they had left off when I came down the stairs.

Elkanah, a tall, dark-haired, energetic thirty-year-old, said, "We have a reply now from Governor Charles Lawrence of Nova Scotia regarding our letter to him about our expectations if we decided to immigrate to Nova Scotia in 1760. He's met all our demands, so we have a decision to make."

His father stroked his white beard and nodded slowly, "I suspect, my son, that you have already decided, and your mother and I are about to leave the place of our birth and the graves of our ancestors and children for the wilds of Nova Scotia."

Elizabeth, his mother, was stirring a pot with her back to her son. "It's going to be hard for us, son, as our children are buried here. And I don't think your sister, Betty, will go. Her husband, Mr. Tallman, seems content to stay in Dartmouth Township."

"What about Phebe and Seth? They're newly married and free to start over in a new land. Does Mr. Winslow fancy going to Nova Scotia?" Elkanah asked.

I noticed a whiff of concern when Elkanah asked about Phebe and Seth. Did he want them to go, I wondered.

"I think they plan to go along with us, so our family will consist of your father and I, Phebe and Seth, you and Rebecca, and your children—ten altogether," his mother replied. Then she looked at me. "What about Caroline?"

Elkanah smiled at me. "Of course, she's coming with us."

I was excited. I would get to see the first of my ancestors to arrive in Nova Scotia!

"Do we know how many families are going altogether?" Elkanah, Sr., asked.

"I believe there are about one hundred and twenty-five families bound for Cornwallis Township and another one hundred and ten or there abouts for Horton Township," his son answered.

"It's a good deal for you and your sons, but I don't look forward to the move for your mother and I," his father said.

"Aye, it is a good deal for my family and the others who sign up: free transportation paid for by the Nova Scotia Government, up to a thousand acres of land with no taxes for ten years, representative government, freedom of religion, and the freedom to run our townships there as we do here. What more could you ask for?"

"What will you take with you?" I asked.

"Well, Cousin," Elkanah said, "certainly all our household goods, and all our farm equipment, as many of our animals as possible, as well as this house."

"You're going to take your house?" I smiled in amazement.

"Aye. We take it apart, of course, then we'll sell our property here in Plymouth, so we'll have some cash to take along as well."

I tried to imagine putting a house on a ship, but no one else seemed to think this at all odd. "How much material can you take with you?" I asked.

"Each family can take two tons with them." Elkanah, Jr. said.

"Goodness, then how many ships are we talking about altogether?"

"I heard there would be twenty-two ships," Elkanah's father said.

"We don't have a lot of time to get ready. We need to leave by mid to late May to be ready to prepare the fields and plant in June. The growing season in Nova Scotia is shorter than in Massachusetts, so we can't waste any time." Elkanah, Jr., said.

"How hard will it be to prepare the land for planting?" I asked.

"Comparatively easy. The Acadians farmed the land until the English deported them to New England and elsewhere in 1755."

"Yes, the Acadian land," I nodded.

"Right you are. I hope those people realize how lucky they are that the English didn't just shoot them when they wouldn't swear allegiance to the King. I know many who were not treated so daintily," Elkanah's father said, referring to the expulsion of the French-speaking Acadians who had lived in Nova Scotia up to 1755.

"Oh, you're right about that," I agreed. "They slaughtered the High-landers after the Battle of Culloden Moor in Scotland in 1746. Chased them down to their homes and killed them in front of the wives and children, then burned their homes and their crops. After that, they forbid them to wear their type of clothing, to speak their language, play their music, and forced them to learn English. It was terrible cruelty."

"That's what I meant when I said the Acadians were treated daintily." He nodded.

"And I guess you would know a bit about how the English treat dis-senters?" I added.

"Oh, aye, our ancestors were forced to flee England to live in Leyden, Holland, to escape the King's ire that we separated from the Church of England. Lots of the people who first settled Plymouth Colony in 1620 and thereafter, had been thrown into jail for their beliefs."

"Well, I do think that the Acadians and their Indian allies were just pawns in the greater war—the French and Indian War—between England and France for the control of North America. Lots of people get caught up in widespread conflict."

They looked at me askance. I suppose because the French and Indian War was still ongoing, and they had often fought with the English in that war. My opinions needed time and distance from all the terrible turmoil of their times. I changed the subject. "So, if I recall correctly, your ancestors were George Morton and Juliana Carpenter, who arrived in Plymouth Colony on the ship Anne in 1623?"

"Aye, they had five children, and we are descended from the youngest, who was born at sea, Ephraim. Ephraim had a son, George, and George had a son, Ephraim, my father. We were all born in Plymouth Colony, so this will be the first time we've moved in one hundred and thirty or so years."

After breakfast, we went for a walk so they could show me around Plymouth Colony. We put on long capes, and Rebecca arranged my hat, a coif, on my head, and we started off. Once out of the house, I could see it was a square, two-story, plank house, with a few windows with glass panes, and a peaked roof and perhaps two chimneys. We walked along a well-worn path towards what seemed in the distance like a wooden palisade. And that's what it was. We entered through a gate and were in a diamond-shaped enclosure. As we walked along a path toward the centre of the space, our path was crossed by another called Leyden Street, which Elkanah said led down to the wharf.

There was a small collection of stores and shops: a blacksmith, a ropemaker, coopers and wheelwrights, barbers and bricklayers, carpenters, butchers, tanners, and a tailor. But, as Elkanah said, the stores existed to serve the surrounding farms, for the chief industry was farming—extensive farming—and parents had to give enough land to their sons that they could have their own farm, and so be able to marry and have children of their own. Thus, the need to move every third or fourth generation to find land.

Rebeccah was keeping her eye on her children, who were behaving very well, I thought, and trying to add to the conversation. "Caroline, the yeomen who own their own land are the basis of our society. We have a few gentry or gentlemen who we address as 'Mr.' and their female relatives as 'Mrs.' or 'Mistress'. There are also husbandmen who farm the land, but their land is often leased, and the unmarried sons of yeomen are the main type in this category."

Lemuel, although only seven but the oldest of the four children, apparently wanted to be part of the conversation after discovering I knew so little of their culture. He looked rather pleased with himself as he reported, "Yeomen and husbandmen are addressed as 'goodman' and their female relatives as 'goodwife,' which we often abbreviate as 'goody'."

His parents smiled at their son and his father concluded, "Then, as you can see, we have merchants and craftsmen who make many of the items the farmers need. If we can't make them, then we must buy them from Boston or England, which is very expensive indeed."

"Oh, there's an inn over there towards the hill."

"Aye, that's Cole's Inn on the north side of Leyden Street. And over there is the courthouse."

There were many people about, as this was a day the court was in session and there was a case involving fishing rights. Many people did inshore fishing using nets and there were always disputes about who could fish where.

"What's that over there in the square?" I asked.

"Oh, that's the stocks. If the court wants to punish someone for serious misdemeanours, they put their head and hands into the openings and lock a second piece over their head and hands. They must stay like that while people jeer at them and sometimes throw things at them."

"Oh," I said.

"Outside the west gate, there's a gallows. There are only a few occasions when it's been used, but its presence is somewhat of a deterrence to those considering murder. In the early days of the colony, it was used more frequently and especially if one of the colonists murdered an Indian. This prevented the Indians from taking revenge on the colony for the killing of one of their people."

"I can understand that. The settlers were surrounded by the native people. It must have been very scary if the native people became upset about something the settlers did," I said.

Then I noticed some Indian men—they had long, black hair, black eyes, and copper-coloured skin—talking to some of the Puritans. It all seemed relaxed and casual and belied the horrible conflict in 1675 called King Phillip's War when the Indians attacked Plymouth Colony as well as Massachusetts Bay Colony because of the pressure put on Indian society by the ever-expanding European need, and desire, for farmland.

We met two women dressed just like us and they smiled. Elizabeth greeted them warmly, as did Rebecca.

"Cousin Caroline, we would like you to meet our Morton cousins, Hannah and her sister, Priscilla."

"Very pleased to meet you," I smiled, while trying to remember the Morton family tree, to no avail.

"I hear you're going to Nova Scotia," Priscilla said.

Elkanah looked around at his family. "I think so, Cousin. There's a lot to think about before we go, though."

"Well, come and see us before you leave, and we will cook you a special farewell meal. It will be sad never to see you again. I do hear the land in Nova Scotia is particularly good."

"Aye, all reports indicate this is a good opportunity. But we will miss all our relatives that decide to remain in the old colony." Rebecca said.

We continued down the South Street and met friends and relatives, all saying the same thing. "Are you the only ones going from Massachusetts?" I asked.

"Nay, but most of the ones going so far as I know are from Rhode Island and Connecticut; they are also friends and relatives that moved from here for land many years ago and now running out of land for their sons once again."

I wondered who else was going from Plymouth. That's when Phebe and Seth showed up. Right away, I could see trouble brewing. They were both hot-headed and dramatic; the kind of people who don't mind having a full-blown argument wherever they are. Family seemed to walk on eggshells around them. I wondered how they would do in a frontier situation where everyone must pull together.

The next few weeks were a blur of packing and goodbyes, as well as negotiations for selling the land in Plymouth Colony. The Mortons were one of the old families, having come in 1623 from Leyden, Holland, on the ship Anne. Their roots were deep, and the goodbyes were many. Each Sunday, we went to the meeting house for the worship service. The sermons were long and the benches very hard, but I was the only one who wiggled and squirmed to try to get comfortable, to no avail.

Towards the end of the preparations, we all walked together over to Burial Hill. Elkanah Sr.'s grandfather, George, had one of the first headstones in the cemetery and his father, Ephraim and his mother, Hannah, had a headstone there as well. It read:

Here lyes ye body
of Mr. Ephraim Morton
who deed Febry ye 18th 1731
in ye 84th year of his age.

Then we slowly proceeded over to the newer part of the cemetery, to see the graves of Elkanah, Sr., and Elizabeth's children.

"Of our seven children, only Elkanah and his two sisters, Betty and Phebe, survived," Elizabeth said. "Ephraim died aged twenty months, Elisha lived thirteen months, then we had another son who only lived five days, finally, our youngest child, Lazarus, was born April 1742 and died in May. They're all here in our little family plot." A tear slid down her cheek as she knelt by the youngest child's grave. "Dear children," she said, "I know you're all in heaven, so why do I feel so sad? I miss you every day and now I will never come to see you again, as we are going far away."

"Now, now, Mother," her son said, "it is not so far that we might not return for a visit."

"Nay, Son, I'm fifty-eight years old and many difficulties lie ahead. I know I shall never return. Why don't you all go home and leave me for a while with my babies."

We left, after giving her a hug. But we hadn't gone far when her husband turned back. "Doesn't seem right to leave her alone," he said, "I'll see you back at the house."

After the land was sold, the house was to be taken apart, so the women and children left Plymouth Township and we walked to Dartmouth Township to stay with the William Tallmans—Betty's husband and children. I grabbed my valise before we left and put everything in it I thought I could possibly use. Elkanah Sr. had land in Dartmouth Township, which he had given to the Tallmans as he had only the one surviving son and thus no need for this land.

"How did you come to have land in Dartmouth Township?" I had asked before we left.

"The governors of Plymouth Colony bought it from Massasoit and Wamsutta in 1652," Elkanah explained. "Then it was allotted out to those interested in moving and our family bought a share, but we stayed on in Plymouth instead."

Betty was busy with several very young children, and Mr. Tallman was plowing his fields to prepare for planting. We did extra baking to have food to take with us on the ship and waited for the word that we were to proceed to the closest port.

The day arrived and Mr. Tallman brought around his ox cart. We put all the Morton children in it along with food and drink and set off to the port. It was a long walk, but the people were used to going everywhere on foot and seemed not to mind it. When it rained, we all climbed into the ox cart and pulled a tarpaulin over us for the duration. We were to meet Phebe and Seth at the docks.

What a hubbub! The men and sailors were still loading the last of the materials into the ships while women—some pregnant, some nursing babies, some with large numbers of little children—waited for their turn to board the ship. Luckily, it was a fine day. Nearby were piles and piles of kitchenware, the last to be loaded to be available first once we landed in Nova Scotia. One little girl was carrying a small dog which seemed quite frightened, and she tried to calm and comfort him. The rest of the animals were already onboard along with their hay, straw, and water. After what seemed ages, we were told it was time to board.

As we were standing in line to cross the gangplank onto the ship, I heard yelling and crying and strained to see what was happening ahead of me. It was the little girl with the dog. "The dog must go down in the hold with the other animals, little girl," the sailor said.

"No, Sammy must stay with me. He is quite afraid."

But the dog was wrestled from her arms. She ran to her mother and buried her head in her mother's skirt. I could hear her mother saying, "Shush, shush, he'll be cared for the few days until we get there." The little girl's sobs continued unabated.

The ship was underway the next morning, its sails filled with a strong wind. After we were out at sea, twenty-one other ships joined us to form a convoy. We were under the protection of a brig o'war pierced for sixteen guns and under the command of Captain Pigot, in case we were attacked by the French and Indians.

We slept in our clothes, in hammocks which swayed with the heaving of the sea. I was thankful that Phebe and Seth were in another ship as I had found it stressful to be around them, always waiting for some outburst or another.

In the morning, we had bread and cheese that our family had brought along. There was a place on the deck, a small shed filled with sand that held a stove, so we could boil water to cook potatoes and corn with ham for supper.

Elkanah said it would only take about five or six days to get to Nova Scotia. The convoy sailed along the Atlantic coast of New England and then into the Bay of Fundy. The sea fog made it difficult to see anything but high hills that hid the interior from our view. There were whales to watch and lots of sea birds that followed the ship, hoping to get some scraps of food.

After two or three days, we heard a rumour that a child was missing. That was every parent's greatest fear when on a ship. Whose child, we wondered. A search party was organized to scour the ship from stem to stern, calling out the little girl's name, "Polly, Polly, where are you?!"

The scene popped into my mind of the little girl with her dog, Sammy. What if she had gone to look for Sammy? I told Rebecca I was going to join in the search and located the steps down into the hold where I believed the animals were kept. It was dark in the hold and the cows mooed as I approached. I could hear the horses stamp their hooves and there were chickens clucking. I was sure the searchers had been here already and found nothing, so I called for Sammy.

"Sammy, Sammy, are you here? Are you all right? Sammy, where are you?"

A little voice said, "Sammy is with me and he's all right."

"Could I see him? I want to make sure you're both well-fed. I've brought you some bread and cheese and I have some cheese for Sammy."

Polly came out from behind a pile of hay carrying Sammy. I gave her the food, and we sat down while she ate it.

"Your parents are so worried about you and Sammy. Do you think you might let them know where you are? Then they could bring you and Sammy food and some milk."

"I get milk from the cows for Sammy and me," she said, smiling, "but I would like some bread and cheese."

"I'll tell your mother that, and I'm sure your father will bring it for you.

"Don't tell my father. He'll be angry with me and make me leave Sammy down here by himself."

"Then, what if I tell your parents you're safe and I'll bring you some food? It's only going to be a few days, maybe even tomorrow afternoon, when we anchor in Minas Basin. I think they'll take the animals off first before the women and children. At that point, Sammy should be allowed on the deck."

She nodded and crawled back to her hiding place with Sammy.

Her parents were so relieved that she hadn't fallen overboard that they forgot their fear and welcomed Polly and Sammy back into the fold with open arms.

The next day, all twenty-two ships turned east and sailed into Minas Basin. They anchored as close to the shore as possible, considering the incredible low tides we had all heard about. Nearly all the passengers were now on deck, straining to see their new land while the sailors waited for high tide. The settlers for Cornwallis Township would first step ashore at Boudreau's Bank, and the settlers for Horton Township would first arrive at Horton Landing.

"That was a pretty smooth trip, Elkanah."

"Aye, let's hope the weather holds until we unload the ship."

The men had much work ahead of them, unloading the ship onto row boats and rowing ashore before unloading onto the land—the land of Nova Scotia. The women and children stayed on the ship until everything had been unloaded and organized and covered with tarpaulins. Finally, fathers waited in row boats while sailors handed their children down to them, before the mothers then climbed down the ship's ladder and into the boats for the trip to what the Acadians had called Boudreau's Bank. There was a steep climb up the bank and, at last, onto the green grass of their new home.

It was a wonderful June day; a little too warm for the heavier clothing we were wearing, so the newcomers removed capes and coats to cool down. Each family group put up their tents and children were put down for their naps, while the women began locating their kitchenware and the men had a meeting to get organized for the next phase of their arrival, feeding the animals.

Nearby were old, weather-beaten oxcarts and ox-yokes. We realized these had belonged to the Acadians. Where we stood as new arrivals was the very spot the Acadians from this area were loaded onto ships, to deport them from their homes. Homes where they had lived since the mid-1600s. Some children were the first to notice the bleached bones of their cattle, along the tree line, that had died during the five winters since the deportation.

For a while, it was an adventure living in tents and cooking out of doors, but it was wearing after months. For the Morton family, it was perhaps more wearing than for others. Phebe and Seth continued to have public rows in which unpleasant words were exchanged; the kind that you can't take back.

One day I ran into Phebe quite by accident while we were helping to prepare supper. I decided to find out what was happening.

"Phebe, forgive me if I'm being nosy, but why are you and Seth always fighting?"

"Well, you are being nosy, Caroline, but if you must know, we were forced to get married because I was pregnant—but then I lost the baby. After the wedding, he started to be away from home most of the time; off with his buddies drinking or going on long trips looking into land deals and dear knows what else. I want him to stay home, and he doesn't want to."

"Oh, dear, Phebe, how sad for you to have had to marry a man who doesn't want to settle down."

"That's it entirely, Caroline. And it makes me mad and I'm not going to stand for it."

"But Phebe, all the yelling and hollering doesn't seem to be making any change in him, and it's causing distress to the rest of the family. Maybe leave him be for a while and let some of the men try to talk some sense into him."

"Maybe, Caroline. But he better smarten up, or else."

I didn't like to think what 'else' might be.

Finally, Elkanah, Sr., decided the time had come to handle what had become a problem for the whole community—a community which needed to be soberly about preparing for winter and not taking sides in unreasonable arguments.

I could only overhear some of what he said as he hauled them both aside. Phebe was to stay with the family and Seth was to stay with a group of single men—who didn't really want him and only agreed to it as a last resort. I'm not sure what would have happened if they had disobeyed

Elkanah. They couldn't even be sent back on one of the ships as they had already departed to pick up some more passengers in Connecticut. But in those days, children were trained to obey their fathers, so the plan seemed to work.

The men were gone from dawn to dusk, preparing a community garden which had to be surrounded with a sapling fence to keep the rabbits and deer from eating all the crops, as well as surveying the land and dividing it into home settlements, woodlots, dike lots, and salt marsh lots. Then they drew lots for who would get which lots, and finally those who had brought their houses could put them back together on the home settlement. Others had to content themselves with building log cabins until they could get the materials for something more permanent.

Another thing the men did was cut down logs to make a little fort where the settlers could withdraw for protection, and they also formed a militia unit for all males from sixteen to sixty. Though most of the Acadians had been deported, there were still—we were told—many hiding in the woods and attacking settlers with the aid of their Indian allies. So, no one felt entirely safe.

The women worked from dawn to dusk caring for little children, preparing meals, laundering clothing, and linens, and hanging it on bushes to dry, gathering wood for kindling, and feeding the animals, who had to be kept in a fenced area with guards at night to protect them from predators. The women and older girls milked cows and made butter and cheese, as best they could in the circumstances. I tried to stay out of the way unless I could help by babysitting or feeding animals.

Everyone felt under great pressure to have adequate lodging before the winter set in, especially since they didn't know what the winters looked like in Nova Scotia.

After Elkanah's house was set up, we had a proper family meal to celebrate the successful readiness for whatever the weather would bring. Phebe and Seth had been allowed to get back together, but nothing changed. I often heard them off by the tree line, hands flailing, bent forward, yelling.

It was shortly after that I discovered what Phebe meant by "or else." I was walking along a path through the woods, going from one part of the camp to the other, when I heard voices. I slowed to be careful, as they said there were still Acadians and Indians in the woods. Moving carefully, I saw a man and a woman, she leaning against a tree and he with his arms around her. I realized it was Phebe and one of the single men. Not knowing how to deal with it, I retraced my steps and as soon as I was out in a clearing, sat down, feeling a little wobbly. *Should I say anything to Elkanah or to Elizabeth? Or just stay out of it?* I felt badly for Phebe. First a bad marriage, and now an adulterous liaison. This was not going to end well, I was sure.

I was later told by Rebeccah that Seth had found out about what Phebe was up to. We waited for the explosion that never came. Did he even care?

I was worried about Elizabeth, as she seemed to be slow and uncertain lately. Perhaps that was due to all the changes she had been through. Elkanah and his father worked together as a team, so that was a positive outcome. Rebecca was always good-humoured and hard-working, so everyone could rely on her. And the children seemed to be adapting nicely.

One day, everyone watched as English soldiers marched into the main camp. Some had their muskets aimed at a group of raggedy men, perhaps one hundred and twenty or thirty. I ran over to Elkanah and asked, "What's going on?"

"Well, the Acadians had dyked the Cornwallis River—they called it the Habitant—and the Canard River so that they would have many more acres of marshland for producing hay for the cattle over the winter, but a recent storm damaged the dykes. The soldiers are bringing captive Acadians to repair the dykes. If they do this and swear allegiance to the King of England, then they can stay in Nova Scotia."

"Will they do it, do you think?"

"I think so. Those who want to return will be given land in a township called Clare, down towards Yarmouth."

Another day, news came that made everyone panic: The French had attacked Newfoundland.

A Monsieur de Tourney had escaped the English embargo of the French shoreline with four ships of the line and a bomb ketch. With a small body of land forces, they arrived at the Bay of Bulls in Newfoundland, razing the English settlements of Trinity and Carbonear and capturing several English vessels. The Town of St. John's was not able to defend itself and a company of soldiers were made prisoners of war, together with the officers and crew of His Majesty's ship Gramont, which was in the harbour.

Martial Law was declared in Nova Scotia, and the Cornwallis Township Militia was ordered to collect the Acadians and march them to Halifax under guard, with the intention of transporting them to Massachusetts. The fort, which had been only partially finished, was suddenly the focus of all energy. Would the French return with their warship and be joined by the Acadians and Indians? Would we soon be under attack?

Nerves were on edge. Men cleaned their muskets and gathered their ammunition. Everyone held their breath. Finally, we heard Massachusetts had refused to take the Acadians, and the transport had to return to Halifax with the Acadians still on board. In the meantime, the English, under Lord Colville, sailed from Halifax to Newfoundland with the Squadron under his command and soon the places the French had taken were recovered.

And the whole affair was over. The Acadians could stay.

Partway through September, there was some news brought to us by the Surveyor-General, Charles Morris. He had surveyed the boundaries for

Cornwallis Township—one hundred thousand acres between the Cornwallis River and the North Mountain and from Minas Basin to the headwaters of the Cornwallis River—and was on his way to survey three new townships at the head of Cobequid Bay: Truro, Londonderry, and Onslow. We would soon have other near neighbours in Nova Scotia besides those in Annapolis and Granville Townships. There were no roads overland in Nova Scotia and the voyage by sea around the south of the province and up the Atlantic coast to Halifax was long and dangerous, so townships around the Bay of Fundy were closest, as were ports in New England.

That fall, after the harvest of the community garden, we took a break from the hard work and walked along the north bank of the Cornwallis River. Every quarter mile or so was a clearing with a house or log cabin and a barn made of logs. Cattle and sheep were grazing in the patches of grass near the river and plans were underway to reap the hay from the intervale for cattle fodder over the winter. The Acadians had kept apple, cherry, and other fruit trees, so these had been harvested and were a welcome change of diet.

One item was missing from the community. The Pilgrims and Puritans had crossed the ocean so they could worship and govern themselves as they pleased, but no minister had accompanied them to Nova Scotia. Despite this lack, we all met after the October harvest to worship God and to prepare a great feast to celebrate Thanksgiving Day. At the service, the families remembered all their blessings in their new homeland, Nova Scotia. After the feast, each of the Morton family gave me a hug and their blessing. I can see them still, sitting around their harvest table, pleased and happy about their decision to come to Nova Scotia.

"Well, Samson, that didn't work out as planned!"
"I wonder what happened? She was supposed to come with us."

"Did you ever invite the Puritans to help Caroline write the book?"

"Aah, well, umm, nay. I thought we were just going to include the Scottish folk."

"Apparently, the Puritans thought otherwise." Martha laughed. "I wonder how they heard about it."

"Word gets around no matter where you are. No secrets here."

"That must be it. She seems to have had a good experience. That should mean we'll have no trouble getting her to come to Cobequid. But you may have to smooth things over with the Puritans since you didn't invite them."

"I'll have a chat with them. I'm sure they're quite pleased that their story is going to be in the book."

The next day, Caroline woke up in her own bed. *What a wonderful dream!* She put on new jeans and a fancy purple t-shirt and padded to her computer in her bare feet. Writing her first chapter was going to be a breeze. She smiled at the thought of her sisters' surprise when they found out she had such an interesting story and started typing. She had been worried she might forget the details of the dream during the day, but all the events remained clear and strong in her memories.

"Caroline, we're over here! Come, have a seat." They smiled as Caroline sat down.

"So, we're already got coffee and some treats and we're all dying to hear your first chapter."

Caroline looked around at her sisters, pulled a sheaf of papers fastened with a clip out of her rather large purse, and took a bite out of her muffin and a sip of coffee.

"Here goes." She looked at them with just a hint of a Cheshire cat grin. "Chapter One: Puritans." She read the events of her ancestors moving from the Plymouth Colony to Nova Scotia. As she read, she recalled the events as if they had happened to her, and only yesterday.

"That's so interesting, Caroline. And to think those are our ancestors. I almost feel like I know them now. I guess all your research paid off. Just imagine, you're on your way. With one chapter under your belt, the rest will be a breeze."

Janice said, "What happened to Phebe and Seth? Did they finally work things out?"

"Well, Phebe and Seth had three children, two boys and a girl: Nathaniel, Hannah, and Elisha. But Phebe was charged with adultery by her neighbours for living with a man who was not her husband! We don't know the outcome of the trial, but we do know that Phebe died around age thirty-three. So, a sad outcome for our Phebe. And we have no idea what happened to Seth, except that he remarried and died in Vermont."

"And their children?" Elizabeth asked.

"At least two of them may have been raised by family in Cornwallis Township and may have descendants there. My research wasn't firm on that. But two of them inherited some land in the township from their grandfather."

"That's so sad," Elizabeth said. "What happened to Elkanah, Sr. and his wife, Elizabeth Holmes?"

"Elizabeth seems to have died in 1761, but her husband lived to 1778. And Rebecca, Elkanah, Jr.'s wife, died around the same time. It could be they died from the smallpox epidemic in the area at that time. However, after they arrived in Nova Scotia, Rebecca and Elkanah, Jr. had four more children for a total of eight. But his oldest son, Lemuel, who arrived with his parents and siblings, is our fourth great grandfather."

"I guess that just leaves Elkanah, Jr. to account for," Janice said.

"Elkanah, Jr. lived to be ninety-four and had two more wives: he married Mary Belcher Lyde in 1779 and when she died, he married Elizabeth Newcomb. He was a Major in the militia, an Elder of the Chipman Corner Congregational-Presbyterian Church, a magistrate, and he left land for more churches and schools."

"So, a person very involved in church and community, as well as our ancestor," Janice said with some satisfaction."

"Well, no time for you to rest on your laurels. When can we expect the next chapter?" Elizabeth said.

"You see, that's the thing. I must wait for some inspiration to begin a chapter. But I'm sure you won't have to wait too long." Caroline took a deep breath. She hoped this was true.

"It's our turn this time, Martha. Let's hope nothing goes wrong."

"What could go wrong, Samson?"

Samson looked at her to see if she was joking. Martha looked back at him with raised eyebrows and no smile.

"Martha, I have no idea what could go wrong, so let's keep our fingers crossed."

Chapter Three

TRAITORS — THE MOORES

1776: The American Revolution and Truro, Nova Scotia

I arrived one summer morning on a dock in a river. It was early in the morning, fog still hugging the ground. I heard voices in the mist.

"Look Samson! There she is—on the dock."

"Martha, she's in her nightgown! She looks confused. Did you explain to her what was going to happen?"

"No, I didn't really know how it would happen. Did you?"

"Well, no. Anyway, we must get her to the house and find some clothes."

The sun was just coming up so I couldn't see Samson and Martha too well, or the surroundings.

"There you are, my dear," Martha said. "You're in Truro Township. Come with us."

Samson looked around to see if any of the neighbours were up and about yet. "Let's hurry. Here's the path from the dock across the marsh to the upland. You can see my house just at the brow of the hill."

As they hurried me along with a hand under each arm, I could feel the dew on the grass dampening the toes of my slippers. At the door of the house, Samson went in ahead of me and helped me over the door sill. It was dark inside except for the warm glow of the fire.

"How should we dress her? Samson asked.

"Well, we could dress her either in a house dress or a Sunday dress," Martha said.

"Could I make a suggestion?" I asked, tentatively.

"Aye, my dear. I guess we forgot you could hear us now. What are your thoughts?"

"What about a riding outfit? You know, a rather heavier, above-the-ankle skirt worn over riding boots with a fitted, buttoned-up jacket and a woman's tricorn hat."

"I've only seen such a thing on a woman in Halifax."

"Well, I live in Halifax."

"Oh, so you do. What do you think, Martha?"

"Oh, well, if a woman can dress that way in Halifax, then that would explain it to the neighbours."

Martha seemed to think she could just imagine me in such an outfit—and she did. One minute I was standing there in my blue pyjamas with little yellow ducks on them, and after Martha twirled me around a few times, I looked down to see my new brown skirt. Feeling my chest, I touched buttons and wool—a black riding jacket, and I saw a pair of riding boots in the corner.

"Oh," I said, "what wonderful boots!"

Samson smiled. "I make shoes and boots," he said, looking pleased.

Then we all noticed I had no hat. Martha looked perplexed. "Well, a few more twirls, Caroline, and that should work." I was getting dizzy from all the twirling, but Martha was right. A hat appeared, and a very nice one, at that, and Samson placed it on my head. I imagined I must look pretty good in my new outfit and with my curly brown hair pulled back and tied with a ribbon.

At their urging, I sat to rest for a moment. Martha stoked the fire and started making porridge for breakfast, in a big iron pot. Soon, their children joined us.

"Children, I would like you to meet Miss Caroline Morton from Halifax. She's a relative of Elkanah and Rebeccah Morton of Cornwallis Township. She will be visiting with us for a few weeks."

"But how did she get here, Father?" one of the children asked. The rest nodded and waited for an explanation.

"Well, let's say, hmm, well, right then, a ship brought her to Cobequid Bay, and she was rowed ashore to our dock. There. That's how she got here." He looked relieved. I realized only Samson and Martha knew the real story.

The children looked skeptical as Samson began our introduction. "Miss Morton, this is our oldest son, James. He was born in Londonderry, New Hampshire, August 9, 1755, and received his own land grant here in Truro Township when he was only ten years old. James is named after my father, one of the charter members of Londonderry, New Hampshire. He's twenty-one this year."

James smiled and nodded. He told his father he was going out to feed the animals and left.

"This is our second son, John. John was four when we arrived in Nova Scotia in 1761 and now he's nineteen."

John said he hoped I enjoyed my visit. He was as tall and robust as his older brother.

"Our oldest daughter, Eleanor, is named after Martha's mother, Eleanor Orr. She was only a baby when we arrived in Nova Scotia. She has a beau, but as she is only fifteen, her mother and I feel she is too young to marry yet."

Eleanor curtsied. I smiled. Like her brothers and sisters, Eleanor had dark brown hair and blue eyes.

"And this is David. David, you're twelve this year, right?"

David nodded.

"Alice is our second daughter, born in 1766, aged ten."

Alice curtsied. I smiled back.

"Here is Samson, Jr. my namesake. This is Daniel, our youngest son. And, finally, our youngest child, Martha, born in 1773, is just three years old."

Right away, I recognized little Martha as the child in the dreams who invited me to come with them. She smiled at me, and I smiled back.

"Children, I am so pleased to meet you all." Just as I was about to ask a few questions, James yelled from outside the front door.

"Father, Father! There's a big ship in the bay! Come and look!"

Samson ran to the door. When he turned around, he looked pale and shaken.

"What is it, Husband?" Martha asked.

"The English. I'm going to change into my best clothes now and go to meet them wherever they dock. But first, I'll call out the men for a township meeting. Children, you may smile and say hello to the people from the ship, but do not talk to them. If they ask any questions about me or the township, just say that you don't know."

The children nodded their heads.

"John, saddle my horse and see if you can borrow a horse for Caroline. Now, children, go and do your chores and when you're finished with them, begin your lessons ... and listen to your mother. Do whatever she tells you. Do you understand?"

The children nodded vigorously.

"Now, go."

They all scurried away except for James. "Father, I'm going with you."

Samson looked intently at his son and nodded. "First, tell John to borrow a horse for you, then go down river and let Alexander Miller or James Yuill know about the meeting." James left on the run.

"Martha, just keep the home settlement running smoothly. I'll send James back with the news." He was changing his clothing behind a little screen as he spoke.

Martha nodded.

Little Martha, his three-year-old daughter, toddled over and stretched her arms up toward her father. He picked her up and gave her a big hug and a kiss on the forehead. "Go and help your mother," he said, as he put her gently down on the floor.

Samson, now dressed in his best clothing, remembered I was there.

"Caroline, come with me. You may be allowed to attend the meeting. If so, just sit at the back quietly. If anyone asks, you're my guest and have come to the township to visit my family."

I nodded and wondered what the meeting would be about.

We set out along the path by the river. The warmth of the July sun was burning off the dew from the grass. The sedges and cattails that lined the river tossed lazily in the breeze. Red-winged blackbirds clutched taller grasses; dragonflies flitted from perch to perch. The river was red with tidal mud. I had to hurry to keep up with Samson and James, who were walking quickly and calling out to the men in the houses along the river. Each house had a pathway down to the River Road with flowers on either side—marigolds, sweet William, lavender, and lupins, and so on, all prettily arranged. Many of the houses were plank buildings, but there were still log cabins.

"Ho! John and James Johnson. Ho! George Howe, William Gilmore, William Downing, Matthew Fowler, James Faulkner, John Savage, Jean Long, Andrew Gammell! There's a meeting at the meeting house!"

I could hear some names being called from further down the river—Alexander Miller, James Yuill, Alexander Nelson, John Caldwell, Adam Johnson, John and William Logan, Thomas Gourley, Thomas Dunlap. James returned and we continued together to the meeting house.

We were quickly joined by the men, and the group swelled until we reached the meeting house. Even as we entered, I could hear calls to men, probably those living on the other side of the meeting house.

After all had arrived, Samson stood before the men and asked, "You've seen the ship?"

"Aye."

"I'm going to ride over towards Londonderry Township, where they're heading—probably to the wharf at Debert—and try to discover their purpose for coming to Cobequid. If they come to Truro, my plan is that we greet them with a meal and show them around our township, except for the river. Would any differ with these plans?"

The men nodded in agreement.

"I'm sure the other townships have seen the ship by now. We also need to alert our wives so they can prepare a feast for the officers and men."

The meeting broke up immediately and each man walked away with a grim face.

I had to run to catch up with Samson and James, who were now heading back home to get the horses. "What's happening?"

Samson stopped. "Caroline, we dare not tell you. Your life could be in danger if you were even to speak of our meeting. But you will see we are all united as a township."

"You mean the people on the ship might kill me? And united in what?"

"Nay. The people in the township might do you some harm if you betrayed them."

"Betrayed them! But I don't even know what's happening."

"And that will have to do for now. You may come with me to Londonderry. James, tell your mother the plans." James ran toward their house.

I felt a little dizzy. I knew the plans, but not the reason for all the secrecy. What was going on?

James and John arrived back with the horses. Samson rode quickly. I hurried to keep up. As we rode, I noticed how handsome Samson was—about forty years old with dark brown hair and hazel-green eyes. He was not much taller than I, but muscular. He was wearing breeches with stockings and buckled shoes. His long green silk vest was adorned with silver buttons and his long, black jacket was also decorated with silver buttons. He looked quite splendid, except for the perspiration on his forehead. Just as we arrived at the dock in the Debert River, he removed his hat and wiped his brow with a handkerchief.

There were many of the township folk arriving at the dock, including the magistrate and the Member of the Legislative Assembly for Londonderry Township, John Morrison. Mr. Morrison greeted the officer in His Majesty's Navy, who was ferried to shore by Isaac Deschamps of Windsor, his guide from Windsor to the Debert River.

"Greetings. Welcome to Londonderry Township."

"Greetings, all. I have come to announce that our new Lieutenant-Governor, Mariot Arbuthnot, has arrived to pay you a visit. He wishes to bring you greetings from His Majesty's Government in Halifax and to show his interest in how you are prospering."

Mr. Morrison responded with equal politeness and formality. "Give the Lieutenant-Governor our greetings and say that Cobequid—the Townships of Truro, Onslow, and Londonderry—invite him to come ashore and enjoy our hospitality.

"I will take your warm greetings and invitation back to the Lieutenant-Governor."

"It seems like a friendly visit, Samson?" I whispered.

"Aye, I think so. But it will not remain a friendly visit if we do not keep him away from the Salmon River."

"Because?"

"You will have to wait for an answer."

Once again, I knew the plans, but not the reason for them.

Shortly, the Lieutenant-Governor was rowed ashore and helped up the ladder attached to the dock. He was a plump man dressed in the full regalia of an English naval officer, including a sword and a firearm. He had an aide-de-camp attending him, as well as Isaac Deschamps, a government official.

There was a trading and shipping post on the Debert River, as this was the only place where even medium-sized ships could dock. James explained to me that most of the trade was with Boston and other smaller ports in New England as there was no decent road to Halifax—only a trail through the woods with logs attempting to provide a bridge over swamps and streams. Not fit to take a cow over, someone had said, and going by ship was long and dangerous. Cobequid sold hay, oats, and timber to New England. New England brought tea, sugar, rice, rum, ale, and luxury goods—cloth for women's dresses, parasols, men's dress clothing, silver buckles, and the like—to Cobequid. Friends, relatives, and businessmen also travelled from Cobequid to New England and back.

After introductions were made, including Samson as the Deputy Provost Marshall for Halifax County, and plans finalized—there would be a feast at supper time and a military parade of the militia in the evening—Samson said to me, "I need to speak to our former magistrate,

Mr. Archibald, before we call out the militia to be ready. Let's return to Truro Township."

Mr. Archibald, of course, had seen the ship and been given news of the meeting.

"What are your thoughts, Mr. Moore? Is this a friendly visit or a scouting mission?" Mr. Archibald was an imposing man with a big voice. He suddenly noticed me. "Who is your companion, Mr. Moore? Can we trust her?"

"Mr. Archibald, I'm pleased to introduce you to Miss Caroline Morton of Halifax. We are relatives. She has no notion of what is happening. As she is a near relative of mine and I have cautioned her to keep silent, I believe she will keep our secrets."

"As you wish, Mr. Moore, but it seems a little dangerous to rely on the word of a stranger. I think the other township people will agree with me."

"I will take full responsibility for her. You have the authority to call out the militia, Mr. Archibald. I think the Lieutenant-Governor would appreciate the opportunity to review them this evening."

"Consider it done, Mr. Moore."

We were off again, though Samson kept a slower pace. We rode back to the river, dismounted, and walked down to Samson's dock. Across the Salmon River, I could see another dock, which must have belonged to the large house and barn. There were men working there, perhaps repairing a ship. Samson took his hat off and wiped his forehead once again with his handkerchief. After watching the activity across the river for a while, we started back to the house.

"Samson, James says our visitor is the new Lieutenant-Governor?" Martha asked.

"That's right, Martha. Cobequid is going to entertain the Lieutenant-Governor, and he's going to review our militia."

"I've been preparing a big pot of salmon chowder, and there are biscuits in the oven. I'm organizing our bowls and spoons so we can take them as well. We'll need the ox cart ..." Martha paused, hands on hips, moved her head to one side and looked at Samson, probably picking up on some of his concern.

A slight but strong woman, Martha was wearing her workday clothes—a blue linen skirt over a petticoat, colourful blouse, all of which was covered by an apron that went over her shoulders, down to her feet, and tied in the front. A linen cap covered her hair. She had wooden shoes. Whatever was worrying Samson, she seemed less concerned and even cheerful.

"Samson Moore, don't you worry. It will be fine. All the townships are united in giving guests wonderful hospitality. Each family is bringing several quarts of cider and rum. His Majesty's representatives will be well entertained."

And they were. There was roast beef and chicken, ham, potatoes, turnip, bread and butter, rum, ale, cider, and dessert puddings, and, of course, Martha's salmon chowder made with diced potatoes, onions, and carrots and swimming in cream and butter, the biscuits being a perfect accompaniment.

The Lieutenant-Governor stood up when everyone was thoroughly sated and thanked the townships for the wonderful welcome and the excellent feast. He told them that Governor Francis Legge had been recalled to London, and that he was the administrator for the province until another governor was appointed by the King.

I was sitting near Samson while we were eating. "He seems like such a nice man, Samson. Cheerful, good-natured, and genuinely happy to be visiting you. Have you ever, in the fifteen years you've been in Nova Scotia, had a visit from the Government in Halifax?"

"Never, Caroline. This is the first visit. I agree that Lieutenant-Governor Arbuthnot seems like a good man, but naïve."

"What do you mean, naïve?"

"We cannot discuss that here." He turned and smiled toward the Lieutenant-Governor and lifted his cup of ale in a salute. The gesture was returned with a cheerful smile.

The men of the townships looked more relaxed than I had seen them so far. Was that because the King's men were more than a little tipsy? But there didn't seem to be a cloud on the horizon.

A few hours later, the King's men and the townspeople gathered in the parade square. The militia began forming, directed by their captains and lieutenants. None of the militia had uniforms, only their work clothes—blue linen trousers and unbleached linen shirts, usually covered with a vest. It was too warm that day for jackets. They wore leather shoes. But each one of them had a musket. Mr. Yuill and Mr. Morrison, being majors in the militia, walked with Lieutenant-Governor Arbuthnot as he reviewed the troops.

Afterwards, the Lieutenant-Governor was effusive in his praise. "My dear magistrates, what a fine militia you have. Five hundred well-trained men with muskets! Surely enough to drive off any rebel attack and protect the Province of Nova Scotia from those traitorous revolutionaries in His Majesty's Thirteen Colonies. I shall report back to the Council on the fine state of your townships and your readiness to protect Nova Scotia."

Samson was standing close to Mr. Yuill and overheard Lieutenant-Governor Arbuthnot. When the Lieutenant-Governor left, I watched them look each other in the eye and heave a sigh of relief. Relief, I believed that stemmed from their desire to impress the King's representative.

"That went very well, Samson," I said.

"So, it would seem," he replied.

"You're a Deputy Provost Marshall. What does that mean?"

"It means I work for the Government of Nova Scotia in Halifax and attend the sittings of the Supreme Court of Nova Scotia in order to carry out their orders in Halifax County. Cobequid is in Halifax County."

"Oh," I said enthusiastically. "I guess that makes you an important person."

"Important enough to get myself hung," he said flatly.

After that, we walked back to the house in silence.

James had brought the ox cart back with all the cookware. Martha was already cleaning up the kitchen, having put the smallest children to bed. "The English seemed to enjoy themselves, Samson. Overall, a great evening."

"So far, so good," said Samson. "Are the children ready for Sunday service tomorrow?

"Aye, they've all had their Saturday bath and washed their hair."

"Good. Let's get some sleep. What are the plans for Caroline?"

"We'll put her in the cot by the fireplace. Her nightgown is in her valise. We, and the children, will sleep in our usual places."

Sure enough, beside my cot was the same valise I had found in my room in Plymouth Colony. However did it get here? But what a relief. I didn't really want to sleep in my attractive new outfit, so I hung my new clothes on a hook near my cot and put on my pyjamas. I smiled at how incongruous my blue pyjamas with the yellow ducks looked in Samson's plank house.

The boys climbed up the ladder into the attic. The girls rolled out a featherbed in the far corner of the kitchen, and Samson and Martha climbed into the bed with curtains around it.

I woke when Martha stirred the embers in the fireplace and put some kindling on the fire. Seeing I was awake, Martha greeted me cheerily, "Come on, Caroline, get up and help me make the bread."

Thankfully, that was one thing I knew how to do, as I made my own bread at home.

"Do you use bread pans, Martha?"

She looked at me quizzically. "When you've finished kneading it, make it into two rounds and put it on the baking paddle. Once raised, you put it in the oven." She pointed out a door on the side of the brick fireplace.

The bread came out just fine and I breathed a sigh of relief. Nothing else in the kitchen—and the house was just one large room for cooking, eating, sleeping, for everything—was different from what the Plymouth people used: the dishes were made of wood, as were the spoons. The cooking utensils were made of iron. All cooking was done over the fire in large iron pots or frying pans with long handles.

Samson and the children sat around the kitchen table, and we had bacon, eggs, and fresh bread and butter. Everyone ate a lot and then ran off to do their chores. Martha told me that the boys took care of the animals and, every day but Sunday, hoed the crops of corn, potatoes, turnips, flax, and whatever else they might have in. They also went regularly to their woodlot and brought back logs to be chopped for firewood. The girls milked the cows and made butter and cheese. The women also tended the kitchen garden. Eleanor looked after the smallest children while Martha cooked and made bread. Martha, Eleanor, and Alice spun wool into yarn and flax into thread. During the winter, Samson or Martha would weave the yarn into clothing and blankets and the flaxen thread into towels, shirts, sheets, bedclothes, and potholders. They sold the excess flax thread and yarn.

As today was Sunday, only the most basic chores were done. As much as possible, Martha had everything prepared the day before, and everyone soon dressed for church. Martha looked so different in her beautiful green flowered dress with lace petticoats. Her bonnet was tied under her chin in a soft bow, and she carried a parasol. I thought I would stay in my usual costume, and no one disagreed with me.

We all set off up the river path to the Truro meeting house. Samson's brother, Joseph, and his family came over to greet us and I was introduced.

Joseph looked at me with consternation but said nothing. I was introduced to other family and friends.

Before the service in Truro Township, Samson left to go to Londonderry Township, to attend service there and see the Lieutenant-Governor. When we were all back home after services, Samson related that the Lieutenant-Governor and his officers looked a little the worse for wear after consuming so much alcohol the day before. He thought that the Truro minister, Reverend Cock, was a better preacher than the Reverend David Smith of Londonderry. At the end of the Sunday service in Londonderry Township, Samson told us he had approached the Lieutenant-Governor and invited him to Truro Township to show him around and provide a meal of sandwiches and ale before they had to return to their ship.

The next morning, Samson and James Yuill toured the Lieutenant-Governor around Truro Township. I was invited to ride along and was still struggling to understand why the Cobequid people seemed less than forthcoming when I asked questions. *I guess time will tell.*

The people were extremely proud of their township, and I could see why. Houses were well built, fields were full of flax, grain and vegetables, pastures were full of healthy-looking cows, sheep, and pigs, and the woodlots were a source of excellent firewood. The marsh, or intervale, on either side of the Salmon River was lush and green with the grass needed to feed the animals over the winter. The Lieutenant-Governor frequently remarked about the strong and healthy-looking people in Cobequid.

The whole place was close to Cobequid Bay with its fishing enterprises, but we did not go near the mouth of the Salmon River.

The Lieutenant-Governor left in the late afternoon high tide. At the dock, he addressed the people. "My dear township people, I must thank you again for all the hospitality you have arranged for us. I shall go back to Halifax and report to the Assembly and Council that your well-organized and neat farms, your fine meeting house and school, and the excellent militia, all proclaim that Cobequid is the finest township in all of Nova Scotia. The Government will be pleased that your militia is available to defend the province from the rebels in New England. As you know, the Legislative Assembly and Legislative Council in Halifax have proclaimed their loyalty to the King. I am sure that when the King's representatives come to Cobequid to have the inhabitants swear an oath of loyalty to the King, all will enthusiastically put their names on the list."

He paused ever so slightly but there was no reply, so the Lieutenant-Governor once again offered his thanks and he and his men went back to their ship.

Samson stood and watched them go. He looked both relieved and concerned.

The next day, the men of the township met again with Mr. Archibald, the former magistrate. I understood rightly. He had been relieved of his post by the former governor for suspicion of disloyalty. It seemed Mr. Yuill was now the only magistrate; except I heard Mr. Archibald was going to be re-instated by Lieutenant-Governor Arbuthnot as he believed Mr. Archibald was loyal to the King.

"Men," Mr. Archibald said, "we have already decided where our allegiance lies, but our Lieutenant-Governor plans to have us take the Oath of Allegiance to the King. Whatever we decide here today, we must all agree to stand together. There can be no dissenters. Some of us—those who are employed by the Government—are in an even more difficult position than most. But they must decide, here and now. So, I ask you, one and all, are we still united in our previous resolve?"

Although he said nothing, Samson scowled and looked at his shoes. If they were planning to do what I guessed they were going to do, everything was at stake.

Mr. Archibald insisted on a show of hands as he called out each man's name. When it came Samson's turn, he raised his hand—as did each of the other men.

I was afraid to ask what had just happened, so I just walked silently beside him until we were home.

Martha looked at him with concern as we entered the room. Besides the light from the candle, there were only the embers in the fireplace. Except for James, John, and Eleanor, all the children were in bed.

"Was everyone united?" she asked, looking up from her knitting.

"Aye. Every one of us."

"Samson, shall we tell Caroline?"

He looked at me and I could sense his weariness. "Aye, as soon as the time is right. It's been a long day; let's all go to bed."

The next day, Samson and I and the older boys went out to the barn to feed the animals and put them out to pasture. The boys soon finished their chores in the barn and left to hoe potatoes. Samson had managed to get me a horse, so I had to clean out her stall and brush her. Luckily, I had learned to care for a horse, as horseback riding was one of the chief joys of my childhood. Samson was cleaning out the stall of his horse, so I looked around, and, seeing no one, asked Samson the burning question.

"Samson, I think we're alone. Please tell me what's happening. I can feel the tension in the township meetings and the grim determination of the township people." Having cleaned out the stall, I brushed my horse as I waited for his answer.

Samson was wearing his work clothes—coarse linen trousers, dyed blue, a coarse linen shirt, wooden shoes, and a broad-brimmed hat. Looking around to check out my observation that we were alone, Samson leaned on his dung fork and considered what to say.

"Caroline, you already know from your research that most of the families in Cobequid came from Londonderry, New Hampshire, to Nova Scotia in 1761. Before that, many of our parents had come from Londonderry,
in northern Ireland, to Londonderry, New Hampshire, in 1719. But our
families had not been long in Ireland. They called us the Scotch-Irish because in the 1600s our families came to Ireland from the south of Scotland.
It was a plan of King James the VI of Scotland—who in 1603 became
King of England as well—to settle English-speaking Protestant people
in Gaelic-speaking Roman Catholic Ireland. The English hated the Irish
with a passion because the Irish were Roman Catholic and loyal to the
Pope in Rome. James I of England was determined to turn Ireland into a
Protestant country with the King as the Head of the Church of England."

Samson went back to forking out the stall for a few minutes before
turning back to our conversation.

I said, "I've read about all the wars and massacres that followed the
settlement of Scottish Protestants in northern Ireland. But despite the fact
the English preferred the Scottish Presbyterians to the Roman Catholic
Irish, they still wouldn't let you vote or hold office unless you were willing
to take Oaths of Allegiance and take communion in the Irish Episcopal
Church—the name for the Church of England in Ireland. I'm not sure
about all the details, but I know that your parents and many of your friends
and relatives set sail for the New World to escape the ongoing violence."

"Quite right. Now we find ourselves in support of our friends, relatives
and neighbours in New Hampshire who are determined to overthrow our
English rulers and rule our own selves instead," he said, with a whiff of
pride.

"You mean the whole of Cobequid are in support of the revolution!?" I
immediately realized I had said that too loudly.

Samson looked around again to be sure we were alone. "Caroline, everything is at stake, so silence is essential," he whispered.

I nodded, feeling embarrassed at my outburst. The horse shifted slightly,
pinning me against the stall. It took quite a push on her side to get her to
move.

"You are comfortable around horses," he said approvingly.

I nodded and whispered, "The whole of Cobequid is in support of the revolution?"

"We are. We have had secret township meetings—as have all the other Nova Scotia townships who were settled by New Englanders. All the townships have voted to support the American Revolution."

"That would be treason!" I whispered, standing with my brush in hand.

"Aye," he nodded and, having finished cleaning the stall and putting down some hay, he turned to brushing his horse.

"But Samson, you're employed by the English Government in Halifax. They are loyal to the King of England." I was so taken aback by his revelation I had completely given up brushing the horse and was just standing there, eyes wide.

"Aye, so you can see my predicament." He was brushing so hard, the horse turned around to see what was happening.

"If you're caught, you'll be hung as a traitor." The brush fell out of my hand, and I had to reach under the horse to pick it up.

"Not only that, Caroline. You know what the English did to the Acadian French when they wouldn't take an Oath of Allegiance to the King of England?" He was still brushing with such vigour that the horse was moving away from the source of discomfort.

"Oh, yes. They were rounded up and expelled from Nova Scotia." I dropped the brush again.

"Aye." He stopped brushing and rubbed the perspiration from his forehead with his sleeve.

"Oh, Samson, if you take the oath, Cobequid will consider you a traitor to their cause. If you don't take the oath, the English will consider you a traitor to the King. The people of Cobequid could be expelled from Nova Scotia." The enormity of what the people of Cobequid were planning was slowly sinking in.

"Aye." He untied his horse and led him out of the barn and into the pasture. I followed with my horse and caught up with him as he opened the gate. We walked in and untied the ropes from their bridles so the horses could run free. We both looked around to see if we were alone.

"No wonder you look concerned. You must be anxious about your family, as well. Does Martha know about this?"

"She does, and James, John, and Eleanor as well. I am trying to spare the younger children the worry, at least for now." He sighed, and we left the pasture and closed the gate behind us.

I asked no more questions, having more than enough to digest before I could think clearly.

Three days later, at a meeting of the three townships, the men of Cobequid decided to write a letter of thanks to the Lieutenant-Governor for his visit. David Archibald, Esquire—now re-instated magistrate for Truro—was to write the letter which all grantees would sign.

Two days later, the same people gathered again to hear the letter read and to sign it on behalf of their townships. I was there and was struck by the tone of the letter. Once Samson and I were away from the meeting house, I whispered, "Samson, I listened very carefully to the reading of the letter to the Lieutenant-Governor. It was so friendly and generous in the praise and appreciation of the Lieutenant-Governor. It sounded like the kind of letter loyal subjects of the King would write."

"Aye. That is the impression a reader would rightly have from reading the letter." Samson was calm and factual.

"But nothing could be further from the truth. I'm beginning to feel sorry for the Lieutenant-Governor. He seemed like a genuinely well-meaning man. Everyone said so, after he departed."

"Cobequid does not want to cause any disturbance with the Government in Halifax until our plans for capturing Nova Scotia are put into action." Again, the calm, factual response.

"You're really going to join the American rebels who plan to attack Nova Scotia?" I was whispering loudly, and he put his index finger to his lips as he looked around once again.

"That is the plan."

I felt a little dizzy. "I really don't know what to say, Samson." My field of vision was getting darker. Was I going to faint?

Samson took off his hat, smoothed back his hair, put his hat back on, then looked me in the eyes. "I suggest you say nothing. You might be in danger if you do."

I sat down on a tree stump. Samson continued into the house.

When I finally stopped feeling dizzy, I went to the dairy to see if any of the equipment needed washing. I needed to buy some time to digest what Samson had told me.

I had been trying to learn to milk a cow. Eleanor was an excellent teacher, and I did a little better each time, I thought. The cow did not agree. Whenever Eleanor or Alice milked her, she quietly chewed her cud, but when I sat down on the milking stool, she would turn and look at me with consternation. I didn't blame her.

I was a little better at making butter. After milking, I went into the dairy and poured the fresh milk into setting dishes and waited for the cream to rise to the top where I would skim it and put it in the butter churn. The milking pail, the setting dishes, the skimmer, and eventually the butter churn, all had to be washed. The butter was put in moulds and together with the by-product of butter-making, buttermilk, was stored in the icehouse. It was quite a process.

Later that week, Martha and I were walking up the River Road after visiting a neighbour who just had a baby. As we moved closer, we could see a group of men gathered. Thinking it might have been a spontaneous wrestling match or a game of some sort, we walked over. Instead, a man I recognized as the now re-instated magistrate, David Archibald, was holding a pistol against the chest of another man.

"Well, Squire Patterson, I'm sorry to hear you're on your way to Halifax to obtain copies of the Oath of Allegiance for the residents of Pictou County."

"Mr. Archibald, I'm surprised you would treat one of the King's loyal subjects with such a lack of hospitality and respect."

"You may be as surprised as you wish, Mr. Patterson, but I tell you truthfully that if you begin down the Halifax Road, I will shoot you."

"I can understand now why the former governor had turned you out of your office as magistrate. And are these friends of yours willing to be accomplices of murder?"

The men shifted from foot to foot and looked at each other. One of them spoke up,

"Mr. Patterson, it grieves me to see this rift between Cobequid and Pictou after our many years of friendship, but we are quite determined to support the desire of our friends in New Hampshire to govern ourselves."

"It grieves me as well that you would conspire against the King and those loyal to him."

"What is your decision then, Mr. Patterson? Will you go back the way you came, or shall I shoot you?"

The men surrounding the two antagonists hung their heads, as Mr. Patterson picked up his hat from the ground, slapped the dust off, and placed it on his head.

"I do not think you will be successful in your plans, Mr. Archibald, but I will not test your determination to kill those who disagree with you."

Mr. Patterson turned back towards the Pictou trail. Mr. Archibald re-holstered his pistol as the men gathered around the confrontation walked away silently.

"Martha, this is getting more serious by the day," I whispered.

Martha nodded calmly. I had learned that it took a lot to agitate Martha.

A few days later, Samson and I rode over to Londonderry Township. I waited as he served a subpoena that required attendance at the next sitting of the Supreme Court of Nova Scotia on a grantee who had been named in a property dispute.

I was getting to know my way around Cobequid. Everything was so neat and well organized. Farmers were out in their fields hoeing their crops, the sawmills were busy sawing boards for the plank houses that were gradually replacing the log cabins, the grist mills ground grain for porridge and bread. One of the more interesting things I had learned was that bread was considered essential to life. The farmers could have cheese and milk and butter, meat and fish and fowl, but none of this was considered essential, only bread—bread made with whole grains coarsely ground, yeasty, satisfying and slathered with freshly made butter and served with a big cup of cold buttermilk. Yum. Martha baked bread every day and we had bread with every meal. I didn't complain. Bread is my favourite food.

While I was daydreaming about bread, Samson noticed a commotion down on the north side of the Salmon River, so we rode over. The yelling seemed to come from Charles Dickson's wharf and involved the crew on two ships tied up close together. Close to the wharf was Dickson's house, tavern, and store house which we rode past on the road down to the river.

Samson handed me his reins and jumped down from his horse. He walked down onto the wharf and ordered the antagonists to cease and desist. The crew on the schooner, *Fairwind of Windsor,* took a step back but the crew of the smaller, rough-looking boat, called *Raven's Duck,* kept up their threats and name-calling until they realized the crew of the *Fairwind* would no longer participate. It seemed a tense and fragile peace.

After a short ride from Dickson's wharf, Samson said quietly, "The men on the *Raven's Duck* are American privateers and, as well, there are escapee prisoners of war from His Majesty's jail in Halifax. They are being aided to escape back to New England."

I nearly fell off my horse. No wonder Samson didn't want to show the Lieutenant-Governor what was happening on the Salmon River! "So, everyone in Cobequid knows who they are!?"

"Aye. They often came to Tupper's Tavern in Truro Township and talked freely about why they are here."

"Why are they here?" I was starting to feel rather frantic about what was going on in Cobequid.

"One of the privateers captured an English ship off Canso and took the men and cargo aboard their ship, *General Gates*. Shortly thereafter, the privateers were sighted by one of His Majesty's ships, chased and run aground on the rocks. Fourteen of them swam ashore and made their way to Pictou County, where they were directed to Cobequid—where they would get a warm welcome and help to return home."

"What about the prisoners of war? How did they get here?"

"The others were prisoners of war taken from the American privateer fleet led by the brig *Washington*. General George Washington commissioned them to interrupt English supply vessels and get him desperately needed provision and ammunition. Captain Sion Martindale was in charge. They were seized by the English on their second voyage, transported to England, then returned to Halifax. They were waiting to be exchanged for English prisoners of war when they escaped from jail. Six of the thirteen made it to Cobequid."

"But why Cobequid?" This place was surely a hotbed of treachery and treason! I thought.

"They all know about Cobequid, so if they can escape from jail, they head through the woods to Cobequid hoping to get help. It's sixty miles through dense forests and swamps from Halifax to Cobequid, so they often take a chance and walk on the road where they usually get caught by

His Majesty's soldiers who are searching for them. But some make it here to a warm welcome and all the help we can give."

"Are you going to report the privateers or the prisoners of war to the Lieutenant-Governor?"

"Most certainly not. And neither will the magistrates, militia officers, or any other person in the township."

Once we arrived home, we did not speak about the incident. Martha and I worked on the preparations for supper while Eleanor taught the smaller children how to print and write. After supper, Samson went over to Dickson's wharf to find out the state of affairs. He was gone quite a while.

"Samson," asked Martha, as he returned to the house, "is the situation resolved?" Martha always seemed to know what was going on. I think the women kept an eye on both their homes and their neighbourhoods.

"Nay, the *Fairwind* doesn't dare leave the wharf until the *Raven's Duck* is off and away. They fear the privateers will only capture their ship as soon as it is out into the bay. In the meantime, some of the township folk are threatening the owners of the *Fairwind*."

"What are they threatening them about?" I asked.

"The threat is that the *Fairwind* will never be allowed to return to Cobequid if they tell anyone in Windsor about the *Raven's Duck*—and that is not all."

"What else are they threatening?" Martha and I asked at once.

"They are threatening that if Michael Francklin arrives in Cobequid to administer the Oath of Allegiance to the King—as Lieutenant-Governor Arbuthnot indicated—they will take Mr. Francklin through the woods to hand him over to the rebel Congress."

"Who is Michael Francklin?" I asked.

"Only the Lieutenant-Governor's right-hand man. Francklin had been Lieutenant-Governor himself under Governor Francis Legge. Francklin

went to London to ask the Lords of Trade to recall Legge before he gave
the townships any more reason to rebel. Legge was recalled to England
because he was, I think unintentionally, upsetting all the power groups
in Halifax as well as the people of the townships. Once back in England,
he engineered the removal of Francklin. The new Lieutenant-Governor,
Mariot Arbuthnot, oversees the province until the King appoints a new
Governor. Francklin would have accompanied the Lieutenant-Governor
on his travels around the province, but he was ill. It is he who will be sent
to administer the Oath of Allegiance to Cobequid."

"Kidnapping the representative of the Lieutenant-Governor and taking
him to the rebel Congress would be considered treason, would it not?" I
was sure I knew the answer to this question.

"You are right, Caroline. Do you see that even talk like this is very
dangerous as it gives away the intentions of the townships?"

I did see and nodded my concern. I was thinking to myself that this was
all going very badly. But nothing happened right away, so we let down our
guard.

Samson and the boys were out in the fields hoeing corn and potatoes.
Martha, Eleanor, Alice, and I were in the kitchen making supper. I had
been relieved of milking the cows as I, and the cows, agreed I had no
aptitude for it. Martha sent me out to the icehouse to get some buttermilk.

"I'm getting a taste for buttermilk, Martha. On a hot day it is very
refreshing." Martha and Eleanor looked at me askance.

"Honestly, Caroline, living in Halifax has certainly limited your household skills," said Eleanor. "When I learned you couldn't spin or weave or
milk a cow, I had to wonder what your mother taught you."

I was saved from having to explain my lack of skills when Samson and the
boys returned. I poured each of them a cup of buttermilk which they guz-
zled down. Hoeing is hot and dusty work. We had roast chicken, little new

potatoes—white, creamy, and melt-in-your-mouth, and peas just shelled before supper and tasting of garden goodness—with lots of bread and butter. It was superb. My grandmother often told me how much better the food tasted when she was a girl, but I always imagined that was because being older her taste buds weren't working as well. But in a prosperous township with all the food being unprocessed and completely fresh in the summertime, I knew she was right. Fresh out of the garden is better.

That evening Eleanor invited me up to the attic to see her hope chest. I gladly agreed. "I'll hold the ladder while you climb up, Caroline." Once in the attic, I couldn't see a thing as it was so dark. But Eleanor was right behind me, so I had to move, nearly hitting my head on something hanging from the beams, I imagined. It turned out to be herbs hanging to dry.

Over by the tiny window at the far end of the attic, there was a small trunk. We knelt in front of it and Eleanor opened it carefully. Covered by a protective cloth, the trunk contained linen towels and sheets, linen nightgowns, and a dress that Martha called her wedding dress. It was a strange-looking affair: there were strings hanging off here and there; none of it made sense.

"Eleanor, what are all the strings and ties about on this dress?"

"Well, Caroline, the wedding dress is made to accommodate pregnancies. So, the ties allow the dress to expand as the pregnancy advances, and this over-piece here can be moved aside so you can nurse the baby."

"How very practical, Eleanor," I said, thinking there was nothing too romantic about this design.

By now my eyes had adjusted to the dim light and I could see a large loom in the far corner of the attic and the places that the boys slept at night. No cots, just linen-covered straw pallets with wool blankets, which surely would not be needed in the summer heat. The heat of the attic was also the best place to dry herbs, corn, apples, and many other foodstuffs.

"Who is your beau, Eleanor?"

"John McCabe of Pictou District. His family came there in 1767 from New England with the Philadelphia Company. They were the first European settlers in the area, I believe."

"How will you get your trunk over there? It's a long way through the woods and over Mount Thom."

"John will come for me with a horse. We'll tie the trunk on one side and some furniture on the other side to offset it and we'll walk from here to Pictou."

"I know you'll make an excellent wife, Eleanor. And I'm sure your husband will appreciate your cheerful attitude."

We climbed back down into the kitchen and helped prepare supper.

When I awoke one morning in late August, Martha was humming a merry tune and making what looked to me like a cake.

"Aye, it is a cake, Caroline. Some of my neighbours are coming this morning for a tea party."

"A tea party! How lovely. Will your guests all be women?"

"Oh, aye. The men get together at Tupper's Tavern for ale and discussions about grain prices and politics and such." She always seemed surprised I didn't know these things.

"Do the women ever go to the tavern?"

"Nay." She looked perplexed. "Only men. Women have their tea parties. Look, here is my tea set."

I picked up a dainty cup to admire it. "Martha, it's so pretty—white China cups and saucers with pink and yellow flowers—and a teapot to match."

"Aye, and the tray is also part of the set and eight matching tea plates."

"You must be very proud of your tea set."

"Aye, Aye, it is my most special possession." She bent over to test the cake.

"I'll put the tea set on the table. Will you need spoons or napkins?"

"Look on the tray. There should be two little silver spoons, one for the cream and the other for the sugar." She stood up for a moment and looked at me. "They were my mother's. She brought them from Ireland. Very special. A wedding present." Her mother, Isabel, would be my fifth great grandmother. It was an honour just to touch them. I felt my eyes get moist. Strange what things affect you. How I wished I could have met Isabel, too.

"And there should be some linen napkins and wooden spoons right there on the cupboard."

She went back to baking, and I watched as the cake rose in a pot over the coals.

"I'll serve it with fresh blueberries and thick, sweet cream."

"I hope I can attend your tea party."

"Well, I hope so, too, Caroline, as it is in your honour."

"My honour. How very kind of you. I look forward to meeting your friends and eating cake and sipping tea."

The women, dressed like Martha in their weekday clothes, soon arrived and took their places around the kitchen table. It was covered with a fresh linen cloth, with the tea set proudly sitting in the middle, beside the cake. Beside Martha were the blueberries, in a pretty pottery bowl which matched the bowl containing the cream. Eleanor and Alice were in attendance both to assist their mother and to learn to preside over a proper tea party.

I was introduced. "Caroline, I would like you to meet my friends and relatives. I'll begin with the wives of James and John Johnson, our next-door neighbours. This is Margaret McRoberts, wife of James, mother of three, and stepmother to seven." Margaret smiled. I thought she looked a little tired, and who wouldn't with ten children!

"Pass this plate over to Margaret, will you, Caroline." The plate held a big wedge of cake almost completely covered in whipped cream in soft peaks and sprinkled with lightly sugared blueberries.

"Does that ever look good, Martha," Margaret and I chimed. And Martha smiled with pleasure.

"Beside Margaret," Martha said, "is her sister-in-law, Sarah Hogg, wife of John, mother of six, including Mary, here."

"Oh, I suppose your children are mostly grown, Sarah?"

"Oh, nay, Mary is my oldest girl. I have many younger." She, too, looked a little weary.

"Mary," Martha clarified, "is the wife of James Dunlap and mother of ten. Next to her is Margaret Robertson, wife of Alexander Nelson and mother of fourteen."

Mother of fourteen! "You need a lot of energy and patience," I suggested. She nodded.

"And here's Eleanor Taylor, widow of Samuel Archibald and mother of eleven. And, finally, here is my sister, Janet Orr, wife of Thomas Archibald and mother of nine children." They greeted me with smiles.

I was amazed at the number of children. Seven women had sixty-six children. If you included Martha, then eight women had seventy-four children! "I'm very pleased to meet you all and look forward to chatting as well as eating Martha's cake."

Martha poured the tea and Alice passed the cups to each of the guests while Eleanor took the cream and sugar around to satisfy their preferences.

I had a burning question. It took some time to get the courage to ask, but when there was a lull in the conversation, I took my chance, "Do you women support the desire of your menfolk to join the revolution?"

"Oh, Caroline," Martha said quickly, "each of us support our husbands' decisions."

"You mean you have to support the men?"

"Our husbands represent our family in public. We would never challenge their decisions in public or even among friends. The honour and status of our family depends on the status of our husbands."

"Caroline," Janet Archibald, Martha's sister said, "in our beds at night we tell our husbands our thoughts and feelings, but once they have decided, wives and children support his decisions."

"I can tell that this would be good for family unity," I said, the most neutral response I could think of in the moment.

The party went back to chatting about their children, their kitchen gardens, and dairies.

"You know you could lose everything if there is a war!" I thought perhaps they didn't understand the potential outcome of a war.

"Caroline," said Martha, "we do understand and as women and mothers we would not wish anything to harm our husbands and children, nor would we wish to lose our farms."

"Thank you, Martha. I just want you all to be safe."

"We know you do, Caroline."

"Would anyone like more tea?" Martha smiled as her daughters brought around the teapot.

September was a beautiful month. Everyone turned out for the most important event in the world each year—the harvest. Potatoes and turnips had to be stored in the cold room in the cellar. Corn was hung from the rafters to dry. Apples were cored, sliced, and hung to dry or made into cider. Flax was cut and submerged in streams, the first part of the extensive process of making linen. Hay was cut with scythes, stacked in the fields to dry, and loaded on ox carts to be carried to the barns. The women made preserves from blueberries, strawberries, and cranberries. The whole month up to mid-October was a whirl of business.

As the season ended, the farmers were able to look with satisfaction at their full barns and storehouses, and the housewives were proud of their preserves and drying fruit and vegetables, certain they could feed their families over the winter.

I asked Samson if he expected the turbulence to settle down over the late fall and winter.

"I don't know if Michael Francklin has recovered or if he has heard about the threat to his person. For the time being, all the drama seems to have dissipated."

He could not have been more wrong.

The beginning of November, a Cobequid spy in Windsor let Cobequid know that Michael Francklin was in Windsor and had deposed both owners of the *Fairwind*. The spy believed that Francklin was setting out by boat with thirty armed men to find out what was happening in Cobequid. However, the spy explained, Francklin was attacked by American privateers who had already captured the Partridge Island ferry. Francklin fought off the privateers and rescued the ferry. It was the Partridge Island folk who told him of a planned attack by the American rebels on Fort Cumberland.

But the people of Cobequid already knew this. Before they heard about Michael Francklin, two men from Cumberland Township arrived in Londonderry Township bringing a letter to Magistrate John Morrison. The letter, from the Cumberland Safety Committee, invited the people of Cobequid to join the rebellion and support a planned attack on Fort Cumberland. The two men continued on to bring a similar letter to Magistrate Archibald. He sent them away without an answer, but told fellow magistrate, James Yuill, also a Major in the militia.

Samson returned from Tupper's Tavern one evening following a discussion of the letter from Cumberland Township. He shared the gist of the conversation with Martha, James, John, Eleanor, and I.

"Who is Colonel Jonathan Eddy?" I asked.

"He's a grantee in Cumberland Township. He was an officer in the English Army during the French and Indian War before he came to Nova Scotia at the end of the war. He is deputy provost marshal for Cumberland County and their Member of the Legislative Assembly from 1770 to 1775."

"So, another person paid by the English in Halifax as part of their government?" I asked, surprised at the picture I was getting of who was involved in the plans to participate in the American Revolution.

"Aye."

"What will you do, Samson?" I asked. Martha, James, John, and Eleanor waited for the answer.

"I won't participate in the attack on Fort Cumberland but that means very little in the long run."

"What do you mean, Father?" James asked.

"It is my duty as a representative of the King to report treason—in this case, high treason—against the King. If I don't report it, and the rebellion fails, I will be considered guilty by reason of failing in my duty."

Only days passed when several men went running down the River Road yelling, "The rebels have arrived in Cumberland Township!"

Soon men were running up the River Road towards the meeting house. I went along to find out if they would let me into the meeting. It was a little surprising to find no one noticed my presence—or seemed to care if they did notice.

Mr. Archibald and Mr. Yuill were there along with Mr. Morrison from Londonderry Township. There was a great low murmur in the room and the air was electric with excitement. Mr. Archibald spoke first, "As you know, Cumberland has sent a letter to us asking that we join the rebels who plan to attack Fort Cumberland. What is your wish?"

"Some people say that Colonel Jonathan Eddy has three hundred men," yelled someone.

"Some say that Colonel Eddy and his men are coming to Cobequid," another yelled.

There seemed to be little solid information upon which to make a decision. In the end, the men sent the Truro Township tavern owner, Eliakim Tupper, to Cumberland to assess the situation.

A few days later, Mr. Tupper explained that Colonel Eddy had very few men of his own and very little arms and ammunition. He was trying to force Cumberland Township people, Acadians, and Mi'kmaq to join him. A few did. He may have three hundred men total, Mr. Tupper told the meeting.

That cooled the excitement, although a few men were determined to join the attack on Fort Cumberland. The rest wanted to hear more. If the rebels succeeded, then the rest of Cobequid would join in and the American Revolution would start in Nova Scotia.

The spy in Windsor let the Cobequid people know that a runner from Fort Cumberland had brought news to Michael Francklin in Windsor that the fort was going to be attacked. Francklin had dispatched a ship to Chignecto Bay to find out what was happening there, as the runner continued to Halifax to report to the Lieutenant-Governor.

In his wisdom, the Lieutenant-Governor sent a troop of regular soldiers to Chignecto in *HMS Vulture* and sent letters to Cobequid to request that Cobequid Militia supplement the regular soldiers in protecting Fort Cumberland from the rebels. People read the letter and shook their heads in disbelief. The Lieutenant-Governor still believed in the loyalty of Cobequid!

While all this was going on, the rebels under Jonathan Eddy attacked the fort several times without success.

Men from Cobequid arrived just in time to find out that the soldiers from the fort, together with the regular soldiers, had attacked the rebel camp and the rebels had all run into the forest to escape. They learned some returned to the American side, while others turned up in Cobequid to tell what they knew. Some rebels were captured.

To say that the atmosphere in Cobequid was tense was an understatement. Would the prisoners tell the English the truth to avoid capital punishment?

That week, Samson told Martha that he had to go to Windsor to serve a subpoena. I asked to accompany him. Windsor was an important shipping port and lots of rich people from Halifax had summer homes there, so perhaps a nice place to visit. But I had a hidden agenda. The plan for the day was to kill chickens and pluck them. You had to scald their dead bodies in hot water to get the feathers off. I would do almost anything to avoid that process. We left in the morning from Dickson's wharf. After about six hours, we were in Windsor. Samson served the subpoena, and we had supper and slept in the home of an older couple who had rooms to spare. In the morning, we would return on the next tide.

We were standing on the wharf enjoying the sunshine and the cool breeze of November. We were both wearing our winter capes. Samson and I were chatting about the tides in the Bay of Fundy when he turned with a look of—well, I wasn't sure. In any case, as the man in the official-looking clothing approached Samson, I stepped back out of the way.

"Mr. Deputy Provost Marshall, good morning. I won't beat around the bush. I have deposed the owners of the *Fairwind* and several people from Cobequid who are on the wharf this morning. I intend to depose you and determine what is going on in Cobequid."

"Certainly, Mr. Francklin. What would you like to know?"

"I want to know if all of Cobequid is in league with the rebels."

"Well, Mr. Francklin, there are a few—no more than ten or a dozen—who have rebel sympathies. But they are not among the important people. And besides, Cobequid is very deficient in arms and ammunition."

"It has been reported that rebels have stayed in Cobequid and were helped to return to New England. I have heard the name Dickson—who, by the way, is located just across the river from your home—according to reports."

"I have heard that Mr. Dickson supplied the needs of American privateers while they repaired an old boat so they could sail home. But I have no first-hand knowledge of this. Since I last returned home from being on the King's business, I have been ill and remained in my house for the last three months."

The official, Michael Francklin, moved away when he saw another person from Cobequid.

"Samson, that was Michael Francklin!"

"Indeed. And I was very sorry that you had to hear me lying to Mr. Francklin."

"If you wanted to save your life, you didn't have too many choices."

"Still, it is not a proud moment for me."

Now, I felt badly that I had overheard the conversation and, thus, caused Samson pain. We returned to Cobequid silently. Samson must have been very distressed as, to some degree, he had betrayed Cobequid. He didn't report his encounter with Michael Francklin to anyone, but that made no difference. The next thing that happened disclosed that the Lieutenant-Governor had finally learned the truth.

The Reverend David Smith of Londonderry Township received a letter that was shared and discussed within Cobequid. In it, you could hear the shock and disbelief of the Lieutenant-Governor upon learning that he had been lied to and duped into believing that the people of Cobequid were loyal subjects of the King. He wrote that, "as I have no duplicity in my own conduct, I was not prepared to meet it in yours." The listeners were silent and gave no indication of their feelings. I would have been stung by the Lieutenant-Governor calling out my lack of integrity.

Ever a man of good will, despite how he had been treated, the Lieutenant-Governor promised "that if the Cobequid people act as dutiful and loyal subjects my glory and happiness will be increased to render theirs complete as human affairs will permit." He also warned, "if you attempt any longer to trifle and do not send me substantial proofs of your loyalty, I shall consider you rebels and treat you accordingly."

"Samson, I wonder what the Lieutenant-Governor means by 'substantial proofs of your loyalty'."

"He probably is referring to the taking of Oaths of Allegiance to the King."

"Will Cobequid do that or are they still thinking of joining the American Revolution?"

"This is a setback, but we are all quite determined to overthrow the English and rule ourselves. We are waiting to hear what the prisoners taken at Fort Cumberland will say to the Lieutenant-Governor."

The older members of the family were sitting around the kitchen table one evening. Samson was smoking his pipe. Martha was knitting, James and John were playing a game of cards, and Eleanor was putting away the materials used to teach the younger children to read and write.

"Father, do you know who was captured by the English at Fort Cumberland?"

"Aye. Thomas Faulkner of Debert. He has had several run-ins with the English in the past and so is well known by them. Also, James Avery, Jonathan Eddy's commissary officer, as well as Dr. Parker Clarke of Eddington Township on the Penobscot River, Benoni Danks of Cumberland Township and, to my surprise, Richard John Uniacke of Hillsborough Township."

"What happened to them?" John asked.

"They were put on *HMS Vulture* and taken to Windsor. Benoni Danks died there of his wounds. The rest were marched through the snow to Halifax."

"What will the English do to them?" Eleanor asked.

"Well, my dear, I suspect they will be charged with treason or high treason, tried in the Supreme Court, found guilty and hanged, but not before they reveal the names of others in Cobequid who also participated—or failed to report the plan to attack the fort."

Martha lifted her eyes from her knitting and looked into Samson's eyes with real concern. He held her gaze for a minute or two in the secret language of husbands and wives. Neither said anything, but James furrowed his brow and Eleanor looked away, keeping her feelings to herself.

All the families in Cobequid were consumed with worry, going about their daily tasks silently, their faces grim. If they spoke about the revolution at all, they whispered, hoping not to pass their feelings to their small children.

Then the news arrived from Halifax about the fate of some from Truro Township. Samuel Archibald, Member of the Legislative Assembly for Truro, and the militia officers—Truro Militia Captain Matthew Tayler, Samson's neighbour John Savage, Thomas Archibald of Truro (married to Janet Orr, Martha's sister), Samson's next-door neighbour Lieutenant John Johnson, and Joseph Scott of Onslow—were all charged with comforting, aiding, and assisting Martingale and Carleton and their associates belonging to the *Washington* and the *Gage*, rebel privateers.

Up to this point, Martha had been confident and cheerful, but finally she was visibly upset, a tear running down one cheek as she heard the name of her sister's husband.

"Samson, we need to go and see Janet. She must be really worried."

"I'll ride over tomorrow, Martha."

The next day, Samson returned to tell Martha that regular soldiers had been sent to read Thomas the charges against him. He was taken to the small ship that would transport all the prisoners to Windsor where they would walk to Halifax under guard.

Samson related that all nine of Thomas's children were crying as Thomas was led away. Samson and his family watched helplessly as their neighbours were charged and taken into custody. They could see the wives and children standing outside the doors of their homes, calling farewell.

Back inside the house, David, one of the younger children, said, "I wish Jonathan Eddy had captured Fort Cumberland!" His brother, James, cautioned him, "David, whatever we feel it is not safe to say such things aloud. You could put our family in jeopardy." Samson nodded in agreement.

Later in the day, we rode over to see Janet again. Martha sent some stew and bread in case Janet didn't feel like baking. It was always very hard for women to leave their home settlement as they had so much to manage, including the care of little children. On the way back, Samson, in response to my question, said he had secretly felt relief that his name was not on the list of men charged. He exhaled briefly, but it was too soon.

Soon, charges were laid against Charles Dickson, owner of the wharf and tavern where the American privateers and the escapee prisoners of war, had planned their escape to New England. This was just across the Salmon River from Samson's dock. Dickson, too, was charged with comforting, aiding, and assisting the rebel privateers.

Just when it seemed the bad news would be endless, a small ship arrived from Windsor. On it were, to the surprise and delight of the whole township, Samuel Archibald, Matthew Taylor, John Savage, John Johnson, Thomas Archibald, and Joseph Scott. Township folk ran to the dock from every direction yelling to their neighbours as they went. The returnees were met with great rejoicing, for they had been released by the English due to lack of evidence.

Thank heaven for English law and due process, I thought. The townships were too busy celebrating the return of their friends and kinfolk to think about English law. Reverend Daniel Cock, minister of Truro and Onslow Townships, called all the people to a celebration of thanksgiving, "for what we thought was lost is restored to us." The people met that evening at the meeting house and joined in heartfelt songs and prayers.

It was not over yet. In April, during the meeting of the Supreme Court, with Judge Isaac Deschamp presiding, Thomas Faulkner of Debert and Dr. Parker Clarke of Eddington Township were tried and found guilty, Faulkner of high treason and Clarke of treason. They were sentenced to be hanged, although carrying out the sentence was delayed so there could be an appeal.

In the early morning, a few weeks later, there was a knock on Samson's door. Answering in his nightshirt, the caller said that Thomas Faulkner and Dr. Parker Clarke and four others had escaped from jail and were hiding out in a barn. Samson threw on his clothes and followed the caller.

Later, he told Martha that they had helped the escapees get to Debert and warn Magistrate John Morrison that he was charged with high treason, and along with twenty-six men from Cumberland Township would soon be arrested.

Morrison, Faulkner, Clarke, and the four others were able to board a ship heading to Newburyport on the Merrimac River. They were delivered to safety within rebel lines, reported the ship owner on his return.

When all was said and done, no one was ever hanged for treason concerning the Eddy affair, the attack on Fort Cumberland.

"Samson," I asked, "why did so many men escape from jail and avoid hanging?"

"This is my suspicion, Caroline. There are about eight thousand New England men in Nova Scotia, all with muskets. The Lieutenant-Governor doesn't want to alienate them by hanging other New Englanders. It is probably a wise choice. And it doesn't give the New Englanders any reason to rebel. Also, a wise decision."

"And letting prisoners escape after sentencing them saves the Government the embarrassment of not trying them or not carrying out the sentence of hanging?"

"Aye, and I also suspect that Lieutenant-Governor Arbuthnot has no real desire to punish individuals, but to bring the townships over to signing loyalty oaths."

"But couldn't someone just sign the oath but continue to rebel against the Government?"

"Caroline, how can you even consider that! A man's oath is sacred. It is his bond. A man who would go back on his word is not to be trusted by anyone. No one would associate with him or do business with his either. No, either refuse or sign the oath, but there can be no going back on an oath!"

"I can see that this is a great point of honour with the men of Cobequid."

We left it at that.

Early in 1777 there was more news of rebellion.

"I hear that one of Colonel Jonathan Eddy's friends is trying to gather a militia and return to capture Fort Cumberland," James said, as we all sat around the table in the evening.

If the spies and rumours were right, John Allan, a landowner in Cumberland Township, also Justice of the Peace, Clerk of the Supreme Court, Sheriff, and Member of the Legislative Assembly for Cumberland Township, was advocating with the Congress in Massachusetts for another attack on Fort Cumberland. A successful attack would rally the Townships of Nova Scotia to the American cause. Early in January he began to assemble an armed force.

But English Loyalists in Massachusetts got word to Lieutenant-Governor Arbuthnot. He sent five warships to the Bay of Fundy: two at the entrance, one at Minas Basin, one near Fort Cumberland and a smaller vessel "to keep the inhabitants up the Cobequid Bay in order." The Lieutenant-Governor and Council also moved to prevent an overland invasion by issuing orders to Lieutenant-Colonel Gorham at Fort Cumberland.

Council also ordered that: "The inhabitants of Truro, Onslow, and Londonderry be call'd on to take Oaths of Allegiance, Supremacy and Abjuration at Special Sessions of the Peace to be held forthwith for that purpose in the Township of Onslow and that Mr. Cunningham with another magistrate proceed there on that business."

Hearing the order read, the angry men headed for the meeting house. I followed Samson as usual, and was ignored, as usual. Magistrate Archibald tried to calm them in order to speak, but to no avail. Finally, someone shot a musket into the air and the chaos came to an abrupt halt. The minister, the Reverend Daniel Cock, climbed up to the pulpit.

"Men, you know that Presbyterians of the Burgher persuasion are absolutely dead set against the state forcing us to take oaths. I am sure your fathers told you that unless they took oaths of Supremacy and Abjuration and took communion in the Church of England, they could not vote or hold public office back in Ireland. As well, you were all promised by the English Government who invited you to come to Nova Scotia in 1759 that you would not be asked to take such oaths even for officeholders and representatives of the townships. To add to our sense of revulsion, the English require us to kiss the Bible instead of just raising our right hands to take an oath. This we believe is idolatry. We must stand firm against this assault against our liberty and rights that were granted."

A huge "Aye!" arose from the gathering.

"Stand firm. Stand together. Resist the Government's intrusion into our freedom and our religion!" the Reverend Cock shouted.

I had heard the Reverend Cock preach many times by now. He was a pleasant and genial man, and his sermons were far from fiery or demanding. It was my thought that the men of Cobequid had given the Lieutenant-Governor ample reason to hang them all. Having them swear allegiance to the King seemed like the least aggressive move on his part.

"Samson, what will you do? Will you take the oaths?"

"Most certainly not. We will stand against this assault against the liberty promised to us."

Shortly after this, Cobequid got word that this second attempt on Fort Cumberland had failed to materialize. That didn't seem to deter the people from continuing to resist the orders of the Lieutenant-Governor. When the two magistrates, Mr. Cunningham and Mr. Pyke, arrived to administer the oath, they met with universal refusal. So, the Lieutenant-Governor threatened them further. He said that if they continued to refuse to take the oaths, he would treat them like popish recusants.

"What's a popish recusant, Samson?"

"It is only the worst thing possible you could call a Presbyterian: a Roman Catholic. In England and the south of Scotland, as well as in northern Ireland, Roman Catholics are hated. They have no civil rights. They cannot vote or hold public office or even worship in public. Here in Nova Scotia, it is illegal for Roman Catholic priests to come into the province. It would certainly mean I could no longer keep my job as Deputy Provost Marshall, nor would the magistrates and militia officers keep their jobs."

I feared for Samson and for Cobequid. The Lieutenant-Governor was ramping up his threats as his anger grew ever more furious against Cobequid. They were going to swear their loyalty, or they were going to pay for their duplicity towards him. I didn't blame him. No one likes to be publicly humiliated.

That evening Samson, Martha, James, and Eleanor sat around the flickering fire. Perhaps they were each considering what might happen to them and their township, to Cobequid.

Martha spoke quietly. "Husband, all this talk of war has brought us to the brink of disaster. I am afraid we could lose all we have worked together for in Nova Scotia. What do you think will happen next?"

"Martha, I'm sorry that it has come to this. I was looking forward to a bright future for us and our children. I thought that joining the American Revolution and getting free from English rule was best. All the townships did. If the Americans win the war and we are left under English rule, we may never see our relatives in New Hampshire again. I guess I am re-thinking everything."

They fell silent again.

Finally, James spoke, "Father, I think that Cobequid is not northern Ireland. I know many terrible things happened in northern Ireland, but Nova Scotia is not northern Ireland. I don't want to go to war. We came to New Hampshire to escape war and massacres. We can have a good life here in Nova Scotia—if it's not too late. That's how Eleanor and I feel. That's what we want for our brothers and sisters."

I could feel that Samson was touched by his children's observations about all the talk of war. Where were they going, where would they end up if the townships took up arms against the English? It would mean killing people to rule themselves. Did they want to go back to killing and being killed? Who knew how the American Revolution would end up? Who knew if the system of government they designed would actually be better than the current system?

Samson and I were riding along the River Road in the spring of 1777. He had recently learned that the Supreme Court of Nova Scotia was going to proceed against the residents of Cobequid to take all their movable property, including their animals. The Lieutenant-Governor was planning to charge them with outlawry and take away their land.

"What will you do, Samson?"

"Well, Caroline, I do not want to lose everything and see my wife and children homeless. I hope the Lord will see that much as I am loyal to my fellow township people and to my religion, I cannot put them in harm's way."

"Samson, I think the Lord does not so much care for loyalty as for love. You're doing the loving thing, and it will all work out in the long run, you know."

Later that month, Samson joined the others in Cobequid as they took the Oaths of Loyalty to the King of England and His Government in Nova Scotia. I stood and watched as the men lined up inside Tupper's Tavern and tried to read their faces. I knew Samson had come to terms with his decision, but what about the rest?

James and John Johnson, Samson's neighbours, were there, and they were glum and fidgety, one twisting the button on his jacket and the other kicking one foot against the floor. Further down the line was James Dunlap, staring at the toes of his boots and rocking back and forth looking as if he'd like to be anywhere but there. Alexander Nelson, father of fourteen, stared straight ahead, shoulders drooping, hands shoved in pockets. Samuel and Thomas Archibald seemed to be whispering together but in a desultory manner. Samson stood quietly, knowing that each of the men must be struggling with the choice between what they thought was right and what Lieutenant-Governor Arbuthnot had presented them with.

Choose, the Lieutenant-Governor had said, between signing the oath or deportation. "One order from me and soldiers in transport ships will set sail from Halifax and arrive in Cobequid Bay to start loading you and your families to go back to the colonies that are at war with England. This is what happened to the Acadians when they didn't sign the Oath of

Allegiance, and it will surely happen to you if you refuse to sign the oath. You must choose."

And they did choose. They signed. Lieutenant-Governor Arbuthnot wrote them a warm letter telling them of his great pleasure that they had become loyal subjects of the King.

One evening that summer, the whole Moore family joined me on the dock in the Salmon River. I told them how thankful I was to spend time with them and get to know them. Martha, Samson, and the girls gave me a hug. The boys shook hands with me. Little Martha gave me a kiss on the cheek and waved goodbye with her little hand.

Caroline woke up that morning in her own bed, exhilarated that she had had a dream adventure. As she drank her morning coffee and munched some toast, she realized she could now write her second chapter.

What day was it? Tuesday. *Only three more days to get this chapter written before meeting with my sisters. Best get going.*

Her fingers flew over the keyboard as she filled in the sketch about the lives and adventures of Samson and Martha. She thought about what to call the chapter. Rather ruefully, she realized that her dear ancestors had been traitors to the King and Government of Nova Scotia. But it was the truth.

"So, Caroline, what have you got for us?" Joan asked, looking up expectantly from her green tea.

"You're a little late, aren't you? Janice smiled.

"Where's Elizabeth?" Caroline asked.

"She's a bit late herself. Just getting a muffin, I think."

"Okay, I'll wait to read you what I've got until I get something for myself."

As she left the table, Joan and Janice looked at each other with raised eyebrows. She couldn't have written an entire chapter since they last saw her, but she was looking rested.

"Now, of course, it still has to be edited, but here it is. 'Chapter Two: Traitors.'"

As she read, the sisters made little sideways glances at each other.

"Well, done," Elizabeth said, looking at the twins.

"Yeah," they both said together.

Caroline smiled.

"So, we're descended from a bunch of traitors," Elizabeth said.

"Afraid so."

"What happened to Samson and Martha?" Joan asked.

"Well, Samson moved, and we don't know the reason, to the other side of the Shubenacadie River where he had bought perhaps fifteen hundred acres which he agreed to pay for in four instalments over several years. Besides farming, he was also getting into fishing in the Bay of Fundy just off the mouth of the Shubenacadie. After about three years, he, James, his oldest, and John, his second son, were out fishing when their boat was overturned somehow, and Samson and John drowned. So, the land was given back to the owner and James was given land back in Truro Township where the family moved. Eventually James got land elsewhere and gave his land in Truro Township to his brothers. Martha lived with one of her younger sons in Truro Township.

"Well, I'm sad to hear about Samson and John. What happened to little Martha, our ancestor?" Janice said.

"Martha married Robert Stewart and moved to West River, Pictou County, Nova Scotia. They had fifteen children and seventy-three grandchildren! One of the grandchildren, James, married Janet Begg, and they are our great-great grandparents."

"Fifteen children! I can't even imagine that! Well, anyway, you've made amazing progress. Can you keep it up?"

Caroline put down her coffee cup. *Could she*? "Oh, sure," she said, acting more confident than she felt.

"Do you need another two weeks or a month?"

"Better make it a month. Still some research to do."

The sisters were smiling as they collected their belongings and headed back to their cars.

As she drove home, Caroline pondered her good luck in having such a wonderful dream; a dream that let her imagine the lives of Samson and Martha, and especially their little daughter, Martha Moore.

What if I never have another dream and have to make it all up from my research notes? It would be a very different type of chapter than this. But then, what if just any dream wasn't what she needed to write chapter three? How could she dream just the right dream?

Caroline read and re-read all her research notes, took another melatonin, and hoped she had just the dream she needed. The next morning, she couldn't remember any dream, let alone the right dream. She felt quite distraught. *Maybe too much melatonin.*

The next night, still no dream she could remember. She took half the amount of melatonin and went to bed early. No dream.

Having tried every combination of possibilities, the next night she just went to bed, pulled up her covers and went to sleep. In the morning, as she made her breakfast, she thought maybe expecting just the right dream at just the right time was a hope too good to be true. She could feel a migraine starting so she took a painkiller and waited for some relief before finishing her porridge.

McDonald was holding his sides laughing at all of Caroline's attempts to dream her next chapter. The others had smiles on their faces as well.

"Well, Samson and Martha, you certainly provided her with an interesting adventure and your chapter seems like a great success," Margaret Nicolson said.

Samson and Martha smiled at each other. "It turned out rather well for us. Now, what about the rest of you? Who's next?"

"That would be us," David Stewart said.

"I feel sorry for her," Mary, his wife, said. "She's never experienced real physical hardship. I wonder if she can handle it?"

Her husband nodded in agreement. "But we agreed 'nothing added, but nothing omitted either'."

The others nodded in agreement, but the mood had turned more sober and reflective. Even McDonald was no longer smiling. "You had a bloody hard time, for sure. Well, we'll see if she really wants adventure or only thinks she does."

The rest sighed and nodded. This adventure would certainly make or break her.

"Who's going to invite her. Maybe you better get little Martha like the last time," David suggested.

"Do you think so?" Samson said. "Seems rather disingenuous. This time she really wants to go. Mary should invite her."

That night, Caroline heard a soft voice with a Scottish accent ask, "Would you like to come with us?"

Caroline said, "Yes."

CHAPTER FOUR

CANNIBALS — THE STEWARTS

1774: SCOTLAND TO PRINCE EDWARD ISLAND, AND ON TO NOVA SCOTIA IN 1776

I was awakening when I heard a rap on the door.

"Miss, are you awake? You have visitors in the drawing room."

"Hello, come in. Who are my visitors?"

"Why, your relatives, Mr. and Mrs. Stewart."

The young woman who now stood just inside the door of my bedroom curtsied. She wore a grey plain floor-length dress with a white apron. She had a cap with a gathered edge covering her hair. I wanted to ask, "Where am I?" but thought better of it.

"Miss, I'm here to help you dress."

"Oh, just leave the clothes and I'll dress myself."

"No, miss. It's my job to dress you and you'll not be able to get into the dress yourself." She looked puzzled at my suggestion that I could dress myself.

I looked around. A bright ray of light shone through a slight opening in the heavy damask curtains, illuminating the room. I was in a four-poster bed with a canopy. There was an oriental rug on the smooth wood-plank floor by the bed. Across the room, I could see a pitcher and basin on a stand. Wherever and whenever I was, it was a pleasant place.

The young woman was laying out the clothes. I glimpsed a long pink dress and other unfamiliar articles of clothing. "Miss, I have poured some hot water into the basin and there is cold water in the pitcher. I will go out for a few minutes while you wash. There is soap and towels beside the basin." With that, she closed the door behind her.

I washed. Feeling refreshed but still wondering where I was, I opened the door to the room and found the young woman waiting outside. She entered and as I took off my night clothes she handed me a long linen shift to put on. After that came several petticoats and a corset; a contraption used to keep your breasts in place, less you be called a loose woman. This had to be laced. Then came the dress. It was made of a beautiful taffeta material with stripes of pink flowers alternating with larger pink roses and lace trim. This, too, had to be laced up. It was lovely, but quite low in the front. Not something I would have chosen for myself.

Next, I sat down on a chair in front of a dresser with a mirror and the young lady, Miss Robertson, a lady's maid she told me, along with her name, brushed my hair, and arranged it carefully. She wasn't surprised to see me or curious about my hesitations. Over my hair, she placed a pale blue wide-brimmed hat decorated with flowers and ribbons. Silk stockings and buckled shoes completed the outfit. Looking with pleasure at her handiwork, Miss Robertson led me to the stairs, which I descended with great care. Waiting in the drawing room were two well-dressed people, a man and a woman, who came forward to greet me with smiles and hellos. I was very glad to see people who were glad to see me.

The man was wearing knee breeches with stockings and buckled shoes. His long jacket covered a long green silk vest with gold buttons. His dark brown hair was pulled back in a queue. He was quite handsome, as was his wife, she in a green floral dress with her red hair coiled on top of her head under a cream-coloured hat with various shades of green ribbons, showing off her lacy gold earrings.

We walked together to the dining room, which was full of similarly well-dressed people having their breakfast and chatting quietly. As we were seated in the dining room, I asked hopefully, "Where are we?"

"Oh, my dear, we are so sorry. I forgot that you have not met us. My name is David Stewart, and this is my wife, Mary Wilson. You are at the Red Lion Inn in Annan, Scotland."

"Oh."

"You're not displeased with us, are you?" David seemed genuinely concerned.

"No, no. I am surprised but very pleased. Do you know who I am?"

"Of course. We have invited you here as our guest, Miss Morton." Mary smiled encouragingly.

"Miss Morton. Then you must know Samson and Martha?"

"We most assuredly do." The husband and wife looked at each other and smiled.

"And this is a dream?"

"Right again," David said. "Although we should keep that to ourselves. I must tell you it is the practice here to burn or drown witches, so we must never give the slightest hint of anything out of the ordinary which might encourage suspicion."

"I understand. I would not be happy to draw the slightest attention to myself. But I have always been curious about your lives."

"We should also say that, although there are a lot of Morton families in Scotland, we plan to introduce you as a visitor from His Majesty's Colonies in North America, Nova Scotia specifically." Both David and Mary looked me directly in the eye and nodded to emphasize the importance of this information.

To indicate I understood, I suggested, "Miss Caroline Morton from the Province of Nova Scotia, relative of Elkanah and Rebecah Morton of Cornwallis Township. Descended from George Morton and Juliana Carpenter, who arrived in Plymouth Colony, Massachusetts, in 1623?"

"Aye. That will arouse no suspicion as to your connections in Scotland." David nodded.

Breakfast arrived. Poached eggs on toast with a delightful and tangy sauce, fried potatoes, and fresh green beans. And, thankfully, lots of strong, hot tea. I worried the whole time that I would spill something on my beautiful dress.

As we were finishing breakfast, I heard the sound of horses' hooves coming closer.

"There's the stagecoach!" said David, as he rose from the table and gave his hand to his wife to rise. I rose too, and asked, "Are we going somewhere?"

"Indeed. We are going to my tenancy so you can see how we live. Our landlord promotes the best agricultural practices and equipment so that we are the most advanced in Dumfriesshire in farming and husbandry."

"Then I am excited to see your farm." I smoothed out my skirt and realized that although my shoes had a bit of a high heel, they were comfortable. I followed my hosts toward the door.

"Let's hurry. The coach will only be here for fifteen or twenty minutes. Just enough time to water the horses and let the other passengers off." I realized David was trying to keep us on some kind of schedule.

The coach and four pounded into the courtyard. The horses tossed their heads and snorted as they slowed down. You could see the perspiration on their bodies and smell the wonderful pungent smell of the animals. I had always loved horses and considered going over to touch them, but then remembered about not drawing any attention to myself. Their manes and tails were woven with red ribbons and the coach had red lion insignias on the doors, much like the sign on the inn.

David paid the driver and escorted us to the coach. A coachman put a step stool below the door and helped me into the coach. David gave Mary a hand into the coach and followed her. There was a well-dressed gentleman inside and he nodded to us in a friendly manner.

There was a padded bench at the front and back, with handles by the seats and leather straps from the ceiling. The driver called, "We are ready, ladies and gentlemen!" The second blew a trumpet to warn that the horses were about to move as we started out of the courtyard and toward the road.

We were soon galloping down the road at breakneck speed. The coach pitched and rolled. David and Mary seemed quite inured to the experience, as did the other passenger. I loved the sensation of roaring through the countryside. It was exhilarating, but I found out what the handles and straps were for.

The stagecoach stopped at a beautiful, thatched cottage surrounded by fields. There was an enclosed garden at the front, filled with varieties of roses. Roses made their way up the side of the cottage and a spiral of smoke rose from the stone chimney. We descended from the coach and walked through the flowers to reach the front door. Inside was the coziest cottage you can imagine.

Waiting for us to arrive were David and Mary's children.

"Miss Morton, I would like to introduce you to my son, Robert, just turned sixteen. Robert, this is Miss Caroline Morton from His Majesty's Province of Nova Scotia. She will be visiting with us for a few weeks."

"Miss Morton, I am pleased to make your acquaintance. I hope you will have a most pleasant stay." Robert bowed.

"Thank you, Robert. I am pleased to meet you."

"And this is our daughter, Jennet, aged fourteen." Jennet smiled and curtsied.

"A pleasure to meet you, Jennet.

"Robert will accompany us on our tour of the farm. Mary and Jennet will prepare our lunch."

The three of us left the house. David waved his hand to indicate I should follow him down a country lane. "We will walk a way down this lane to see my fields of crops and herds of animals."

It was a beautiful late spring day. The trees swayed in the wind and the leaves made soft swooshing sounds and they blew this way and that. Rows of trees and hedges marked the fields, which were a hazy green from the early shoots of grain a few inches high. Further along, we leaned on a fence and watched his black cattle graze. Several of the cows had calves who romped about their mothers on spindly legs. Further along was a large field of sheep with many lambs hopping and skipping about in a happy, playful manner.

"Your house and your farm look so prosperous, David."

"Indeed, we are prosperous. After I sell my crops and pay my landlord, I have money left over. I am part of the farmers' association in Annan—a group of very prosperous farmers. At our recent meetings, we have discussed the idea of taking up land on the Island of St. John. The island has been divided into lots and the lots awarded to proprietors who are looking for people to emigrate."

"But why would you want to do that?"

"Well, the proprietors of the Island of St. John have promised very low rent and so we stand to make even more money than we do here in Annan."

"Who is the proprietor of the part of the island to which you are going?"

"No less than the Lord Advocate of Scotland! His name is Sir James Montgomery. We'll be going to his holding—Georgetown at Three Rivers—on the east of the island."

"Have you plans to get there?"

"We are amid finalizing our plans. In fact, there will be a meeting this evening to hear more about what we will need to take with us, especially farming implements, seeds, saws to cut timber, provisions, and all the details we can learn about the land and the weather."

"Have you already arranged for a ship?"

"Yes, indeed, we will be going to see her right after lunch." He smiled.

"Excuse me for changing the subject. Is that a river on the far side of the field of oats?"

"That is the River Annan. They say it may have been named after the Celtic goddess, Anu. I can't say this for a fact, of course. The Town of Annan is just a few miles upriver from the estuary of the Annan and the estuary empties into Solway Firth."

"Oh, perhaps that was what I was seeing on the coach ride here. There seemed to be sizable areas of flat sandbars."

"Yes, there are miles of red sand bars when the tide is out. The tide seems to come in quickly and it's best not to be caught on the sand bars when that happens."

Robert was quiet on our tour of the farm. He seemed to hang on his father's every word. Sometimes he ran ahead to get to a good spot to see the view before we caught up to him. I was impressed with his friendliness and good manners.

Soon we were back to the cottage and our lunch of fresh, hot scones with butter and preserves. There was cheese as well and plenty of strong, hot tea.

"Did you make the scones, Miss Jennet?" I asked.

"She did indeed," said her mother proudly. "She is an excellent cook."

"I agree. The scones were delicious."

She smiled.

David began to describe the ship they had chartered, when we once again heard the sound of horses' hooves and the trumpet sounding the approach of the carriage. We hurried out to the stopping place. This time the children were coming with us, so we all squeezed into the seats as the trumpet sounded again and the horses began their wild ride toward Annan and its seaport.

We rode through the Town of Annan with its red sandstone buildings. The seaport was a bustling place. The docks were surrounded with buildings used to store material to be shipped and those to be received. Ships rocked gently beside the docks, their sails furled, cargoes waiting to be loaded or unloaded. There were many workers and horse carts and ox carts for conveying materials to and from the storage buildings.

There were lots of unsavoury materials—animal dung, tar, spoiled food stuffs that had waited too long in the sun. The air wasn't too thick thanks to the brisk breeze blowing in from the Solway Firth. The incoming tide was raising all the ships, and it would soon be time for those ships that were loaded and ready to cast off their lines, to leave the dock, and head down the Solway Firth to the open ocean and to points unknown to me.

"There," said David as he paid the carriage driver, "there's our ship, the Lovely Nelly. Now I know she's not the biggest ship, but she seems sturdy and easily manoeuvred. Let's head over and I'll give you a tour. Mary and the children have seen the ship before, so they are going shopping."

We walked over the cobblestones toward the dock. From what I could see, the ship was everything David had said—on the small side but looking in good shape.

"Here's the gangplank, Caroline. Would you like to come on board?"

"Most certainly." I wasted no time boarding, only needing David's help to step down onto the deck.

We looked at the quality of the wood on the deck and the masts. The sails were all furled. We examined the wheelhouse and then went below deck to look at the accommodations. There were bunkbeds along either side of the space. Beside the lower bunks there was a bench running alongside. In the middle of the space was a table that stretched the length of the ship, with benches along either side. There was an area for storing food supplies. David opened the hatch to the hold, where the farming and logging equipment, as well as the trunks belonging to each family, were stored. There were barrels of food—salt beef and pork, potatoes, oatmeal, peas, flour, barley, tea, molasses, ham, beer, rum, cheese, butter, hard bread—as well as barrels of water. My elegant costume prevented me from going down to take a close look, but the Puritans had taken many of the same supplies with them to Nova Scotia. There being no refrigeration, salting or storing in brine was the only method of preservation for meat.

"How many people are going to go, David?"

"That's what the meeting tonight is for. We are waiting for the last of the potential settlers to make up their minds and pay their fare. The leaders of the settlers are Wellwood Waugh and John Smith. They have the most money invested in the charter of the ship and the provisions."

"Why Wellwood Waugh and John Smith?"

"Well, John Smith is an agent for some proprietors on the island. Wellwood is from Lockerbie and the rumour is that he inherited a tidy sum from his family and wanted to invest it in an estate in the Island of St. John. It is he who has chartered the ship."

"Oh, yes, Prince Edward Island," I said. David looked puzzled. Then I realized that Prince Edward probably hadn't even been born yet. I made a mental note not to get ahead of the timeframe. "So, he plans to buy land? I heard that, unlike most of North America, the land is only for rent from the proprietors. Do you plan to buy or rent?"

"Well, rent. I don't have an inheritance to invest in land."

"I hear that the King will give land grants to settlers in the other English colonies. I think there is still land to be had in Nova Scotia."

"Well, Miss Caroline, I don't have any knowledge of these things. John Smith and Wellwood Waugh have asked us if we want to be part of this emigration and from what I have heard, I am quite optimistic. I wouldn't take my wife and children if I wasn't as certain as a man can be that this is a good plan. And remember, the proprietor is Sir James Montgomery, Lord Advocate of Scotland. If he has faith in this plan, then I feel certain that with some hard work, we will thrive in our new surroundings."

That evening, we had supper at the inn. After supper, the men considering going to the island met in the tavern. Mary, Jennet, and I sat close by while Samson, Robert, and the men asked questions of John Smith, the agent for the proprietors.

"What will the rent be in the Montgomery holdings?"

"One shilling per acre," replied John Smith. "Right now, you're paying three and five up to twenty-five shillings per acre, depending on the quality of the land, right? So, this is a very good deal."

The men looked at each other and nodded. It seemed they thought this was a good deal.

"How many people live on the island right now?"

"Presently, about twelve hundred people, but we are anticipating a huge immigration in the next few years. Those who go this year will get the best locations."

This, too, seemed to be what the men wanted to hear.

The ship master of the Lovely Nelly, William Sheridan, was also present to hear the discussion and answer questions about the ship. He told the assembly that the Lovely Nelly was a snow. Most of the farmers and tradesmen didn't know what that meant, so he explained that it meant a square-rigged vessel of no more than a thousand tons with two masts, supplemented by a snow or small mast immediately behind the main mast.

"This is the perfect ship for your purposes, gentlemen, as it can hold a lot of cargo and deliver it speedily. And speed is important for another reason that you will understand immediately—the snow is the preferred ship of pirates and privateers. This means that if we are sighted by a pirate ship and they decided to give chase, we have the best chance of outrunning them."

"We can definitely appreciate the snow's speed now that you mention pirates, Mr. Sheridan," said David, and the rest of the men smiled their agreement.

"There are even more advantages to appreciate. For one thing, the snow can operate with a crew of as few as thirty-five men and has a draft of ten feet."

"That draft means you can bring the ship in close to shore to be loaded or unloaded?" asked Wellwood Waugh.

"That's right," Mr. Waugh. "As you have a lot of people and materials to unload when you reach St. John's Island, that will be an asset. And, of course, the smaller crew means less cost for those who charter a snow."

The questions continued until everyone seemed satisfied. Most present—about eleven families and quite a few single men and a few single women—signed up for the year 1774 and a few for 1775.

David and Robert re-joined us and were all smiles.

"So, Mary, my dear, and Jennet, my darling, we are going to become pioneers! It will be hard work for a couple of years, but then we shall have many acres of land with very low rent. What an adventure!"

Mary didn't look excited, nor did Jennet. I couldn't tell about Robert. I think he wanted whatever his father wanted. He seemed a sturdy, practical young man. David would certainly need his help with what was ahead.

The family left me at the inn, and they headed back to their farm. Before they left, I asked when the ship would be leaving. "Caroline, my dear, we are leaving in a week's time. Just time enough for you to prepare for the voyage."

I didn't know what to say. I hadn't thought about what David's plans meant for me.

I went to my room, where Miss Robertson helped me undress. "Miss Robertson, if you had a chance to sail across the ocean, would you do it?"

"Oh, yes, Miss. It would be very adventurous. Just the very thought of sailing on the high seas makes me quite excited."

"Do you know how long it takes to sail across the Atlantic Ocean?"

"No, Miss. I should think at least a week."

"A minimum of seven weeks if all goes well. One can be blown off course or becalmed or caught up in a severe storm."

"I would still want the adventure, seven weeks or more."

"You're a braver woman than I, Miss Robertson. I hope you get the opportunity to go if that is what you want."

"I think my fiancé and I will be married next year and then we will go to the colonies. Perhaps I will see you there?"

"Perhaps you will. And congratulations on your engagement. May you be blessed with a long and happy marriage."

"Thank you, Miss Morton. I feel certain that my future will be wonderful."

I was still wondering what to do when I fell asleep.

Miss Robertson brought my breakfast to my room, as I needed time to ponder my decision. As I ate, I realized the dream had brought me here for the adventure, so of course I would go, and informed Miss Robertson.

"Well, Miss Morton, you'll have to have a new outfit. You can't go aboard ship wearing such a lovely gown. If you please, I can go with you while you shop for something appropriate."

What would be appropriate, I wondered. I needed ship-worthy clothing but had no idea what was available. I asked Miss Robertson for suggestions.

"May I suggest something like a riding outfit? The skirt is less full than the one on your dress and a little shorter. It is made of sturdy material. Under it you wear high boots. The jacket is close-fitting and buttoned up to the high collar. You wear a lady's tricorn hat with this."

"Perfect." I knew that would be comfortable and practical, having worn it before. "Let's go shopping. You can show me how to find the shop. How much will this cost?"

"You should not concern yourself about that. Mr. Stewart has left you a purse for your expenses."

When David next arrived at the inn, I had bought two outfits along with an ankle-length cape. I had a valise with my nightgown, towel, hairbrush, and some soap. The carriage was waiting with the family inside. Off we went to board the Lovely Nelly.

After several days at sea, lying in my upper bunk, I got over my seasickness, and set about getting my sea legs, which took less time than on the previous voyage from Plymouth to Nova Scotia. By then, we were just past Ireland and out into the North Atlantic Ocean.

I was out for a stroll on the deck with David and the family when we met up with Wellwood Waugh and David Smith. I learned Wellwood's wife was Helen Henderson and they had four boys and a girl, the oldest being ten years. John Smith's wife was Margaret McVicar and they had two children, William six and Mary four. After the introductions, the men talked among themselves.

As I listened, I gained impressions of Wellwood, a plump man in his early thirties wearing gentlemen's clothing—knee breeches, a long blue brocade vest with silver buttons and a long jacket with big cuffs and decorative buttons. He was a cheerful and friendly person, but with a sense of superiority from, I guessed, receiving a substantial inheritance and being able to charter the Lovely Nelly and underwrite the venture. The passengers seemed to accept Wellwood's superiority as it was due to his initiative that they had this opportunity.

Wellwood's partner in the venture, John Smith, a lean and muscular man, was in his forties, and, David said, with experience working for St. John's Island proprietors. He seemed capable and confident. He wore worsted wool trousers and a workman's jacket of similar material.

I also got to know the other passengers from the Annan area—other families had boarded at points along the Solway Firth—and their hopes and dreams. For the most part, it was David who made sure I was introduced. This would usually happen on fine days when we were out strolling on the deck.

"Caroline, here are our friends, Charles Blaikie and his wife, Jannet Herries. They have four children. Charles and Jannet, I would like you to meet my relative, Caroline Morton. She is from the colonies—Nova Scotia."

"Pleased to meet you, Miss Morton. Please tell us a bit about Nova Scotia."

"Well, Mr. and Mrs. Blaikie, the closest part of Nova Scotia to St. John's Island is called Pictou County. It was first settled in 1767 by New Englanders. They called themselves the Philadelphia Company. There were only six families originally, so they arranged for many Highlanders to come over six years later in 1773 to begin to settle their land grant, the Philadelphia Grant, which is near Pictou Harbour."

"Highlanders!" said David with disgust. "Why would they invite those savages to live near them?"

I was shocked. I had never heard David speak with hatred before. "David, what is your concern about Highlanders?" Knowing many of my ancestors were Highlanders, I felt quite concerned and knew there were already Highlanders on Prince Edward Island.

"Well, Lowlanders know how dangerous and warlike they are. We've all heard the stories of the raids and wars. They supported Prince Charles Edward Stewart, a Roman Catholic, against King George only twenty-five years ago. Who knows what they are planning after that!"

The Blaikies changed the subject. "Miss Morton, I'd like you to meet our children. Here is John, six, William, four, and James is three. Jennet is carrying the youngest member of our family, Ann, just ten months."

"Very pleased to meet you. Are you excited about starting over on St. John's Island?"

"Of course," Mr. Blaikie said as he glanced quickly at his wife. "We will soon have more land at lower rent."

As we chatted, John Crocket and his wife, Margaret Young, and their three children, James, six, William, four, and Joseph, one, joined us. Soon, the men were talking about their plans once they arrived. The women were focused on their children's safety as the deck of a ship is no place for young children.

As time went by, I got to meet eleven families with a total of thirty-six children, fully one-third under five years of age. In addition, there were thirty-six young men, mostly in their twenties and thirties, one of whom was Wellwood's half-brother, William Campbell, aged twenty-four. There were also five single women among them: William Campbell's sister, Margaret, aged twenty-six, and Wellwood's cousin, Catherine Colvend, thirty years. Among the men were four masons, one blacksmith, two wheelwrights, two farmers, three joiners, which was what they called carpenters, nine labourers and one sailor.

All the men saw their new life on St. John's Island as a great opportunity—one that they would never get in Scotland—to rent a large amount of land at a very low price. The women kept their reservations to themselves as there was no going back, even if they had the money to return. Their homes were now rented out to others by their landlord, their possessions sold to buy a share in the venture.

"Mr. Waugh," David asked one overcast and rainy day when he and all the passengers were below deck, "will there be a representative of Sir James to meet us and assign us to our tenancies?" Mary and I, sitting nearby, stopped talking to listen to the answer.

"Nay, Mr. Stewart, there will be some men there organizing Sir James' materials—fish and timber—for shipping back to Scotland. Mr. Smith and I have decided we should spend our time first getting to know the area and how best to get through the first winter. Then we will be in much better shape to decide how to assign each man his property."

The men, listening in, nodded in agreement.

"That seems perfect, Mr. Waugh. I imagine no one man can cut logs and build cabins by himself. Cooperation is the way to go." David seemed satisfied with the plan.

Another man asked, "What directions have you received from Sir James about settling on Lot 59 at Georgetown, Three Rivers?"

"Why, Sir James has left the whole affair in our hands and so we are quite free to determine our future."

"Mary, what do you think?" I whispered.

"Caroline, strictly between you and me, Sir James has provided no help or support—but, of course, he will be glad to accept our rent. No one knows for sure what must be done. We are on our own."

That wasn't a comforting thought, but I tried to relax and enjoy the voyage. No sense fretting and being tense, I told myself. Maybe David was right. Maybe everything would work out. None of the men seemed the least worried.

We settled into a routine. The women were up and dressed early. On the deck, the ship's carpenter had built a shelter around the stove, which sat in a box full of sand. Each morning, the ship's chandler filled the women's pails with water from a barrel on deck. Then the women poured the water into several large pots, where they boiled the daily supply of oatmeal into porridge and served it with butter and molasses. If it was a fine day, all but the smallest children and their mothers ate on the deck. Every fine day, the passengers spent as much time as possible on deck, as the passengers' quarters were cramped.

After breakfast, tea was made for all. Lunch was usually bread and cheese with perhaps some ham. Supper was a stew, made from salt beef or pork, well rinsed, along with onions and peas. Peas were also mixed with suet, flour, raisins to make a pudding, which young and old enjoyed. There was beer and rum to drink, for no one would drink water that had not been boiled first. I had always liked beer, but this stuff was weak and watery. At least the alcohol content killed off most of the germs.

It was a beautiful summer day somewhere in the middle of the Atlantic Ocean. As we often did, David, Mary, and I leaned on the railings and watched the seabirds skim the tops of the waves, following the ship. I tried as much as possible not to think about how many miles it must be down to the bottom of the sea. David was in a cheerful mood.

"Caroline, what an adventure! I'm happy you decided to come with us. Every day I wake up imagining my farm on St. John's Island. Now it will be difficult for a year or two, but then I can see Mary and I sitting on our front porch enjoying all we survey—our little estate."

"Mary," I asked, "how are you feeling about the great adventure?"

"Caroline," she looked at David with a furrowed brow, "I admire David's enthusiasm, but I am concerned about the amount of heavy work there will be. I'm fifty and David is older than I. I don't have the energy of the young people on this voyage."

"That's where our young people come in, Mary," David said. "Robert is sixteen and Jennet is fourteen, and with their youth and strength, we'll have no problems. And think of the land we can leave them in the future. It will be in their interest to put all their effort into getting settled."

"As long as we don't run into any unknown difficulties, I guess you're right, Husband."

On clear days, I spent hours whale watching—or more specifically looking for whales to watch. I was surprised to be joined by a little girl called Susie—maybe seven or eight and the daughter of a couple I hadn't met yet. She was young to be on deck, but the crowding in the underdeck areas was difficult for everyone.

Susie would chat happily about her hopes for her new home. She would help plant the kitchen garden and learn to make bread and pudding. She especially liked pudding. Susie was good company. I assumed her mother was busy managing younger children. The greatest fear for mothers was that a child would crawl out onto the deck.

One morning I awoke and saw women dressing their children and hurrying them up to the deck.

"What's happening?" I asked from my top bunk.

"Two babies are sick. We don't know why, so we are taking the healthy children up on deck," said one mother, as she herded her brood toward the ladder where her husband was waiting.

The parents of the sick children, who had not boarded at Annan but at later stops as we sailed down the Solway Firth toward the sea, held their sick children, rocking and singing to them trying to give them some tea or a bite of bread. Their older children watched helplessly as their parents became more and more desperate. Finally, some of the single women came down from the deck and took their older children up with the rest of the families.

After having dressed, I stayed in my bunk, hoping I might be of some service. It was excruciating to watch as the two babies struggled to live, and the parents cried and prayed. Finally, it was over. That night, another family's baby died.

In the morning, the ship's carpenter made three little coffins, filled them with sand, and drilled two holes in them, so they would sink. The passengers and crew gather on the deck as the fathers placed the babies, wrapped in their little blankets, into the coffins while the mothers knelt and wept. The captain said a prayer and benediction as the sailors lowered the little coffins down into the sea. Breaking away from their friends, the parents ran to the railing and, seeing their babies now in the sea, wept and called their names.

But the coffins did not sink. They bobbed along in a little convoy and were soon in the ship's wake. The sun sparkled on the waves and a light breeze encircled them. For a time, the rising sun was too bright to see what was happening, and by the time the sun was higher in the sky, the coffins had disappeared into the light.

It has always struck me as strange that even amid such grief, daily tasks must be done. The women cooked breakfast, but the parents of the babies remained at the railing, refusing food and drink. Finally, at sunset they were persuaded to eat and drink before going to bed.

"Your other children need you," the other mothers told them. "You must rest and eat for their sake."

The next day was the Sabbath, and all were in attendance as the captain led the worship service. The hymns and prayers comforted everyone, now joined by the memory of the little coffins sailing away on a sunlit sea.

After the service, David looked sad and, for the first time since I met him, seemed deflated. "I never imagined that such a thing could happen to us on our own ship. Other immigrants must sail in ships over which they have no control about the food or the cleanliness, but this ship was chartered and cleaned from top to bottom before we brought our families aboard."

Mary said, "My heart breaks for those parents, not even the comfort of burying them in the parish churchyard where they could visit and bring flowers. I don't know if I could survive seeing my babies buried at sea."

"I know, Mary. I wonder if they would have come if they knew the danger?"

"Oh, aye, they would have come anyway because they want a better future for their children, and they believe that the future lies on St. John's Island."

It was shortly discovered that the cause of death was foul water. A barrel had a dead bat floating in it. It was the smell that led them to the source of so much misery. The babies had been bathed in it before they died, presumably ingesting some of the water. The barrel was thrown overboard, and the parents eased their concern that childhood diseases had infested the ship.

A week later, we were somewhere in the middle of the North Atlantic. I was chatting with some of the women with very young children and the talk seemed to be, once again, about breast feeding. The women usually breastfed until the baby was over a year old. Besides being the only form of feeding babies, it was a way to space out pregnancies. We also discussed teething and other concerns of mothers.

I excused myself and went to look at the whales swimming alongside the ship. We often saw whales and seabirds, like terns and puffins. Frequently, we would see large flocks of migrating ducks or geese or swans. I was enjoying the bracing sea air and salt spray when the captain warned us that there was a storm on the horizon. We were to secure all our belongings and stay below deck until the storm had passed.

This was just what I feared—a storm at sea. The clouds rolling towards us, pushed by a fierce wind, were not dark but black and huge. I could see that we could not outrun them. The wind also raised the waves. The first flash of lightning was followed by a tremendous clap of thunder, which then rumbled on until overtaken by another flash. Not just one flash, but lightning that branched out in all directions, lighting up the sky. Soon the whole world was jagged lightning striking the sea, followed by rolling thunder filling the air.

Then it was dark. The crew closed the hatches, to prevent the waves that were washing over the decks from running down into the space where families huddled in the bunks, parents trying to prevent their children from falling onto the floor.

We were one small ship tossed on gigantic waves, below us the depths of the ocean and above us the chaos of the storm, and in our hearts the growing fear that this might be our day to die. The ship pitched and rolled and shuddered. Would she break up? I could hear the captain yelling orders to the crew. I tried to protect a couple of the older emigrants, or maybe we just all held onto each other. Someone began the Lord's Prayer, and everyone joined in with a sincerity that might not always have been obvious in regular worship or devotions.

As the storm worsened, no one spoke. Everyone held on. I couldn't hear anything above the sound of the wind and the waves pounding the ship. What had happened to the captain and crew? Were they swept overboard? What about the masts? Were they intact? Would we survive or would the ship break up? Would we soon all be at the bottom of the sea?

To the extent I thought anything at all, these were my occasional thoughts. It took all my strength just to hang on to the side of the bunk. Then I heard an ear-splitting crack. We had been struck by lightning and could smell something burning. Was our ship on fire?

Some men wanted to open the hatch and find out our situation, but the hatch was locked! Our fate was completely in the hands of the captain and crew, and no one knew if they had survived or were swept away by the giant waves. I'm pretty sure we were all praying; I know I was.

After what seemed an eternity, someone said, "I think the storm is lessening." We listened intently.

"Don't let go too soon," someone else said. "Maybe the ship has turned in another direction."

We waited.

It seemed safe to let go of the uprights we had been clinging to in desperation.

We waited.

No one wanted to ask the obvious question, "What about the crew?"

After about an hour, we heard someone unlocking and moving the hatch.

"Are you alright?" asked a voice.

"Yes," we said. "Are the crew alright?"

"We've lost two men," was the answer. "The captain says you must stay below for at least another hour while we clear the deck and make repairs."

"We will," we called back. Most people fell asleep out of sheer exhaustion.

Once people had recovered from the terror of the storm, the captain held a memorial service for the two crew members who were lost overboard. They were only young men. One had a wife and child. Everyone prayed in a most heartfelt way for their souls and for their family and friends.

It's amazing how danger bonds people together. There was a sense that all on the Lovely Nelly were closer to each other than before. That was probably the only positive thing, other than our lives, of course, that came out of surviving the storm.

The voyage continued with pleasant weather. When a sailor pointed out the most northerly tip of Cape Breton Island, we could see it in the distance. That meant we had entered the Gulf of St. Lawrence and were within a week of reaching our destination. We all felt relieved and excited—relieved that we had survived the ocean crossing and excited that our goal was in sight.

Mary, Jennet, and I were perambulating the deck on a fine but windy day. The men were spending all their time planning for the arrival. The women were fretting about how to keep their young children and babies safe once we arrived. Were there not bears and other dangerous animals?

We heard a shout from the crow's nest. The wind blew the sound away, so everyone ran towards the sound. "Pirates! Pirates! On the horizon!"

Every head turned in the direction the sailor in the crow's nest was pointing. To our horror, we could see a ship heading directly toward us.

Captain Sheridan appeared on deck yelling orders, "Women and children to your bunks, men as well unless you can handle a musket. Run up the sails, turn her to the south-west and fill the sails! Bring up the muskets!"

David and I held onto the railing, straining to see if the pirates were gaining on us.

"Caroline, I think they're closing in!"

"Oh, yes! They're American privateers—look at their flag!"

"Aye, aye! A blue flag with a top left corner of white!"

Our ship sails, having caught the full breeze, billowed out with the northeast wind. It was flying through the waves with the sea spray being blown back, soaking the deck.

We were so fixed on the sight of the privateer gaining on us that we didn't even realize our clothes were getting soaked. Time stood still as we clung to the railing and rigging, praying that our ship would go even faster. But the privateer was still gaining on us, and the captain handed out muskets to the sailors and passengers on deck. David took a musket, but it didn't look like he knew how to handle it. I refused.

"Load your muskets! Prepare to defend the ship!" he yelled.

Then, with seconds to spare and seemingly out of nowhere, there appeared a massive ship with three masts, the sails filled, heading toward the privateer. We saw the moment the privateer spotted the big ship, as she changed course to avoid the *Antelope*—for it was *His Majesty's Ship Antelope*, a ship of the line and pierced for fifty-four guns—assigned to these waters to capture pirates and American privateers. Her flag, the White Ensign, was flying straight out in the wind as she gained on the privateers.

A huge cheer went up from the deck of the Lovely Nelly as crew and passengers realized that we had been saved from being captured. If we'd been captured, we would have been taken to an American port where the ship and its contents would be sold. Then the passengers and crew would be put in jail until they could exchange us for American prisoners captured by the English.

To the passengers' astonishment, the captain called for our ship to continue racing through the sea.

"What's happening? What's going on? Why are we still heading on this course?" The answer to our questions was soon forthcoming, passed along by the sailors to the passengers—the *Antelope* is hunting American privateers and, as well, hunting young men to press into the Royal Navy. The sailors said there might soon be a war, and the navy needed sailors. If we stayed around, the young men might be in as much danger from the Royal Navy as from the American privateer. We soon put more distance between us and the *Antelope*, and they did not pursue us.

That evening, the day drew to a close under a cloudless sky and the moon rose over the ocean, shining down on the celebration of passengers and crew. Men and women danced on deck to the music of several fiddles and a harmonica, while others sang the old familiar songs as they swayed and clapped their hands to the music. I joined in, happy just to feel part of the soon-to-be pioneers.

We travelled toward the east coast of the island and on August 23, 1774, the sailor in the crow's nest shouted, "Land ho!" We all rushed to the railing to see, floating on the horizon, the first sight of our destination, our new home, St. John's Island. As we sailed along the east coast of the island, we could see the red cliffs topped with a vibrant green forest. Turning west, we entered Cardigan Bay, and finally Georgetown Harbour. Everyone cheered as we anchored in the harbour.

Close to the wharf were some buildings. We could see a few men on the wharf as the ship dropped anchor. The plan was to go ashore and find out what could be gleaned from the men.

John Smith and Wellwood Waugh were rowed to the wharf, and we could see them chatting with the men. Soon they were rowed back. Everyone waited with bated breath for the news.

"At high tide we can tie up to the wharf and unload our materials. We can put them in the storage sheds—which belong to our landlord for storing fish and timber until it can be shipped to England or New England—while we get started with cutting logs and building homes. The men will show us where our home settlement is and answer any questions we have," John Smith said.

We ate some bread and cheese while we waited for high tide.

There being well over ten feet of water by the wharf at high tide, we tied up at the wharf. Leaning over the railing of the ship, we could see the rocks on the bottom through the crystal-clear water. The men disembarked and were shown the storage buildings where they could put their supplies. Mr. Smith later told us that the men were from Stanhope Farm on Lot 34, also owned by Sir James Montgomery. Stanhope was to be a flax farm but after four years it was barely surviving. The men, indentured servants from Perthshire, were from Lot 34 and came over in the summer to cut timber to be loaded on ships returning to England, along with fish caught and dried by fishermen from New England.

In contrast to the men's excitement, the women, their brows wrinkled with concern, were reserving judgment. They could see no houses or shelters visible. Where would they take their children? How would they cook for their families? It took the men several days to unload the ship and put the supplies in storage, while the women and children remained onboard. In the evenings the men brought fresh fish back to the ship and everyone welcomed the change after seven weeks of salt beef and pork.

After the ship was unloaded, the men determined that they would find a suitable clearing in the forest and set up tents and bring up cots, bedding, trunks, cooking utensils and some food. Once they had organized this, the women and children were helped off the ship and led by a path through the woods to the little tent community. For a while we all staggered about. The constant rocking motion of the ship had affected our inner ears balance system. Even going to sleep or getting up you felt like you were rocking.

The trees encircling the community, fir, spruce, birch, maple, and pine, were massive, and many two hundred feet tall. Each tent had a circle of flat stones just outside the opening and a stack of firewood beside it. Lacking any other option, the women organized their family's belongings, started a fire, and prepared to make a meal. In the meantime, some men returned with fresh fish, bought from some fishermen who were on the beach splitting their catch and laying them on the fish flakes—platforms built on poles where fish were laid to dry in the sun and the wind.

David had put up a small tent just for me close to his family's tent. I didn't have my own fireplace as the plan was that I would eat with the family.

"Will this do for you, Caroline?" Mary asked as she peeked inside.

"I can't say I've ever camped for any length of time, Mary, so I guess I'll find out soon enough." No sense complaining that I never liked camping, I thought.

"Nor have I, Caroline. I'll just be so glad when the men build us some cabins. At least our children are older and can help with all the chores. Just imagine all the women with little children and all the household chores to accomplish while camping out." She sighed at the whole situation.

"I know how you feel, Mary, but we'll get through it, I'm sure." I was trying to encourage myself as much as Mary.

She nodded and went back to her tent.

I went in my tent, unfolded the blankets I had been given, and put my valise to one side. What now, I thought. And soon found out the answer—get pails of water to drink and to wash with; help carry firewood the men were splitting by the tree line back to the fireplace; help peel potatoes; wash clothes and hang them on bushes; just no end of daily chores.

That night the pioneers and their children went to bed on their little cots—their first night in their new home.

Although many supplies and equipment had been brought up to the tent community, the bulk of the supplies brought on the ship were stored in the landlord's sheds on the waterfront. This was to tide them over the winter until gardens could produce enough food and they could catch their own fish and seafood.

The men, having had many days aboard ship to plan, went to work with a will. Some cut down smaller trees and chopped them into firewood, which they supplied to each tent each day. Others took the water buckets to the nearby stream and hauled water back to each tent daily. Some men cleared an area to plant a vegetable garden for potatoes, turnips, onions, and oats. A few tried their hands at fishing, bringing back fresh fish from time to time as well as lobsters and other shellfish. Soon fall arrived with its spectacular display of colour and cooler nights. Mothers dug warm clothing out of their trunks.

The community had to guard the garden with muskets as deer, bears, racoons, rabbits, and other animals were enjoying the fresh vegetables. When that proved unsatisfactory, a sapling fence was constructed to encircle the garden. The growing season being much shorter on the island than in the south of Scotland, many of the plants didn't have time to grow or ripen, but at least they were ready for next spring.

I helped the folks near our tent with fetching supplies and watching children to give their mothers a break. That's when I discovered a worrying propensity of children—I don't know how many I caught up with just before they wandered off into the forest or down to the stream. Mothers with many little children just couldn't watch them all and do their chores, so I was much appreciated.

One morning, early in November, we woke up to a snowstorm. It lasted all day and left a foot of snow. During the storm, the men had to leave their tents to brush off the snow lest the tents collapse under the weight of it. David and Robert were reliable in keeping our tents snow free. I often went with them to help others. Everyone in the community helped each other all they could.

During the winter, some men from the Stanhope farm, Lot 34, came over to teach the men how to cut timber and prepare it to be incorporated into a log cabin. The Stanhope men also showed them what materials they would need to cut for framing the roof and shingling it with birch bark shingles. The Georgetown men, as they were now calling themselves, were ready to build as soon as the ground was thawed enough to dig cellars and line them with the stones they were gathering for that purpose.

Most of the men had never seen a two-hundred-foot tree, let alone cut it down. The Lowlands of Scotland are almost barren of trees except along streams or gullies. I could see their anxiety as they first watched the Stanhope men cut down a hundred-fifty-foot white pine. How much strength did it take to chop halfway through such a tree trunk? Which way would it fall? Just suppose you finally got one lying on the ground, then what? And the stumps: how do you get rid of the huge stumps to plow the ground?

Some men got up the courage to cut down their first enormous pine tree and the others limbed it, gathered the boughs into a pile, and set them on fire. This was something they could only do when the forest was wet in the winter and early spring. They eventually learned to plant potatoes around the stumps.

David came home one day from a logging experience, his face red and damp with perspiration and his clothes covered in wood chips. "I helped cut down another pine tree, my dear. We're trying to concentrate on trees that are the right size for log cabins and clearing more space for gardens and pastures. It's hard work, I must say."

"Sit down, Husband, I'll get you a cup of water. Rest yourself. Remember you're not as young as most of the men."

"Oh, don't worry, Mary, our Robert is right there beside me and takes my place from time to time. It's all rather exhilarating and by spring we should have our cabin ready to be built."

The winter was rough because of the cold. Everyone, including me, was losing weight due to the effort needed to attend to the work and the cold. Even with many layers of blankets, it was hard to sleep because I was always cold. Spring came and none too soon.

As the days became warmer, the building and gardening efforts began. Cellars were dug and lined with stone, logs were notched and stacked one on top of the other, roofs were framed and covered with birch bark shingles, and to keep the shingles from flying off in a windstorm, poles were nailed lengthways across the roof. The biggest effort was the building of rock fireplaces. All the women and children joined in bringing stones up from the beach to aid in the effort. Soon one family after another moved into the log cabins, lighting roaring fires to finally feel warm at night.

Regularly, Wellwood and John Smith would walk about talking to the settlers. They lived in rather larger and more 'luxurious' tents a short distance from the rest of the community. They seemed to have over-wintered well. On the first of these occasions, Wellwood said to David, "Well, Mr. Stewart, I see you have survived the winter. We'll soon have this settlement in good order and be able to help the next arrivals."

"Oh, indeed, Mr. Waugh, I have always said that it would take a couple of years but soon we would be sitting on our front porches and enjoying our own extensive farms, and maybe doing a little fishing or lumbering on the side."

"I like your attitude, Mr. Stewart. I am sure Sir James would be proud of what we have accomplished so far. Isn't that right, Mr. Smith?"

"Oh, aye, Mr. Waugh. And it is certainly under your good management that all this has happened."

Wellwood and John Smith strolled on to the next tent, Wellwood still wearing his gentlemen's clothing and looking quite pleased with himself.

In June, the Lovely Nelly brought the next group of settlers to George-town. There were about fifteen families and some ten single men, including a schoolmaster and a clerk. There were two weavers, two joiners or carpenters, a gardener, a chapman, a blacksmith, a mariner, and a farmer, along with twelve labourers. Most were from Annadale, Galloway and Nithsdale in Scotland. Wellwood was there to welcome them and take charge of the next group of settlers. The newcomers were scarcely set up in their tents when the most horrific event happened.

People noticed several rodent-like creatures—I think they were mice—in the settlement in the morning. By noon there were many more, and as the men got together to decide what to do, suddenly a mass, a horde, a wave of the creatures swept into the settlement swarming over and into everything. They ate the food in the garden and flowed into the tents and cabins eating everything in sight. The householders and their children, in utter terror, huddled in the corner of their dwellings, having no idea what was happening. Some creatures even ate the bedding and nibbled on the covers of books and curtains. The waves of rodents kept coming for some hours. Then, as suddenly as they had come, they were gone. The men who followed them said they disappeared into the forest where they could not follow.

There was nothing to do but replant. Wellwood and John Smith were ferried by a small fishing boat, owned by the American fishermen, to Tatamagouche, on the coast of Nova Scotia, where they bought more seed potatoes.

The work of the settlement continued, incorporating the new arrivals. Most of the 1774 settlers were in cabins, but the 1775 newcomers were in tents. Still, we all dared to relax and enjoy summer evenings with music and dancing. There were clam and lobster bakes, along with fresh fish and new vegetables out of the garden.

One hot summer day, David and I were sitting on the wharf enjoying the sunshine on the water and the cooling breeze.

"We are well on our way to success, Caroline. Like I said, a few difficult years and then we shall have our dreams come true."

"David, I am glad you have so much optimism. Do you ever get discouraged?"

"Nay, Caroline, I am the perpetual optimist. I see no future in pessimism."

"Nor do I, David. But it is important to be realistic. Hard to believe there are not more troubles to come."

"Whatever happens I'm sure we can handle it."

"Of course," I said just to be agreeable. No sense worrying."

"There you go, Caroline. There's the spirit!"

Secretly, I liked David's happy, enthusiastic disposition, but I doubted that there was smooth sailing ahead. Would he be able to handle adversity? How would I handle adversity?

We sat for a while longer, watching the American fishing boat crews, not far offshore, as they spent their day catching fish and the evenings splitting and drying them on fish flakes. They often came ashore to enjoy a break from routine and drink rum and tell tales.

One story was about how disgruntled the people in the Thirteen Colonies were with the new tea tax imposed by the King to help to pay for the French and Indian War. The English had fought that war to protect the Thirteen Colonies from the predation of New France and their Indian allies. Now the colonies didn't want to help pay for the war, leaving the burden to be borne by the English people back home.

Later, Mary and I were preparing supper when it occurred to me that she might see things differently from her husband. Mary, I had learned, was not a complainer or a pessimist, but a realist. She dealt with all the everyday problems with a calm resignation. She told me she was waiting for a few years of successful crops before she felt confident about this whole enterprise.

"Mary, have you heard the stories by about the dissension in the Thirteen Colonies?"

"Oh, aye, Caroline. The women think there will be a war as the Americans are all descendants of dissenters, of every shape and kind, who left England so they could do what they wanted the way they saw fit. The women don't know if a war between England and the Thirteen Colonies would affect us here, and we cannot get enough news to decide about that."

"I fear that you and the other women are right. You know that the fishermen that come ashore here are Americans?"

"Aye. And a rowdy bunch of men they are."

My fears of adversity to come were soon proved correct.

First, the mice returned, eating the contents of the vegetable garden when it was too late in the year to replant. It was a terrible blow, with so many mouths to feed and winter coming on, but there was a final blow that put the nail in the coffin of the settlement at Georgetown.

All night, on one of the last days of September, we could hear carousing on the beach. There were loud, bawdy songs, and fighting. The settlers were becoming used to this behaviour as it happened regularly and, besides, no one would have wanted to get involved with the Americans when they were drunk. And certainly, none of the settlers could have guessed what would happen next. In the morning, a settler found Mr. Brine, who managed the storage buildings, unconscious. The fishermen had turned pirate as they had stolen everything out of the storage buildings—everything.

When Mr. Brine regained consciousness, he told the story of the night before. The fishermen had heard that the American Revolution had started, and they determined to sail to New England and join the fight. Seeing the settlers now as the enemy, they raided the settlers' supplies to take with them. Hardly believing what they were hearing, the men searched through the buildings to see if anything was left, but the Americans had taken the whole lot.

What were we going to do? The spectre of starvation rose like a ghost out of a grave. We all saw it and for a time we all became disorganized and depressed. Families went into their dwellings and stayed there for days. What was going to happen to them and their children? Even David, the perpetual optimist, succumbed to despair.

"David, you must rally the settlers and make a plan. Consider your remaining resources. It will soon be too late if the others don't get together and make a plan."

"Caroline, there are no resources. Our garden is eaten by the mice. Our barrels of food and all our tools are stolen."

"David, it is a desperate situation without a doubt. But you will all starve if you just sit in your dwellings and do nothing. Get up for your children's sake!"

To his great credit, David did get up. "Well, I suppose we can gather all the sea food that we can and store it for the winter. And we can go over to that Acadian village and see if they have food to sell. If so, we'll buy some potatoes and oatmeal and bring it home on our backs. At least that's something. At least it's a start."

"There you go. That's the spirit. Get the men together and see if there are other things you could do. But hurry. The snow can start in October. There is no time to waste."

I wondered about buying from the Acadians. They had been living on Ile St. Jean—St. John Island—at a place they called Trois Rivières, very near Georgetown, before the English expelled them at the end of the French and Indian War. Some had hidden from the English, and some had returned after taking the Oath of Allegiance to the King of England. I was sure there would be no love lost on the new settlers who came to occupy their land.

Every man, woman, and child hunted for clams, mussels, lobsters, and oysters, burying them in pits in the cold sand. The Acadians were willing to sell potatoes, but because money was of little value since there were no stores or trading posts, the settlers had to barter with the clothing they had brought from Scotland. That was a frightening prospect—freeze to death or starve to death. It was the decision each family had to make.

David and Robert took some of the family's clothing and went to the Acadian village at least twice in October and brought back as much oatmeal and as many potatoes as they could carry. There were still some dried fish on the fish flakes, and these were divided among the settlers. The few men that had guns went hunting but besides bringing back a few rabbits no one was a hunter, and they were all afraid of getting lost in the dense forest. David and everyone else in the settlement moved slowly and barely spoke. A pall had fallen over the Georgetown people.

After the first snowstorm, the equation became even more difficult. Go through the deep snow to the Acadian village, when you might freeze to death on the way there, or with an added degree of difficulty, while returning carrying a heavy load of potatoes. Every family knew that if the father died, they too would die because no other family had enough to spare. Indeed, no family had enough to keep their own family fed. That meant that some girls sacrificed themselves for their family by not eating their fair share of the food available, so that their fathers and older brothers and little children could survive.

I noticed Jennet was not eating and spending a lot of time in bed. "Jennet, you must eat," I said one morning, when she had quietly taken only a spoonful of her porridge. She looked at me, or rather, through me, and didn't reply.

"Mary, Jennet hasn't eaten her porridge. She needs to eat."

But Mary didn't reply. I could see she was depressed. Then, I realized that she, too, was not eating much. It seemed to me that I should join them. After all, I was an extra mouth to feed. I joined Jennet in her cot, huddling together to keep warm. Mary kept the fire burning.

Later that day, I went down to the beach with a bucket to get our share of the clam cache. The boys chopped the ice-covered brook every day to get fresh water and split firewood. After we ate our daily ration of clam and potato soup, we all went back to bed.

One morning in February, we heard someone yelling hysterically. "He's going to eat her! You've got to stop him!" No one had the energy to get up out of bed to investigate. Later in the day, our neighbours told us that the daughter of one settler had frozen to death and her father was going to try to save the rest of his family by eating her. I didn't ask what happened, and no one spoke further of it, but we all had sympathy for the father, and for his son, who was horrified by the plan.

During the January thaw, a Maritime phenomenon which didn't happen until February that year, I overheard David talking to Mary.

"I am so sorry, my dear, for having brought you and the children out to this wilderness to starve to death. Not being able to provide for my family is the most woeful experience. Please forgive my uneducated optimism and desire for adventure."

"Husband, whatever happens, I know that you would never have intentionally put our family in danger. I had no idea what we were getting into either, but at least we will all die together."

If I had the energy, I would have cried to hear their despair, but I had to save my energy to get some more clams from the cache on the beach and peel some potatoes. The oatmeal was gone. There was only half a bag of potatoes. No one needed to ask what happened next.

The next morning as I awoke, even before I was fully conscious, I knew Jennet had died during the night as, despite my arm around her, there was no warmth from her body. With broken hearts, we wrapped her in her blanket and buried her at sea for fear that she would be savaged by wild animals, or, worse yet, by the starving people in the camp. Each of us felt we would be next and had become resigned to this.

But we survived. Some of the young men, including Robert, made the long trek through the snow, during the spring thaw, to the Acadian village with the last of the clothing the passengers had brought from Scotland. A few men tried ice fishing and, with their remaining strength, sat on the cold ice catching just enough fish to help keep body and soul together.

When the ice in the strait began to break up, a small fishing boat was spotted. Seeing men waiving to them from the wharf, the crew came over to check the situation. The boat was from Charlotte Town. The men quickly hired the boat for someone to go to Pictou to see if there was land available there. They choose David, and he was more than willing to go. We all had had enough of mice and bad luck. Staying meant dying. Maybe it would be best to see what Nova Scotia had to offer.

Those who had the energy went down to the wharf to see David off. He looked almost cheerful, as no one wanted to spend another day on the Island of Doom. I went with him to be of some support. Most of the men were barely hanging on and couldn't even imagine using their energy to go on this trek. Robert stayed to look after his mother. It took most of the day to reach Pictou Harbour as the pilot had to go out of his way many times to avoid the ice flows, the result of the breakup of the ice in the Northumberland Straight.

Reaching the little wharf, near the largest settlement in Pictou Harbour, the pilot tied up his boat and we disembarked. The skipper agreed to wait for us for a couple of days as David had money to pay him for the round trip.

The few people on the wharf looked at us rather strangely, I thought. Then I realized why. It was the first time I had thought about our appearance since winter set in. David was not much better than a skeleton dressed in rags and clutching his blanket round his shoulders—as all the clothing had been bartered for potatoes—and his shoes had holes in them where the mice had tried to eat them. I couldn't see myself, but I suspected I didn't look much better. What a sad sight we must have been.

"We've come from St. John's Island to buy supplies. Who oversees your colony?"

Someone directed us. "I believe you could inquire at Squire Patterson's. He sells supplies. His house is about a mile from the wharf. Turn right at Front Street and just keep walking. His is the only plank house in the town."

The town was a few log cabins scattered here and there. There was no church or school. There was no store or tavern. Front Street might be described as a bridle path, and that would be generous. In many areas of the town there were alder swamps and bogs. Altogether a rather dismal place, I thought. But did they have food to spare? That was the only thing we really cared about.

After walking a long time, that seemed even longer as David and I were exhausted, we came to a plank house and knocked at the door. A man in what had once been rather elegant clothing, but clean and well cared for, opened the door.

"I've just arrived from the Island of St. John. I'm part of a group of settlers who have come to grief in the short time we've been there. Could you spare me a meal and some information about Pictou? My name is David Stewart, formerly of Annan, Scotland."

"Greetings, Mr. Stewart and Mrs.?"

"Miss Caroline Morton of Halifax, a friend of our family and a relative of Mr. Elkanah Morton and his wife, Rebecca Tupper of Cornwallis Township."

"Well, you're both most welcome. Come in. You shall have fish stew and bread and some ale if you please or tea or both. Come in, come in. I am Squire Robert Patterson of Renfrew, Scotland, late of Maryland and part of the Philadelphia Grant."

Soon David and I were eating fresh salmon stew with potatoes and turnip. The bread was so good—finely milled after the rougher bread I'd had, before we ran out of flour—with lots of fresh butter. We both drank a bottle of ale. Mrs. Patterson cut each of us and her husband a slice of blueberry pie and poured heavy cream over it. David looked at her gratefully, ate one piece and asked for more. She cut him another large piece and handed it to him with a smile. After our repast, David asked to lie down, and he instantly fell asleep. I was also shown to a bed and enjoyed my first comfortable bed in a very long time.

The next morning, after a breakfast of oatmeal porridge with cream and maple syrup, David told his story to the Pattersons. "Squire Patterson, Mrs. Patterson, I can't thank you enough for the food and a place to rest. You have been most Christian in your kindness and generosity. Now that I am feeling a little stronger, I would like to tell you about our experience as settlers on the Island of St. John."

"We will gladly hear your story, Mr. Stewart. We are recent settlers as well, but not so recent as yourself. I think my wife might enjoy telling you of our arrival in Pictou. But let's leave that for another time."

"The owner of two-thirds of Lot 59 is Sir James Montgomery, Lord Advocate of Scotland. His agent, James Smith, and a man recently come into an inheritance, Wellwood Waugh, got settlers from Dumfriesshire and a few other shires and began to settle near what was to become Georgetown on the Three Rivers."

"Yes, I've heard of Three Rivers. Trois Rivières the French called it."

"The same place, indeed. Well, we came well-prepared and well-provided. We were all tradesmen and farmers from rich farmland and used to using the best farming tools and techniques. We hoped to farm on good land at lower rent than the arrangement we had in Scotland. And we would have been happy and prosperous on the island if calamity did not strike us three times in a row."

"My goodness," Mrs. Patterson said, "whatever could have happened, Mr. Stewart?"

David told them the whole sad story.

"I heard stories about this," Mr. Patterson said. "They say that you became cannibals, eating the flesh of those who died over the winter."

"It is true that several older people and a few young children died, whether of hunger or disease I do not know. We gave them decent Christian burials." David looked at me, his eyes severe. I interpreted it as if I should say nothing, nor did I.

"The men got together and at least fifteen families decided we couldn't risk another season of being overrun by the mice. We decided to look for a more advantageous place. I was sent by the families to find out if there might be land in Pictou where we might settle."

"Mr. Stewart, please tell your families that they will be most welcome in Pictou. We have land available at no cost. There are terms and conditions for improving the land but to date no one has enforced these terms except for escheating land grants that were given to land speculators once they did not settle enough people on them. There is good land on the West River and on the Middle and East Rivers. The mouths of these rivers are settled by the Hector people but a little further upstream, the land is untouched."

"Who would I see about getting the land surveyed and assigned to families?"

"I am the surveyor for the Philadelphia Company. So, you have come to the right person to survey, assign and register land in Pictou."

"This is the first sign that our luck is about to turn. I am grateful to you, Squire Patterson. I'll return to the island and organize the passage of the families to Pictou."

"Even in this I can help you, Mr. Stewart. I have a ship available if that would be suitable."

"Thank you, again, Mr. Patterson. I will return by the fishing boat by which I came. It will take us a week to get organized and have everyone down to the wharf at Three Rivers. Can your ship meet us in a week, Mr. Patterson? We need to move and get started on planting and building our cabins as soon as possible."

"Agreed, Mr. Stewart. We will be there to bring the families to their new home in Pictou. I have some supplies that I could sell to you, Mr. Stewart, to help in the meantime."

"Thank you, Mr. Patterson. If you could give me some potatoes and some oatmeal, it would be gratefully received. We may not have provisions, but we do have money. Unfortunately, on our end of the island, money is useless as there is no monetary system."

We left Mr. Patterson and his wife after thanking them for their kind hospitality and headed back to the wharf, where the fishing boat was waiting. It was spring and the ice on the strait, having nearly disappeared except for an occasional floe as usually happens, the water of the Northumberland Straight was a beautiful blue reflecting an equally blue sky with a few fluffy clouds. Closer, the red colour of the shores and cliffs enhanced the green of the forest above, the beauty hiding the hunger and desperation of families who were close to starvation. David and I didn't talk the entire trip. What was there to say? We both just wanted the families to be in good enough shape to prepare to travel to Pictou in a week's time.

After docking, we walked as quickly as David could up the path into the forest and reached the home settlement. Seeing us approach the men rose and gathered around us, followed by the women and children.

"What is the news, David? Please tell us that we can escape from this place to safety and security."

"Good news, indeed, people. We are most welcome at Pictou. There is free land available and by great good luck I was directed to the very person who can survey the land and assign us our settlements." David explained about the ship that would come in a week and asked each family to be ready. "In the meantime, I have brought oatmeal and potatoes which we will pay for once we get settled in Pictou. If anyone needs any help, let me know and I will try to find some help. I know that Miss Morton will do anything she can do to help. You just have to ask."

At that point, I felt a tug on my skirt and looked down to see one of the little children. "It's Miss Susie, isn't it?" We all looked so different after that winter.

"Aye, Miss Morton. Miss Morton, will you help me wash my dress? I want to go to Pictou and look pretty."

"Of course, Miss Susie. We'll go over to the stream, and you give me your dress. I have some soap in my valise, and I'll wash your dress and put it on a rock to dry. You can wear my extra jacket while you wait, and we can recite your alphabet. I hope you've been practising."

Susie smiled and gave me her hand. We walked to the stream and chatted while I washed and dried her dress. She was pleased with the result, but I was shocked to see how emaciated she was. I could count each rib and she had not an ounce of fat on her little body. I worried. You can only lose so much weight before your heart and kidneys shut down. Getting everyone to Pictou and getting them fed was the only way to prevent my worst fear.

"Now I'm ready to go to Pictou."

"Will you miss this place?"

"Nay, Miss Morton, every year our crops are eaten by mice and our parents are very worried and sad. I want to go to a place where we can have some food and be happy."

That's what I wanted for them, too.

There wasn't much packing and readying to do. Nearly all their farm implements, and seeds were gone as well as their supplies. Thankfully we still had the tents, cots, and cooking ware—whatever wasn't in the storage sheds. As promised, Mr. Patterson's ship arrived and there were smiles, even a little laughter, as the settlers boarded. Good weather and a quick passage further lifted the spirits of the fifteen families.

When we arrived at Pictou, Mr. Patterson was waiting on the wharf along with a tall red-haired man wearing a kilt. Once the passengers were off the ship, Mr. Patterson turned to the red-haired man and said with great consternation, "Mr. Fraser, look at these poor souls. They look like skeletons. The whole situation is worse than I thought."

"Aye, Mr. Patterson. This will surely test the extent of our hospitality. But we must find a way."

As David approached, they turned to address him and the families. "Mr. Stewart, Mr. Fraser and I welcome you to Pictou. You are, of course, most welcome but we must sit down with you and some of your menfolk and make a plan to help you as best we can."

"Mr. Patterson, Mr. Fraser, thank you for your greeting. Where can I direct the families to go while we discuss immediate plans with you?"

"The women of Pictou have been baking and cooking in anticipation of your arrival. If you lead the families to my house, they will be fed, and you can build a temporary shelter nearby. You have brought tarpaulins and tent pegs?"

"Yes, indeed," said David. "Before we leave the wharf, let me introduce you to John Smith and Wellwood Waugh who are the leaders of our expedition." John Smith and Wellwood Waugh had not fared well during the famine. At least they had never asked for more than their fair share of the cached food and had tried to help with all the physical work. Wellwood, himself, having been from, we believed, a rather privileged background, was not used to physical labour and found the work exhausting. He was one of the last to get off the ship. He was in bare feet, holding a blanket with one hand and carrying a bucket of clams—the only thing he had left to feed his family, despite all the supplies and provisions he had brought from Scotland. Of all the men, David had fared the best and thus led the exodus to Pictou.

"Welcome, gentlemen. Come and be fed and then we shall make our plans," Mr. Patterson said.

As we were speaking, the crew of Mr. Patterson's ship had unloaded what little valuables the families still possessed, and they posted a guard to watch these belongings until the men returned.

The walk to Mr. Patterson's house was a little quicker than might have been expected. The thought of good, hot food drew the people forward. As they approached, they almost broke into a run. They were greeted by smiling faces, pots of stew, and huge chunks of bread to dip into the thick, steaming, delicious, venison dish.

"Sorry not to have enough spoons for all of you. We hope the bread will allow you to scoop out the meat."

Wellwood looked at the women with a great smile. "You need not worry, mistress. Your pots will soon be empty."

After the meal, the men followed Squire Patterson to the area on his land where he thought they could set up tents. The men, being used to this exercise by now, and refreshed with food and hope, returned to get the tarpaulins, tent pegs, and the other belongings from the wharf. Before nightfall, there were makeshift shelters for the families. The Pictou women came by with more bread and milk for the children. There was also ale for the adults.

For the first time since the initial swarm of mice, people felt more secure and confident. Surely, they had finally found the place where they could settle and thrive.

Now that hope was on the horizon, Miss Susie spent time with me, chatting on about having a home once again and learning to make pudding. Several times I encouraged her to eat a little more as, despite her dreams of pudding, she wasn't eating well.

Concerned about her, I asked her parents if I could sleep with her. I thought I could get her to eat a little more before bedtime, but to no avail. However, she wanted a story. We snuggled together near the warmth of the fire, and I told her a story about a little girl who went on a long journey to find a new home. After many trials, the little girl finally found a lovely, new home with a fireplace and lots of food where she learns to make puddings for her family.

Susie smiled happily. "That little girl is me!" "That's right, I said," smiling back at her. Then we both fell asleep.

That night, Miss Susie died. We awoke in the morning only to discover that she had died in her sleep. She seemed so peaceful.

I felt bereft, having become attached to the little girl during our long voyage and the two years on the island. I wanted to go down to the beach to cry but found my legs didn't want to carry me that far, so I sat down where I was and wept. We buried her in her pretty dress in the community graveyard. There was no minister, just Squire Patterson to say the prayers.

Susie's death gave the community pause. They realized they were much too tired and weak to begin immediately to plant a garden and build log cabins. They and their families needed to build up their strength. The next day, when they met with Squire Patterson and Mr. Fraser, they were clear about that necessity.

Mr. Patterson asked the men to be seated. There was only the ground to sit on. "Dear people, I know you are grieving one of your own, but time is not on our side. We must decide almost immediately how we can help you get started in Pictou. I have asked Mr. Alexander Fraser, a leader of the Hector people, to give us advice. His people only arrived three years ago, and they are just barely getting started. The other obstacle for us is that his people only speak Gaelic. They are from the Highlands of Scotland and were brought here at our instigation. They are having a very hard time themselves. I am a leader of the Philadelphia Grant people. We have been here since 1767. Altogether in Pictou County at the moment we have eighty-four people—not families but people. There must be about a similar number of you?"

"That is right, Mr. Patterson. The men have had a meeting and most unfortunately, we find that our state of near starvation of the last winter has greatly reduced our strength and energy. Indeed, many of us have difficulty thinking clearly. We must have rest and good food to return us to health. Our people realize that this will put the utmost strain on the people of Pictou, but if you can just give us a little time and food, we assure you we will be an asset to Pictou. We will pay for our way with cash if that is of any value here. All of us will work to benefit those who assist us and learn from them all we can."

"Thank you for stating your case so clearly, Mr. Stewart. It is my belief that you are people of goodwill and integrity. So here is what we can offer in our own strained circumstances. Mr. Fraser and I will put each of your families with a Pictou family. You will pitch your tent on their property. They will provide you with food and teach you the skills you will need to survive. You will do all that you can, more and more as your strength returns, in labour and with goodwill until you can survive on your own. And I will show you the land available on the three rivers that flow into Pictou Harbour and survey this for you."

"With the utmost of our strength and ability, we will accept your plan and we thank you all from the bottom of our hearts."

"Mr. Fraser, do you want to say a few words to the families?"

"I do, Mr. Patterson. Friends, when I and other of the Hector people saw your people on the wharf at your arrival, we were shocked. We were very poor people who arrived at Pictou in a poor state after eight weeks at sea. But we had never seen people poorer than ourselves and in such terrible condition. We were very moved to do all we could to help. However, you must realize that it will be very difficult for those of you who are placed with Hector people. I, and three others, are the only one who speaks English. The rest speak only Gaelic. If there are any concerns, you must go through me to resolve any problems."

Faced with the kindness of the Highlanders, David's long-held animosity toward them dissolved. "Mr. Fraser, I have often heard about Highland hospitality. Please thank all your people for your gracious kindness. The very thought of causing you even the least concern distresses me. We will do all we can to repay you for your generosity."

With that, the Island of St. John families were divided among the Philadelphia and Hector families. They soon tented in tiny clearings near the log huts of the people who had almost nothing. My little tent was set up beside David and Mary's, near Mr. Fraser's log cabin, as David was now exercising some leadership and needed to consult with the leader of the Highlanders.

It was several months before the Georgetown people had the mental and physical strength to even think about clearing land and building log cabins. In the meantime, they hoed the gardens of their hosts, split firewood, hauled water, and helped to thresh grain. Being farmers themselves, it only took a demonstration of the method for them to understand what they were to do.

A month or two after their arrival, Mr. Patterson, and his servant, a convict serving his sentence by working for no wages for seven years, arrived at the wharf to collect David, Wellwood and John Smith for their first excursion up the West River. I went along. The means of transport was a canoe made from a hollowed-out log. We looked at the canoe with consternation, but having no options, lowered ourselves carefully into this uncertain vessel.

Mr. Patterson and his servant paddled us the mile across Pictou Harbour to the mouth of the West River. The trees came right down to the water but occasionally, as we travelled upstream, there was a small clearing with a log cabin and a barn. Soon we were past all European habitation.

We eventually went ashore and pulled the canoes up out of the water. David turned to look across the river and nearly fell. There, standing on the far bank, were several people looking back at him. They wore almost no clothing except for a loincloth and their long black hair fell across their copper-coloured skin. After regaining his footing, David looked toward Mr. Patterson to see him waving in a friendly manner at the strangers. They responded in a very dignified and considered manner.

"Who are these people, Mr. Patterson? Are they dangerous? I've heard that savages live in the forests of Nova Scotia."

"Do not disturb yourself, Mr. Stewart. These are the Mi'kmaq who live in these parts. They do not trouble us at all and, indeed, they have been helpful to us in times of need."

I was glad to see them looking so strong and healthy. I thought they were a beautiful people and wished I could have spoken to them.

David looked back across the river, but the Mi'kmaq had disappeared as silently as they had arrived.

"Now," continued Squire Patterson, "the land here on the east side of the West River is available for settlement."

They spent some time as the farmers examined the soil and the surroundings. Several of the men, David being one of them, spoke up and asked for Squire Patterson to survey land grants for them on the West River.

"We'll be visiting the Middle River and East River as well this week. I know some of you are living with families on these rivers and have looked at the land. I can certainly give you land grants upstream past the Hector people's land."

Some of the newcomers wanted land grants on the Middle and East Rivers and they were soon surveyed, and the grants assigned to each of the fifteen families who had come from the Island of St. John.

On the West River settled the families of Anthony McLellan, William Clark, David Stewart, William Smith, Joseph Richards, John McLean, and Charles Blaikie. On the Middle River settled the families of Jon Crockett, Robert Marshall, Robert Brydon, John Smith. The families of Thomas Turnbull and Anthony Culton settled on the East River. Wellwood Waugh and his brother, William Campbell, settled near the Town of Pictou.

It was late fall when all was settled. By now, the Georgetown families referred to themselves as the South of Scotland people—others called them the Dumfriesshire people—to distinguish themselves from the Hector people from the Highlands and the Philadelphia Grant people from New England. They would stay with their hosts until spring and would then clear land and build cabins.

One afternoon I went to visit Mrs. Patterson. Her husband had mentioned that she liked to tell the story of their arrival in Pictou, and I hoped she would have time to tell me what happened.

"Come in, Miss Morton. Yes, I would be glad to tell you about our arrival here. Please sit at the table. I've just put on some tea and I'm sure I could tempt you with a scone."

"Indeed, you could. I love your scones. So delicious."

"Let me get myself comfortable. There. Well, at the end of the French and Indian Wars in the early 1760s, land speculators in England and New England began to contract with the Crown, through the Government of Nova Scotia, for land grants. Our company, the Philadelphia Company, obtained two-hundred-thousand acres in this area and advertised for settlers. All the land grants required that the land speculators settle a certain number of families over a certain period of time. The families themselves had to agree to improve their land by cutting down forest and planting crops or providing pasture for animals. In the end only six families signed up to come to Pictou—and one of those families returned to New England."

"Only six families came to Pictou? You would have been the only English-speaking people on the north shore from Canso to perhaps the Miramichi River." At this time, Nova Scotia encompassed the lands that later became New Brunswick, including the Miramichi River.

"True. I still don't know what we were thinking. Robert was so enthusiastic about having plenty of land, there was no room for doubt or deliberation. So, we came on the ship *Betsy*. Captain John Hull, from Rhode Island, was our captain. We left Philadelphia, stopped at Halifax to get directions, and arrived in Pictou Harbour June 10, 1767."

"What was that like—arriving full of excitement at your destination?"

"It was only upon arrival that the enormity of what we had undertaken became clear. The great, primeval forest that covered Nova Scotia surrounded Pictou Harbour and came right down to the water's edge. We stood on the deck speechless. Then, to our horror, we saw fires burning on the beach and men running about yelling and hollering. We were sure they were savages—Indians. Remember, we were only a few years past the French and Indian Wars. We knew all about how Indians conducted warfare and we were terrified. After a while, someone looked at the beach through a spyglass and discovered that the people on shore were white people."

"Who were they?"

"Settlers from Truro Township who had found their way through the forest. They had heard about us after we stopped in Halifax and trekked through the forest to greet us. We laughed at our fears once we realized how easily spooked we were because of the stories we had been told.

"Truro Township would be about forty miles through the forest and over Mount Thom. There would have been no road or even a trail?"

"True. Well, we unloaded our supplies onto the beach, and I walked around surveying our situation. Finally, I just leaned up against a tree and said, "Oh, Robert, take me home!" She took a sip of tea. "The next morning, the ship was gone. Unknown to us, she sailed away."

"Lest anyone might change their mind?"

She nodded. "There we were. Twelve men and women and about twenty children. The youngest child had been born on the *Betsy* just as we anchored in the harbour. Let me see if I can recall a few details."

"There was Dr. John Harris and his wife. He was the brother of one of the Philadelphia Company speculators, Matthew Harris, and an agent on their behalf. Then my husband, Robert, and our five children. Our eldest was nine years old and the youngest three months. James McCabe and his wife had six children. Their son, John, married Eleanor Moore, Samson and Martha's daughter. John Rogers and his wife had four children. Henry Cumminger and his wife had four or five children if I remember correctly. There was a sixth family, but they left almost immediately. And, of course, my husband had his servant, a convict serving seven years through free labour. Dr. Harris also brought two enslaved black people."

"What happened to the enslaved people? Are they still in the community?"

"Why do you ask, Caroline? I think they're still in the service of Dr. Harris. Where would they go?"

"Oh, I just didn't realize that enslaved people were here from the beginning."

Mrs. Patterson furrowed her brow and tilted her head to one side, trying to understand my question. She decided to proceed.

"We began to build shelters and plant a garden at what is now known as Brown's Point, the only part of the harbour that belonged to the Philadelphia Grant. The rest of the harbour was included in Alexander McNutt's grant. He was a land speculator from northern Ireland and had been responsible for settling Truro, Londonderry, and Onslow Townships on Cobequid Bay. However, he didn't have much luck getting settlers to come to this grant and so it was escheated to the Crown in 1770. We were able to get more harbourfront and moved to this better location."

She excused herself and went to check the fire where she was baking something for their supper. She returned with more scones.

I admit I may have eaten several and the serving plate was empty. "Oh, thank you, Mrs. Patterson. You are a splendid cook, and I just can't get enough of these scones. They are delicious with your butter and preserves."

"I'm glad you like them. So, I told you about the colony until 1770."

I nodded, chewing on a scone.

"By 1770 we had a population of eighty-four and livestock consisting of six horses, sixteen oxen, sixteen cows, sixteen young cattle, thirty-seven sheep, and ten swine. Dr. Harris had a fishing boat and a small vessel. That year we harvested sixty-four bushels of wheat and sixty of oats. By 1775 we had a municipal government with Dr. John Harris as Clerk and Overseer of the Poor."

"I can see that you are very well-organized and industrious people. I'm sure it was quite a while before you knew that your colony would survive but now here you are doing so well. A lot to be proud of, I'm sure." She smiled at my praise of their efforts and continued.

"One of the first major improvements was a cleared trail between Pictou and Truro Township so we could travel easily on foot or horseback."

"Could people travel over it with carts, or ..."

"Nay, it was a blazed trail. You could only travel it in the daytime so you could see the blaze marks on the trees. But, for us, this was a huge advancement and we called it a road.

"But it connected Truro Township and your Pictou community so you must have felt less alone?"

She nodded. "That's it, Caroline. That's why our road was so important to us. Well, to meet our obligations to settle more people, we decided to bring people from the Highlands of Scotland. We knew they were in a bad way after the Battle of Culloden Moor in 1746 and probably willing to emigrate. They arrived on the ship *Hector* in 1773. I'm sure you will hear their story."

There was a knock on the door and Mr. Fraser came in.

"Good-afternoon, Miss Morton. Mrs. Patterson, is your good husband around?"

"Nay, Mr. Fraser, he's gone over to the storehouse to meet Dr. Harris. I expect him back for supper."

"Thank you. I'll be back later."

"Will you have some tea and a scone?"

"Thank you, nay. I have some errands to run."

I thought I could detect a bit of tension in Mr. Fraser's voice but could determine no immediate reason. Perhaps I would find out why once I heard Mr. Fraser's story of the arrival of the Hector people from Scotland. I made it my business to discover what discord might exist between the Philadelphia Grant people and the Hector people.

The opportunity arrived sooner than expected. I saw Mr. Fraser the next day just as he left his home. The Stewarts and I were still living in tents near his home while David and Robert built a log cabin on their newly assigned property. Mr. Fraser was a tall, powerful looking man with red hair and blue eyes, always dressed in a kilt. As with all the Highlanders, there was an air of danger about him befitting the warlike nature of his people. I liked that about him.

I ran to catch up with him. He was always on the move either on his own business or helping the Highlanders wherever he could.

"Is all well with you, Miss Caroline?"

"Oh, indeed, Mr. Fraser. We are certain that moving to Pictou was the best possible decision. We are grateful for your help every day."

"No need to be grateful. It was our duty to help those in need. We do it gladly."

I thought again about David's one time hatred of the Highlanders and how wrong he was.

"Mr. Fraser, would you have time to tell me about the Hector people?"

"I would. Come to the beach towards evening. I plan to stay the night at a shelter near Philadelphia people so I can continue my business tomorrow. I will roast some salmon over the fire and eat it with some bread. You are invited to this supper."

We sat on the beach where he had built a little fire and had strips of salmon gently roasting. The bread was on a large napkin. It had been buttered. The sand was warm, and the wavelets made a whooshing sound. The tide was coming in, but we were well above the high tide mark. The food was wonderful, and we washed our hands in the sea water.

"Well now, you want to know about our arrival in Pictou."

"I do. I have heard that you had a hard time."

"To say the least. We were recruited to come to the New World by the Philadelphia Grant people and promised provisions, land, and assistance getting settled by the people who had just settled themselves. It all seemed so promising. Three families boarded at the port at Glasgow, Scotland. The rest of us boarded at Loch Broom far up the western coast. The voyage was a disaster."

I knew what was coming, but it hurt me to hear it from someone who had lived it. My own recent experience of sailing from Scotland was still a vivid memory.

"Instead of the usual seven weeks, we were eleven weeks, the ship being an old hulk. There were children who died at sea due to disease and we ran out of food towards the end. But despite all that, we prepared carefully to come ashore. Ever since the Battle of Culloden Moor in 1746, the King of England had banned the wearing of the tartan, the playing of the bagpipes, the bearing of arms, and many other things. Of course, we carefully hid all that was contraband while we were in Scotland but brought it with us on the voyage. Each of the Highlanders dressed in his kilt and wore his sword, dirk, sgian dubh—and we all came ashore following our piper. Scared the living daylights out of any who saw and heard our arrival." He smiled broadly at the remembrance of that day.

"We thought the worst was behind us, but it was just beginning."

"It breaks my heart to hear what you had to suffer."

"Aye, it's hard to think back to those days, only three years ago. Well, they took us back into the forest—and remember only a few of us spoke English and none of them spoke Gaelic—and told us this is where we were to live."

"And in the Highlands, there are no trees, and this was dense forest with trees up to two hundred feet tall."

"That's right. We didn't know how to cut down trees. So, we wouldn't stay. We also believed that wild animals and savage Indians—and perhaps even fairies—lurked in these woods endangering our wives and children."

"And you were promised a year's worth of supplies, right?"

"Right. But because we wouldn't stay in the woods, they wouldn't release our supplies even though we had none of our own."

"I suppose they thought you would return to your land grants. They probably didn't know much about Highlanders." I smiled.

He smiled. "When we surrounded the supply building and entered with our dirks drawn, I think it began to dawn on them that we were not going back into the woods or see our families starve. We tied up Squire

Patterson and Dr. John Harris and took what was needed, leaving a list, and promising to pay it back as soon as we were able."

"And you did, eventually."

"Aye, we did. But not before they sent to Halifax with word that there was a Highland uprising." Alexander stopped and looked at me with a bit of a scowl. "You seem to have a fair knowledge of the facts, Miss Morton."

I was taken aback. I had a historical knowledge of this story, but it occurred to me I didn't have a reason for that which I could share with him.

"Are you a witch, Miss Morton?"

"No, no, no indeed, Mr. Fraser. I must have overheard some of the Philadelphia Grant people talking about the history of this settlement. Please continue."

He paused, looking at me carefully, the way a cat looks at a mouse, and slowly moved his hand to his dirk. I stood up, feeling too vulnerable sitting on the beach at dusk.

He stood as well, still focused on me, his blue eyes seemed to darken and become menacing. I couldn't move, transfixed by his calm regard.

"Well now, I think we need to clarify who you are. What is your exact relationship to Mr. Stewart?"

"Well," I fumbled, "David, Mr. Stewart, is a relative of mine. My family came from England to North America in 1623 so we rather lost track of our Scottish relatives. I know that there are a lot of Morton families in Scotland, but I forget the exact genealogy."

He stood tense but silent, his hand still on the dirk. My heart was pounding. The Highlanders still believed in witches as did most of the Lowlanders, and I didn't think that David or Mary could get me out of this situation.

Just then, we saw a young couple holding hands and strolling along the beach. Coming closer, she recognized me. It was Miss Robertson, the lady's maid from when I first met David and Mary, years ago, though it didn't seem much time had passed despite everything that had happened since, and her new husband.

"Oh, Miss Morton, I was sure I would see you in the colonies and here you are! Are you well? You look a little pale. Here is my husband, David Murray. Darling, here is Miss Morton, the relative of Mr. David Stewart." With that, she took a breath.

Well, I was never so glad to see a familiar face. "Congratulations, Miss Robertson, sorry, Mrs. Murray. I'm so pleased to see you again. This is Mr. Fraser, who arrived here in 1773. He was just telling me the story of the voyage of the *Hector*. How was your voyage?"

"We are pleased to meet you, Mr. Fraser. Any friend of Miss Morton's is a friend of ours."

Mr. Fraser, who had his hand on his dirk until now, relaxed and removed his hand. "Pleased to meet you Mr. and Mrs. Murray. Did you make your trip by a timber ship?"

"Aye, not the best of arrangements, but we are here," said Mr. Murray. "There is land to be had, so we plan to stay in Pictou."

While they talked, I re-thought my propensity to help him along with his story, demonstrating knowledge I should not have.

After the Murray's left, promising to keep in touch, Mr. Fraser said, "It is my opinion that you are not a witch, Miss Morton."

"No, indeed, Mr. Fraser, I am a storyteller, a seanachaidh. I pick up historical facts and store them in my mind until I can assemble them into a story. I am sorry to have caused you concern. If you would, please continue."

I wish I had thought of this explanation to begin with, for when I had said I liked that Highlanders were dangerous I wasn't thinking I would be the object of their interest. It was scary: the calmness and coldness. I had rather expected agitation and heat.

We sat back down.

"Where was I? Oh, aye, Squire Patterson, after one of our Highlanders had freed him and Dr. Harris, sent word to Halifax that there was a Highland uprising and to send troops. The Government, in its wisdom, sent word to Thomas Archibald who oversaw the Truro Militia to send the militia to quell the uprising."

"The Truro Township people are no friends of the English Government."

"Nay."

"Mr. Archibald sent word to Halifax that if Highlanders were treated kindly, there would be no problem." Mr. Fraser nodded to agree with this assessment.

"So, no militia was ever sent?" I knew the answer but wasn't going to get ahead of the story once again.

"Nay. But when the food ran out, many of us went through the woods to Truro Township and hired ourselves out as labourers. Some families, men, women, and children, indentured themselves as servants to the Truro folk so they could have food to eat."

"So, you came to Nova Scotia for land and freedom and were reduced to becoming labourers or indentured servants on someone else's land, just to survive."

He nodded grimly.

"In 1770, Colonel Alexander McNutt's land grant was escheated and gradually we got land at the mouths of the three rivers that run into Pictou Harbour. Our people started returning from the townships, clearing land, and building log cabins. And that is where things stand today."

"Did you ever get over being afraid of the Mi'kmaq—the Indians?"

"Aye, they were kind and helpful to us. They taught us how to hunt moose and deer, how to collect sap from the maple trees and boil it down to make maple sugar, how to make snowshoes and many other useful things. We were amazed how much their tribal societies resembled our clans. As Highlanders, the English called us savages and took away our language and way of life, forcing us to emigrate. Gradually, the Mi'kmaq, who the English call savages, have lost their way of life and became oppressed. Although our way of life is improving, theirs is not."

"Mr. Fraser, I want to thank you for trusting me with your story and I will remember it and tell it whenever I can."

"I don't know what there is about you Miss Morton. A seanachaidh you say, but also someone who cares about the people in your stories."

"I care more than I can say, Mr. Fraser. You are all very special to me."

"Would you care to join the Highland campfire this Sunday evening?"

"It would be my honour, Mr. Fraser."

Sunday evening, the Philadelphia Grant folk and the South of Scotland people gathered around campfires on the beach to drink ale and sing the familiar songs from the south of Scotland. The Highlanders had their own campfire where they could sing the bittersweet songs of their homeland in Gaelic. I sat by Mr. Fraser so he could translate some songs and conversation. We ate a seafood stew filled with diced potatoes in cream and butter along with some coarse bread. I felt such a kinship with these poor people and their struggle to survive that I felt at home even if I didn't speak much Gaelic. It was a great joy for me to be with them.

As we sat around the campfires that night eating our supper, it was David who rose first to thank the other two groups for saving their lives and giving them land and a future in Pictou.

"If I live to be one hundred, my dear friends, I will never ever forget the help and support of the Philadelphia Grant people and the Highland hospitality of the Hector people. We have truly been blessed." This sentiment was greeted with loud cheers by the fifteen South of Scotland families.

As the bonfires were allowed to burn lower and lower, and people began to take their little children home to bed, David beckoned me to come where he was sitting with Mary and Robert. I said a regretful goodbye to my Highland host and walked over to the glowing embers of the South of Scotland people. As soon as I sat down between David and Mary, I knew they had been thinking of Jennet because their eyes were red-rimmed and their faces blotchy. I was rather in the same state as I also was thinking about little Susie. How I wished Jennet and Susie had been able to see this day. David patted his eyes with his sleeve and leaned forward and asked in a whisper, "What do you think, Caroline? Is our story worth telling?"

"Mr. Stewart, David, I have learned so much from all of you—the founders of Pictou County. I greatly admire your courage and endurance in great adversity. It has been my privilege."

It seemed to me my dream was drawing to a close as I smiled at them, and they smiled back at me.

Caroline woke up in her bed in Halifax.

Two weeks later, the sisters got together again, and Caroline read them the latest chapter of her book.

"Well, you are certainly well on your way now, Caroline," Joan said, as the others nodded.

"When you get started, you get along famously, for sure," Elizabeth said, and Janice added, "Well done, again."

Caroline beamed.

"I thought you said you only preferred well-to-do and well-educated ancestors. There are quite a few sketchy people in this chapter," Elizabeth noted.

"What do you mean, sketchy?" Caroline frowned.

"Well, take those Highlanders. None of them could read or write—or even speak English."

"But, don't you see, they became one of the founding people of Pictou County. That makes them important. And they eventually learned English—though, regretfully lost their Gaelic. Although they did tie up Squire Pattern and Doctor Harris at knifepoint, they paid for all they took; and they only took it to keep their families from starving. So, what else could they do?"

"All's well that ends well, you're saying."

"I suppose so. But, anyway, the South of Scotland people are our ancestors and the Hector people helped save them, so I think they should be admired."

"No argument from me," Joan said. The rest seemed satisfied to eat their cranberry scones, a new favourite, with butter and jam.

"So, when can we expect the next chapter?"

"Give me a month or so, and I'll try to have chapter four ready."

"By the way, Caroline, I like your new outfit. Been out shopping, have we?" Joan asked.

"I thought I'd celebrate my newfound momentum with the book with some more artistic clothing."

"Oh, is that what you call it? A tartan hooded cape with knee-high boots?"

"You don't think I look spiffy?"

"I guess, if you say so." Janice said.

"What tartan is that?" Elizabeth asked.

"Why, Nicolson. Hunting Nicolson. That's what they call this green plaid with a white and red stripe. I was doing a little research and Nicolson is probably a Scottish name. Anyway, it's new and rather attractive for the fall, I think."

"Well, if you like it that's good enough for us," Joan said, and the others nodded.

Now, if only I can do as well on the next chapter, Caroline thought, as the coffee party broke up.

"She did a lot better than I thought," David Stewart said to the others during their meeting.

"Truly, I think she might have been able to handle all our extreme conditions." Mary nodded.

"What a hard time you South of Scotland people had," Flora McKenzie said, looking at her husband, as he nodded his agreement. "I hadn't realized that it wasn't just Highlanders who suffered so much."

"It was only by the grace of God that most of us survived that last winter on St. John's Island," David said. "Our land on the rivers of Pictou County was a real blessing. We could survive and thrive." As soon as he said this, a cloud of distress shadowed his face. He looked at his wife and son. They knew instantly the cause of his distress.

"We are always mindful of our Jennet," Mary said. David and Robert both nodded and David said, "Although we are all united now and what a blessing that is."

"Oh, you did more than just survive and thrive, I'd say," Joseph Begg laughed. "Robert, didn't you have fifteen children and seventy-three grandchildren?"

"He certainly did. That's what I mean by 'thriving'," David laughed heartily and slapped his knee to emphasize the point.

Robert blushed. "Many people had big families in those days, Father," Robert said.

The rest of the group laughed.

"So, now, who's next? The Highlanders or the Beggs?" Samson asked.

"Janet and I are next," Joseph Begg said. "I hope we can provide as interesting a story as the Moore's and the Stewarts. It certainly has its fair share of tragedy. I'm going to get Janet to invite Caroline. And, by the way, it's rather rewarding, don't you think, that she is so interested in our lives?"

"It is good to have our lives recognized. For the most part, I believe everyone, even our own families, has forgotten us. I hope they enjoy finding out about our existence."

No one disagreed with that. There were a lot of happy smiles at the thought of their descendants getting to know them.

Caroline put out an offering of her special homemade oat cookies and a glass of milk. She remembered that as a child her mother would put out treats for Santa Claus so he would have some nourishment on his Christmas Eve journey to the homes of all the little children in the world. This seemed a nice enticement for whomever was sending her such great material for her book. They need to be encouraged; to know how much I appreciate their help, she thought. Once again, she wondered who they were.

Whoever it was, they must have liked her oat cookies as she had another interesting dream.

CHAPTER FIVE

LUMBERMEN & MERCHANTS — THE BEGGS

1798: MIRAMICHI, NEW BRUNSWICK TO PICTOU, NOVA SCOTIA

I opened my eyes to see nothing but mist swirling around me. *Where was I?* After a careful search, it seemed I was on a wharf and dressed in my travelling clothes, a valise at my feet. *Where is my hat? Oh, there beside my valise. Was it early morning or dusk?* There seemed to be nothing to do but sit and wait for the mist to clear and the sun to rise—if it was morning.

After about half an hour, I heard the crunching sound of someone walking on gravel. There must be a road at the end of the wharf! Placing my hat on my head and grabbing my valise, I hurried in the direction of the sound—crunch, crunch, crunch. At the end of the wharf, I could see a form. Yes, it was a man hurrying down the hill.

"Excuse me, Sir!"

He kept moving—crunch, crunch, crunch.

"Excuse me, Sir!"

He finally slowed down, but just a little. I ran to keep up.

"Sorry to be rude, Miss, but I'm late to meet someone."

"Who are you meeting?"

"A woman relative of mine who I have never met, and I can't quite remember where we are to meet."

"What's her name?"

"Caroline Morton."

"I'm Caroline Morton."

He stopped short; his face crinkled in puzzlement.

"You are Caroline Morton?!

"I am."

"Forgive my lack of manners, Miss Morton. I wasn't sure how or where you would arrive. I'm Joseph Begg."

"Very pleased to meet you, Mr. Begg. Where are we?"

"Why, on the north side of the Miramichi River in New Brunswick."

We walked together until we came to a large clearing in the forest. The morning sun was rising, burning off the mist on the river. I could see Joseph more clearly now—late thirties, tall, with blue eyes and blond hair. He was completely dishevelled—his jacket and trousers, besides being wrinkled, had seen better days and his long hair was loose and quite unkempt. Noticing me observing him, he tried to smooth back his hair and re-arrange his clothing.

"Sorry about my poor appearance, Miss Morton. When I heard you were coming, I slept in my clothes just to be ready."

"I'm surprised you have blonde hair. I rather imagined you would have dark hair. Not sure why."

He smiled and relaxed a little.

The air was cool and clear now. Looking around, it seemed like a lumber camp surrounded by the great North American forest on three sides. The trees—pine, fir, spruce, oak, maple, birch, and many other species—towered a couple of hundred feet above us. On the fourth side was the Miramichi River. At the river was a mill with logs on one side and squared timber and full-length pine trunks on the other. Joseph confirmed my assumption.

"Aye, it is a lumber camp and a shipbuilding centre as well as a salmon fishing station."

"Who does it belong to?"

"This land was granted to William Davidson of Banffshire in Scotland and his business partner, John Cort, of Aberdeenshire in 1765. They set up fishing and lumbering enterprises where the northwest and southwest branches of the Miramichi meet and recruited tradesmen from Scotland. When the American Revolution broke out, they were so harassed by American privateers and pirates that they moved inland to Maugersville until the end of the war. Mr. Cort died during the war and William Davidson returned to Scotland in 1784 and 1785 and recruited more tradesmen. I came over in 1784.

"He was a man not easily deterred."

"Nay, indeed. In 1789 he got a contract with William Forsyth of Halifax, a Scottish businessman, for masts and spars. But his luck ran out—he died 1790, aged fifty-two, because of getting caught in a snowstorm."

"Who got the business after his death?"

"A member of Forsyth's circle—James Fraser. He has been very successful and as of 1797 he took over Davidson's estate—land, mills, wharves, various buildings."

"So, you've been here fourteen years?"

"Aye. For all I have to show for it." Men were beginning to arrive for work, all dressed much like Joseph. "Let's go and have breakfast with the men, and then I'll show you around."

The cookhouse was filled with long wooden tables with wooden benches running along either side. We picked up our food from the kitchen—porridge, pancakes with maple syrup, bacon, eggs, ham, bread, butter and lots of tea and rum were on the menu. I had porridge, Joseph had the bacon and eggs. We sat with some men, friends of Joseph, but no one was talkative.

Just as I was enjoying my second cup of tea, I heard a loud whistle. All the men got up, grabbing their caps, and knocking over benches in their rush to get out the door.

"What's happening, Joseph?"

"There's a fire somewhere!! We must find out where and fight it before the whole forest goes up in flames!"

I grabbed my hat and followed him out the door, toward the sound of the whistle, which was the lumber mill.

"Men," the foreman yelled, "grab a bucket and head up the north branch of the river. There's a fire at the old wharf!"

Joseph and I grabbed buckets and ran with the rest towards the smoke and flames, now clearly seen back up the trail we had just come down.

Arriving breathless, we climbed down the riverbank as the men formed a chain from the river, up the riverbank, and across the trail to where the fire was burning two ramshackle buildings. Men at the river filled the buckets and passed them quickly to the next man in the chain as the empty buckets came back down the chain.

Joseph was beside me filling the buckets and he looked frantic, never getting his bucket entirely full before passing it on.

"Joseph," I yelled, "what's wrong?"

"My family lives in the direction the fire is taking!" He grabbed another bucket.

After that I worked twice as hard but, looking up, I could see our efforts were having little effect so far. There was nothing to do but work faster.

We heard the foremen had sent part of the brigade to a creek a mile or so away with the hopes they could prevent the fire from jumping the creek.

As the day wore on, buckets were passed on only half full and water was sloshed on our feet as hands lost control of buckets. Up ahead, the supervisors yelled encouragement.

"We've started to get it under control! Keep going, keep going!"

Late in the afternoon, the fire seemed under control, and I followed Joseph up the path by the river to where his log cabin was located. It was burned to the ground, a blackened heap in a blackened clearing surrounded by a blackened forest. The efforts of the fire brigade had stopped the fire before it jumped the creek on the far side of Joseph's cabin.

Joseph rushed about and found a half-burned pole, still hot from the fire, which he used to pry up the roof of the cabin to peer inside. As I watched, heartsick, at the horrible scene, Joseph collapsed to the ground.

I went over and sat beside him. Hours later, the foreman and some men who had been fighting the fire came and carried him down to the bunkhouse. I followed. I borrowed soap, face cloths, and bandages to wash and bandage his burned hands. I washed his face and combed his hair—not that he cared, but I couldn't think of anything else to do.

After a long while, the door of the bunkhouse opened and an older man entered, tears streaming down his face.

"Joseph, my son, I have just heard the terrible news!"

"Father, where have you been?"

"I left shortly after you did this morning in order to do some masonry work on the new building." Tears continued to stream from his eyes.

His father lay down on the bunk next to Joseph's and they spoke not one word more. I brought them tea and food and although they both drank some tea, neither ate a bite.

Toward the end of the day, the door opened again.

"Brother," said the tall, blond man as he entered, "I just heard."

He crossed the room and sat down by his father. They did not say another word and seemed not to notice me. Tears were flowing from my eyes, so I went and sat on the bunk assigned to me. It was in a corner, with my valise beside it, and with a curtain that could be drawn around it.

The next day, the foreman came to see Joseph.

"Take the time you need," he said, "And if there is anything I can do for you, just let me know."

"Will you take my family out of the cabin and help me to bury them at the cemetery?"

"They have been removed and put in coffins. The men are digging the graves right now, so we can bury them this afternoon. But you all must eat something before then."

I went to the cookhouse and got some pancakes and a pot of tea. The cook's assistant helped me carry the food, plates, and utensils to the bunkhouse. Joseph, his father, and his brother, John, ate a small amount and drank the tea. They dressed in similar fashion—dark wool trousers, a double-breasted navy-blue jacket with rows of brass buttons and a workman's cap.

Then Joseph's friends and co-workers came to the bunkhouse and the Begg men led them towards the cemetery beside St. James Presbyterian Church at Beaubear's Point. The men introduced themselves to me. James Welsh, James Barnett, Benjamin Stennmeist, Peter Bonamy, Jonathan Loughberry, James McComb, James Anderson, and Daniel Dunn.

As we arrived at the cemetery, we could see several open graves with a pile of earth beside each. James Welsh seemed to know the way, so we all followed him to two graves side-by-side close to the church. At the head of each of these graves was a small wooden cross with the names carefully inscribed with white paint:

Mary Begg, wife of Joseph, Jr. died 1798, age 35
Joseph Begg, son of Joseph, Jr. died 1798, age 12

There being no minister, one man who had studied to be a catechist and, therefore, had a Presbyterian service book, led the prayers. Then four of the men attached ropes to the pine caskets and lowered them into the graves. I sprinkled them with some wildflowers before the final committal was read. The Begg men knelt on the ground while the men filled in the graves and smoothed over the final product. Their task completed, they all shook hands with Joseph, his father, and brother, and left the cemetery. I gathered ferns from a stream nearby and placed them on the graves and then sprinkled them with wildflowers—it seemed I needed to do something and that was all I could think to do.

Back at the bunkhouse, Joseph went back to bed—and there he stayed during the day. But, as we were to discover, he roamed the campground at night.

Later that day, I talked with John about his brother.

"Aye, Caroline, Father, Joseph, and I came to the Miramichi together in 1784. Mother died a few years before and so father came with us. We were twenty-two and twenty-four years old, so we thought it was a grand adventure. We had both trained as stone masons, and tradesmen were what Mr. Davidson wanted. We came over in one of his ships. A few years later, Mr. Davidson brought over some lassies as there were no women in the area and that's how Joseph met Mary."

"Were you promised a salary or land or?"

"Aye, a salary, but land only after a few years of labour and that land was to be rented, not owned. I think Joseph had just cleared two or three acres of his land, just enough to grow some potatoes and keep a cow."

"A cow?"

"Somehow, the cow survived. She got away and went down to the creek. She's in rough shape, so we're taking care of her until Joseph decided what he wants to do."

One night, I heard a shuffling sound. I got out of my bunk and looked around the curtain. It was Joseph, putting on his boots. He grabbed his jacket and left. I dressed and followed him down to the river. On the beach, near the wharf and above the waterline, was a canoe. Joseph got in and began working on the struts that keep the shape of the canoe intact. I walked over.

"Good-evening, Joseph. That's a nice-looking canoe."

He jumped, startled. "Caroline! What are you doing here?"

"Joseph, what are you doing here?"

"Well, oh, well, I'm just getting the canoe ship-shape."

"Planning to take a trip?"

"Perhaps."

"We're worried about you. You need to talk to your brother and father."

He slumped back into the canoe and looked at me with tears in his eyes.

"You can't run away from the pain, Joseph. It's called grief and you have to walk through it—and we're here to support you."

"I'm not sure I can bear it, Caroline."

"It seems impossible to bear, but even worse to wish it away."

"Aye, like my wife and son were nothing to me if I want to be rid of the pain."

"You're a man of faith, Joseph. I know that about you."

"All my prayers have turned to dust and ashes."

"Then you must let others pray for you."

He nodded.

We stood together in the moonlight, and I prayed for his wife, Mary, and his son, Joseph, and for Joseph himself that he might be raised from his present darkness and despair into the light and peace of God's presence and that he might be comforted there. We both said, "Amen" and returned to the bunkhouse.

In the morning, I went for breakfast. Joseph's father and brother were there, but no Joseph.

"Where's Joseph?" I asked.

"We thought he was with you."

"No, I haven't seen him."

They grabbed their hats and jackets, and we headed over to the river. The canoe was gone. We all looked at each other.

"Did he say anything to either of you?" I asked.

"Nay." They both shook their heads. John took off his cap and ran his hands through his hair before slapping the cap back on his head. His father stared at the river, perhaps considering the possibilities. His long grey-white hair had become loose and was blowing and swirling around his head adding to the state of confusion we all felt.

What could we do? Upon inquiry at the company store, we were told that Joseph had bought new paddles as well as a tent and blankets, and a musket and ammunition. Joseph's co-workers and friends had no idea where he had gone. That made all of us.

Five days later, early in the morning, I heard a noise on the other side of the curtain. Getting up quietly, I peeked around the curtain. It was Joseph. I decided to wait for morning but in the morning, he was sound asleep. When he woke up around noon, he had to confront his father and me, sitting together on the bunk next to his and staring at him.

"Sorry if I worried you. I wanted to test out the canoe and tent, and I was afraid that you would try to prevent me."

There didn't seem to be any point to telling him how worried we'd been. I took on the role of the grand inquisitor. "Why did you need to test out your canoe?"

"Because I'm going to go to Pictou on Monday."

"By canoe?"

"Aye. There won't be any ship from Nova Scotia for at least two months and by then it may be too late in the year to start over."

"Why Pictou?"

"Caroline, you reminded me that I needed to walk by faith. To do that, I need the support of a congregation and a minister who I admire greatly, the Reverend James Drummond McGregor. I have been corresponding with the Reverend McGregor ever since he came here for a visit as a missionary almost ten years ago now."

"Then when are you leaving?"

"Monday. I'm going to first collect all my back pay and then I'll be ready to leave."

"I'll come with you," said his father.

"Nay, Father, you have John and his family here, and my future is completely uncertain. I don't even know what dangers may lie ahead on my voyage."

John said, "I think Father should go with you, Joseph. I have a wife and children, and my home is here. You will have no one in Pictou. If Father wants to go, you should let him."

I found myself saying, "I'll come with you as well, Joseph," despite my aversion to being on the open ocean ever since my voyage from Annan to St. John's Island with the Stewarts. I still remembered the horrible thunder and lightning storm that we barely survived. There was a Joseph Begg in my family tree, and I felt that was the person I needed to be with, storms or no storms.

"Then," Joseph said, "it's settled. Father and Caroline will come with me. I will miss you, Brother, but once I'm settled, I'll send a letter by the next ship from Pictou to the Miramichi. I may even get back to visit you—or you might come to visit me."

The day of the voyage arrived. We packed the tent, cooking utensils, and food. Joseph secured his salary in a leather pouch, which he tied to his leather belt but hung it inside his trousers.

There was a large gathering to see us off. Joseph shook hands with his co-workers and friends, kissed his sister-in-law and his nieces and nephews, and gave his brother a big hug. Then we were off.

The day was partly overcast and breezy but warm as we took up our paddles and began to paddle down the Miramichi River towards the Gulf of St. Lawrence. The canoe felt balanced, and the paddles were easy to grip. Joseph was at the back to steer and his father at the bow as he knew the river better and could watch for obstructions like floating logs. I was in the middle, just in front of the supplies, with a bucket at my feet in case we needed to bail water.

Joseph figured it was about a hundred and seventy miles as the crow flies, but, of course, it would be longer by boat following the coast. We paddled vigorously until Joseph told us that it was a long voyage and we needed to be mindful of that. So, we would paddle for an hour and then take a ten-minute break, before paddling the next hour—and just enough to keep the canoe from drifting towards shore.

While we rested, I enjoyed the scent of the river, fresh and clean, and the breeze invigorated us with the scent of pine and spruce. There were loons floating on the water until the sight of a fish caused them to dive quickly and return to the surface with their prize. We saw eagles soaring overhead, perching on dead trees, or catching fish with their talons. Late in the day, deer came down to the river to drink. It was a great day to be alive.

We ate supper and slept on the beach at the mouth of the Miramichi that night, not even bothering to put up the tent as the weather was so beautiful. We could smell the sea air close by. In the morning, we ate breakfast and then put out our campfire before pushing the canoe back into the water and turning east into the sunrise as we paddled into the Gulf of St. Lawrence.

The Gulf was certainly choppier than the river had been, and Joseph had to work to keep the bow of the canoe pointed into the waves so we wouldn't be pushed sideways or swamped. We all had to work harder to make progress. At night, we would find a sheltered cove, put up the tent if it was raining, build a fire and make our supper—mostly dried salmon and potatoes. As long as we could find water for tea, our diet suited me. One day, Joseph caught a fish and roasted it and some potatoes—it was a change. In a few days, we paddled into the Northumberland Straight, the water between Prince Edward Island and New Brunswick and Nova Scotia.

"We're getting close to Shediac, Father," said Joseph.

"What's at Shediac?" I asked, not knowing much about the history of New Brunswick.

"It was first settled by the Acadians who were expelled in 1755 during the French and Indian War. Now some of them have returned after signing a pledge of allegiance to the King of England. In 1785 William Hannington, an Englishman, from London, got five thousand acres at Shediac Cape and set up his fishing, lumbering, and shipbuilding centre. He's also into agriculture, importing, wholesaling, retailing, and land speculation, in addition to being the only office holder in the region."

"So, an entrepreneur like William Davidson?"

"Aye, exactly so, Caroline."

As we approached Shediac Cape, Joseph's father pointed into the distance where we could see dark clouds gathering, lit up from time to time by flashes of lightning. Storms at sea are scary and dangerous, but a thunderstorm at sea is terrifying, and a thunderstorm while canoeing is horrifying. Everyone knows that lightning strikes the tallest structure and even a canoe is the tallest structure on the open ocean. My heart was pounding when Joseph yelled to his father, "Head to the cape!"

We paddled like fiends when it was clear that the storm was overtaking us. A lightning bolt struck the water close enough to cause the sea to boil and steam. The resulting waves began to swamp the boat, so I began to bail as if my life depended on it—which it did. But soon the canoe was swamped. Joseph jumped overboard to lighten the load and I followed him into the sea. Grabbing the sides, we kicked as hard as we could and managed to keep the canoe afloat. After half an hour, we were close to the shore, where the waves were breaking onto the beach with a thunderous roar. I still don't remember the final moments. When I came to, Joseph and his father were overturning the canoe to dump out the water before dragging it up the beach to where I was lying, still spitting out seawater.

No sooner had Joseph and his father dropped down beside me, exhausted, than we saw people approaching. As they came closer, we could see that there were two men and a woman. The woman wore a long blue dress with a white apron and cap, and the men had brown trousers, white shirts, and wide-brimmed straw hats. They all wore sabots—wooden shoes.

The woman was the first to speak.

"Bonjour, comment ça va?"

"Do you speak English?" Joseph asked.

"Un petit peu—a little."

"We're from the Miramichi, heading to Pictou."

"In a ... a petit bateau?"

"A canoe. Aye."

"This is my husband, Antoine, and my son, Pierre. They don't speak English. My name is Marie Surette."

"You speak very good English, Madam Surette," I said.

"Acadian women sometimes get part-time work with Mr. Harrington's business, so we have to learn some English."

I nodded and Joseph continued. "I'm Joseph Begg. This is my father, also Joseph, and my relative, Caroline Morton."

"We saw you struggling to get ashore. Come, our house is nearby. My husband and son will bring your canoe along so you can spread out your supplies to dry." Madam Surette spoke to her husband and son in French to explain the plan.

We were so grateful that these Acadians would help us out since the Acadians and the Indians had been the foes of the English during the French and Indian War. Of course, we weren't English, but they didn't know that. "Merci beaucoup, Madame Surette, Monsieur Surette," I said in my petite amount of French.

They smiled.

We had bread, cheese, and hard cider, before removing our clothes to be dried by the fire and wrapping ourselves in blankets. We slept for about twelve hours, awakening to find the kitchen full of men with muskets who were speaking French, as well as several Indians—Mi'kmaq, I thought—who wore only breechclouts and buckskin moccasins. Their long, shiny black hair was braided down their copper-hued backs. They carried muskets, bows and arrows, and knives.

"What is happening, Madam Surette?" asked Joseph.

"Before we can send you on your way, we want to know who you are and why you are travelling from Miramichi to Pictou."

"If you would be good enough to let us dress, then we will answer all your questions."

"Very well."

We quickly dressed and felt a little less powerless.

"As you know, Madam, we did not choose to come ashore here, but were forced to when our canoe was almost hit by lightning and was swamped. I and my father have been working on the Miramichi for fourteen years, brought out by William Davidson in 1784. A few weeks ago, my family were killed in a forest fire, and I am on my way to Pictou to start a new life. Does that answer your questions?"

"Somewhat. Who is the woman with you?"

Oh dear, I thought. This isn't good.

"Miss Caroline Morton lives in Halifax, but her family is from Cornwallis Township in Nova Scotia. She is a relative of mine."

I could see the Mi'kmaq looking at each other and suspected that the cause was the mention of the name Cornwallis—the founder of Halifax. Cornwallis Township was named in his honour. The Mi'kmaq hated and despised Governor Cornwallis as he had ordered a bounty for their scalps after confrontations between them and his fledgling colony.

After a few minutes of consultation between the Acadians and the Mi'kmaq, Madam Surette asked if I was related to Cornwallis or part of the establishment of Halifax in 1749.

"No, Madame, my family came up from New England in 1760. I don't know who named the township, but I suspect it was those in a leadership position in Halifax. Beyond that, I have no information."

Luckily, they accepted my explanation. Had I been part of the Cornwallis family or part of the founding of Halifax, I might have been in trouble, so great was the understandable hatred of the native people toward Governor Cornwallis. After they searched all our baggage, including my valise, they seemed satisfied, and we were allowed to go on our way.

We thanked the Surettes for their hospitality, perhaps a little less enthusiastically than before. Joseph and his father packed the supplies and loaded them in the canoe before carrying it to the beach.

In a complete change of mood, the sea was quiet—little waves lapping the shore and the water of Shediac Bay quite calm. We were all relieved when we got far enough offshore that we seemed safe from the Acadians and the Mi'kmaq—just in case they changed their minds about us.

As we neared Cape Tormentine, we had to paddle further out to sea to round it easily. I was glad when that was over, and we could keep closer to shore.

Another night on the beach near Pugwash, Nova Scotia, and it was time for the final push to Pictou.

We paddled into Pictou Harbour about midday. Though the town was larger than my last visit in 1776, the primeval forest still came down to the water's edge in many places. The harbour was filled with sailing ships of all sizes and descriptions and even some of His Majesty's warships. I counted about thirty, but there were certainly more. We headed towards the docks near the town, tied the canoe to a pier and, as it was low tide, we had to climb up a ladder to the wharf itself.

We just sat down on the grey, weathered boards of the wharf, and dangled our feet over the edge, watching the hustle and bustle of the waterfront.

"What do we do now, Joseph?" I asked.

"Not sure," said Joseph.

A man soon showed up and introduced himself as Thomas Harris, Sheriff. He invited us to come with him to meet the local magistrate, Squire Patterson. I had previously met Squire Patterson when I came with the Stewarts from St. John's Island and wasn't sure if I wanted him to remember me. It would be too complicated to explain.

I needn't have worried. Squire Patterson was getting along in years and needed spectacles to see. A short man, he had gained weight over the years and was now as broad as he was tall, causing him to waddle when he walked. He wanted to know our business in Pictou, so Joseph introduced us and told the Squire our reason for coming to Pictou. The Squire, always a kind-hearted and genial sort, expressed his sympathy and pointed us to McGeorge's Tavern and Inn on George Street, where we were able to have fish and potatoes for supper and then be shown to our rooms.

I fell asleep right away and didn't wake until the sun came up early in the morning. Joseph and his father were already in the tavern, having breakfast. I had pancakes and maple syrup and tea.

We went for a walk around the town, and I noticed many changes. I'd say there were about sixteen to eighteen commercial buildings altogether and plenty of wharves. Many of the ships in the harbour were near a large lumber mill. We were told that it belonged to Edward Mortimer, the richest man in Nova Scotia.

"I wonder what the main business is in Pictou," I said, as I recalled the earlier state of affairs.

"It's timber and fish for the old country, just as it is in the Miramichi and Shediac, as well as all the large harbours all along the coast of New Brunswick and Nova Scotia," said Joseph's father. "The English have an insatiable need for timber to build their sailing ships, including the Royal Navy, since they long-ago cut down their own forests."

"Well, there's a lot of timber here," I said, glancing at the forest that surrounded the town on all three sides.

We passed taverns, stores, and blacksmith shops, homes made of logs, or planks, or stone. There was even a new jail, as of this year, one of the townspeople pointed out with pride. It seemed like a peaceful place in the early morning. We should have guessed from the number of taverns that Pictou was not as quiet as it looked.

After our tour around, Joseph decided to go back to see Squire Patterson to see about getting some land in the town. "I'm thinking of starting a store and becoming a merchant, Caroline. What do you think, Father?"

"My son, I'm sure you would be good at anything you turn your mind to. What kind of merchant?"

"A general merchant. I think there would be a market for sailing goods—sail cloth, ropes, and so on, as well as dry goods for the townspeople and perhaps some types of food and drink. The town is growing and there is probably room for another store."

"I think you're right, my son. Where would you set up shop?"

"I see a piece of property on Coleraine Street at the corner of Water Street."

We walked over to see it, and it certainly seemed a central location. We continued over to Squire Patterson's place.

"Aye, Mr. Begg, we do have land available, and a store would be a splendid idea, but first you have to prove you are fit to be a merchant."

"What do you mean, Squire?" asked Joseph.

"Here is my recommendation, Mr. Begg. Show up at Mr. McKenzie's store on Water Street about seven this evening. I'll let him know you're coming. After that, we'll talk again."

"Agreed," said Joseph.

We arrived at the designated place around seven and were welcomed by the merchant. He introduced us to two of his clerks and was about to show us about the store when a whistle blew loudly and persistently.

"Here's your cudgel, Mr. Begg. Come with me!"

They left the store. His father and I stood outside the door to see what was happening. Moving up from the waterfront was a large group of men carrying cudgels and yelling and hollering at the merchants and their servants, who were pouring out of their stores and businesses, carrying cudgels as well.

When they were within feet of each other, Mr. McKenzie called out, "Halt right there, you ruffians! Come no further. You know you are not allowed in the town."

The order was met with derogatory yells and without warning, the men from the waterfront raced forward to meet the merchants.

From our vantage point, partway up the hill, we could see cudgels swinging and men limping away, holding their heads, or arms or legs. When it was almost over, among those still standing was Joseph, landing his cudgel blows with effect. The men from the waterfront decided to retreat and then it was all over—for the time being.

Mr. Murdock said, "Mr. Begg, you certainly proved yourself tonight. I'll let the Squire know that we would be pleased to have you join the merchants of the town."

Squire Patterson later explained that seamen, sailors from the Royal Navy, and dock workers, were not allowed in the town because of their propensity to get drunk and disorderly, leading to destruction of business and fights with local men. There was another danger from the Royal Navy—their press gangs. Always needing more men to sail the big warships, raiding parties would come ashore and carry away unsuspecting men from the town. By the time their families knew they were missing, the navy had sailed to distant ports.

"Mr. Murdock, who were the young women screaming at the town men during the fight?" I asked. I thought I might know the answer but felt it always better to ask than to make assumptions.

"Oh, Miss, those were the ladies of ill repute from Criton Street. Rosie the Red McLeod runs a boarding house for sailors and those ladies also live in that house. It is best for you never to go over to Criton Street. It is a very disreputable place."

"Are the ladies from the town?"

"Nay. They arrive in the timber ships at any harbour where there are a lot of sailors and go elsewhere once the timber ships and Royal Navy leave."

"Isn't what they do illegal?"

"Oh, nay, or at least the Sheriff leaves them alone unless they get drunk and disorderly."

On the way back to our inn, I said to Joseph, "Well, Joseph, I didn't know you were a fighter."

"Caroline, I never start a fight, but I do know how to end one."

"You certainly do."

"Has Joseph always been a fighter, Mr. Begg?"

"Well, he was a very happy and peaceful child, but he joined the local militia when he was sixteen and soon, he was fighting with the best of them."

The next day, Joseph bought a piece of land on Coleraine Street and he and his father set about to build a log building where they would live and run the store. The Squire and Mr. McKenzie were always available to give advice about where to get the best deals on sailing materials—rope, sailcloth, tarpaulins, buckets, oars, and other nautical items—which were ordered from Halifax along with cloth, ribbons, buttons, and other dress-maker notions. The supplies usually arrived several times a month until the Northumberland Straight froze over. There were forays into the coun-tryside to make deals with millers for flour, oatmeal, barley, etc. and less perishable food. The farmers usually brought vegetables, fruit, meat, and more perishable foodstuffs to the market square each week. And fishermen also brought their catches to the market square. From the beginning, Joseph determined he would not carry the ubiquitous rum. This would turn out to be a problem.

The store was built in a couple of months, and he stocked it with fishing and dressmaking supplies, as well as household items including twine, butter churns, looms, and spinning wheels. He also carried foodstuffs such as maple syrup, flour, sugar, and some candy. Mr. Begg did the accounts, I kept the shelves in good order, and Joseph served the customers.

It was a good life. I continued to live at the inn which Joseph paid for instead of giving me a salary for working in the store. We all ate together at the inn.

One of our first visits outside the town was to the home of the Reverend James Drummond McGregor, the first and only minister in Pictou Dis-trict from 1786 until he was joined recently by the Reverend Duncan Ross.

Reverend MacGregor had been away on a missionary visit to Cape Breton and had just returned. We knew both ministers took turns preaching at the Harbour Church on Prince Street at the corner of Water Street. Joseph held the Reverend McGregor in the highest regard as did I. It would be fair to say that the Reverend McGregor is a hero of mine, as my Pictou County cousin had given me her copy of the Reverend McGregor's grandson's biography of his famous ancestor, so we were both excited about the upcoming visit.

We had to cross Pictou Harbour in the canoe and find the mouth of the East River—the largest of the three rivers that empty into the harbour and the closest to the entrance of the Harbour. It was a great day in late September, the hardwood trees, birch, elm, oak, maple, and many others, turning the forest into a festival of colour. We wended our way through the many ships tied up at buoys and all facing into the northeast wind, until we reached the channel which was kept clear for ships to come and go. A short time after crossing the channel, we saw the mouth of the East River and began our journey upstream.

On either side of the river were small clearings with perhaps twenty by twenty-foot homes, mostly log cabins. Each cabin had a large garden, a barn, and outbuildings of various sorts. We saw men, women, and children engaged in many tasks, such as hoeing, hanging out laundry, and watching the cows and sheep down in the intervale, the grassy fringes of the river. Some of them waved to us.

After about a mile or two, we saw a house that had been described to us as belonging to the Reverend McGregor and his new wife, Ann MacKay, daughter of Roderick MacKay—educated in Halifax and an accomplished seamstress. We had been told that Mr. McGregor had a house built for himself and his bride. Before his marriage, he had lived in the attic of Mr. Donald MacKay's house. As we pulled the canoe up on the little beach, a man of middle height with dark brown hair and a serious demeanour came striding towards us. He greeted Joseph with great friendliness and was gracious towards me as well.

We were invited in for tea, served in the parlour by Ann, who was obviously an excellent cook—the cranberry scones with butter and strawberry preserves were so delicious that I had two!

"So, Mr. Begg, we meet again. How are your wife and child—and your father and brother, as well?"

Joseph told them the story and the Reverend McGregor was shocked to hear the news.

"Oh, to have such a tragedy fall upon your family, Mr. Begg! I cannot even imagine the sorrow you must feel and the pain you must be suffering. Please accept my sincerest condolences, my dear sir, and to your father as well. May I offer prayers for you and your dear departed?"

"Aye, Mr. McGregor. It was to have you as my minister that I came from the Miramichi to Pictou. I need the support of a congregation and a minister like yourself to not completely despair."

"I can assure you of my complete support, my dear sir." With this, the Reverend McGregor prayed for Joseph's wife and child, his father and brother.

The conversation continued as Joseph told the Reverend McGregor about his store and they discussed the present and future of the Town of Pictou before Mr. McGregor turned to me.

"Well, Miss Morton, it is good that you have been there to support Joseph and his father through these trials and tribulations. But there is something about you that I cannot quite put my finger on. If I believed in fairies and such, I might be suspicious of you."

"Why, Mr. McGregor, you are one of my heroes. I know the story of you being sent here from Scotland two weeks after your graduation from theology school, your arrival in Halifax and trek through the forests and swamps of Nova Scotia to Truro Township and thence to Pictou. I know that you were the only minister in the Pictou District for nine years and have heard of your many missionary journeys to Prince Edward Island, New Brunswick, and Cape Breton. I also know you paid the cost of having enslaved people freed and publicly admonished those who held people in slavery. Your dedication to the Gospel is truly inspiring and I hold you in the highest regard."

"Thank you for your kind words, Miss Morton, but it is still puzzling that you know so much about me."

"You have many admirers, Mr. McGregor, and as Joseph knows, I collect stories so that I can write about them so that even more people can appreciate your heroism."

"I'm not certain that your kind words entirely explain your knowledge of me, but I see that you don't intend to satisfy my curiosity any further."

We left, both looking forward to attending Harbour Church on Sunday morning.

"Thank you, Mr. McKay. I appreciate your business," said Joseph, as a small ship owner left his store with some rope and sailcloth.

I was arranging some bolts of cloth at the back of the store and remarked to Joseph, "It seems like business is picking up every day."

"Aye, Caroline, I'm thinking I've finally found a place where I fit in. It was a good decision to come to Pictou and begin a business."

I went back to organizing the dry good section as another customer entered the store.

"Good-afternoon, Mr. Begg. A fine establishment you have here."

"Thank you, Mr. ...?"

"Mr. Smith. I've come to make you a generous offer you would be wise to accept."

I turned around, puzzled.

"I don't get your meaning, Mr. Smith," Joseph said mildly.

"My associate is interested in buying your establishment ... at a fair price, of course."

The man walked about the store picking up lids on barrels and helping himself to a hard candy from a glass jar on the counter.

"Thank you for your offer, Mr. Smith, but I'm happy with my business. By the way, who is your associate?"

"Why, Mr. Edward Mortimer, Esquire. Some say he is the richest man in Nova Scotia."

"Well, thank Mr. Mortimer for me. Tell him I hope to meet him at church very soon."

"I'm afraid you don't understand, Mr. Begg. The only thing that I take back to Mr. Mortimer is the deed to your property."

"I'm afraid you don't understand, Mr. Smith, I said, nay."

"Then we will have to persuade you to change your mind, Mr. Begg."

"And how will you do that, Mr. Smith?"

"You will soon see, Mr. Begg. Thank you for the candy. I bid you good day."

When he was gone, I rushed over to Joseph. "Joseph, what will you do? He's threatening you!"

"Aye, He'll probably try to destroy my inventory or burn down the store."

"What will you do? What can you do?"

"I'm going to have a talk with Mr. Mortimer. Come with me. I may need a witness. Father, take care of the store. I'll be back soon."

We followed a path along the harbour to Mortimer's Point. Arriving, we saw a busy wharf with timber ships being loaded. Nearby was the sawmill and further along a large store. We entered to see it was stocked with many of the supplies Joseph sold in his store.

"Would Mr. Mortimer be available? I want to talk to him about Mr. Smith's offer."

The man smiled in recognition of Mr. Smith's name.

"You're in luck, Mr. Begg. Mr. Mortimer has been expecting you."

Mr. Mortimer's office was an enormous room over the store with a vast mahogany desk on beautiful carpets, from India perhaps, damask curtains and large, plush chairs. He rose from behind the desk, a tall, broad-shouldered man with a big belly, the style among the rich, with blonde hair and blue eyes. He wore gentlemen's clothing.

"Welcome, Mr. Begg. I see you've wisely decided to accept my offer. Sit down, sit down. Some whiskey, perhaps?"

"No, thank you, Mr. Mortimer. I'll come right to the point. My former co-workers and friends are all from the Miramichi, brought out from Scotland by Mr. Davidson to build his business. A business which is even more successful now that Mr. Fraser has taken over. So, I am very knowledgeable about such business ventures. I know that if anything were to happen to my store, my friends would come to my rescue. And we all know how quickly forest and timber go up in flames."

Mr. Mortimer didn't blink once or seem unduly disturbed by Joseph's counter-threat.

"I take your point, Mr. Begg. I wish you nothing but success in your new business. I hope to see you at church on Sunday."

"Thank you for your understanding, Mr. Mortimer. Church begins at nine, does it not?"

"Yes, indeed, Mr. Begg."

Mr. Smith was in the outer office and sneered at Joseph until he saw Mr. Mortimer shaking hands and smiling at Joseph. Then his jaw dropped.

"Afternoon, Mr. Smith," said Joseph and I nodded in his direction, as we left the building.

"Joseph, would you really have burned down his property and called your friends to help you?"

"As I said, Caroline, I never start a fight but if it's a fight they want, I plan to win."

"I admire you, Joseph. No one bullies or intimidates you."

"Caroline, there is no point in letting people bully you. Stand up right from the start."

"That might be easier for a man to do than a woman in this society."

"Oh, aye. I will give you that, certainly."

I waited to see if this was the end of the threats and pressure to sell, and hoped it was.

On Sunday, Joseph, his father, and I went to Harbour Church at the corner of Prince and Water streets. A log building, inside it was plain: a pulpit and communion table at the front, rows of benches that filled the room, and a stone fireplace taking up much of one wall. This Sunday Mr. McGregor was preaching, and the Elders led prayers and singing of hymns and psalms. It was our first visit since the Reverend McGregor returned.

When the service was over, the Reverend McGregor introduced Joseph and his father to the congregation, telling them about the tragic deaths of his wife and son, and asking them to support their new brother-in-the-faith. Mr. Mortimer was the last to shake Joseph's hand and welcome him to the Town.

"You can count on my support, Mr. Begg. Welcome to Pictou."

Could we trust him?

We were sitting in Lindsay's Tavern one evening listening to the talk of the upcoming election—the polls opened December 5, 1799, at James McPherson's barn at Fisher's Grant.

"So," Joseph said to one man at our table, "this is the first time that people from Halifax, Colchester and Pictou will vote for their own candidates?"

"That's right, that's right, Mr. Begg. Colchester and Pictou were always a part of Halifax County and all the candidates for office were from Halifax, but we became unhappy that all decisions were made in Halifax and for the benefit of the Halifax merchants. This is the first time Halifax, Colchester and Pictou are running their own candidates."

Joseph had to yell whenever he asked a question as the ever more heated discussions all around us became louder and louder. "So, who is running in Pictou District?"

"Why, Mr. Mortimer, of course."

"And are there political parties?"

"Oh, aye, there's the Town Party—that's what we call Halifax—and the Country Party—those in Colchester and Pictou."

"Anything else I should know about voting in the upcoming election?"

"Aye, have you made out your will?"

"You're joking, aren't you?" asked Joseph's father.

"No, indeed. Things can get pretty serious."

Joseph, his father, and I looked at each other in consternation. Could this be true?

"Who's running for the Town?" asked Joseph.

"That would be Michael Wallace, the Provincial Treasurer, Charles Morris, and William Cottnam Tonge. The other Country Party candidate is James Fulton of Londonderry Township in Colchester. Mr. Fulton is a moderate man who is a Justice of the Peace, a judge, militia officer, surveyor, as well as a politician."

"He sounds like my kind of candidate," said Joseph.

"Oh, aye, but, of course, we in Pictou have to vote for Mr. Mortimer, do we not?"

"I think we are free to choose the best person to represent our interests. That is what voting is all about, as I see it," Mr. Begg said.

"You should think twice about that theory, Mr. Begg," our table guest said.

It was an early, cold winter, so Pictou Harbour was frozen, making travelling easier for those wanting to get from one side to the other. The day of the election arrived. We dressed in woollen clothing with warm scarves, hats, and mittens and ventured out onto the ice. It seemed thick enough and lots of other people were headed in the direction we were going.

We could hear the crowd before we could see them. Upon climbing up the riverbank, the large, noisy gathering consisted of men carrying banners representing their favoured candidate, but more ominously most of the men were grasping sticks, stones, bottles—some broken—and pitchforks. It no longer seemed like a crowd but a riot. A man walked up the two steps to the platform, raised his right hand and yelled the name of his candidate, Mr. Mortimer. A cheer went up from the crowd as the scribe wrote the man's name on his voting list along with Mr. Mortimer's name.

Joseph let the vote counter, a Mr. McDonald, know that he and his father were there. The vote counter inquired about his father's qualifications to vote. Only land holders could vote in this election.

"Mr. McDonald, what is the meaning of all this disturbance?"

"Mr. Begg, I have asked that only those eligible to vote be present and that they leave as soon as they have voted. As you can see, no one has listened in the slightest to my request. Many are here, including employees of candidates, to intimidate voters to choose their candidate."

Shortly, Joseph's name was called, and he mounted the platform.

"Please raise your right hand, and speak the name of your candidate, Mr. Begg," the vote counter yelled over the crowd. I had read enough about elections in Pictou County to know about this method of voting.

There was a pause in the noise, as Joseph raised his hand. "Mr. James Fulton, Esquire."

As he stepped down from the platform, a group of the men booed and jeered, yelling that he was a traitor to Pictou County. I saw the glint of something flying through the air—a bottle—which struck Joseph on the back of his head, and he collapsed to the ground unconscious.

His father and I raced toward him, grabbed him by the arms and dragged him to the outside of the crowd. As he lay on the light sprinkling of snow, a pool of red began spreading out encircling his head.

While we tried to think what to do, a small, stooped, wrinkled woman with stringy grey hair approached and knelt. She fished around in an old bag that she carried and, finding what she was looking for, applied it to the back of Joseph's head. I recognized her from the town—it was Grannie Joe. Some said she was a witch and people went to her to have their tea leaves read or for remedies for sickness. How did she get to the voting station?

"What are you doing, Grannie?" I asked.

"Cobwebs to stop bleeding."

"Oh."

Joseph was beginning to wake up and Grannie held up his head and gave him some rum to drink. Then she poured rum on the back of his head, as he winced and drew away. Looking towards the source of his discomfort, he asked, "Grannie, what are you doing here? Caroline, Father, what has happened?"

"Joseph, you were hit by a bottle, and you have a ten-inch cut on the back of your head. Grannie stopped the bleeding with cobwebs and poured some rum on it as an antiseptic."

"Who threw the bottle?"

"It seemed to come from a group of men carrying a banner and yelling for Mr. Mortimer."

Grannie gave Joseph another drink of rum. The political parties were handing out alcoholic drinks to gain votes. Grannie could always get some more, as no one refused Grannie anything.

"Thank you, Grannie," said Joseph. His father and I echoed that sentiment emphatically.

Grannie smiled, her teeth full of gaps, and went on her way.

Joseph tried and found he could stand. So, I thought that was the end of it, but no.

At church on Sunday, Joseph showed Mr. Mortimer the red line of the wound on the back of his head.

"My goodness, Mr. Begg, whatever happened?"

"One of your men hit me with a bottle just as I finished voting, Mr. Mortimer."

Mr. Mortimer said nothing, his brow knit in consternation, his eyes unfocused. Finally, as others from the congregation listened, he said, "My men must have gotten out of hand at the voting place. What can I do to make this up to you, Mr. Begg?"

"Find out who it was, Mr. Mortimer, and send him to me for a cudgel match—a fair fight rather than a bottle to the back of the head."

A few days later, a small man with a frightened look on his face showed up at Joseph's store. "Mr. Begg, it was I who threw the bottle that injured you. I have come to apologize."

"What is your name and where is your cudgel?"

"My name is Andrew Young, and I've heard of your prowess with a cudgel, Mr. Begg, but I have no training or experience."

"Well, what do you excel at besides throwing bottles?"

"Really, nothing, Mr. Begg. I just run errands for Mr. Mortimer and live in his bunkhouse."

"So, I have no hope of giving you a good thrashing?"

"I hope not, Mr. Begg."

"Well, I must have my satisfaction, Mr. Young."

Mr. Young just stood there shaking.

"Here is what I have determined. You will begin attending church with me each Sunday and I will hire you as my servant in the store. I will inform Mr. Mortimer personally. You will sleep in the store at night and eat with me and my family."

Mr. Young, Andrew, began to cry, "Thank you, Mr. Begg. I've been so ashamed and so scared. Thank you for not thrashing me as I deserved. I will be a loyal servant."

That settled, Joseph, his father and I took some whiskey, which was harder to come by than rum, but much appreciated, and some money to Grannie Joe. She was busy preparing a potion to protect a cow from the fairies, so we left the gifts beside her door.

Joseph seemed to be thriving in Pictou, but I sensed unhappiness, perhaps from missing his family. It occurred to me that he might be ready for and wanting a second wife. He expressed no interest in either Criton Street or courting any of the women in town, though he did rely on me and take me into his confidence .... *Perhaps? No! What a strange idea.*

The election results were posted at the town jail. Elected were James Fulton of Londonderry, Colchester District, and Edward Mortimer, Pictou District, for the County party and William Cottnam Tonge and Charles Morris for Halifax. The rumour was spreading that the defeated Michael Wallace was furiously angry about his loss and vowed revenge against those who had won, especially Mr. Mortimer.

We were having supper at Lorrain's Tavern, the one frequented by the upper class of Pictou, when we overheard a plan being discussed to run some merchants out of town—those who were speaking up about the evils of demon rum and who would not carry it in their stores.

"These merchants are portraying us as rascals and drunken scallywags despite the fact our fathers are among the elite of the town. I say we get rid of them before our fathers get the idea we should give up our carousing and work for a living," said the one with his back to us. The others, their faces flushed, and their speech slurred, nodded in agreement, "Why should we work, our fathers are rich. Besides, we do the town a lot of good spending our money in their taverns and over on Criton Street." The rest cheered their approval at the mention of Criton Street.

One thing we had learned since coming to Pictou was how much everything depended on rum. No transaction no matter how small could take place without a glass of rum, no visit to relative or friend could take place without a drink or two of rum, no barn could be raised, or building built without puncheons of rum, and all the lumbering in the woods during the winter was fuelled by large kegs of rum. Many men only worked three days a week so they could be drunk for four. Being admonished by the two ministers in Pictou District or by men like Joseph who refused to have anything to do with the rum trade, was ignored or scorned by the rum drinkers.

After supper, Mr. Begg explained that the problem was even wider than what was happening in Pictou County. "Caroline, the rum trade begins with the growing of sugar cane in the Caribbean. To grow and harvest and process sugar cane to get molasses and rum you need a workforce that can cut sugarcane in the tropical heat, and that would be African slaves. So, demon rum destroys the lives of the enslaved Africans, the people who drink the rum in Pictou and all other places in the English dominions, as well as the souls of those who are willing to bring so much misery on others to enrich themselves."

"You are so right, Mr. Begg. I admire the Reverend McGregor and the Reverend Duncan Ross for speaking the truth and trying to end this evil. And I admire you, Joseph, for being willing to risk your livelihood by speaking out and by refusing to sell rum in your store."

Joseph looked troubled. "Caroline, Father, these troubles leave me unsure that Pictou is the place for me. Despite all that our ministers have done to correct the people, even some of the church Elders who are merchants are selling rum in their establishments. Among those plotting at the tavern, are the sons of some of the Elders. It seems like just one fight after another just to stay in business."

"Aye, aye, my son. This is a violent place because of the rum."

I was watching Joseph's face as his father spoke. His eyes were so sad and tired. He had tried to re-build his life but there seemed to be no relief from every sort of challenge.

"Joseph," I suggested, "what about talking to Mr. Hugh Denoon? He's a Justice of the Peace and a judge, as well as a merchant. Perhaps he could defuse this situation before it comes to a head." I knew about Hugh Denoon from my research.

"Mr. Denoon?"

"Yes, he has a store about a mile from Pictou. We could go there."

We did. Joseph explained what he had overheard, and Mr. Denoon said he would talk to the other magistrates, Robert Pagan, John Dawson, Nicholas P. Olding, and Edward Mortimer, about the situation.

Thinking it was too dangerous to stay in the attic of the store, Joseph and his father moved down into the store along with Andrew Young. I decided to stay in the store as well. They brought their cudgels, including one for Andrew who was taking cudgel lessons from Joseph. No one was sleeping much as we waited to see what would happen first. Would the magistrates act in some way, or would the young men arrive before they could act?

One evening we dared to relax. It had been better than a week since the event in the tavern. Maybe the young men were too drunk to remember their scheme. We had no sooner laid down on our blankets than something caused my hair to stand up on end. I tapped Joseph on the shoulder and pointed toward the street. He tapped his father and Andrew and they rose quietly and peeked out the window. Coming down the street was a large group of young men and some of their followers, carrying torches and cudgels.

Joseph opened the door and went out followed by his father and Andrew. I watched from the window, horror-stricken.

"Go home, young men, and I will not report you to the police and to your fathers."

"When we're finished with you, Mr. Begg, we won't have to worry about our fathers. We hear you're quite the fighter with a cudgel and we hope you can teach us a few lessons."

"Indeed, I can, young man, but you will not like the result."

"As you can see, I have those who can replace me, so I'm not worried." With that, the young spokesman, took a step forward and had his cudgel knocked from his hand by a blow from Joseph's weapon. Angered, he yelled, "Get them, gentlemen, and set their store on fire, too!"

So engaged in the battle were the young men that they didn't hear the sound from down the street until it was too late. Marching up the street were many men. Were they a gang from the docks, the sailors, or the press gang? No! It was the Pictou District Militia led by Hugh Denoon and Edward Mortimer. We were saved!

The militia surrounded the young men, with muskets drawn. Mr. Denoon ordered, "Hands up, gentlemen! Captain, march these miscreants over to the jail and lock them up. I will be along shortly to charge them," said Mr. Denoon.

"Good-evening, Mr. Begg, Senior, and Mr. Begg, Junior. We will deal with these scallywags who think they can threaten, and assault respectable merchants like yourselves. It is people like you that we want in our community. Please be assured that our militia is here to protect all law-abiding citizens like yourselves."

Joseph nodded, a look of relief on his face, "Thank you, Mr. Denoon, Mr. Mortimer. I was truly afraid they were going to destroy my business and drive me out of Pictou."

"Nay, Mr. Begg, you should not leave Pictou. Stay and be a positive influence, along with our two ministers."

Joseph nodded slowly, "I think I've found a new life here, gentlemen."

For tonight, it had ended well but I doubted all would be smooth sailing in a town like Pictou.

Joseph and I were walking back to the store, after supper at Reverend McGregor's, when we had to leap out of the way of a two-horse carriage. It was driven by a young man, whipping horses without mercy. He roared by, spraying mud and horse dung from the street on all who were not spry enough to get out of his way.

Angry, Joseph started toward the Sheriff's. Then we saw a young woman clinging to a nearby railing and crying loudly. I ran over and Joseph followed. We could see the problem right away. One side of her dress was splattered with mud and horse dung.

"Caroline, take her back to the inn. I'm going to see the Sheriff."

After she had a bath and I had washed her dress, we chatted. The incident on the street was only the last of a series of calamities.

"My husband and I were married just before we started out for a new life in Nova Scotia, then he died at sea. Now I am here alone. I know that he had some relatives in Nova Scotia, but I could not find them. Perhaps they have moved on to another district, but no one knows of them."

"What is your name, my dear?" I asked.

"Janet Henderson from Glasgow, Scotland." I knew Janet was the name of my second great grandmother!

"My name is Caroline Morton. I'm from Nova Scotia. The man I was with is a relative of mine, Joseph Begg, originally from Aberdeenshire, Scotland." I told her a little about Joseph, his losses, his work, and his faith. She grew tired, and I asked where she was staying.

"I just arrived two days ago on a timber ship and am still sleeping aboard. I haven't the funds for a place like this. Some women down on the docks and they said they could get me a room at their place on Criton Street."

"Oh, no, you must not go there. The women are prostitutes!"

She gasped and began to cry. "Is that where I will end up, Miss Morton?"

"No, indeed, Mrs. Henderson. I'll figure out another plan ... and you should call me Caroline. Get some sleep. I'm going to find Joseph."

As I left the inn, I saw Joseph marching down Church Street toward Coleraine Street, so I ran to catch up.

"Joseph," I panted, "slow down. What happened at the Sheriff's office?"

"Well, he is much concerned that this behaviour be stopped before someone is injured or killed. This is not a new occurrence, drunken young men racing their carriages through the village streets. We must put a stop to it. How is the young lady?"

I told him her story. "Joseph, we can't let Janet be lured to Criton Street out of desperation."

"I agree, Caroline, but what can we do?"

"You could marry her."

He stopped and looked at me with eyes opened wide. "What?"

"You could marry her. She has no friends or relatives in Pictou. Where would she go? What could she do? But you and your father need the help of a good woman."

"Did you propose this to her?"

"No, no. It just jumped into my mind after I left her to sleep. But it's brilliant, right?"

"Brilliant? Caroline, I have only briefly laid eyes on her."

"But this decision can't wait. She is still sleeping on the timber ship, but it will sail in the next few days, then she will be totally without even a place to sleep."

"Caroline, I can't believe you're suggesting this, and I can't believe what I'm going to say, but I will talk to father. I'll come to see you and Mrs. Henderson tomorrow for breakfast."

Joseph and his father arrived early at the inn and were already seated at a large table when we went down. I let Janet go ahead of me and stand, until I pointed out Joseph's table. In the morning light, it was obvious Mrs. Henderson was a pretty woman, and her clean, fresh clothing highlighted all her best features—blue eyes, chestnut brown hair, and clear skin. The men stood as we approached their table.

I introduced Janet to Joseph. "Mrs. Henderson, I would like you to meet my relatives, Mr. Joseph Begg, Senior, and Mr. Joseph Begg, Junior. They have come from Scotland by way of the Miramichi and have only been in Pictou a few years."

"A pleasure to meet you, Mrs. Henderson. Welcome to Pictou. Our condolences on the loss of your husband and all your hopes and dreams for your future." Joseph's father nodded and smiled warmly.

We sat. I could see Joseph was nervous. "Mrs. Henderson, I have explained your situation to Mr. Begg, and we discussed ways he might help you. Mr. Begg, after some consideration, may have a suggestion for you."

Mrs. Henderson and I looked expectantly at Joseph.

"Caroline, I assume you have made your suggestion known to Mrs. Henderson?"

"No, Mr. Begg, I have not."

"Then, Mrs. Henderson, this may come as a bit of a surprise to you. Caroline has suggested that I marry you and that is the offer I make to you today."

Janet began to cry.

Not knowing what to make of her reaction, Joseph continued. "I have a small store on Coleraine Street. I am just getting started, but you are welcome to live above the store with father and I until we get to know each other, and until I can build a house. But we would have to marry first."

Janet continued to cry.

"I can see I have distressed you, Mrs. Henderson."

"Only in a good way, Mr. Begg. I am crying in sheer relief that I will not have to live on the streets, or worse. Aye, Mr. Begg, I will marry you and make very sure that your kindness will not be in vain. God bless you."

By then, we were all smiles and tears of happiness.

Caroline woke up in her bed in Halifax, stretched, and smiled.

"A great story, Joseph and Janet." The firsts smiled at the success of their plan. All was now smooth sailing. Caroline was on board with their plan, and they liked the stories she was writing.

"We're looking pretty good in these stories, Martha," Samson said. The Stewarts and the Beggs nodded with smiles.

"Our descendants will have a lot to be proud of," Martha said.

"We haven't gotten to McDonald's story yet," William McKenzie said, with a slight rolling of his eyes.

"My story will be the epitome of manners and correctness," McDonald said, trying to keep a straight face.

That caused such laughter in the group that they were all holding their sides at the very thought of McDonald and the word manners in the same sentence.

"I will say that you have a good sense of humour, McDonald," Samson said, trying to be positive about something.

McDonald grinned. His wife, Ann, put out her hands, palms up, in a gesture of 'what can you do.'

Martha said, "And you do have good taste in women, McDonald."

To that everyone agreed.

"A great story, Caroline," her sisters said. "Have you got a date for the book to be finished?"

"Not yet, but soon, I hope."

Chapter Six

DREAMS OF SUCCESS

Present Day: Halifax, Nova Scotia

C aroline began to dream about finishing her book and having it published; of being elevated from writer to author. Meanwhile, her sisters met without her, to discuss how they might recognize Caroline's progress.

"She's really doing well. It feels good to see her close to achieve her dream of writing a book. We should celebrate her progress," Joan said, as she thumbed through a new book she had just bought at the Indigo bookstore.

"Couldn't agree more," Janice nodded. "Stop fiddling with that book, Joan!"

Joan looked up with a scowl, but put the book back in the bag.

"I know," Elizabeth said, "let's take her to a book launch so she can get to see what her future holds. The Writers' Federation of Nova Scotia notifies its members of book launches, and I see there's one from Somewhat Grumpy Press coming up next week. It's at the Halifax Central Library." Elizabeth had just bought a Sudoku puzzle book, and it was sitting next to her pasta salad.

"Perfect," Joan and Janice agreed. Joan left to get some more hot water for her green tea and returned with a date square.

Elizabeth tapped out Caroline's phone number.

"Caroline, guess what? There's a book launch at the Halifax Central Library next week. The twins and I want to take you so you can get the feel for what it's going to be like for you when your book is published."

"Let me think about it. Sounds interesting, but will it be crowded? You know I don't like crowds."

"I don't think there's any way to know that in advance, but if it's too crowded, we won't stay, okay?"

"Okay. Email me the details."

Elizabeth smiled. "She agreed. Joan, can you pick her up? Why don't we go out to supper first? Everyone likes *Il Mercato*, right?"

The plans complete, the three sisters headed back to their cars.

"Thanks for picking me up, Joanie. Is this a new Jeep?"

"Brand new."

"Nice colour. Four-wheel drive, too. What was wrong with your other car?"

"After five years the warranty was finished, and it had hundred thousand kilometres on it, so I just decided to trade it in."

"I don't know if I can ever get another car. Maybe if a get a job."

Joan quickly changed the subject.

"Well, I hope this will be an exciting evening for you, Caroline. We're excited, too."

"Whose book is being launched?"

"It's another one by Alicia Jonasson, published by Somewhat Grumpy Press. I think you read her first book?"

"I did. It's about that town in Cape Breton. Shocking story."

After supper, they made their way to the library parking lot and took the elevator to the first floor where they got directions to the location of the book launch.

They found the room filling up with people and the author sitting behind a large table. There was a pile of the new books in front of her and two posters displaying the cover of the book on either corner of the table, along with a splay of business cards. The author was occupied signing books, so the sisters located the snack table where the editor and publisher of Somewhat Grumpy Press were chatting with the visitors.

Caroline was just thinking about how crowded the room was getting and feeling rather edgy.

"Caroline, so good to see you. It's been a while." Caroline turned toward the voice.

"Ruth! Oh, my goodness." They hugged and then held each other at arm's length to examine each other.

"Ruth, don't say, 'You look as young as ever!'" Caroline laughed.

"That's just what I was about to say," Ruth teased.

Elizabeth came over with a cookie in her hand to say hello to Ruth, her sister's old school friend.

"Guess what, Ruth?"

Ruth smiled and waited for Elizabeth to swallow the bite of cookie.

"Caroline is writing a book; maybe more than halfway through, right, Caroline?"

Ruth raised her eyebrows and smiled. "You are! Well done, you! What a big deal."

"Oh, well," Caroline said, "it's my first attempt. Who knows if it will ever get published? Just a hobby, really."

"Ruth," Elizabeth said, frowning at Caroline's lack of enthusiasm for her own work, "She's doing a great job and I'm sure someone will want to publish it."

By then, Janice had her snacks and joined them, and soon Joan showed up.

"Caroline, I just bought a book from the author. She thinks she may have met you at her last book launch. Come on over and have a chat."

Reluctantly, Caroline followed her sisters and Ruth over to the author's table.

"Alicia, here's Caroline. I told her you might remember her. She's writing a book, soon to be published, I'm sure."

Everyone around the table clapped their encouragement and Alicia said, "If you need any advice, let me know," and handed her a business card.

After leaving the author's table, Ruth suggested to Caroline that they meet for lunch soon. They made the arrangements to meet at McKelvey's Seafood Restaurant the next week.

Shortly, Alicia took a seat on the stool next to the microphone and did a great reading from her book. Caroline smiled and clapped with the rest of the crowd.

As she followed the crowd out of the library, the edginess was still there. *Why didn't this feel right?*

Ruth was already there when Caroline arrived at McKelvey's. They ordered wine and the catch of the day.

"Now, Ruth, you have to tell me about your new hairdo."

"Just couldn't be bothered to keep going to the hairdresser," she said, as she pulled the long braid over her shoulder. "Besides, it sort of fits my new business image."

"I heard you had finished your course in Jungian dream analysis down in the States. You've been away quite a while."

"That's right. I know we've chatted a few times by phone since Malcolm died, so I'm awfully glad to see you in person."

"How did you know I'd be there at the book launch?"

"Elizabeth called me. She said she thought you were ready to get out and meet up with an old friend."

"I see," Caroline smiled wryly. "I guess I should be grateful my sisters are trying to encourage me to get on with life."

Ruth smiled.

"Well, I'm glad you suggested we meet for lunch. But it does feel strange. Malcolm and I used to eat here quite a bit." She sighed. Ruth patted her hand.

"Ruth, tell me about your business."

"Okay. After I finished the course, I had to figure out how to set up a business, so I finally got a business loan and that allowed me to hire a technical person to develop a website. Now, I'm offering dream analysis online. So, I'm all set."

"Okay. Let me be one of your first customers. Give me an appointment."

They chatted for hours about old times; and enjoyed their excellent meals, parting later in the afternoon after a little stroll in the downtown.

"I don't like the sound of that dream analysis," Samson said. The rest nodded in agreement.

"We'll have to see," Martha said.

Caroline arrived at Ruth's place for her appointment. It was the same place she knew so well, an older home off Robie Street near the Willow Tree intersection. The older style, slightly worn, plush furniture and the hardwood floors covered with flower design carpets always made her feel warm and comfortable. She was leery about the whole idea of dream interpretation but intrigued as well.

"Come in, Caroline, and take a seat on the sofa," Ruth said as she settled into a comfortable chair nearby. "Let's have some herbal tea and relax for a bit."

Teacup in hand, Caroline said, "First of all, Ruth, congratulations again on completing your studies on dream analysis. I checked out the process online and it looks quite rigorous."

"But very enjoyable, too. I started taking it as I was having so many dreams that I didn't understand and needed help. As time went on, I got interested in doing analysis myself. So, Caroline, how are you doing? Is the depression lifting? Can you see a light at the end of the tunnel?"

Ruth had known Caroline's late husband and all the pain she had been through, so her questions were purely out of concern for her friend. Ruth was a real friend, Caroline thought. Kind and honest and she had surely gone through a lot herself: a mastectomy for the same kind of cancer that had killed her mother when she was only twelve years old. Ruth had lived in fear of the same fate all her life.

"I think so, Ruth. It's taken a long time, but I finally seem to be moving ahead. I know you're very familiar with depression, too."

"I surely am. But you're not here to talk about me. This is a professional appointment." Ruth smiled encouragingly.

"Well, then, let's talk about my dreams." Caroline took a deep breath. Where to start?

"You can talk about anything you want, Caroline. Just start and go wherever seems best."

"I've been having really vivid dreams. Dreams that have helped me write my book, but I have no idea why or how or if the dreams will continue until I finish the book."

"Caroline, I'm sure you're a good writer who doesn't need to rely on dreams to finish your book, but I'm intrigued, so tell me more about the dreams. How did they start?" Ruth looked relaxed and professional in her cream-coloured pantsuit and white blouse.

"Just out of the blue, really. I was struggling to write my book. Spinning my wheels, with only outlines after over a year. Then I found a little pebble on a gravestone and took it home and then dreams started, and I was able to move forward. But what if the dreams stop?"

"You probably did a lot of research, and your subconscious finally brought it all together in a dream."

"Well ..." Caroline felt doubtful.

"Jung believed that dreams are symbolic and to understand them, you must analyze the symbols accurately. Thus, the need for dream analysis."

"Yes, but ..." Caroline didn't recall there was anything too symbolic in her dreams.

"So, why don't we look at one of your dreams so I can see the symbols that are being used?"

Caroline told Ruth the story of the second dream; the one about Samson and Martha in Truro Township and the plans to rebel against the Government of Nova Scotia and join the American Revolution.

"These are vivid significant dreams, about things that are central to your inner self, and not easily forgotten. Jung would say you need to understand what these dreams are leading you to, and that, I think, is obvious—your book.

"But they're so detailed, Ruth. And so specific to my research and what I'm trying to write about ... so far. What if they stop? That'll be the end of my book. And then what do I do? I don't think I can get a job yet and I need something to do with myself." Caroline felt that little pang of despair arising from somewhere deep inside and she shuddered slightly.

"Caroline, I know you. You don't need dreams to write your books. Just have faith in yourself ... and write."

The two friends hugged goodbye, promising to meet up again soon. Caroline wished Ruth good luck with her new dream analysis business and Ruth said she looked forward to reading Caroline's book.

Besides being glad to spend time with her good friend, Caroline wasn't sure how to feel. As she turned the key to the ignition, she felt as though all her sisters' and her friend's and even the author's encouragement was overwhelming. Why did she feel so uncertain?

She wondered what Malcolm would think about her getting on with life. *How can I just move on? Malcolm's only been dead a little over a year.* It didn't seem right, not at all.

Before putting the car in gear, she felt the familiar aura of a migraine beginning in her left eye—jagged flashes of light. Knowing the pain and nausea were not far behind, she headed home and to her bed, the only place to be until the migraine was over.

That night, she had another dream.

CHAPTER SEVEN

HIGHLANDERS — THE MCKENZIES & MCDONALDS

1801: SCOTLAND TO PICTOU, NOVA SCOTIA

The horse knew where she was going, I thought, but, alas, I did not. Careful observation of the hills and trees suggested we were in Scotland, perhaps in the Highlands, and I was wearing my travelling clothes. *Where was my valise?*

The horse continued. After about half an hour, I saw a rider coming towards me. *Should I be relieved or concerned?* As he came closer, he reined in his horse and, smiling, removed his hat. "Good morning, Miss. A fine day, is it not?"

"Mr. Denoon!" I had last seen Hugh Denoon in Pictou, a few years earlier.

"Miss Morton? My dear Miss Morton, whatever are you doing here?"

"I've come to visit a relative, but I am quite lost.

"Well, you're very close to my brother's place. It looks like rain, so let me take you there and we'll sort this out over breakfast."

He turned his horse and I followed, the bridle path being only wide enough for one rider. He was right about the rain. It began with a fine mist and soon turned to a steady downpour.

We trotted past fields of oats and barley and smaller plots of potatoes and peas before meeting up with the main road—only a horse and cart track. A little further along and up ahead was a towering stone gothic-style church, surrounded by a stone fence also enclosing an ancient graveyard.

The sign said 'Church of Scotland, Parish of Kilearnan.' I was right, we were in Scotland.

Just past the church and across the road was a sprawling two-story stone house with many windows, perhaps five on the main floor and as many above, and a chimney with four smokestacks—an impressive and imposing building. Hugh turned up the lane to the house. At the top of the lane, we dismounted and turned our horses over to a stable boy. Large flagstones formed the walkway to the double front door, decorated with a gold lion's head doorknocker. Hugh pushed open the door and we entered a spacious front hall.

"Let me take your hat and cape, Miss Morton. I'll hang them here on the hall coatrack. Oh, there's Jannet. Jannet, may I introduce you to Miss Caroline Morton. She's from the colonies, Nova Scotia. She's here to meet a relative. Caroline, this is my sister-in-law, Jannet Grant—Mrs. David Denoon."

She was an elegant person, wearing a dark blue dress with a light blue collar and cuffs which brought out the blue in her eyes. Her shiny dark brown hair was coiled at the nape of her neck. She gave a welcoming smile. "Come into the parlour, Miss Morton. There's a bright fire to warm up such a damp day. Shall I bring you some breakfast? Eggs, toast, and tea?"

"That sounds just right, Mrs. Denoon. Thank you."

"Hugh, do you want the same?" she asked.

"Aye, thank you, Jannet. Where's David?"

"In his study. I'll rap on the door and let him know you're back."

Almost immediately, Hugh's brother appeared and greeted me with warmth and friendliness. He was elegant like his wife. Tall, with black hair and blue eyes, his hair pulled back in a queue, a long black vest with silver buttons over black knee breeches, white stockings, and buckled shoes. He looked like Hugh, who I think was thirty-four and David four years younger.

"You'll be having some breakfast, Miss Morton?"

"Your wife has gone to get us some, thank you. May I be bold enough to ask about your home, Mr. Denoon? It's quite impressive."

"Oh, aye, impressively drafty in the winter, but I should not complain, as the laird is very generous and keeps it in good repair."

"Oh, then could this be the manse for the church we just passed?"

"Sorry, Caroline," said Hugh, "I forgot to introduce you to my brother, the Reverend David Denoon. David and I were brought up in this manse by our parents, the Reverend David Denoon, Sr. and our mother, Mary Inglis. It was a good place to play as children, as there are so many rooms and hiding places."

Hugh and David smiled at each other at the remembrance of their boyhood days.

Jannet appeared to say that one of his parishioners had entered through the back door and wanted to see David about a baptism.

"Send him in, my dear."

The man was tall and thirtyish, with blond hair and blue eyes underneath his blue bonnet, a sprig of holly under the clan badge. He wore a wool jacket over his woollen trousers and around his body was a plaid—a long tartan shoulder mantle one and one-half yards wide and about four yards long—fastened on the left shoulder with a large silver brooch. His brogues were laced over woollen stockings. Despite his less than elegant attire, he stood erect and with pride.

David stood. "Welcome, Mr. McKenzie. Have a seat here by the fire. You've just had a new baby, your first son, I believe?"

"Aye, Mr. Denoon. And congratulations on your first son, as well. I hope your wife is doing well?"

"Very well, Mr. McKenzie, thank you for inquiring."

"You remember my brother, Hugh, I'm sure. He's visiting us from Nova Scotia. And this is Miss Caroline Morton, an acquaintance of his from Nova Scotia."

Mr. McKenzie shook hands with Hugh and stared at me. "Miss Morton, I found a valise just outside the door, so I brought it in. Would it be yours?"

"Indeed, it is, Mr. McKenzie. I can't imagine why I would have left it outside. Thank you very much for returning it to me."

"I dreamed of meeting a relative of mine. She was carrying a valise."

"Miss Morton," Hugh said, "you will soon learn if you stay for any time in the Highlands that Highlanders are always talking about dreams, second sight, ghosts, and fairies. No amount of rational discussion will dissuade them, so you must pay them no heed."

So, I thought, it's Mr. McKenzie I'm here to meet! "May I ask your wife's name, Mr. McKenzie?"

"Why, it's Flora McMillan. We have a daughter, Isobel, and now our first son, John."

"Congratulations, Mr. McKenzie, please pass on my best wishes to your wife."

Mr. McKenzie smiled and nodded. While I sipped some more tea, he and David Denoon discussed plans for the baptism. In the meantime, Hugh had taken his teacup and gone to look out the window facing the church. He seemed deep in thought.

The details of the baptism settled, Mr. McKenzie joined us for tea. Then Hugh called his brother over to the window to point out something of interest.

Mr. McKenzie leaned towards me and whispered, "It was you in the dream?"

I nodded. We both smiled. Breakfast arrived and Mr. McKenzie took his leave, saying, "I hope to see you again, Miss Morton."

"I'm sure we shall, Mr. McKenzie." So, now I knew who I was here to meet. What adventure lay ahead?

As I enjoyed breakfast and my second cup of tea, I overheard some of the whispered conversation between the brothers over by the bay window.

"I don't think it's a good idea, Hugh. The laird will greatly frown on you interfering in the running of his estate. You know that."

"David, the laird can't do anything about it as far as I can tell. It's up to the tenants."

Realizing I was listening in, they left off their argument and had another cup of tea. What was Hugh up to?

That evening, after a dinner of chicken, roast vegetables, and a delicious, steamed pudding with a brown-sugar sauce, I accepted an invitation to stay with the Denoons. Jannet led me upstairs to a huge bedroom with a twelve-foot ceiling and tall windows framed by the same material as the bed. And what a bed! A four-poster with a green damask canopy and curtains, sitting on a carpet with a green background and rose, white, and chartreuse flowers.

There was a stale smell, as if the room had not been aired out in a while, but Jannet threw open the casement windows, allowing a splendid view of Beauly Firth, and a cool breeze soon freshened the air. Even though it didn't get dark in the Highlands until about eleven o'clock, I went to bed and early and fell asleep immediately.

I woke with the sunrise around five-thirty. I looked around for my clothes and remembered I had been wearing my usual costume yesterday—heavier ankle-length skirt with a tight-fitting jacket and riding boots. *Had I been wearing a hat?* I searched around and found everything in the armoire. *Did I put it in there last night? Strange.* I dressed and checked for effect in the armoire mirror. Not too bad, I thought. Just what an adventurous woman would wear!

That's when I heard what seemed like a whispered argument. I quietly opened the door, just a crack. It sounded like Hugh and David, in the lower hallway. I waited a moment, then decided to go down and find out when breakfast would be served, since I was quite hungry. But as I reached the first step of the stairs, the voices stopped, and it was quiet and tense when I entered the breakfast room. The family were all there. I guess you get up early with a new baby and two little children in the house, or maybe this was their routine.

"How did you sleep, Caroline?" asked Jannet. She had a lovely Scottish accent.

"Very well, thank you." I looked at Hugh and David, but they were quietly eating and didn't look up at me. Maybe they thought I'd overheard them?

"I don't think you've met our children. They have their supper early, then their baths before stories and finally bedtime. Here is our oldest, Isabella, five, and Mary, four, and this is the reason you haven't seen much of me so far, our first son, David Junior, only one month old and needing to be nursed regularly. We do have a maid to help with the meals and the housework, for which I am very grateful."

"Good morning, children. What are you going to do today?"

"We're going to go outside and take our dollies for a walk," offered Isabella, holding up her pretty doll with a bisque face and blonde hair, dressed in the latest fashion.

"What a good idea. And what about the grown-ups? What are the plans for today?"

"Well," said Jannet, "David is baptizing little John McKenzie in the parlour at ten o'clock, so several Elders will be coming over to witness the sacrament."

"Oh, I hope they'll let me attend."

"By all means, Caroline. You'll be very welcome." Jannet was such a lovely, gracious woman.

"I'll go for a walk first and then attend to my horse."

"Nay, the stable boy will take care of her for you," David said.

"Well, I'll check on her, anyway."

I wandered down the lane and over the road to the church. Finding an iron gate, I pushed, and it creaked as it swung open. As I walked along the rows of gravestones, I saw most were covered with moss and lichen, but I found the graves of David and Hugh's parents. Would any of my McKenzie ancestors be buried here? Probably not. If I recalled correctly, the McKenzie's lived in another parish but worked for the laird in this parish.

Strange how drawn I was to old cemeteries; all the people who had lived full lives in generations past. They had experienced joy and probably much sorrow. I didn't want them to feel abandoned or forgotten but remembered as part of the communion of saints. I imagined them keeping an eye on their descendants and caring about our lives.

"Oh, excuse me," I said, as I almost walked on a little grave. Kneeling and rubbing off some of the lichen, I saw it was the grave of a small child: Annie McDonald. She died fifty years ago. "Sorry, Annie, I'll try to be more careful," I said and smiled, thinking that she might be watching.

Leaving the cemetery, I tried the church door, and it was open. Inside the dark gothic structure was a beautiful sanctuary painted a cream colour with light flooding in from the stained-glass windows, filling the space with little sparkles of colour—red, violet, blue, gold—and tranquility. I stayed for a while. When I left, the clouds held the promise of rain, so I retraced my steps back to the house and out back to the barn.

The barn had several box stalls with David and Hugh's horses in them, and finally the stall with my horse. It was clean and full of straw for bedding, and some hay and oats for munching. The black horse came over and put her head over the stall door, obviously looking for someone to scratch her ears and neck, which I enjoyed doing. *I wonder what her name is?* The name Blackie came into my mind. "Blackie," I said to her, and she looked at me and nodded.

"Have a good day, Blackie," I said, as I left the barn.

The McKenzies were already there when I arrived back at the house, and they greeted me with pleasure. After the baptism, I got to hold the baby and chat with little Isabel McKenzie.

"How old are you, Isabel?"

"Five." And she held up one hand and spread her fingers.

"What do you think about your new brother?"

"Well, mother has to spend a lot of time with him, so I try to help around the house."

"I'm sure your mother appreciates all your help, Miss Isabel."

She smiled happily.

"Miss Morton, we would like to invite you to our cottage for tea tomorrow," said Flora, as she picked up the baby off my lap.

"Splendid. I was hoping to visit you both."

"Then around mid-afternoon?"

"Agreed. But how will I find your cottage?"

"Oh, William will walk over to the manse and show you the way."

"I will be ready."

After dinner, the Denoon family and I sat around the fire in the parlour sipping whiskey while Hugh told us about his adventures during the American Revolution and his business in Pictou County.

"So, your business is going well, Brother?"

"Oh, aye. But we need more people in the district of Pictou, so the businesses can thrive."

David looked at his brother askance. "Is that the real reason you're back in Scotland?"

"Not at all. There's plenty of land in Pictou, and I just want the farmers here to know about their options."

My curiosity got the better of me, so I asked, "Mr. Denoon, what options are you talking about?"

David looked at Hugh and Jannet with a bit of a scowl.

"Miss Morton, it is best you do not know, as my brother is planning to bring down trouble on the family. Please accept my apologies for not being forthright with you."

At that, Hugh got up and stomped out of the room, followed by David.

"I won't be long, Jennet. I expect Hugh and I will go for a ride," he called from the front door.

During the evening, Jannet played the piano and sang several spritely songs as the two girls danced around to the music. Hugh and David returned long after the children were in bed. We had some more whiskey before turning in ourselves.

The next morning, once again, I heard David and Hugh arguing in loud whispers. I found out why they stopped before I entered the breakfast room—the top step on the stairs squeaked.

After a breakfast of porridge with milk and butter, Blackie and I went out for a long ride along the Beauly Firth. That afternoon, William McKenzie arrived and we set out walking across the fields towards his village. There were many black cattle and small Highland sheep grazing in the fields, but a short distance away was an enclosure containing large sheep.

"What type of sheep are those, William?"

"Cheviots."

"Cheviots are an English breed, aren't they?"

"Indeed."

"William, are these the sheep the laird is bringing in to make more money?"

"Indeed."

"I read they crop the grass so close to the ground that it makes it difficult to raise your black cattle." I was so engrossed in the conversation I almost stumbled once or twice on the uneven ground scattered with rocks and little hillocks and tufts of grass.

"Aye."

"William, why are you just giving me such curt answers to my questions?" He hadn't really looked at me the whole time we had been talking.

"Caroline, I have no choice but to accept such things. We have found no way to resist the determination of the laird to stock his estate with Cheviots and other English breeds and to bring in English shepherds to herd them."

"And the sale of your cattle is the only way you can make money to pay the rent to the laird and buy necessities for your family?" He grabbed my arm just in time to keep me from falling down a little dip in the field.

"Aye. Our farms are owned by the laird, and we don't even have a lease to provide the smallest amount of security. Any day the laird can put you off your farm and give it to another who promises to generate more rent."

"They're very keen, the lairds, to improve their estates to get more income."

"Indeed. They want us to change from using oxen and our current plows to using horses and a newer type of plow. Now, it would take us about five years to pay off the cost of these expenses and, again, we don't know if we have any security from one month to the next."

"The farm labourers must also be very concerned about the changes going on around them?"

He finally looked at me and nodded slowly. "Well, as each farm is given over to raising sheep, fewer labourers are needed during seed time and harvest, so they are all wondering what will happen to them."

"Couldn't you influence the Government to make changes in your favour?" I kept trying to think about what could be done to improve the situation.

"Nay, only landowners can vote, and property law always favours the landlord."

"You must feel backed into a corner with no way out; no way to stand up for yourselves." In the near distance, I saw a few houses and, as we came closer, I could make out a row of low, stone buildings, each with a chimney and a thatched roof. Across the lane was a plowed field with a green haze over it, the new oat, barley, or potato crop. Little children were playing, drawing patterns with sticks in the dust of the lane. As we started down the lane, a few small sheep wandered past us, and then we were at the door of one of the cottages.

William opened the door, and Flora greeted me without turning away from the fireplace.

"I can't talk for a minute, Caroline. Don't want my scones to burn. There, they're done."

The baby's crib was close to the fireplace and little Isabel was sitting at the table playing with her doll—a scrap of woollen cloth stuffed with wool, probably, with button eyes and nose.

"Caroline, come and sit at the table. The tea will soon be ready. There is cream and butter on the table, and a little honey. And, oh, there is brambleberry jam, as well."

She placed the piping hot scones on a serving plate and Isabel passed me a plate. As I enjoyed my scone, I took a moment to look around. The wooden mantle over the fireplace held several candles in candleholders, some serving platters and dinner plates, and a large Gaelic family Bible. There was a spinning wheel near the fireplace. I could see two other doors, probably to bedrooms, and a ladder going up to the attic. A humble home but almost a mansion compared to those of the Dumfriesshire settlers in Pictou District, and other one-room homes I had visited.

Flora was a pleasantly plump woman in her early thirties. Her brown hair was covered with a mutch—a bonnet with frills which framed her face and tied under her chin with a bow. She wore a long blue dress covered with a very large white apron. But her most outstanding feature was her cheerful, friendly blue eyes.

The whole family were in their bare feet despite the mud floor, shoes only worn for long treks or special occasions.

"Well, Caroline," asked Flora, "what do you think of our plans?"

"What plans?"

"You mean Mr. Denoon didn't tell you his plans—our plans?"

"No, not at all."

Looking at William, she asked, "Didn't you tell her, Husband?"

"Nay. I was certain Mr. Denoon said we should keep our plans secret."

"Oh," said Flora, looking first at me and then back to her husband. "Oh." After a few minutes of consideration, she sat up straight and said, "Then I'm going to tell her. Why else is she here?"

"I suppose you're right," said William.

"Caroline, we will soon be leaving Scotland to go to Pictou, Nova Scotia."

"When? How?" I put my half-eaten scone down on the little plate.

"Probably in June. Mr. Denoon is organizing some ships to take us all from our homeland, where we are losing ground every year to the Cheviots, to a place where we can have our own land."

"Which no one can take from us," said William vehemently, rapping the table with his index and middle fingers.

I was surprised at the upwelling of anger, despite his previous claim to be resigned to the helplessness the farmers and labourers all felt about the lairds' decision to choose income from sheep over people.

So, the secret was out! Now I could see why David was so upset with Hugh. The lairds would be angry and might well try to stop this exodus. As well, David's placement at Red Castle on the Black Isle—for that is where we were, as I had been told the first morning at breakfast—was at the pleasure of the laird. The plans would certainly cause some problems for him.

At the end of our visit, Flora and William waved goodbye at their doorstep. I thought I knew the way back to the manse and I needed time to think.

Should I support the Highlanders' decision to leave Scotland only to brave the high seas and years of labour to build homes in the wilds of Nova Scotia or encourage them to fight the decision of the lairds in Scotland to turn their estates over to sheep raising? The question was, could they win such a fight?

I knew in 1792, the farmers from many estates had worked together to round up all the English sheep and herd them south out of the Highlands, only to have the leaders of the demonstration jailed and the property laws strengthened in the favour of the lairds. No more demonstrations had taken place since that time. Besides emigration, the only alternative for farmers was to move to the Lowlands and work in the factories twelve hours a day, six days a week, while their families lived in tenements and hovels. Or a single man could always go into the English Army and serve in wars in foreign countries.

In the end, I had to conclude that emigration was the best choice, although I greatly regretted that people would have to leave their homeland to find land and security. *How dare the lairds exercise such complete control over the Highlanders!*

I hoped Hugh knew what he was doing. Crossing an ocean in a sailing ship was fraught with endless possibilities of what could go wrong and lead to disaster. The Mortons and the Moores and their companions had been invited to Nova Scotia and were well organized. Many of them had been to Nova Scotia during the French and Indian Wars and knew where the best land was located. Even then, it was a struggle to establish themselves. The Stewarts, too, had been invited to go to Prince Edward Island and what a disaster that was. We barely escaped with our lives.

I knew from my research and past dreams that the Highlanders were often not wanted in Nova Scotia and would be given no help in getting land and being successful. And although in the future, Highlanders would be cleared from their land by the lairds, at present the lairds still wanted their labour and would resist them leaving. It would be such a perilous adventure.

When I arrived back at the manse, Hugh and David were having another heated discussion, but they both stopped and looked at me as I entered.

"Don't stop your discussion on my account, gentlemen.."

"How was your visit with the McKenzies?" Hugh asked.

"Very enlightening." I smiled.

"So, you know?" David said, brow furrowed.

"In general, I think I know." I continued to smile.

"It was to be kept a secret," Hugh said, looking directly at his brother.

"I don't plan to say a word, Hugh. You have my word."

"Whose side are you on?" Hugh demanded of me.

"I fully support the best interests of the Highlanders," I said with pride.

"And what is the best interest of the Highlanders?" David asked.

"From what I have heard and read, they have no good option but to emigrate to the colonies."

"Because?" asked David. I had the sense this was the burning question for him.

"Because there they can own their own land, they can maintain their way of life, and they can vote to choose their representatives in government. David, I wish there was some other way, but I can see none. Besides, they have made up their own minds, whatever you or I might think."

David nodded his head. "Aye, I have slowly come to that conclusion myself."

"So," said Hugh, "there will be a gathering tonight on the beach. Will you both come?"

David and I both nodded.

Later, in the evening, we went along a well-travelled path to the beach. A large gathering of men—the women being at home looking after the children—encircled Hugh, who pulled David, William McKenzie, and me into the centre with him and introduced us.

"Mr. McKenzie is one of your leaders. Miss Morton is going to write about your story, and Mr. Denoon, my brother, will pray for you and support you wherever he can."

"Men," yelled Hugh, "I have been able to charter two ships out of Fort William." At that point, some men spat on the ground, a look of total disgust on their faces. I had forgotten how much the Highlanders hated King William, the English replacement for King James Stuart, who had been exiled to Rome. The Highlanders loyalty to King James resulted in the Battle of Culloden Moor in 1746 and the 'pacification' of the Highlands by the English.

"Sorry, men," said Hugh, "I mean An Gearasdan. The ships will leave in early June. For those who wish transportation to the colonies, the fee is £5 for adults and £2 for children under sixteen. You must bring your own food and supplies. We will have to leave here in the middle of May to reach An Gearasdan and to stow your luggage on board before we sail. I will gather you again as soon as the plans are firmer."

There was great excitement among the men, but I could also see some sadness in their eyes. What must it feel like to leave the place where your ancestors had lived for over a thousand years? What must it feel like to leave behind some of your friends and relatives who decided to stay or could not afford to go? It would have taken a lot to force these semi-nomadic cattle herders and very communal, traditional people into this decision.

On my way to William and Flora's home one fine day, I noticed something reddish move just on the brow of the hill. Investigating, I ran towards the hill. The sheep and cattle, surprised at someone running towards them, sprinted off in all directions. Reaching the top of the hill and looking about, I saw something reddish at the top of the next hill. It was hard to make out in the distance, but could it be a man? At the top of the third hill, I looked down to see a glen—a stream with bushes and small trees on either side. Moving down the steep side of the hill, I found a tree and some bushes I could hide behind to survey the situation.

"Ciamar a tha sibh, an duich?"

I turned to see a red-haired man about six feet tall wearing Highland regalia: dark green tartan, a dirk hanging from his belt, a sprig of crimson heath in his blue tam, and a sgian dubh, another knife, stuck in his stocking. He smiled as he waited for my reply.

It took me a moment to regain my composure and recall my Gaelic. "Tha gu math, tapadh leibh. Ciamar a tha sibh, fhein?

"Meadhanach math, tapadh leibh. Tha i brèagha an-duigh," he replied.

"Tha gu dearbh."

He continued to smile at my discomfort and confusion.

"Dè 'n t-ainm a tha oirbh?" I asked.

"Uilleam MacDhòmhnaill."

"William McDonald!"

"Aye. I see you speak English, and hopefully better than Gaelic."

After several courses at Gaelic College in Cape Breton, my Gaelic was, to be generous, pathetic at best. "Do you know who I am?"

"Certainly, Miss Morton."

"Why are we meeting here?"

He laughed. "We are meeting here because you followed me here. And, because I don't want to meet up with the Sheriff."

"Because?" I was holding onto the little tree beside me and hoping not to lose my balance and tumble down the hill.

"Well, let us just say he objects to my means of earning a living."

"Which is?"

"Come into my cave and see."

I let go of the tree momentarily, but then grabbed it again until I could get my bearings.

We climbed over rocks large and small as we moved further down into the glen, then through some trees and bushes, and suddenly we were in a cave. It was cool, dark, and damp, and I sat down on a rock to wait for my eyes to adjust to the darkness. There, against a rocky outcrop, was some kind of metal contraption flanked by burlap sacks. I looked at William. "What is this?"

"Would you like to taste my recipe?" He had a jolly grin and seemed to enjoy teasing me and laughing at my confusion.

"I guess so."

He opened a spigot on the front of the contraption, poured out a small amount, and handed me the cup. "Uisge-beatha!" I said.

"Aye, whiskey. Do you like it?"

"It's very good. So, I'm guessing this is an illegal still and you are an outlaw?"

"Outlaw is a little harsh. I prefer 'unlicensed distributor'," he said, grinning.

"Can I have some more?"

He laughed heartily as he poured me a quarter of a cup. "So, Caroline, how is Mr. Denoon coming with the plans?"

"Oh, you know about that?"

"Oh, aye, did you not see me at the beach when Mr. Denoon told us about the ships?"

"What were you doing there?" I felt a little light-headed as the warmth from the whiskey spread throughout my body.

"I brought some of the men their whiskey."

"Are you going to go to Nova Scotia?"

"The thought of leaving breaks my heart, but I am considering it."

"I wish none of you had to leave, but I can't see how you can stay. Would you be happy working in a factory or going into the King's army or navy? At least in Nova Scotia, you can have your own land."

"I could not work in a factory, and I will not fight for the King, but the Sheriff, when he hears about this plan to emigrate, will certainly have customs officers on the look out for me."

"Because of the still?"

He hesitated. Still grinning.

"William, what else?" I had begun to see him as quite a rascal.

"Well, then there's the Cheviots."

"What about the Cheviots?" I wasn't sure I wanted to know.

"Well, they've been known to head off to the trysts and be sold to the Lowlanders."

"So, you're a sheep rustler, as well?"

"Did I say that? Can I help it if sheep are easily led? It's a great fault of the woolly race."

"You really are an outlaw, William McDonald!"

"Well, Caroline, nobody gets hurt, and I get to live a bit better than my farming friends."

"Do you live in the cave?" It surely didn't look inhabited.

"Nay. Do not ask me where I live, for that is what the Sheriff would like to know."

I didn't tell William, but I was rather happy to have an such an outlaw in the family. By now, I had guessed that our meeting was not a coincidence. My mother's second great-grandfather was William McDonald of Pictou County.

"Are we related, by any chance?" I asked, certain of the answer.

"It depends," he said with an enigmatic smile.

"Depends on what!"

"You've just called me an outlaw. Do you want such a person as your relative?" He had his hands on his hips and waited for my reply.

I thought about my adamant statement to my sisters that I wouldn't want to include anyone in my research that wasn't an asset to our family. *Did he know about that?* Suddenly, I had a change of heart. "William McDonald, you are just the kind of person I want in my family."

He nodded slowly. "Perhaps then I'll admit that we are related."

"And we were intended to meet?"

"Certainly."

So now I had an outlaw in the family. I hoped he wouldn't get caught. *What might happen next?*

I went on my way to the McKenzie's, and we had a lovely tea. Flora was such a chatty and outgoing person and little Isabel followed her mother around trying to help with the chores. At one point, I saw her with a twig broom twice as tall as her, trying to sweep the ashes off the hearth. She had on a little blue dress and a white apron.

"Will Isabel soon be going to school?" I asked Flora.

"Nay, Caroline. There is no Gaelic school. Come to think of it, there is no school of any kind. The laird and his tacksmen pay for tutors for their children."

"How then do you learn to read and write?"

"We do not. There is nothing in our lives that requires these skills, except for understanding our Bibles. We are all trained from childhood to have excellent memories. We memorize everything—stories, songs, poems, genealogy, and, most importantly, long, long passages from the Bible. A catechist comes around to the villages and reads a Bible story until we can memorize it, and then we never forget it. And, of course, we all learn the stories and songs and genealogy by going to the cèilidhean."

"Cèilidhean, that means house parties or something like that?"

"Aye, get-togethers. We have them often, particularly in the winter months when there is not so much farm work to do. We're having one tonight, Caroline. I hope you can come."

"Flora, I wouldn't miss it. Where and when?"

"On the beach. There will be music, food, singing and dancing and, of course, recitation of long poems. The young women flirt with the young men and many a match has been made at a cèilidh." She smiled to herself. "And, oh, the men usually have wrestling matches or games that involve hurling heavy stones. At the end, the women and children leave first, followed by the men. Young lovers usually linger until dark."

"Only until dark?"

"Aye. After that you must worry about the sìthichean or bean-sìthichean as well as each uisge."

"So, the fairies, both male and female, water horses or kelpies—any other concerns?"

"Well, also the gruagach, but he's only seen at the dairy."

"Anything else I should know?"

"Certainly. Our house is well-protected. We have rowan trees planted nearby which ward off witches and fairies, and as well, we have a piece of iron buried at the gate which protect us from supernatural beings of all denominations. And, as I'm sure you know, if you offer a gruagach milk, he or she will do you not harm."

I really didn't know that. "About the gruagach, do you see him or her often?"

"In our case, it is a male. Aye, we see him nearly every day unless he goes to visit his friends."

"What does he look like?"

"He has blond hair and wears a brown suit and a yellow hat."

"Could I see him?"

"Well, come with me." We went out the door and around to the dairy. There were two milk cows waiting to be milked, their calves already nursing vigorously. "There, sitting on the roof of the dairy, do you see him?"

I didn't. "No, Flora. I can't see anyone."

"Really, Caroline? He right there smiling at us—which is a good sign."

"No, I can't see a thing."

"Do you have any Sassenach blood?"

"Unfortunately, yes."

"Well, then, hold my hand as I think that will overcome your disability."

As soon as she held my hand, I could see the gruagach lying on his side with one hand propping up his head. She was right, he was smiling and looked very entertained by what it took for me to see him. "Should I say anything?"

"Nay, best just to smile and wave."

Which I did, and then turned to ask Flora a question. When I glanced back, he was gone.

"That was exciting, Flora. I have just seen my first gruagach."

Flora shook her head in amazement.

"By the way, Flora, what do you do if you meet up with a fairy?"

"You must quickly draw a circle around yourself and make a cross within it. The circle must be drawn deasil—that is, in the direction of the path of the sun."

I was going to say 'clockwise' but thought better of it as the Highlanders had no clocks.

"Will the circle and cross also protect you from kelpies—water horses?"

"Aye. And making the sign of the cross—but that's mostly for witches."

"How would I recognize a fairy or a kelpie?"

Again, she looked at me with dismay. "Kelpies are demonic Celtic monsters. They can look like a horse or a handsome young man with sand and seashells in his hair. If you are not careful, they will drag you down into the water to their lair where you become a meal. So be wary whenever you are near a body of water. Fairies are tricksters—they like to play tricks on people, and they're easily offended. They can be mean."

"What size are they?"

"They can be very tiny or the size of a young man or woman. Mostly they wear brown or green, sometimes crotal—a yellowish brown.

"And the witches, should I be afraid of them?"

"Well, there are black witches and white witches. The white witches work for good and prepare potions and spells to help their neighbours. Black witches, needless to say, are dangerous."

"How do I tell them apart?"

"Well, all witches can perform spells and make potions. All witches can transform themselves into animals to escape detection and, as well, they often appear out of nowhere or disappear in the same way. But black witches cause harm and death with their spells, while white witches only do good—they heal and protect. There are laws that require witches to be hung if they are caught practising magic."

"Thank you for explaining all that to me, Flora. Now, about this evening, will I get to meet some of the village folk?"

"Aye. They've all been watching and wondering who you are."

"Who I am?"

"Aye. Most think you are a fairy or a witch. I've told them you are from Nova Scotia, but they feel you appeared out of nowhere—none of their relatives along the road from An Gearasdan to Easter Ross ever saw you or heard of you."

"How do the people feel about witches?"

"They will do you no harm as long as they believe you are a white witch."

"Flora, I want to assure you that I am certainly not a witch or a fairy. I am a person just like you. I intend to do no one any harm."

"Caroline, I believe you and have already assured the other that you are a white witch."

What! I thought to myself but realized that I might as well save my breath—a decision had been made.

That evening, I was at the village early and helped carry some of the food and children down to the beach. The people were very friendly. There were a lot of McDonalds—all related somehow—Grants, MacIntoshes, MacKenzies, a few MacGregors, Camerons, a Chisholm and a MacMillan.

As soon as everyone arrived, the fiddlers and the pipers took turns providing the music and the children and young people got up and danced while the women spread out the meal—chicken stew with more potatoes than chicken—bread, butter, milk, scones, tea, and whiskey.

After supper, the best singers led the people in beautiful, haunting, bittersweet songs about love and loss and love of homeland—all in Gaelic. No English spoken here.

A young man came forward and, looking at a particular young woman, sang this song to her. I only understood the chorus on which we all joined in.

> A Mhàiri bhòidheach, 's a Mhàiri ghaolach
> A Mhàiri bhòidheach gur mòr mo ghaol ort
> A Mhàiri bhòidheach gur tu a chlaoidh mi
> 'S a dh'fhàg mi brònach gun dòigh air t'fhaotainn
>
> Beautiful Mary, darling Mary
> Beautiful Mary, great is my love for you
> Beautiful Mary, forever and always
> I will be sad that I couldn't win you.

Another song I really loved was called "S e Tìr Mo Rùin-sa Ghàidheal-tachd—I Dearly Love the Highlands." There was a chorus, and long series of verses.

> Air fà lè liù hò ro hù
> 'S e tìr mo ruin-sa Ghàidhealtachd
> (I dearly love the Highlands)

Air fà lè liù hò ro hù

Afar one sees the cows and their calves
On the sheilings throughout the glens

A milkmaid goes to milk them
With a big pail in each hand

You will get plenty of it to drink
And you'll not pay a penny for it

There will be girls carding
For the women who are spinning

You will get salmon there and venison
And fish to your heart's desire

You will get oat cakes and barley bread
That's what I ate when I was young

There the sun rises early
My desire is to live there

There the birds sing early
I am desperately sad that I left

And you wouldn't be wakeful all the night
In the glens of Berneray

There the young women waulk the tweed
How I loved the sound of their laughter.

Suddenly a man in his late thirties stood up and roared,

"Enough of this maidenly singing. I long to hear a song of warriors and battles even if I am the one to sing it."

It was obviously a song that everyone knew, as they immediately joined in the chorus.

> Hoilibheag hilibheag hó ail il ó
> Hoilibheag hilibheag hó ró i
> Hoilibheag hilibheag hóail il ó
> Smeòrach le Clann Dómhnaill mi
> (A mavis [thrush] of Clan McDonald, I)
>
> If every bird praises its own land
> How then should I not praise mine?
> Land of hero warriors, land of wandering poets,
> Fruitful land; generous, esteemed land.
>
> I was raised amongst Clan Donald:
> Sea-faring people, under bright banners,
> Swift ships on the wide ocean,
> People not slow to unsheathe gray blades.
>
> My beloved people, not mild-tempered,
> A people easily roused to strife,
> A people ambitious to grasp their swords,
> Beneath the flying banners.

At the end of the song, I looked down the beach to where many of the men had retreated. Instead of the wrestling matches and stone hurling I expected, William McKenzie took the men a way down the beach where they practised fighting with knives—dirks, swords, and sgian dubhs. It didn't seem casual entertainment. They seemed deadly serious.

As I watched the swordplay, a man of perhaps forty years and wearing Grant tartan stepped into the light of the fire and sat down on a flat rock. The people all gathered round, each vying for seats closest to the man who Flora told me was one of their poets. I sat close to Flora and Isabel, hoping Flora would help me with understanding the Gaelic.

The poet looked around at the gathering and began.

> As I look steadfastly, my mind is troubled with sadness and dejection; as I gaze around me, I see the peasantry adrift; if some of them will gain, others will not reach shore; many of them are broken, the situation does not surprise me at all.

> It does not surprise me if they do not recover or recoup; land has never been so expensive, ever since the world began; the North has been massacred, even since this current oppression began; the landlords took their people from the lands and each day their toil is increased.

> Their toil increases; it is the nobles who have raised the rents; people no longer feel pity, and frigidity is taking its place; a noble's word no longer stands and currently it carried an ill reputation; the truth and justice of this era are to be found in the goose's quill.

> Truth and justice, they were perverted long-ago in this place; greed and ill-will are so plentiful that they will never run out; kindness has departed from everyone and the cry of the commoners is wretched every day; the nobles are mowing them down, as they learn to do in luxurious London.

> Love has turned its back on us, and the nobles of our land are so disagreeable, spending so recklessly all that ruins and injures the poor; taking their assets away from them, even if

they had not put much aside; and with all of it that they have accumulated, the blessing of God's son will not be theirs.

There will not be the blessing of God's son and He will not gladly help one bit given all the toil that is accumulating as people's burden; the nobles will not distribute charity to the poor, even if they come inside; it is a cause of grief to hear all that I have to read about their faults.

It is no surprise that we have no wealth given everything that is constantly hounding us; there is never an assembly or forum that does not involve expenditure, despite whatever joy or solace, grief or sadness accompanies it; everyone who hears this song will drink a toast to my health.

It is time for us to be going while we have at least a little wealth before they take it away from us and before our children will be heir to poverty; despite the opinion of the nobles, we will gain the upper hand regardless and we will traverse the oceans to arrive in bountiful America over yonder.

With Flora's help, I was able to understand the Gaelic so I could remember the poet's offering. I felt so dejected and unhappy for the Highlanders, being forced from their homes to survive in the dense forest of North America. The poet is right, the lairds will not receive any blessing for their cruelty to the people. But there was that hopeful note in the poet's address: 'despite the opinion of the nobles, we will gain the upper hand regardless.' It was not all grief and sadness. The Highlanders felt anger and defiance towards their oppressors. A good sign.

It started to get dark. I was standing with the people watching the fire when I felt a touch on my shoulder and turning there was William McDonald. Without a word, he began to wrap a plaid around my body and, having arranged it to his satisfaction, he fastened it in place with a silver annular brooch. Then he was gone. The people nearby laughed at my surprise and pleasure.

Two days later there was bad news.

"Caroline," said David, "did you hear? William McDonald was caught leaving the cèilidh and is in the jail in Beauly?"

"David, what happened? How did he get caught?"

"Not sure. He was on his way to visit his wife and baby when the Sheriff's men just happened to run into him."

"Did he fight them?"

"Oh, nay. Too outnumbered."

"David, can we go and visit him to see what can be done?"

"Surely."

We rode from Red Castle to Beauly and tied up our horses in front of the jail. The jailer was a jolly fellow and was pleased to let us see his famous captive.

"Aye, aye, Mr. Denoon, Miss Morton, you can visit that outlaw, William McDonald. Come this way."

William was lying on a small cot in a room with bars on the windows and door. He jumped up when we arrived.

"Caroline! Mr. Denoon! How good of you to visit."

"William, what will happen to you? How can I help?" I asked.

"Well, the trial is tomorrow so then I will know my fate. Probably hanging for the sheep stealing."

"What! Hanging! No! Shouldn't you just get a fine or a jail sentence?" I was shocked.

"The laird wants to make an example of me to prevent the practice from gaining any more momentum."

He seemed way too cheerful, I thought.

"David, can you talk to the judge?" I asked in desperation.

"I will, Caroline, but I doubt it will do any good."

David did talk to the judge, but the sentence was still hanging—within the week. I was in tears when David and I visited William after the sentencing.

"Caroline, don't weep. I took the risk, and I lost."

"Aye, Miss," said the jailer, "he pled guilty, and the laird wanted an example made of those who chose to rustle their sheep."

"But he has a wife and baby. What about them?"

"Caroline, the McDonalds will care for her," David said.

"William, shall we have a prayer?"

"Aye, Mr. Denoon, I need all the forgiveness I can get from heaven."

We all knelt while David held William's hand and they said the Lord's Prayer, then William made his confession of sin and David offered the assurance of pardon. We stood, and I grasped William's hand and held on until David and the jailer pried me away.

When I awoke on the day William was to be hung, I could hear the Denoon family in the breakfast room chatting merrily. For a moment, I thought of not having breakfast with them, but on second thought, I decided to go into the room and demand to know how they could be so unfeeling.

On entering the room, they all turned and smiled at me. I was at a loss for words. How could they act like nothing terrible was happening today?

"Did you hear?" Jannet asked. "William has escaped from jail."

It took a few minutes to sink in. "He's safe?"

"Aye," David said.

"How?"

"Someone pulled the bars out of the window."

"Who?"

"Ah, we should not ask that question. We do not want to know," David said.

"Do you know, Hugh?"

Hugh and Jannet smiled and said nothing.

"I'm so happy and relieved. I just wish I could thank whoever freed him."

"Well," said David, "maybe someday you will get your wish, but not today."

"Will he be coming to Nova Scotia?"

"That," Hugh said, "is up in the air. The Sheriff will be looking for him, especially at the ports and borders."

It seemed I would have to leave Scotland without knowing what happened to William McDonald. I smoothed the plaid that he had given me and thought this might be the only thing I might have to remember him.

While I waited and hoped to hear some news about William McDonald, plans were moving ahead for the emigration.

Sadness and tiredness seem to go together and so I had been going to bed early. One night, I was awakened by a faint rustling sound. Turning toward the window where the light of a full moon was shining into the room, I could see the casement was open and someone was pulling him or herself into my room. When he stood up from a crouch, I could see it was a man. I reached under my pillow for my sgian dubh as he approached the bed.

"Caroline," he whispered, "it's William." Seeing the glint of the knife, he laughed softly, "So you were going to stab me!"

"I didn't know it was you. I'm so glad to see you!" I whispered.

There was more rustling at the window, and another person fell into the room.

"Caroline, I would like you to meet my wife, Ann."

I got out of bed and hugged her, having never expected to ever meet her. In the moonlight I could see she was above average in height for a Highland woman and with the most beautiful, curly strawberry blonde hair. She wore a long, blue, woollen skirt with a bodice over a linen blouse under her arisaid—a dark green length of woollen cloth held on around her waist by a thick leather belt and at her throat by an annular brooch with still enough cloth left over to pull it over her head if it rained. It fell almost to the floor.

"Where is your little boy, Finlay?"

"With my sister, for the moment, until we get a plan to escape to the colonies," she whispered.

"Do you have any food, Caroline?" William asked.

"I'll get some. Come with me, Ann."

Creeping as softly as possible, and avoiding the squeaky step, we went into the pantry and took several loaves of bread, some cheese, fruit preserves, and a jug of milk. All was silent in the house as we returned.

"Glè mhath, a Charoline. Aran, im, bainne, caise, tapadh leibh," William said.

William and Ann ate ravenously and fell asleep on my bed. I dressed to be prepared for whatever might happen next.

What happened next were several sharp raps on the front door right after sunrise. It was the Sheriff following a lead that William might have come towards Red Castle.

William and Ann, who had been sleeping lightly, woke up and I hid them behind the voluminous curtains around the bed.

"Caroline," David called from the entry hall, "are you able to come down to speak to the Sheriff?"

"Certainly, Mr. Denoon, I'll be right down."

The Sheriff was a tall, dark-haired, severe-looking man, no doubt much disturbed by the escape of an outlaw from his jail. "Good morning, Sheriff," I said, upon stepping on the squeaky step.

"Now, Miss Morton, we do not want to alarm a guest of Mr. Denoon's, but William McDonald has been seen in this neighbourhood. We are aware that you know him and even visited him in jail, so we want to know if you have seen him since you visited him in jail?"

"Strange you should mention that, Sheriff. As a matter of fact, I dreamed about him just this morning. He was boarding a ship to, well, I'm not sure where it was going. You know what dreams are like."

"You sound like one of them, a Highlander, talking about dreams and such. Mr. Denoon, since your guest has shown such interest in our escapee, with your permission we will search Miss Morton's room."

"Oh, aye, Sheriff. Please search any room you wish. I'm sure Miss Morton will agree?"

I did not agree, but what could I do? My heart was pounding as I followed them upstairs and into my room. I watched helplessly as they pulled the bedding apart, threw open the doors and searched the armoire, pulled up the rug, and pushed aside the curtains around the bed. At that point, it occurred to me that hopefully William and Ann had escaped out the window.

Looking frustrated, the Sheriff turned to me, "I see you eat your meals in your room, Miss Morton."

"I have migraine headaches, Sheriff, and become really hungry. Sorry, Mr. Denoon, for eating your bread and cheese."

"My dear Miss Morton, you are our guest, we should have been more solicitous about your needs. You are more than welcome to any of our food."

The Sheriff turned on his heels and left, followed by his deputies, the last of whom turned to me and with a smile whispered, "Miss Morton, you should probably clean up the breadcrumbs behind your bed."

I just stood there, frozen. He knew but had kept silent. Why?

After they were gone, I asked David, "Who is the young man who spoke to me just as they were leaving?"

"One of the MacDonalds from Urquhart Parish. Why do you ask?"

"But he's one of the deputies?"

"Aye. Don't worry, Miss Morton, I'm sure they don't suspect you of hiding the outlaw in your bedroom." He smiled reassuringly.

After breakfast, I decided to take Blackie for a ride. We both needed some fresh air and I needed to ponder what had happened to William and Ann. I hoped their escape out the window had gone unnoticed and they were heading somewhere safe.

When I returned to my room to get my hat, there were William and Ann having breakfast on the leftover bread, milk, and cheese. They smiled as I entered. *What is going on?*

"You're probably wondering where we went while the Sheriff was searching the room?" William said, smiling.

"Oh, no, the thought didn't occur to me—of course, I want to know!"

William looked at Ann and smiled, "Our relative seems a little annoyed with me, my dear."

"Caroline," said Ann, "my husband is a bit of a tease. Just ignore him."

Seeing that the two women were in no mood for teasing, William stood up and gestured for me to come and look behind the bed. Seeing nothing but what I expected, he said, "Put your hand here and push."

With great ease a little door, invisible unless you knew what to look for, opened smoothly and quietly.

"How did you know?"

"We didn't," said Ann, "we just leaned against the wall, trying to decide what to do, and it opened."

"Do you want to look inside?" she inquired.

I nodded. Stooping to climb through the door, it was surprising to find a bed and washstand with a bowl and pitcher. The bedding looked fresh as did the towels ... so had someone just prepared the space? What was going on?

I couldn't ask David or Jennet for permission for William and Ann to stay in their house, but this would be a perfect place for them to hide while the manhunt went on. Would I be putting David in danger if I said nothing about them hiding in his house? What else could I do?

Life in the Denoon household went on as usual. The plans for emigration proceeded apace. Hugh was going further and further afield in his effort to recruit emigrants and his message was carried by word-of-mouth even further into distant parishes. David and Hugh seemed to be on the same page now.

William, Ann, and I fell into a daily routine. As soon as the maid had made my bed and picked up the dishes from the day before, William and Ann would leave their hiding place and have their breakfast on the supplies I had gathered the night before. It was surprising there was always plenty of easily portable food, as if someone knew I would be raiding the pantry. After my breakfast with the Denoon family, I would return to my room, and we would spend hours listening to William tell me about our MacDonald ancestors and their life in the Highlands.

"Now, I know your mother was a MacDonald, Caroline, so you should know about our ancestry which we trace back to Ireland. Indeed, the MacDonalds are originally from Ireland, and related to Conn, High King of Ireland. This means we are of royal blood."

Well, I thought, that would explain the haughtiness that the MacDonalds often displayed, especially to Sassenachs. I decided to be very silent about my own English ancestors and many Lowland ancestors. But it was charming to think that we were of royal blood.

"So, William, how far back are we talking about? When did Conn live and when did our ancestors come to Scotland from Ireland?"

"I cannot say, Caroline. We do not keep time like the Sassenachs, but the next person you need to know about is Somerled."

"Oh, I have heard of Somerled. He chased the Norse Vikings out of the southern Hebrides. Yet strangely, he married Ragnhilda, daughter of the Norse Viking King of the Isle of Mann."

"Very good, Caroline. It is most pleasing to me that you know some clan history. Then you would also know that Somerled, who lived in Argyll and Islay, was killed in a battle he instigated with the King of Scotland."

"And three of his sons, Dougal, Reginald, and Angus, took over his territory."

"Aye, aye. And Reginald's son, Donald, began the Clan Donald." William said.

Ann, who had been silent all this time, spoke up. "And Donald's descendants became the Lord of the Isles, the great Gaelic Kingdom and was the headship of all those who spoke Gaelic."

"True," William said. "And in that kingdom, all that is good flourished. Poets, bards, harpists, pipers, physicians, priests and monks, craftsmen well-trained in wood and metal work as well as the creators of the wonderful standing stone crosses."

"Don't forget the lawyers," Ann said. "They had a very ancient law code with judges and lawyers in every part of the kingdom."

Not wanting to be outdone, I mentioned the great sea power of the kingdom.

"One thing we learned from the Vikings, how to build sea-going ships and to sail them as well as the Norse. It was really that skill that helped Somerled and his descendants drive the Norse out of the Hebrides," William said.

"I hesitate to ask this question, William, as I don't want to offend you."

"Nay, Caroline, we are family, you can't offend me. Ask your question."

"William, it has been my impression that Clan Donald, indeed all the Highland Clans, were quite warlike."

His eyes brightened and he smiled broadly.

"Oh, aye. Most warlike."

"Would you say, dangerous?"

"Aye, aye, most dangerous."

"Ask him to recite some of the Clan Donald Incitement to Battle, Caroline." Ann said.

I looked at William.

He stood, smoothed out his clothing, and drew himself up to his full height.

O Children of Conn of the Hundred Battles
Now is the time for you to win recognition.

O raging whelps,
O sturdy heroes,
O most sprightly lions,
O battle-loving warriors,
O brave, heroic firebrands,
The Children of Conn of the Hundred Battles,
O Children of Conn, remember
Hardihood in the time of battle.

"There are forty more lines, Caroline, but I think you see the High-landers great love for battle. Clan Donald was a warrior society with the best of them enshrined in songs and poems recited by the bards at great gatherings of the Clan," Ann said. Ann was a great companion for William. She was bright, quick, and energetic, but able to direct William's energy away from more troublesome goals.

William's eyes shone as he recalled the greatness of Clan Donald. Then, suddenly, they turned dark and sad. "But those days are gone now, and we have to leave everything dear to us for a strange land leaving our ancestors distant and alone."

I too felt sad. There was no need for words.

Our wonderful time together came to an abrupt end.

Mairi, the maid, went up to my room early, to retrieve one of the many plates that were stacking up after William and Ann's late-night snacks. I was in the breakfast room with the Denoons when we heard hysterical shrieking. We were all halfway standing, pulling our napkins off our knees, when she raced into the room and screamed, "Fairies, fairies, in Miss Mor-ton's room, in her bed! Oh, Mr. Denoon, what shall we do!"

David pulled out a chair and said in a kindly voice, "Mairi, sit here. Jennet, pour her a glass of milk. Don't worry, Mairi, Miss Morton and I will investigate. Come with me Miss Morton."

We ran up the stairs, two steps at a time. My heart was pounding, not just from the exertion, but because now my secret was going to be found out. What would happen from there?

David opened the door to my room and, there, seated at the little tea table, were William and Ann, trying to arrange their clothing and their hair.

"Really, William," David said, "shame on you for scaring Mairi."

"She doesn't usually come into the room so early. We thought we had lots of time."

I wondered what they were doing in my bed, but I decided this was not the time and, besides, I could guess.

"So, what are we going to do now?" asked William.

"Well, it's best that we agree that you are fairies, rather than outlaws. I will try to calm Mairi, so she won't tell her family and friends. Then, I think you will also agree it is too dangerous for you to stay here. So, I'm going to arrange for two horses to take you to Loch Broom. Hugh is chartering another ship from there."

I realized that David had known all along that William and Ann were in his house and I couldn't contain myself.

"Mr. Denoon, David, you knew they were here all along?"

"Aye, Caroline. I sent them here."

"What do you mean? How did you know where William was after the jailbreak?"

William laughed with great merriment, obviously enjoying my complete bafflement. "Caroline, it was David who broke me out of jail and gave me directions of where to hide."

"A minister of the Church of Scotland broke you out of jail and hid you from the Sheriff?" I asked, quite shocked.

"Aye."

"David, I shall always have the deepest gratitude and regard for you. You are a hero to me. What would happen if you got caught?"

"I would lose my position and my place in the Church of Scotland. And, perhaps, be imprisoned for a long time."

"Then let's go down and re-assure Mairi before anything else happens."

That evening, after dark, William and Ann lowered themselves out the window of my room and onto waiting horses.

"God speed," I whispered, as they waved goodbye.

Would I ever see them again?

I was amazed how many men showed up on May 15 to pay their fee. There were families from the Black Isle and many other parishes. Hugh told the gathering to be in An Gearasdan by May 30.

The following Sunday, the church was filled with Highlanders as David preached and led the people in prayer. It was their last worship service in Scotland. No word was spoken about the plan as some of the laird's family were there. Following the service, many of the people went into the graveyard carrying little pebbles in their hands. After visiting the graves of their ancestors, they placed a pebble or two on the gravestone before leaving.

Days before our exodus was to begin, I rode Blackie out toward Ord Hill. My mind was on all that had happened and was to come next, so I was surprised when I found Blackie taking us up the hill. I often wondered about Blackie. How had I come to be riding her when Hugh first met me? At the top of the hill, there was a wonderful panorama out over the Black Isle and Beauly Firth. I dismounted and found a suitable rock to sit on and survey the scene. The sky was soft blue with little clouds nudged along by the wind and the air was so fine and light I could easily believe we had arrived in heaven. Far out towards the mouth of the Firth lay the North Sea and surrounding the hill were the fields of the Estate, already green with new growth.

I looked over to check on Blackie and she turned and looked at me. There was a look of merriment in her eyes, I thought. *Could she be ...?* No. But then why did I have such a strange feeling. Probably because I had become so attached to her and was worried what would happen to her when I left with the Highlanders. *What would happen to her?*

After breakfast on the day we were to leave, I thanked David and Jennet with all my heart and they both hugged me. Then I heard a strange sound and, stepping outside, saw the beginning of the line of people coming over the hill. The sound was stronger, a low murmuring and moaning.

I saddled Blackie and rode out to the road. The whole crowd of people were lamenting, a sound that one usually heard at Highland wakes and funerals. The people were grieving the loss of their beloved homeland. As the sound rose and fell, I realized how much anger I felt over this sad departure.

Hugh rode out to the front of the line and David stood by the road, with his hand raised in blessing, as the people passed. I looked for William McKenzie and could see him organizing a group of the men to walk on either side of the column, to support the women and children, I imagined. I joined the exodus and rode with Hugh.

As we journeyed along the road from the Black Isle, people from the parishes we passed joined the column—Kirkhill, Kilmorach, Kiltarlity, Strathglass, and other parishes—all with ox carts or horse-drawn carts filled with their movable possessions. All the people were wearing plaids, that most indispensable Highland garment, which kept off the rain and the cold during the day. At night everyone wrapped themselves in their plaid and slept near the road.

The road to An Gearasdan ran along the north side of Loch Ness. It was slow going as the road was just a cart track and the oxen plodded along at their own pace. The gorse was blooming a cheerful yellow, and the bracken was bright green, but they would never see the heather bloom again, never see the beautiful pink and white flowers cover the hills in beauty. By August, God willing, they would be in far away Pictou, Nova Scotia.

On the third day a group of horsemen—the lairds' men—rode by the line of people and reached the head of the line where Hugh and I were on horseback. Just behind us was William McKenzie, the leader of the people.

"What is the meaning of this?" The angry man demanded. "Who is in charge here?"

Hugh rose in his stirrups, "I'm in charge."

"By what authority are you leading these people away from the lairds' estates?"

"These are free people, are they not? Why would they need to consult any authority to move freely?"

"These people are obliged to farm the lairds' estates."

"Show me their leases or any document that describes their obligations to the laird, or his obligation to them."

"These people cannot read or write. What good would a lease do? By long tradition, they have always farmed the estates."

"They farmed the estates because they had no other option. But now they have a good option. Land of their own which no one can take from them. And as free people they are not going to wait until the lairds take their farms and replaces them with Cheviots. I'm sure you can understand that. Perhaps you would like to go with them?"

The men looked at each other, perplexed. "We'll be reporting this rebelliousness to the lairds, and then we shall see how much further you can get."

"No one is rebelling. Each Highlander is simply exercising his right to seek a better situation for himself and his family. If the lairds had offered long leases and rewarded his hard-working tenants, they would still be living happily on the estates. As it is, he will have to rely on his Cheviots to provide him with a living."

The men rode off.

The next morning, the Sheriff and his men arrived to insist to Hugh Denoon that he turn the people back to the estates.

"Indeed, I will not, Mr. Sheriff. You have no legal authority, and we will be continuing to our destination."

Some of the Sheriff's men began to ride along the column of Highlanders, assessing the situation. I noticed that each Highlander had his right hand inside his plaid. As the Sheriff's men rode by, each man drew his hand partway out of his plaid. They were all grasping the hilt of a dirk, a long stabbing knife. The steel that showed glinted in the sunlight, making it clear what the Highlanders were signalling. The Sheriff's men wheeled around and came riding back to the front of the line. The Sheriff looked at them, puzzled.

"They're all armed, Sheriff!"

Hugh said, "You well know, Sheriff, that there are no people on earth better fighters and more dangerous than Highlanders. They are not looking for a fight, but if it's a fight you want, we shall oblige."

"Thank you, no, Mr. Denoon. I will tell the lairds that they will have to find another way to stop you if that is their wish. Good day to you."

There were no more emissaries from the lairds, so Hugh felt we were out of the woods.

William and Flora thought it might not be over yet. "The lairds are used to getting their own way. We doubt they are through trying to stop us."

"But what are their options?" I asked, "since no one has a lease."

"Oh, but they have friends in the Government. They may try to get them to pass legislation that would prevent us leaving and force us back to the estates."

I asked Hugh if he had thought of that.

"Nay, Caroline, I hadn't thought of that, but I don't doubt that he would use that option if it was open to him."

Upon reaching An Gearasdan, Hugh found out that indeed one of the lairds was trying to get the Government to stop the emigration of his tenants. The application had gone all the way to the Lord Advocate for Scotland, Charles Hope. Satisfaction did not ensue for the laird, as the Lord Advocate ruled that, it is "clear that there is no law for keeping the people in the country against their will."

Hugh and the people were delighted by this news. There was singing and dancing that evening. Some of the men performed the sword dance to the sound of the bagpipes. The children tried their best to imitate the dancers but with varied success.

In the morning, Hugh and I went to speak to the customs people and look at the two ships he had chartered, the *Sarah* of Liverpool and the *Dove* of Aberdeen. The Sarah was the bigger of the two, but the two of them didn't look spacious enough to accommodate all the Highlanders that had arrived at the port.

The customs man, a Mr. Campbell, approached Hugh, "Ah, Mr. Denoon, it seems you have made quite a name for yourself, whisking away our farmers and labourers. The laird is still looking for a way to stop you and so we have been ordered to search your ships for all possible infractions of existing laws."

"Very well, Mr. Campbell, let us proceed with the search."

After an hour or so, the two men re-appeared.

"Well, Mr. Denoon, you thought you could hide that extra row of bunks, but you are not so clever as you imagine. Now that those bunks are removed, let us see if you have room for your passengers."

Hugh said nothing.

Mr. Campbell continued. "You have 199 adults and 151 children under sixteen for a total of 350 passengers. The *Sarah* is only 350 tons, so I advise against so many passengers for such a long voyage."

Hugh took in a deep breath, "I was hoping that we might agree that children would not be counted as adults. My thought is that you add up the ages of the children and divide by 16, we could arrive at an equivalent of the number of full passengers under sixteen. Having done so, the number I get is 51."

"So, you have reduced 350 full passengers to 250 full passengers by simple mathematics, Mr. Denoon. Brilliant, I must say. I suppose you propose to use the same formula for the passengers on the *Dove*."

"Aye. Using the same formula, you will see there are 149 adult passengers and 70 under sixteen, and thus we arrive at 180 full passengers for the *Dove*."

"Unfortunately, Mr. Denoon, there is no law against what you are doing, but I would point out to you that according to the slave trade regulations, you are overcrowded by 200 passengers."

This seemed to be news to Hugh, and he seemed taken aback.

"As well," Mr. Campbell continued, "I need to advise you that all your passengers should be vaccinated for smallpox."

I could tell from the look on Hugh's face that he had not thought of this.

"Also, Mr. Denoon, you have enough water and provisions for a voyage of average length, but not enough if your crossing takes longer than average."

Hugh nodded, "Thank you for all your good advice, Mr. Campbell."

Mr. Campbell took the passenger lists for the *Sarah* and the *Dove* and approved the two ships for clearing the port of Fort William for June 8, 1801. They were on their way to the New World and a new life whatever that might be.

"Hugh, will you provide more water and food and get everyone vaccinated?"

"Nay, Caroline. The laird is surely still looking for some way to stop us and it would be disastrous if all these folks had to turn around and go back to their estates. We must take this one opportunity for there may not be another." With that he was gone, giving orders for the Highlanders to line up to begin boarding, women and children first, then the elderly, and finally the men.

I was standing with Blackie when the young MacDonald Deputy-Sheriff, who knew that William had been hiding in my room, came up to me.

"Good day, Miss Morton. Well, you're all soon going to be leaving us."

"There is no joy in it, Mr. MacDonald."

"How can there be?"

"Are you here to say goodbye to a relative?"

"Nay, the Sheriff has sent me here to find the outlaw, William MacDonald."

"That is why the Sheriff has sent you here, but why are you here?"

"To take care of your horse."

"You're going to care for Blackie? I'm so relieved."

I handed the reins over to Mr. MacDonald.

"It's not that she needs my care, but she wanted to ease your mind."

"I don't understand."

"You don't need to."

I gave her a big hug and a kiss on the forehead, and he led her away. Then it occurred to me! *No one saw me riding her from Fort William to the Black Isle when I arrived because she's a fairy horse!* We were in the Highlands after all, so why didn't I suspect that?

The night before departure, all the people boarded the ships and found spaces in the crowded areas below deck to sleep. All were in a very sober mood. Would they survive the crossing? Where and how would they live when they arrived in Pictou? Had they made the right decision?

On the morning of departure, as the sailors untied the ship from the dock, the Highlanders lined the railings on deck. They struggled with their feelings as took their last look at their homeland and it receded below the horizon.

"We have to hold to our decision, Flora, and look forward now to the future of our family in Pictou," said William, as he watched Flora's tears fall from her eyes. She nodded her assent, but this did not stop the tears, so, of course, she didn't see the tears in William's eyes.

It was clear from the beginning that the *Sarah* and the *Dove* were over-crowded, and we all hoped for a swift voyage of seven or eight weeks. I felt no excitement and only dread. Sailing ships are unpredictable; so many things can go wrong: storms, becalmings, being blown off course, reefs, shoals, pirates, privateers, and the Kings Navy, always on the lookout for young men to impress into service—and those were only the things I could think of off the top of my head. Oh, and scurvy and the spread of disease in closely packed living quarters. But sailing ships were how all my ancestors got from Europe to North America and so I could not avoid what must needs be. Of course, I knew from my earlier journeys, never mind what Mr. Campbell had pointed out to Hugh, that they were woefully unprepared.

At first, there was a great sense of freedom among the passengers. They stayed on the deck in the evenings singing and dancing, telling stories of heroes and battles from long-ago and reciting long poems—all in Gaelic. They no longer needed to speak English or have their Gaelic translated into English for the Sassenachs. It was a great relief. But the sense of relief was short-lived.

"Flora, what's happening?" I asked as I heard lamenting from below deck.

"Smallpox," she said grimly.

This disease was one of the most lethal in the world, carrying away many children and adults every year, and leaving the survivors with horrible disfigurement, blindness, pox-marked faces, and suffering from the trauma, along with their families. A means of prevention had been found—an amazing blessing—vaccination. But vaccination had not yet reached all the parishes in Scotland. Luckily, the McKenzies were from a parish where everyone had been vaccinated against smallpox.

Day after day, as we sailed westward, we left a trail of coffins, lowered into the sea, floating along behind the ship until the sandbags inside and holes drills in the sides finally pulled the bodies down into the deep, dark ocean. I stopped counting after thirty-eight children succumbed to the dreadful disease, and numerous adults died as well. The horror continued until every single adult and child not vaccinated died of the disease. We all became almost inured to the suffering and death, the weeping and mourning. Even when one had experienced death a sea before, it was too much to bear.

Besides the horror of smallpox, there was another sense of doom. We had been seven weeks at sea and were nowhere near our destination. Despite the loss of so many, the food and water were getting low, and it seemed there was nothing to be done by passengers or crew to speed the ship. At eleven weeks we neared Newfoundland, and the people felt a sense of hope rising until another bad omen appeared.

There, on the horizon, was one of His Majesty's warships, and she was closing in on us. Our ship, the *Sarah*, was not built for speed as had been the one the Stewarts sailed on. We hadn't seen the *Dove* in days. There was nothing to do but wait for what at least the crew knew was coming. Although we continued sailing, the warship had no trouble cutting us off and coming alongside.

Sending a signal that she was sending sailors to board us, everyone looked around for Hugh, but he was nowhere to be seen. William McKenzie signalled the Highlanders that they should arm themselves and be prepared to fight if possible. By then we all knew what was coming—a press gang.

Where was Hugh?

The lieutenant who led the press gang boarded the ship along with his crew and began pointing out the young men to be tied up and brought to the deck to be loaded on the boats from the warship. The mothers and fathers followed their sons, pleading for the King's men to let them go, to no avail.

Just then, Hugh Denoon appeared striding across the deck, dressed in the fine clothing of a gentleman, his hair slicked back into a queue and wearing the finest tricorn hat I had ever seen. He had taken the time to dress and present himself as a magistrate and representative of His Majesty's Government.

"What is this? What is this? Who is interfering with the plans of His Majesty's Government for the colony of Nova Scotia? My dear lieutenant, I am the judge for Pictou District transporting Highlanders to populate and improve that district and would you be bold enough to steal away the very young men needed for this enterprise?"

The lieutenant was taken aback. "Mr. Denoon, I too serve His Majesty and have authority to press men into the King's service."

"Then we are at cross-purposes, my dear sir, and nothing is to be done but to sail to Pictou and let the magistrates sort this out. Until then, I will keep the young men with me. When can we expect you in Pictou?"

The lieutenant thought for a moment and then decided. "Mr. Denoon, the captain has no orders to sail to Pictou currently. You may continue, and I will consult the captain as to when we can arrive at Pictou."

"And, by the way," said Hugh, "please explain to your captain that this is a plague ship. We have had fifty-seven deaths from smallpox."

At the mention of smallpox, the lieutenant and his men could hardly wait to get off the *Sarah*. Hugh had saved the day! After weeks of distress, this was the first positive sign. We only hoped that the *Dove* didn't run into the Royal Navy.

We arrived in Pictou Harbour on September 10, 1801, after thirteen weeks at sea, and found the *Dove* hadn't arrived yet. We anchored out in the harbour and Squire Patterson was rowed out to greet us.

"How was the voyage, Mr. Denoon?" the Squire, looking not much changed from when I last saw him in 1798, was standing in the rowboat with difficulty, as he shouted up to the deck of the Sarah.

"Thirteen weeks at sea, Mr. Patterson, and we have had fifty-seven small-pox deaths."

The rower began to row backwards, almost upsetting Squire Patterson.

"I am sorry to be so officious with you, Mr. Denoon, but you must not leave this ship until I have consulted with the Government officials. I will be back to you as soon as I can."

"We only had food for seven or eight weeks, Squire Patterson. My people are starving and starting to get scurvy."

"Tell your people that we will immediately bring food to the little island you can see quite close by and leave it there for you to pick up. Your people can also leave the ship and spend time on the island after the food has been dropped off each day. We will bring fresh water as well and there is some fresh water on the island when the people can bathe and wash their clothes."

Almost a week later, Squire Patterson was rowed out again.

"My dear Mr. Denoon, I wish I was not the bearer of bad news, but we will have to keep you on this ship until every person in Pictou District has been vaccinated. Please tell your captain that he can anchor at the Beaches."

The same fate awaited the *Dove* when she arrived five days later.

Upon hearing of the plight of the Highlanders, the people of Pictou were distressed, many of them being Highlanders themselves. They raised £1,000 for the relief of their countrymen and women. The Nova Scotia Government sent relief to them as well.

Toward the end of the quarantine, I saw Hugh sitting near the bow of the ship, head in hands, looking quite dejected.

"Hugh, I'm sorry you're feeling badly."

"Hello, Caroline. Aye, I feel so responsible for all the deaths. I should have made sure everyone who boarded had been vaccinated. Mr. Campbell warned me, but I was in such a rush to leave in case the lairds found some way to stop us, that I ignored his advice. And he was right about the overcrowding and the amount of food and water. I wonder if the Highlanders will ever forgive me, I wonder if I will ever forgive myself."

"Hugh, I don't think the people are angry with you, they knew the stress you were under to get away quickly."

"Caroline, how can they not be angry with me? Many of them have lost spouses and children, nearly starved, and now they are quarantined on this ship."

That evening, I told William McKenzie what Hugh was feeling.

"Nay, Caroline, I know my people and they do not hold a grudge against Hugh. He made many mistakes, but now we are here and about to begin our new lives. We have no time or energy for anger and grudges. Leave it to me."

A few days later, William gathered the Highlanders on deck, and I knocked on Hugh's door to ask him to come with me. When he saw everyone on deck, he looked taken aback, almost frightened.

"Mr. Denoon," said William, "we hear that you are feeling badly about all our troubles on the voyage."

"Aye, Mr. McKenzie. Now that you are all here, let me apologize for the disaster I have caused for all of you. I was over-confident I could manage this emigration and under-prepared for all that could happen. I wonder if you could find it in your hearts to forgive me?"

"Mr. Denoon, on behalf of all of us I want to acknowledge that you have been truthful about your leadership of this emigration, but having acknowledged all that has happened, we want you to know that we forgive you. We cannot be free and begin our lives anew unless we let go of the past and are willing to move forward. You must accept our forgiveness and move forward with your life as well."

"Thank you all from the bottom of my heart. You are the kindest and most generous people I have known, and I know you will be a great asset to Pictou District."

A week later, the *Sarah* and the *Dove* were given permission to disembark. Arrangements were already made for them to stay with the Highlanders already settled on the East River. William and Flora McKenzie were invited to stay with Colin and Isabel McKenzie on the East Side East River. He was long-established there, having arrived on the ship *Hector* in 1773. His family being grown, he had space to spare for one of his clan.

As I waited my turn to go ashore, I noticed a sloop, named the *Hope of Lossie*, sailing into the harbour. Wasn't that the ship from Loch Broom that Hugh had chartered?

I had already said goodbye to all my Highland friends and, especially, William and Flora and their children, Isabel, and John. I planned to go and visit either Joseph and Janet Begg in the town or David and Mary Stewart on the West River.

As I walked along the dock, still wearing my plaid with the silver brooch, I heard a familiar voice say, "Ciamar a tha sibh, a Charoline?"

There stood William McDonald, his wife, Ann, and their baby son, Finlay.

"You escaped! You're here!"

Without thinking, I ran to him and gave him the biggest hug I could muster. He laughed and so did Ann. Then I hugged her, too.

At the end of the wharf, there was a group of Highlanders waiting to see if any of the passengers of the *Sarah* and *Dove* needed accommodation. William walked over and said cheerily, "My name is William McDonald and I'm from Urquhart on the Black Isle."

He and Ann and Finlay were immediately claimed by James McDonald of the East Side of the East River at Bridgeville. James was a former soldier in the 84th Highland Immigrant Regiment and had been given two hundred and seventy acres by the Government.

"I'll come and find you after you're settled, Ann." And I kissed Finlay, who seemed to be handling it all with aplomb.

I didn't know how long I had been in Scotland, but I guessed the best part of a year. What had happened to the Stewarts and the Beggs in that time? I had to find out. I went to find Joseph and Janet Begg in the Town of Pictou.

Joseph had replaced his log cabin store with a stone building. I entered the new doorway to see Joseph, his father, and Andrew Young all serving customers. The store looked prosperous—full shelves loaded with shipping and fishing supplies but also barrels of foodstuffs such as flour, oats, barley, cheese, maple syrup, sugar, salt, along with plows, spinning wheels, bolts of cloth, and a great assortment of smaller things, especially my favourite, barley candy.

Joseph saw me first, leaving his customer and greeting me with a huge hug, as did Mr. Begg and, surprisingly, Andrew Young. Andrew, I was to find out, was now a member of the family or thought of himself as such.

"Glad you're back from Scotland!" Mr. Begg said, smiling.

"Oh, you knew I was going there?" They all nodded, and I didn't ask further.

"Where's Janet?"

"Oh, I have such a surprise, Caroline. But let's let Janet tell you herself."

We went upstairs to the living quarters where I got an enthusiastic greeting from Janet, now six months pregnant. Joseph was beaming from ear to ear.

"How wonderful for the both of you! You've both been through so much and now such joyous news."

We sat and talked for hours. I told them about William McDonald, leaving out the part about his outlaw proclivities, and William McKenzie, saying I hoped they might meet them as soon as the newcomers were settled.

"I can't wait to meet them, Caroline. I'll do all I can to help if they need it."

Then the talk turned to David and Mary Stewart on the West River.

"Do you know David, Joseph?"

"Certainly, he goes to Harbour Church, I see him nearly every Sunday. But, Caroline, he hasn't been looking good lately. Perhaps a visit is in order."

"And what about his son, Robert?"

"He and Katherine Cameron had two sons and then Catherine died in childbirth with their twins. Robert remarried and he and Martha Moore now have fifteen children."

"Fifteen children. Amazing."

I went to see David and Mary Stewart, paddling across the harbour in a canoe and leaving it at the mouth of the West River as there had been a dry spell and I wasn't sure if I could get all the way up the river. After following the trail along the river and asking directions from the folks with farms along the river, I finally found David and Mary's farm. David did not look well but was happy to chat about our shared 'adventure' on St. John's Island. Mary looked concerned whenever she glanced in his direction, but they did not say anything about what was making them anxious.

"Pictou has been good for us, Caroline. Our farm is very productive. Robert is doing well, with several land grants."

"Knowing what you know now, would you have stayed in Scotland or come to St. John's Island and Pictou?"

"Well, I would never have gone to St. John's Island. You tried to steer me away from that plan, but I felt that was our chance to get ahead with more land and less rent. I don't know. Mary, what do you think?"

Well, husband, I could have done without St. John's Island and, of course, I miss our daughter, Jennet, every day. Whenever I think about burying her under the ice, I could just break down and cry all over again. But now, after all this time, I am satisfied that we came to Pictou County for Robert's sake. How do you feel?"

"I feel the same way, my dear. We lost our dear Jennet, but Robert and his children will have a better future now that he has lots of his own land. Heaven knows he needs it with the future of fifteen children to consider."

After hugs and kisses, I left feeling content that the family was doing well. I didn't tell them about the McKenzies and the McDonalds as they seemed to have enough on their minds.

I made my way back along the trail by the West River and watched the river move slowly towards Pictou Harbour. In the swampy areas, the leaves of the maple trees had turned red and those of the birch yellow. The spruce trees had an abundance of cones clinging to the tops of the trees and I heard the chittering of a squirrel warning me that this was his territory, and I should move along. I picked up my canoe at the mouth of the river and paddled leisurely across the harbour, smooth as glass except when a cheerful breeze ripped the water. I watched as the water dripped off my paddle and left little watery circles on the surface. It was one of those perfect days in the fall of the year when all seems right and perfect with the world; a day when you feel how glorious it is to be alive and happy.

I reached one of the wharves at the Town of Pictou and tied up the canoe, retracing my steps back to Joseph and Janet's store.

"How did David look, Caroline?" Joseph asked.

"I'm worried about him, Joseph. Mary looks fine but worried as well. Could you keep an eye on them for me, just in case?"

"I'll let the Reverend McGregor know of your visit and how you found them and check with Mary at church on Sunday."

That made me feel better.

The rooms over the store were crowded with the family so I got a room at the inn where I had stayed before. I spent the days helping Joseph in the store to earn a little money for my room and board. A month or so later, I decided it was time to paddle up the East River and see if the McDonalds and McKenzies had settled in with their Highland hosts.

After crossing the harbour, I found the broad entrance to the river and paddled past the homes of the first settlement with its log cabins and large expanses of intervale on both sides of the river, where the farmers could reap hay for the winter. Most had extensive areas of cleared land for planting crops and grazing cattle and sheep. Some of the log cabins had been replaced by frame houses, but for the most part people were living in their original cabins.

Colin McKenzie had quite a bit of cleared land and extra rooms. I felt like I had joined a clan get-together. Isabel, his wife, made lots of Highland food and, of course, there was the ubiquitous rum, seemingly necessary for every occasion. William and Flora had been busy filling them in on what had been happening in the Highlands and about their friends and relatives still across the sea. They were also slowly learning about life in Nova Scotia.

"Caroline," Flora said, "did you know you can get sugar from the trees here?"

"You mean maple syrup, Flora?"

"Aye, aye. It is the most wonderful thing I've ever tasted."

"I agree," I said. "I put it on porridge or pancakes or use it in cooking. It's so good."

"Oh, I forgot. Our hosts tell me you've been here before."

"Oh, yes, at least twice. I do hope your family will be happy here. Have you heard anything about getting a land grant?"

She turned and looked at her husband.

"Not yet, Caroline. I guess the Government is going to take their time with us Highlanders," William said.

"I hear it can be a long process for some folks unless the Government invites them. I'm sure Hugh Denoon will work very hard on your behalf to get you some land of your own. In the meantime, you have a place to stay and I'm sure your hosts will teach you everything you need to know."

They both nodded. Their hosts smiled. All was well. Isabel sat in my lap the whole time I was there, which pleased me as I had grown fond of the little girl. They were singing Gaelic songs as I left to visit the McDonalds.

Past the first settlement, there were scattered houses on both sides of the river until, past the island where the East and West Branches of the River joined, the next settlement was at Bridgeville. I pulled up my canoe at James McDonald's homestead.

James McDonald, William and Ann's host, had a wonderful story to tell about how he came to the East River. His ship, bound for New York at the beginning of the American Revolution, had been commandeered by the English Army. He and the other Highlanders were forced to fight for the King for eight years in the 84th Highland Emigrant Regiment. At the end of the war, he and the other Highlanders were given land in Douglas Township, Nova Scotia. The grant had no rivers, no roads and was not suitable for farming, so, finally, they petitioned to be granted land in Pictou County.

The other men of the now disbanded 84th regiment who got land on the East River in 1784 were Donald Cameron, his brothers Samuel and Finlay, Alexander Cameron, Robert Clark, Peter Grant, first elder of the settlement, James McDonald, and Hugh McDonald on the east side of the river. James Fraser, Duncan McDonald, John McDonald, brother of James, John Chisholm, drowned at the narrows with Finlay Cameron, a second John McDonald, and John Chisholm, Jr.

So, William, Ann and Finlay were surrounded by Highlanders. Everyone spoke Gaelic, indeed, the whole population of the East River spoke Gaelic, so William and Ann felt right at home. Thoughts of petitioning for their own land grant were put aside for the time being as they hoped to learn all they could from their new neighbours about building log cabins, felling trees, and farming around the tree stumps. But they could see this in their future, a future they, and the McKenzies, could never have had in Scotland.

Someone had loaned William McDonald their bagpipes and he was playing a lively tune while his hosts and all their neighbours clapped or danced or sang. I knew that many difficulties lay ahead, but that was in the future. Today, there was music and happiness on the East River of Nova Scotia, and it did my heart good to be part of it.

I waited until morning to return to the Town of Pictou and the last image I have is of William, Ann, and Finlay waving goodbye from the little wharf on the river.

I fell asleep in my bed at the inn only to awaken in my own bed in Halifax.

CHAPTER EIGHT

ENOUGH OF DREAMS!

PRESENT DAY: HALIFAX, NOVA SCOTIA

C aroline didn't write down her dream as a new chapter in her book. Instead, she sat in front of the computer for hours, pondering what to do next.

Why not do something adventurous? she thought. All my ancestors took big risks and had big adventures, and all I'm doing is dreaming about them. Maybe it's time I took some risks, got out of my apartment, got a job, and made some new and interesting friends. Maybe that's what the dreams are trying to tell me. Go have your own adventures and write about them. That seemed right; at least she had to try. Yes, she would have her very own adventures.

She remembered an advertisement she saw the last time she went to her favourite bookstore: clerical help wanted. She had spent enough time at the Archives that surely she could do that work. It was not a big adventure, but she applied. It would at least get her out of her apartment.

"There's our author! How's your new chapter coming?"

Caroline looked at her sisters and smiled. "Guess what? I just got a job at the bookstore."

Silence.

"Say again," Joanie said, with puzzlement written all over her face. "You got a job at the bookstore?"

"That right. Nine to five, Tuesday through Saturday, and perhaps half-time on Sundays from time to time."

Silence.

"What about your book?" Janice asked.

"Oh, I can work on that on my days off. You've always wanted me to get out more. Think of all the people I'll meet. And if they're not busy, I can do a little of my own research. Aren't you happy for me?"

"It's not that," Elizabeth said. "You were doing so well on your book. Why not finish that before you get involved in a job?"

"Just because you write a book doesn't mean you're going to get it published."

"I suppose not, but if you don't finish it, for sure you won't get it published."

"But there's no rush. It takes time to write a book. You have to edit and re-edit, and so on. In the meantime, I can have a little income and make some acquaintances—all the things you've all been encouraging me to do."

"Okay, sure, you're right. Income and friends are all good things, for sure."

"Let's have some lunch," Janice said. "Joan, how's your new Jeep? I like that deep green colour."

The sisters finished their lunch as they chatted about their jobs and families and dogs and cats. But their dismay was obvious.

"What do we do now?" Martha asked.

"Not much we can do," Samson said glumly.

"Did we do something to cause her to stop writing?" Malcolm Nicolson asked.

"Couldn't have. She didn't even write down the last dream we gave her. I'm confused."

"All we can do is wait, I guess," William McKenzie said.

"I guess nobody will know our stories now. Sad." Ann McDonald said.

It was wonderful to have a job after all these years of being on her own in her little apartment, Caroline thought, as she clipped her staff identification card to her new blazer and hung up her raincoat in the closet at the back of the bookstore.

"Good morning, Caroline," Susan Lydiard said, as Caroline closed the closet door. Caroline knew Sue from long-ago when they worked as volunteers for a summer at the local hospital. The first thing she noticed about Sue as they met again was her beautiful long hair and her well-manicured and painted fingernails. Some things never change.

"There're some new folks who need help getting orientated to how to use the computer. Can you take care of that?"

"Right away, Sue," Caroline almost skipped over to the three uncertain looking women standing by the information desk.

"Morning, ladies. My name is Caroline and I'm going to help you find your way around. Let's start over at a computer." The morning was filled with answering questions and working at the cash register.

At lunchtime, her co-workers chatted about their husbands, children, and upcoming vacations. Although Caroline continued to enjoy working with the customers, she began to spend her lunch hours by herself, working away on her own research, before returning to re-shelving books, opening boxes of new books and shelving them, and tidying up the store.

Soon, another employee was hired, a young woman who was taking her master's degree in library science and in need of a summer job. Caroline found her compatible, and they always had lots to chat about. They enjoyed lunch hours together, and an occasional dinner at a local restaurant, until she left at the beginning of a new school year.

Not long after starting her job, Caroline met Ruth for lunch and shared her new activity.

"I'm glad you're enjoying working at the bookstore, Caroline. How's the book coming?" Ruth had ordered a chopped salad with crispy chicken, and it arrived looking tasty.

"I haven't worked on it in a while, Ruth." Caroline was poking at a grilled cheese sandwich with fries.

"Because?" Ruth looked up, fork in hand.

"Because ... maybe because ... because I'm not sure I can finish it." Caroline picked up a French fry, dipped it in ketchup, and bit it in half. She had only taken one bite out of her sandwich.

"You mean you're not dreaming anymore?" Ruth had stopped eating and her wrinkled forehead showed she was struggling with what was happening with Caroline.

"No, I'm dreaming, but I can't see the way forward. I have all these dreams, but nothing to hold them together and make them into a book. Maybe if I just leave it alone for a while, the way forward will become clear to me." She ate the other half of her French fry.

"And maybe not. Why are you having doubts now? I don't get it. Are you afraid of failure?" Ruth had abandoned her salad while she waited for an answer.

"Maybe. And maybe I saw how courageous my ancestors were, and how they risked everything for a new life. I felt that I needed to be more like them. At least get out of my apartment and try new things, for heaven's sake." Caroline was feeling pressured. *Weren't they supposed to be enjoying their time together?*

"You don't think it would be just as courageous to finish your book? That would be a genuine achievement and you could meet all the new people you want at book launches and promotional events." Their server came over and asked if everything was okay with their meals. She obviously had noticed neither of her customers were eating. Both Ruth and Caroline nodded, and the server left.

"No, I don't think so. Besides, my migraines are getting worse, and I don't think I can do both the job and write the book. Just too much stress." Caroline felt the symptoms of a migraine beginning and desperately wanted to stop the cross examination.

"When you were writing the book, how were your migraines?" Ruth seemed genuinely concerned.

"Manageable." Caroline took another bite of a French fry. It was cold.

"Humm." Ruth seemed to realize the conversation was going nowhere and went back to her salad.

Then perhaps feeling the need to sum things up, "You know, Caroline, my friend, sometimes you're just meant to do something; to risk complete failure to follow your dreams. You need to think of that."

"I will, Ruth. How are you feeling these days? How's the business going?" Caroline relaxed, the examination being ended.

"I have to go in for some more tests to make sure my cancer hasn't returned. But I'm feeling pretty well and enjoying my business, so I'm not too worried."

"Well, let me know the results of the tests. I'll worry about you until then."

Caroline and her sisters still met for lunch or coffee regularly, but as their advice on keeping on with her book seemed to fall on deaf ears, they mentioned it less and less. A new topic of conversation was Caroline's cat, Pangur Ban.

"We knew you liked cats, Caroline, but your apartment is pretty small for having a pet, don't you think?" Elizabeth said. She was drinking a banana smoothy.

"He's a very little cat, and they were going to euthanize him at the animal shelter, as they had way too many cats." Caroline was buttering a cranberry scone.

"Well, it will be nice for you to have some company. How did you come up with his name?" Joan just arrived from the Second Cup with green tea and a brownie.

"Oh, an old Celtic poem that I remembered from a book I read." Caroline took a sip of her coffee.

"What does the name mean?" Janice was munching a huge date square, almost as big as the plate.

"I've never been able to find an answer to that. But the poem is about an Irish monk who sits in his scriptorium all day searching for words for his manuscript, as his cat searches all day for mice. The monk says, 'Tis a like task we are at'."

"Who are you like, the monk or the cat?" Joan asked, smiling at her sister.

"The monk, I think. I live alone." Caroline smiled back. She knew this was just gentle teasing.

"But you're not searching for words anymore," Elizabeth said, frowning a bit.

"I knew you were going to bring it around to my book, once again. No, I'm not working on my book. I'm enjoying my job and my new friend. And I'm worried about my old friend, Ruth. Haven't heard from her for a while. She was going for tests. I should call her soon."

Before Caroline could call Ruth, a mutual acquaintance called Caroline, and told her Ruth was not doing well and Caroline should call her.

Thinking that 'not doing well' meant her business was not working out quite as she imagined, Caroline didn't call right away. When she did, Ruth said, "I need you to come over right away, Caroline. I'm at my daughter's place." Ruth put her daughter, Pauline, on the phone to confirm the address.

Caroline headed over to Dartmouth, wondering what was so urgent. Ruth's daughter let her in and said, "She's in the living room."

Completely unprepared for what happened next, Caroline was shocked to see Ruth in a bed in the living room. "Ruth, what's going on? What's happening?"

"I'm dying, Caroline."

Caroline was silent. Stunned. Unbelieving. Confused.

"Ruth, what is it?"

"I got terribly sick and had to go to the hospital immediately a week or two ago. The cancer is all through my body. They say I have about two weeks to live."

Caroline started to cry. "Ruth, it's what you've been fearing all your life!"

"I thought I had overcome it when I had that prophylactic mastectomy a year or two after the first mastectomy. But it was just growing and metastasizing, unbeknownst to even the doctors."

Caroline went over and kissed Ruth on her forehead, then she sat down at her bedside.

"I've come to terms with it, Caroline. I'm prepared and I think my family is too. I just wanted to say goodbye to you."

"I love you, Ruth," Caroline said through her tears.

"I love you, too."

The drive home was a blur. The next few days were a blur. Then came the phone call Caroline had been dreading. Caroline cried through the funeral and went home and cried some more. Her friend, her dear friend, her good and kind friend, was gone.

As bad things come in threes, within a few weeks she received news that her mother, who had been suffering from dementia for several years, and her brother in Toronto, both died of strokes. For days, she sat in her bed with her cat on her lap. She watched re-runs of home decorating shows until she could fall asleep. Her migraines were constant. When she finally returned to work, she wasn't surprised when her boss called her into the office. She knew she had missed too much time from work because of the deaths and the migraines.

"Caroline, I hate to do this; I really do. But you need to take some time to care for yourself and I need to have someone here for my customers. Do you see where I'm going?"

"I understand, Portia." Portia was a large black woman with the best head for business that Caroline had ever seen. She felt badly that she had put her boss in this position.

"You're a good worker, Caroline. I feel bad about all that happened in your family. When you're feeling better, come back. If I have a position open, I'll hire you, for sure."

"Thanks, Portia. I'll collect my things and go home."

Portia sighed.

Caroline slowly unpacked the few personal things she had brought home from work and put them on her desk. Pangur Ban sat on her open dictionary and watched, his yellow eyes narrowed, and his pink nose wrinkled. But, being a cat, he couldn't help himself when he saw the rubber finger used for turning pages and he batted it onto the floor and leapt on it, sending it scooting across the room. Caroline went after it, snatched it out of his claws, and stuck it into the desk drawer. Then she scooped him up and held him upside down in her arms.

"Well, Pangur Ban, it's a good thing that I still have you. There's another thing we have in common. You were down on your luck when I met you, and now I'm in the same position."

Pangur Ban looked at her with his big yellow eyes, pink nose, and long white whiskers. She thought he understood, and she carried him into the living room and sat down on the sofa and sighed.

After her husband's death, she thought she could handle grief, but she could tell now this wasn't the kind of thing where practice makes perfect, she thought ruefully. *Where do I go from here? My decision to be adventurous and outgoing has failed miserably, and I'm back where I started.*

Over the next six months, Caroline and her sisters still met every two weeks for coffee or lunch. Elizabeth and Joan were working on the conditions of their mother's will. Janice was working more overtime as a nurse. Mostly, the sisters reminisced about their mother and brother or other family issues. There was no energy for new things.

It was two o'clock in the afternoon and Caroline was still in her pyjamas. Remembering she might have a peppermint in her little bedside table, she was searching with one hand through the odds and ends, feeling for a peppermint, when she felt something satiny smooth with rough edges. She pulled out the black stone. She showed the stone to Pangur, who seemed unimpressed.

"I wonder what this stone is all about, Pangur? I found it on a gravestone, and it seemed so important at the time. Now, it's just one more thing clogging up my bedside table. I'll put it in one of the flowerpots out on the balcony."

She put it on the bedside table until her next foray into the living room and onto the balcony.

"Do you think she's ready for another adventure, Martha?"

"Nay, Samson. She's not even ready to get out of bed. I fear there is nothing more we can do."

The rest of the firsts nodded. But there was someone else listening to this evaluation of Caroline's situation who had never been included in the plan to help Caroline write the book. Someone who had an entirely different take on the situation.

That night, Caroline had a dream about an ancestor she had never researched, had never heard of, and would have ignored if she had known about. But that ancestor would have the most influence on her.

CHAPTER NINE

VIKINGS — THE NAKYLSSONS & NICOLSONS

1160: SCOTLAND, AND SCOTLAND TO PRINCE EDWARD ISLAND IN 1841

I was sitting on a rock at the head of Loch Snizort Beag, watching a long boat being rowed down the loch. I could see a figure at the bow, perhaps scanning the shoreline. Just before the oarsmen ran the boat up onto the beach, it became clear that the figure at the bow was a woman—a woman wearing a black, fur-lined cape and hood over her deep blue tunic and black trousers. As she leapt out of the boat onto the beach, I could see she wore leather shoes with leggings tied up to her knees. She walked directly towards me across the rocky beach. Her white-blonde hair was braided in several rows from her brow and temples towards the crown of her head and it fell from there in a silver river down her back. I could feel her pale blue eyes fixed on me. Her hand was on the hilt of an eighteen-inch dirk.

I stood up. She was a few inches taller than I.

"Hallo, Caroline Morton."

"Hallo. Am I here to meet you?"

"Indeed."

"You look like a Viking."

"I am the daughter of Nakylsson, the King of Ljodus—the Isle of Lewis. We are the ruling family of that island as well as an area on the mainland, Edyrachillis, Durinish, and Assynt. We hold our land in the name of Olaf

the Red, King of the Isle of Man and the Suderays—the Hebrides. He, in
turn, owes allegiance to the King of Norway."

"Do you live here on the Isle of Skye?"

"Not on Skuy. We live on Ljodus. That is where we are going now. Come
with me."

I grabbed my hat and valise and followed her to the boat. We were helped
on board by a man who spoke to her with great respect. At her order, men
pushed the boat back off the beach and headed up the loch towards the
sea. The sky was overcast, the sea dark except for the whitecaps on each
wave, the wind brisk. It was early spring and cold. I pulled my cape closely
around me and raised the hood.

There was no opportunity to talk due to the sound of the oars striking
the water and the wind snapping the single square sail with red and white
stripes. Above the sail a white banner with a raven design in the middle
flew straight out in the gusty wind. So, I had time to observe.

The boat was wide in the middle, narrowing to a point on either end
that rose perhaps ten feet into the air, ending in a spiral. The oarsmen, six
on either side, were brawny men wearing tunics over trousers with leather
shoes and leggings wrapped up to their knees. Over their wool clothing,
they wore wool capes. Their hair was tightly braided.

Having taken stock of the boat, it occurred to me that I hadn't asked the
woman her name. Leaning towards her, I yelled, "What is your name?"

"Signi," she yelled back.

So, I was on my way to Ljodus with Signi, Nakylsdottir, in a Viking
longboat. She must be my relative, else why was I here? That being the case,
I planned never to tell her that I knew little about Vikings except for the
usual bad press, and that I entirely disliked them and doubted that would
change.

We were soon out into the North Minch, the sea passage between the
Isle of Skye and the Isle of Lewis. After three hours of rowing, we arrived
at Stjarnavgr—Stornaway—the largest Viking settlement on the island.
Close to the shore I could see what looked like a castle with walls of stone
blocks perhaps twenty-five feet tall, and the central keep flying a raven flag.

We were assisted out of the boat and onto the beach. We entered the castle through the water gate, crossed a courtyard of cobblestones, and came to the keep's massive wooden doors, held together with ironwork. Two armed men opened the doors, and we entered a spacious room with a massive fireplace. Having become chilled by the sea voyage, I ran over to the blazing fire.

Signi laughed at my shaking and shivering as I tried to get warm. She didn't seem to mind the cold.

Servants, I assumed, ran into the room, taking her fur cape and asking in broken Norn what she would like to eat. She ordered our supper and led me to a table near the fireplace, seeing that I was reluctant to leave my newfound warmth.

Mutton and barley soup served with substantial chunks of oat bread revived me and I was determined to find out what I could about my circumstances. Before I could begin my investigation, there was a great commotion. A servant rushed back into the room and flung herself at Signi's feet.

"Mistress, the Sheriff has accused my brother of trying to escape. He wasn't trying to escape, just get away from his master who was beating him. They're going to execute him! Please, please spare his life," she cried.

"It is not my place to interfere in the law against runaway slaves. Leave me!"

I stood, aghast, as the Gaelic servant—no, slave—ran out of the room. I remembered from the little I had read about Vikings that they were slave raiders and traders, one of the reasons I disliked them so much.

Turning toward me, Signi must have seen the look of horror on my face. "I see you do not approve, Caroline Morton."

"Approve of having slaves or murdering slaves because they want to be free? No, I do not approve, and furthermore I'm also sure I do not want to be here. I've seen enough!"

My anger didn't faze Signi at all. "Perhaps you will feel better tomorrow." She rang a bell and a slave—the same slave that had just been begging for her brother's life—appeared, picked up my valise and hat, and motioned for me to come with her.

I was so agitated I scarcely paid attention to where we were going, except it was up a spiral staircase. My room was larger than any other room I'd stayed in, warmed by a fire in a grand fireplace. The bed was huge, enclosed by heavy curtains and covered with sheepskins. There were sheepskin rugs on the floor.

A great wave of tiredness washed over me, and I just wanted to lie down and sleep, perhaps to wake up in my own bed. Before the slave left, I said in my pathetic Gaelic,

"I am so sorry about what happened."

Tears ran down her face, but she didn't say a word before leaving.

In the morning, I opened one eye just a little. No, I was still in the castle. Before I could get dressed, the same slave brought me my breakfast and put another log on the glowing embers from the night before.

"Are you able to speak to me?" I asked the slave. She shook her head.

"Even to say your name?"

"Mairi." Mairi was perhaps in her thirties, thin, with red hair and grey eyes. Her grey knee-length dress was almost too big for her and was too thin for the brisk wind that roared around the castle, finding a way in through every nook and cranny. Her feet were bare.

"Hallo, Mairi. Forgive my terrible Gaelic."

She smiled, or rather, the corners of her mouth turned up just the faintest bit.

"Are you from Ljodus?"

"Eire."

"Ireland?"

She nodded and ran out of the room.

I ate my porridge as I pondered what to do. Should I stay? If not, where could I go? Were the Vikings really any worse than other people of their day? Shouldn't I get to know Signi and her family since I was here? The thoughts swarmed, bit, and stung like gnats.

I dressed and decided to creep down the stairs to look around before anyone saw me, but there in the great room with the fireplace was Signi. Her clothing was finer than what she had worn on the sea voyage yesterday, and the flames in the fireplace danced in the gold and silver jewellery she was wearing.

"You're looking rested," she said. I was surprised to realize that I understood Norn—the language the Vikings spoke in the Hebrides.

"I am, thank you." I said, coolly polite.

"I have plans for today." She stood with her hands on her hips, a person in charge.

"Executions, maybe?" My anger was still burning hot after the scene yesterday.

She ignored my remark. "We will ride to the north of the island and see farms and fishing stations." She turned on her heel and headed to the door. Two armed men opened it at her approach.

Crossing the courtyard, we entered the stables, stone buildings with slate roofs, and found the horses already saddled and bridled. We rode out through the Watergate and took a road, really just a cart track, north along the seacoast.

The day was overcast but mild and it felt good to be riding again. We were on the east side of the island and there was a forest of small trees interspersed with cleared farmland. The fields on our left were filled with sprouting grain, oats, and barley, being hoed by slaves, called thralls, and the pastures were full of cattle and sheep. The landowners, called boendr, had their land in absolute title and so could bequeath it to their descendants. There was no rent except for civic and military duty. Signi explained all of this to me as we rode. The island was prosperous and well-kept. I was impressed by the Viking laws of order and good government but wasn't going to tell Signi that.

"Are any of the boendr women?"

"There are several women boendr and women own a share in any marital holdings."

Now that was a surprise—women having property rights. But the practice of slavery overcame all thoughts about the good points of Viking society.

We finally reached the top of the island, called the Butt of Lewis, and turned west to the very northwest point. We dismounted and strolled around. Looking west there was only the North Atlantic Ocean until you reached North America. Far out on the great ocean, we could see fishing boats trawling for their catch. The gusty wind, the smell of salt air, the ocean crashing on the rocks below, and the seabirds gliding on the wind above was enlivening. I threw my arms open and twirled around, to Signi's amusement.

Both Signi and I examined a towering stack of firewood built in a pyramid shape.

"It's a beacon. When Olaf the Red wants to send a ship from the Isle of Man north along the islands, perhaps as far as Norway, each island sets the wood on fire so the ship can find their way."

"Could it work the other way? Could the King of Norway send a ship south in this way?"

"Either way would work. Let's head south along the west side of the island. You'll find the trees are even shorter on this side because of the strong northwest wind."

As we rode south, I saw a wooden building surrounded by a stand of trees. Each of the trees had a man hanging from it! It seemed to me that these men had been hung recently. I turned to Signi in disbelief.

"You don't approve, Caroline Morton?"

"What's going on, Signi? I can't believe what I'm seeing!"

"This is what you might call a temple. The hanging men are offerings to the god, Thor."

I urged my horse into a trot to get away from that ghastly sight. I didn't mind if Signi stayed behind. I could find my way back to the castle on my own. Yes, their society had some good points, but slaves, executions, human sacrifice? That was too much.

I came upon some people walking along the road speaking Gaelic. Should I approach them? I really didn't have an easy way to avoid them, and it might give the wrong impression; that I was an enemy of some sort, or an escaped slave. I just didn't know.

"Ciamar a tha sibh?" I tried to look friendly.

"Tha gu math, tapaidh leibh," they replied, smiling.

"Are you thralls?"

"Certainly not! We are Gaels, Gaelic speakers. It was our island before the Vikings arrived. Now we share it with the Gall—the foreigners, the Vikings."

I had heard of the Gall-Gaels: more dangerous and warlike than any other of the peoples of the Hebrides and Ireland. And that was saying something! Despite the fact the Gaels had been Christians since after the coming of St. Columba in the 500s, the Vikings worshipped the gods Odin and Thor, among others as best I could recall my brief reading about them.

"Are the Vikings Christians as well?" I asked, to check my understanding.

"To some extent. A few still practice the old religion."

Signi caught up to me and the Gaels went on their way. Being alone on the road among the Gall-Gaels scared me enough that I was almost glad to see Signi. At least she knew who I was and why I was there. So, I determined to at least be civil and stay close to my Viking ancestor.

As we returned to the castle, Signi pointed out ships just arriving at the mouth of the bay. I didn't ask questions, having decided whatever it meant, it wouldn't be anything good if it involved Vikings.

I was right.

After lunch, I returned to my room and watched from my window as the boats discharged their booty from raids on the west coast of Scotland. Their cargo included about twenty slaves, chained by the neck to each other. They were marched from the beach to buildings inside the walls of the castle.

There was a rap on the door, and I called, "Come in!" thinking it was Mairi. It was Signi.

"There will be a banquet tonight in the great hall. You will meet my father and brothers who have just returned."

I nodded. She left, probably having had enough of me for one day.

Moments later, Mairi entered, carrying clothing.

"What is this, Mairi?"

"Your clothes for the banquet, Miss Caroline."

"I prefer my own clothes, thank you just the same."

"The princess insists, and I will be in trouble if you refuse."

"Don't worry, Mairi, I will do it for your sake."

I changed my clothes and Mairi braided my hair in the Viking style. Soon, the transformation was complete. Caroline Morton looked every inch a Viking, according to Mairi. I put my clothes in the valise.

Signi arrived to lead me to the great hall. As we entered through the huge wooden double doors, the scene was one of energy and merriment. Flaming torches in sconces lined the stone walls and a crackling fire leapt in the stone fireplace. The room was filled with Vikings sitting around tables laden with roasts of meat and containers of fish, platters of cooked grains, bread, butter, cheese, cakes, and puddings. The men, and there were only men seated at the tables, were drinking from kegs of beer and mead. I thought I saw wine at the head table.

I wasn't looking forward to the banquet but was curious about Signi's father and brothers, my relatives. It was a noisy and chaotic place as the drinking continued. The serving women—were they slaves? — were pulled onto the laps of the drunken men, who roared songs and slogans and offered toasts to the success of their raid on the helpless Gaels of Scotland.

Then the King entered with his entourage. The shouts became even louder. Tormod Nakylsson was about forty years old, tall, blond, everything you would expect of a Viking ruler. His name was a Gaelic derivative of the Norse personal name, Thormodr—Thor, plus mind—courage. He wore a fine red wool tunic and trousers under his fur cape. Gold cuffs sparkled from his wrists and a large, intricately designed clasp held the sides of his cape together. He wore a gold circlet on his head. After grasping a large silver chalice filled with wine from the table, he raised it and toasted, "To the men of Ljodus, for their success!"

They roared back, shouting his name, and toasting his fame as their King. After the roar settled, Signi beckoned me to attend her and as I approached, she touched her father's arm and introduced me.

"Father, this is Caroline Morton, my guest and our relative. She has come here to meet us and learn about our way of life."

Tormod stood up to his full height—about a head higher than me. He put both hands on my shoulders and proclaimed, "Welcome, kinswoman. We welcome you to our home and our kingdom. I know my daughter, Signi, will assure you of having a wonderful visit with us. Please ask for anything you want or need, and I shall make sure your wishes are fulfilled."

"Thank you, sir. Signi is indeed a good host, and I appreciate your warm welcome."

Signi's brothers, Erik and Harold, also greeted me warmly before I returned to my seat. Slave raiders and traders with good manners! *Confusing.* I must have drunk too much mead and not eaten enough food because I don't remember the rest of the evening or even winding my way up the staircase to my bedroom.

Late in the morning, I opened my eyes, just a slit. I was still in Ljodus, but what was the noise that had awakened me? Climbing out of bed and putting on my sheepskin slippers, I wrapped my shawl around my night-gowned shoulders and shuffled across the wooden floor to the window. Men were heaving warships, dragon boats they called them, off the beach into the bay. Capable of taking a crew of sixty—thirty to row and thirty to fight—the high prow was fitted with a dragon's head.

Mairi came into the room with my breakfast.

"Mairi, what's happening? Why are they putting the dragon boats into the water?"

"I don't know. They must be going to battle somewhere."

Just then Signi arrived in my room and told me to eat my breakfast and dress quickly as we were leaving soon. Before I got a chance to ask Signi, she informed me that we were going to Morvern on the coast of Scotland to put down an insurrection. We would be meeting up with the Olaf the Red, King of Mann and the Sudereys, before the battle.

"We're going to go in a dragon boat and fight with people?"

"Most certainly."

"And what if I don't want to fight people? What if I would rather stay at the castle and wait for you to return?"

"That is impossible. You are my responsibility and so you must come with me, but you will not be required to fight, of course."

"Can I bring my valise?"

"Certainly."

This battle might be my chance to get away from the Vikings and join the Gaels. After all, I was related to them as well. If an opportunity arose, would I take it?

King Nakylsson was in the lead ship and Eric and Harold were in two ships sailing close behind. Altogether, there were thirty boats. Because I was slow to dress in my new Viking clothes and finish my breakfast, Signi was left to be in charge of our ship.

Men in chain mail and helmets filled the boats. In the hold were double axes, spears, javelins, and swords, as well as bows and arrows. You would not want to meet up with these men, these Vikings. They are terrifying people with a well-earned reputation for rape, pillage, and plunder—and to my great dismay, my ancestors.

The thirty dragon boats set out for Morvern, wherever that was. Certainly to the south of Ljodus. Two days later we arrived in what must have been Morvern, and the men hauled up the ships onto the beach near where a stream ran into the sea. This sea voyage wasn't as scary as the ones across the ocean or in the canoe. I knew Vikings were masters of the sea and of ship building, and that made me feel more secure.

Signi had given Mairi to me as my personal slave. Mairi and her husband, Malcolm, were to keep me away from the fighting. Signi herself planned to join the fight, having trained with her brothers. I thought that was a bad idea. I thought the whole expedition was a bad idea.

The King and his men were busy with battle preparations. The slaves and I slipped off into the woods just as Olaf the Red's fleet arrived. From our hiding spot, we watched Olaf's fleet. It was an impressive sight. Perhaps fifty dragon boats, each with that red and white sail and the raven banner fluttering above. I saw Olaf, the High King, come ashore and meet with Tormod and the kings of the other Hebridean islands, who held their positions at Olaf's pleasure.

Thinking we should move further away from the beach, we explored and soon found a path that led inland. We followed it for some time, and the sound of the surf grew fainter. Hopefully, the path was leading us to somewhere safe from the Vikings, and maybe a way for Mairi and Malcolm to escape.

Just as it seemed we had made some headway, I was grabbed from behind and felt the cold metal of a knife on my neck. Mairi and Malcolm were in a similar position.

"Well now, they look like Vikings to me. What do you think, Iain?"

"Vikings for sure."

"No, no, we're not Vikings," I said. "We're Gaels. Mairi and Malcolm are from Ireland and I'm from ...."

"You're from where?"

"Well, I was captured by the Vikings when I was on the Isle of Skye. They took me to Lewis."

"So, you're all slaves?"

"Mairi and Malcolm are enslaved. I am not." I just prayed that Malcolm and Mairi didn't say I was a guest of Signi and her family.

"So, you are?" they persisted.

"A seanachaidh. I write stories about great kings and princes. Perhaps you know a king or prince that would like his story told?"

The armed men relaxed their grip and considered my request. "Indeed, we do. Come on, men, let's take them to our leader."

After walking at least an hour, we came to a clearing filled with tents. A short distance away was a large cave. There were armed men in chainmail standing at attention, listening to another armed man in chainmail. He stood on a knoll where the sunlight filtered through the trees and high-lighted his red-gold hair. After he finished speaking, the men holding us hostage led us over to their leader.

"Look what we found heading toward us on the path from the beach. These two are husband and wife, slaves of the Vikings from Lewis who have just arrived. This woman, dressed like a Viking, is a seanachaidh who wants to write the story of a great man."

"Sit them down under that tree while I consider their fate." A young Gael was posted to keep us from leaving, but he seemed more interested in the upcoming battle than guarding us.

Sitting under the tree and watching the leader, I could see he was hand-some, with a vigorous and active physique. But, alas, his clothes were very rough and, as far as I could tell, he lived in the cave. Hardly a hero I could praise in a story or poem.

I felt bad for this leader and his men—especially for the young man guarding us—and angry at the Vikings for what was about to happen. The Gaels, who had been forced by the Norse invasion of their coastline to flee back into the forest and caves for many, many years, were about to head into battle with the Vikings. The Gaels had never won against the Vikings, and this felt like the last battle before they were annihilated. Yet the warriors seemed to have total confidence in their leader and in their own ability.

Their leader was naturally thinking about other things besides Malcolm and Mairi, so we began to consider our options.

"What do you think, Malcolm?" I whispered, "do they believe we are not Vikings?"

"I think they believe us, Caroline, and this is our chance to slip away as soon as the battle starts. We hate to leave you, but we may never get another opportunity to escape back to Ireland."

"I understand, Malcolm, and that is what I want for you and Mairi. Please go as soon as it is safe."

"What will you do, Caroline?" He kept an eye on our guard to make sure he wasn't overhearing us, but our guard was talking to one of his friends about the upcoming battle.

"I'm not sure yet. I think I'll stay until the battle is over. I'm worried about Signi—and I can't believe I'm saying that."

"Then be sure to wait here until the battle is over and it's safe to go back to the beach. They'll have guards posted in this camp to keep the place secure."

"Do you think the Gaels will win?"

He looked at me askance. "Nay."

"Good enough. Then we have a plan. I wish you a blessing for your journey. I hope you reach Ireland and your families safely."

We watched as the leader and his men left for the battle with their spears and bows and arrows. Most had swords. Our guard hesitated, then ran to catch up with his unit. Since those guarding the camp were posted at the coastal side entrance and none towards the back of the camp, we were sure we could escape without notice.

I was sad watching them leave for what was certainly their last battle—one that few of them would survive.

Soon we could hear the roar of battle, even at our distance from the shore. Malcolm and Mairi faded away into the forest and I was on my own. It seemed best to change into my travelling clothes while everyone was preoccupied. I packed my Viking clothes in my valise.

After an excruciatingly long time, a runner arrived and spread the surprising good news. The Vikings had been defeated, and those who were able were pushing their dragon boats off the beach to get away. The guards were ordered to leave their posts and help with the mop-up operation on the beach.

I got up and ran for the beach, knowing I had to find Signi and make sure she had survived.

The slaughter was terrible. Dead Vikings lay everywhere on the beach, floating face down in the water, and even in the woods, where some had tried to escape the wrath of the Gaels under their new leader.

In shock over the carnage, I was still determined to turn over every body until I found Signi, all the while hoping and praying she was on a ship heading back to Lewis.

A short distance into the forest I found her, lying on her face. *Was she dead or unconscious?* I rolled her over and she groaned, but before I could take time to search for a wound, one of the Gaelic warriors saw us and ordered me to move. I knew why. He was part of the mop-up operation and was going to kill Signi.

I threw myself over Signi and began to yell at the top of my lungs, "No! No! Help! Help!"

Just as the warrior grabbed my arm to fling me aside, the leader appeared, assessed the situation, and ordered his man to stand down.

"You're one of the three people we captured and left back at the camp, the one who composes stories and poems about great men."

"Yes, yes."

"And who is this Viking you're protecting with your life?"

I pulled off her helmet and her long, white-blond hair spread out around her beautiful but blood-stained face.

"And who is she?" he demanded.

"The daughter of the King of Ljodus, Signi Nakylsdottr."

"And who is she to you?"

"My kindred. I know the Gaels are loyal to their kindred and so am I to Signi. Please let me examine her to see where she is wounded."

"Great loyalty is something to be rewarded and you shall be rewarded, Miss?"

"Caroline Morton, from Skye."

I removed her overclothes and chain mail and, finding a sword cut in her shoulder, bandaged it with strips of cloth from her overclothes. Straightening out her leg and using a couple of small tree branches, I made an improvised cast by wrapping her leg with strips of cloth. Hurrying to complete the task before someone changed their mind, I paused when I noticed a tattoo on Signi's right arm. It was the same design as the etching on the little black stone!

When I finished, the leader ordered one of his men to carry her back to the camp and put her just inside the cave. As we reached the camp and entered the clearing, I saw Mairi and Malcolm standing near the cave.

"Caroline, is that Signi?"

"It is. She has a shoulder wound and her leg may be broken. What are you doing back here? I thought you were on your way to Ireland?"

"We heard that the Gaels won the battle, so we came back. Where are the Vikings?"

"Gone. Beaten by the Gaels. As far as I can tell, they even left without their dead."

"Mairi, that means we're free!" exulted Malcolm.

"No longer slaves of the Vikings!" Mairi said in amazement.

"I think so, Mairi. Come, help me make Signi comfortable."

Mairi didn't move.

"I understand, Mairi, but would you do it for my sake?"

She nodded, and we cleared away rocks and tufts of grass and laid her on her outer clothes with a piece of clothing folded up as a pillow.

"Malcolm, will they come back for her?" I asked.

"Her father will want them to, I'm sure, but they may not have the strength to return. Were a lot of the Vikings killed?"

"I counted at least fifty while I was searching for Signi. I've heard that two of their war chiefs were also killed."

"Not the Nakylssons?"

"Not sure."

"Caroline, you realize this is the very first time that the Gaels have won against the Vikings. They have a great leader. Who knows what else he may achieve?"

"What is his name, this great new leader?"

"Somerled."

"Somerled! The Somerled?"

"Indeed. His father GilleBride—the name means servant of St. Bridget of Ireland—was the thane of this region, part of the old Gaelic Kingdom of Dal Riata in Argyll, before the Vikings forced him back to Ireland. That is where Somerled was raised."

My research of my Highland ancestors started to come back to me. Gille-Bride returned from Ireland with an Irish army, but until now they were unsuccessful. The Gaelic men of the Isles then asked his son, Somerled, to be their leader. And what a leader he was! It was Somerled who pushed the Vikings out of Kintyre and the Hebrides. That was before 1160! *Oh my, this is what I'm seeing. Amazing.*

Signi groaned, opened her eyes, and recognized me. "Where am I, Caroline Morton?"

"In a cave at the camp of the Gaelic leader, Somerled MacGilleBride, Thane of Argyll. We found you among the dead and brought you here."

"Caroline Morton, get me a sword! They will try to kill me!"

"Too late. They already tried to do that but were prevented by Somerled."

"But why? I would not have spared him!"

"Oh, I know that Signi, but right now you are his captive, and we are allowed to take care of you. You need water and a little soup so Mairi and Malcolm will prepare your supper. Are you in pain?"

"If I was, would I tell you?" Signi was a brave person, but I could see the pain in her eyes. The heavy lids and dark circles, and restlessness, answered my question.

"Of course not. Well, I'm going to wash you to get the blood and dirt off and then I'll put on clean bandages."

"Malcolm, take care of her until I find my valise."

"Are both my slaves here?" Signi asked.

"Signi," I said, "they are not your slaves anymore. You are a captive, and they are free. They came back to this camp instead of returning to Ireland to help me help you. Any help they give is out of the kindness of their hearts." *Not that you would know anything about kindness.*

Signi was silent. We gave her some mead to ease the pain. After her meal, she fell asleep.

"She will try to escape as soon as she feels better," Mairi said, "and if she can kill a few of her enemies in that process, she will be happy."

"Where would she go if she escaped?"

"She may not know that the Vikings have been defeated and driven out of Morvern. She may think she can reach their camp."

"Mairi, Malcolm, we will have to guard her day and night."

They nodded.

I thought the Gaels would post a guard, but they were re-organizing in case the Vikings came back and since Signi couldn't walk, I doubt they thought she could escape. But she would probably be of some value to them, if the Vikings had taken any prisoners. Perhaps she could be exchanged for them. I'm not sure if the Gaels had any women fighters. I hadn't seen any, and that would make Signi quite an anomaly.

"Why are you pouring whiskey on my wound, Caroline Morton?" Signi was suddenly awake.

"To keep it from becoming infected, Signi. It was quite a deep wound. You're lucky to be doing so well."

"Then it is time for me to be going back to my camp."

"Signi, you have no camp. The Gaels won over the Vikings and those who survived left in their dragon boats. They're all gone."

"Are my father and brothers alive?"

"I think so. When I searched for you after the battle, I looked at all the bodies and didn't see your father and brothers. I was lucky to find you and keep you from being killed. Again, you have no camp."

To the extent that Vikings let you see their feelings, I could see how upset Signi was.

"Signi, Malcolm, Mairi and I will care for you and, if we can, find a way for you to return to Ljodus."

She nodded. I don't know if she believed me.

One of Somerled's men came to visit Signi. He was a good-looking Gaelic warrior and perhaps the one who had originally been posted to guard Signi before the battle.

"Princess, my name is Calum. I brought you some meat, as I see your friends have only bread and cheese to offer you."

Knowing Signi, she would see this as an offer from an enemy. "You can keep your gift of meat, Gael. Leave!"

He did.

"Signi," I said, "Calum was only trying to be kind to you."

She looked at me with disdain. "I would rather die than accept such an offer."

I knew she meant it. However, the following day and every day after, Calum returned with the same offer. Would Signi ever relent?

Towards the end of the second week after the battle, Malcolm returned from a meeting in the camp with news. "Mairi, Caroline, I've joined Somerled's band! Of course, not as a warrior as I am not trained, but as a transporter of food and supplies for the camp."

I looked at Mairi and she was beaming, so proud of her husband, now no longer a slave of the Vikings but a part of Somerled's action to clear the coast of Argyll of Norse rule.

"Husband," said Mairi, "we now have the freedom we have so long desired. My only sadness at this happy time is the remembrance of my brother, who was executed for trying to find the same such freedom."

"Mairi, let our freedom and choices of what we do with it be done in his memory." Malcolm put his arm around his wife as they celebrated this bittersweet event.

Signi, of course, did not celebrate the freedom of her former slaves. I thought she might at least thank Malcolm and Mairi for their faithfulness while she was healing, but no, that would be too much to expect from a Viking.

Her leg, though still badly bruised and swollen, may not have been broken. She had been trying to stand a little more every day, and she pulled herself up now. "Caroline Morton," Signi said, "I want to bathe."

"That's a good idea, Signi. I'll help you over to the pool by the river. I've saved my Viking clothes so you will have something fresh to wear."

To my surprise, she leaned on my shoulder on the way to the pool. I gave her some soap from my valise and helped her down into the water. She threw her old clothes back on the ground and Mairi took them away to be burned.

"Caroline Morton, help me wash my hair. I can't lift my wounded arm above my shoulder."

Soon she was fresh and clean and, upon pulling on the clean clothes she looked every inch a princess. She really was beautiful, in the way a hawk or falcon is beautiful, yet dangerous.

Back at the camp, Malcolm and Mairi had cleaned up her sickbed and found a small chair for her to sit in and watch the goings-on in the camp. At suppertime, Calum arrived with a generous piece of meat and to my everlasting surprise, Signi accepted it.

He continued to bring meat, and each day he spent a little more time with her. On the surface, I was happy for them, but underneath I didn't trust her, the beautiful hawk.

Calum returned to the camp one day, having taken Signi for a walk down the path towards the beach, with a wound in his side. Signi had found a sword left over from the battle and, escaping from Calum, left in one of the small boats belonging to the Gaels. The hawk had flown.

It was obvious to all at the camp that Signi, with her wounded arm, could not row to Ljodus. Perhaps she thought she could find Vikings further up the coast.

A day and a half later she returned to the camp and, most surprisingly, she began to care for Calum's wound. They were never apart after that, taking long walks to the beach or along the paths that led away from the camp. They were so handsome together.

"Signi," I asked, "I know why you returned." I smiled.

"I found no Viking encampment further up the coast," she stated flatly.

Was that the reason, or had she fallen in love with Calum? I decided not to ask.

One night, after we had all gone to bed, if you could call lying on rocky ground a bed, I woke up slowly, disturbed by some noise. After a second or two, I heard a 'psst'.

"Who's there?" I whispered.

"It's Malcolm, Caroline. Listen carefully. The Gaels are leaving in two days to continue up the coast to root out the Vikings living there—settlers rather than a military camp; those who pushed out the Gaels and took over their farms. Signi was looking for the Viking camp and I'm pretty sure there isn't one; that the Vikings have gone over to the Isle of Mull. Some men have determined to kill Signi and perhaps you as well before they leave."

"What about Calum?"

"They will send him away on a pretext so he will not be here to object or protect you. I must go now before they find me missing."

"Thank you, Malcolm. Take good care of Mairi."

And he was gone. Should I tell Signi now or wait for morning?

But she—who slept like a cat—had overheard. Just before dawn we gathered our few possessions together and told the guards we were going to the pool to bathe. Once out of the presence of the guards, we hurried to the beach. Signi lifted a small boat and underneath located a sword. She smiled and began pulling the boat towards the water. I grabbed the other side, and we soon had it afloat.

I knew why she smiled. On one of her walks with Calum she had managed to locate a sword and hide it where there was a boat of a size we could manage. Not every woman is star struck over a handsome man.

We knew that Somerled's war band was heading north along the coast. To the east and the south were the Gaels newly freed from Viking rule, so west was our only hope.

I had already climbed aboard the boat when I saw Calum striding across the beach, sword in hand. Signi turned to confront him and drew her own sword.

Calum spoke first. "You were going to leave without even saying 'Goodbye'."

"Goodbye," Signi said.

"Calum," I pleaded, "they were going to kill Signi, and me before they started north. We must escape."

"Then let me go with you."

"No, Gael, you have no life with the Vikings, and I have no life with your Gaels. Find a Gaelic girl."

Signi sheathed her sword and pushed us further into the water before climbing aboard.

Calum stood silently on the beach, sword in hand, as Signi rowed us toward the Isle of Mull, the closest land to the west, and Viking territory.

We took turns rowing as Signi's arm still bothered her. Since the water was calm, we arrived within two hours. We pulled the boat ashore and hid it up a little stream that flowed into the sea.

The feeling of relief was short-lived. We had a little bread and cheese that I had grabbed before leaving. Neither of us knew the Isle of Mull. Tomorrow, we would have to explore our options, but for now Signi needed to rest her arm.

In the morning, we set off up the banks of the stream looking for food and any signs of habitation. There was no sign of either for some time. Then I heard something and stopped to listen.

Signi looked at me.

"I think I heard a cry!" I whispered.

We moved up the hill on our left and, reaching the wooded area at the top, we paused. There it was, definitely a baby's cry. After a quick search, we found a tiny baby wrapped in a blanket and lying on a bed of pine needles.

Signi put her hand on my arm. "The child is being exposed. We must leave it alone."

"What?!"

"The child's father or grandfather has not accepted the child, so it must be left to die."

"Who says so, Signi!"

"It's our practice."

"Well, it's not my practice."

"Very well, but you have no way to feed the child."

This was true. I picked up the baby and attached to the blanket was a small, gold ring.

"This is the child of high-born parents. Best not to interfere."

"Signi, I'm not leaving the baby to die."

She sighed in resignation.

I folded my cape to make a pouch and Signi put the baby inside.

"We have to find a nursing sheep or goat," I decided.

That suited Signi, who was hoping for some milk to drink.

After an hour or so, we found a pasture filled with sheep and goats. It being spring, most of the ewes had lambs and the nanny goats had kids.

"I'm going to catch a goat," Signi said.

"Make sure to get the kid as well."

"Why take the kid."

"The goat will only produce milk as long as the kid keeps suckling."

After a few tries, Signi had both a nanny goat and her kid, so we were ready to milk the goat. But what to put the milk in? Finally, we made a square of birch bark rolled into a cone with some pine pitch to seal the edges and the point of the cone.

Signi held the cone, and I milked the goat. She drank the first cone full and I the second, but how to feed baby?

We made a smaller cone and didn't seal the point, so that a few drops at a time fell through into the baby's mouth. Baby cooperated, and we were able to give quite a bit of very rich milk. I was so relieved.

Despite the child, and the pasture, there was no sign of any settlement in the area, and the Isle of Mull was mountainous. We decided to row northwest along the coast to find a settlement. We returned to the boat with the baby, the goat, and its kid. Signi carried the goat over her shoulders, still limping from her injured leg, and the kid, who was very agile, followed her mother. I carried the infant, now fed and content. Once at the boat, we rested while the goat grazed and the kid gamboled about. Signi looked tired, but we had to find a settlement, so we loaded the goats into the boat and set out, Signi rowing and I looking after the baby.

We saw no settlements or any other signs of people that day and spent the night by another stream. I imagine Signi was hoping we would soon have more food than goat's milk. I certainly was. I had become very attached to having food available after my experience of near starvation on St. John's Island.

Late in the afternoon, the following day, we came around a point of land to see some buildings—a Viking settlement—surrounding a small bay full of dragon boats.

"Look, Signi, isn't that one of your father's dragon boats, there in the midst of the fleet!"

"Indeed."

"Let's head right over there now!"

I knew that Signi couldn't keep up with the rowing much longer, so I was very relieved. And, of course, the baby needed a wet nurse and nanny, and the goat and her kid needed to be returned to their owner. That's as far ahead as I had thought.

Reaching her father's boat, Signi called for the captain, who appeared quickly.

"Erik, it's Signi!"

"Sister, you're alive! What happened? How did you get here?"

"It's a long story. Help us aboard, Brother. I hope you have some food, and we need a wet nurse for, for ...."

"For Toramagh," I said.

"Who is Toramagh, Sister?"

"That is what I intend to find out as soon as I get my strength back. You remember my guest and our kindred, Caroline Morton?"

"Of course. Welcome, Caroline. We will take care of you all. What do you want us to do with the goat?"

Signi looked at me. "Ask Caroline Morton."

"Erik, could one of your men return it to the farm back by the second brook that flows into the Sound of Mull? The goat came from a pasture a couple of hours upstream from where we spent our first night—a wide creek that flows into the Sound of Mull. There's a clearing on the north side, and wooded hill close behind. I hope that's enough to find it."

"I know the place, or, rather, I know a man who knows the place."

I gave nanny and her kid some pats, scratched their ears, and thanked them for their cooperation before they were rowed away.

A wet nurse soon arrived on board, Olga by name. She came carrying her own infant.

"Give me that baby," she said, as she plucked him out of my arms. Finding a seat, she pulled aside her blouse and began to nurse both babies.

"Olga," I ventured, "do you have a lot of experience with babies?"

"Ha!" she said, "this is my fourteenth—eight boys and six girls."

"Oh, my!" was all I could think of to say. "What does your husband do?"

"A boendr. He farms oats and barley as well as raising sheep and goats."

"Is that a good living?"

"Well, he better make it a good living as he is the father of fourteen and he would bring down my wrath if he didn't feed his family."

I had a feeling I wouldn't want to cross Olga. I looked at a nearby hammock, where Signi was sound asleep. Tomorrow we would have to find a way to bathe and wash our clothes.

After Toramagh was asleep, Olga went ashore and brought us back two shifts. I had to awaken Signi and then we removed our clothes to have Olga wash them and have them dry by one of her return visits to nurse the baby. In the morning, we bathed in a small tub on the ship and by late afternoon we were dressed in clean clothes.

"Olga," I said, as she nursed the two babies, "I need to find out a secret."

"You mean you want to know who Toramagh is?"

"Why, yes. How did you know?"

"Because you have not told me who he is. I believe he is not yours or Signi's."

"That is true, Olga. Are you able to keep a secret?"

"Well now, who would I tell a secret to? My husband is always away farming or fighting. My sons take after their father and my girls are interested in finding husbands. My friends might be interested but they would be afraid to repeat anything I said—if I said anything at all. You can trust me to find out who the baby's parents are."

Signi and I met with Erik. He, of course, wanted to know what happened to Signi, and she wanted to know what happened to her father and other brother, Harold.

"Signi, where did you disappear to after the battle? We looked for you, but we could not stay as the Gaels were swarming all over the beach, killing our warriors. We had to save as many as possible."

"The Gaels say they won the battle. Is that right?"

"Indeed. We lost a lot of men and had to withdraw. We couldn't even set up a camp further north on the coast. Father took all the wounded and headed back to Ljodus to get them treatment and re-stock our supplies. I came here with Olaf's fleet to be part of the discussions about what our next plans should be. Father and Harold and our warriors will be back here shortly. But I want to hear what happened to you, Signi."

"I was wounded during the battle. I tried to hide in the woods before I fainted, as I was losing a lot of blood. Caroline Morton found me and prevented me being killed by the Gaels, then she nursed me back to health and we escaped to Mull."

"Caroline," Erik said, "on behalf of our family, I thank you for rescuing our Signi. We will remember your courage."

"I wasn't courageous, Eric, I was afraid the whole time. But Signi is my kinswoman and I had to do what I could."

"As I said, we will not forget your loyalty to our family. There's something else I would like to know. Whose baby are you caring for?"

"Olga is trying to find out right now. We found him just after we arrived on Mull."

Olga arrived to feed Toramagh and with knowledge of his parentage. She pulled me aside and whispered her news.

"Toramagh is the son of Arne, the Prince of Mull, and a high-born woman, but the King would not accept the child."

"Why not? Or why not just let the mother raise the child?" I asked.

"The King had been dealing with the King of Ljodus in order to marry his son to Signi. But Signi refused to marry anyone."

"But," I said.

"But, the King of Mull still has hopes to marry his son to a princess in order to make an alliance and bring more property to his family."

"So?" I asked.

"So, the King decided to expose the baby as the child might grow up to be competition for his throne and the young woman's family were afraid to go against the King."

"What would the King do if he finds out Signi has the baby?"

"If I were Signi, I would return to Ljodus immediately and take the boy."

I showed Olga the little gold ring we had found on the baby's blanket.

"This is a wedding band. The King's son must have given it to the boy's mother to make the child legitimate. It should be kept safe until the child grows up and wants to claim his parentage."

Signi was looking healthier each day, and sword practice had given her some of her range of motion back to her injured arm.

"Signi, you're looking very well and back to your old warlike self," I teased.

"Caroline Morton, we have been through a lot together."

"Keeping company with Vikings is never dull, I will say that."

"Have you learned to appreciate your Viking kinsfolk?"

"I struggle with it, Signi. But I have learned my other kin, the Gaels, aren't much better. So perhaps I must accept my kinsfolk, Viking and Gaels, love to fight and are really good at it. But if you are asking how I feel about you, Signi, I respect you and admire your bravery and courage. I can see you as a future queen of Ljodus."

"I respect you as well, Caroline Morton. You saved me from being killed and nursed me back to health and we escaped captivity together."

"I wouldn't have escaped without you, Signi, and you've been patient with my desire to save Toramagh."

"What will happen to Toramagh when you return to your home, Caroline Morton?"

"You're going to adopt him or foster him, whatever the right word might be."

Signi scowled and said nothing for a few minutes. I felt I had to say more. "Toramagh exists because you rejected the Prince of Mull. He secretly married another and upon discovering this, the King of Mull required the child to be exposed."

Signi was silent for a while. Then she said, "I have become fond of Toramagh, and it seems my decision to reject the Prince has had unintended consequences. I feel I owe Toramagh his life. What is the significance of the gold ring?"

"The gold ring is a wedding ring. The Prince gave it to Toramagh's mother to establish his paternity. It contains the mark of the Prince." I took it off my ring finger and gave it to Signi. She examined it carefully and put it on a chain around her neck. There was a little golden hammer already on the chain. I frowned as I knew the symbol as Thor's hammer. She dropped the chain inside her garments.

"So, it is a symbol of Toramagh's birthright. The Prince wanted it known who he was in case he was rescued."

I nodded. "Signi, I think we should try to let the King's son and his secret wife visit the baby. Imagine a mother or father suffering because they think their child is starving or being eaten by wild animals."

"Caroline Morton, it would be very dangerous to bring them here. If the King found out about our plans for Toramagh, he and we would probably be killed."

I had never thought about that. Still, there must be a way. "What about bringing a healer on board to help with your wound?"

"How would that help?"

"Well, most healers are women. We could bring Toramagh's mother on board as a healer. Her husband, the Prince, could row her out to the boat.

"It's risky business for us, and especially in the midst of a war with the Gaels."

I decided to keep silent for a while so Signi could think it through. Being courageous and a risk-taker, Signi finally agreed after discussing it with Erik.

"Erik will meet with the Prince and propose the plan, including bringing the child's mother as well," Signi said one afternoon, as I was playing with Toramagh.

Late one rainy summer afternoon, a man and woman wearing capes with hoods raised were rowed out to Eric's ship and helped aboard. Eric greeted them and led them below deck where Signi and I were sitting with Tora-magh.

Without lowering their hoods, the parents reached out to touch their son and to lift him into their arms. They said nothing to prevent being overheard. Astrid, his mother, gave him a stuffed toy and his father placed a fine gold chain around his neck.

Then the Prince said quietly to Signi, "Princess, we will never forget what you are doing for our son. If I should become king, I will send for my son to be with me. I entrust him to your care."

I had been sitting silently as the parents had the joy of knowing their child was alive and safe and the sadness of having to give him up to save his life. "Princess Signi," I asked, "could Toramagh's mother come with us as his wet nurse?"

"Caroline Morton, I am sure your suggestion will lead us into another degree of danger, but I will leave it up to the parents."

Immediately, Astrid nodded enthusiastically, and the Prince nodded as well.

Then, as quickly as he had arrived, the Prince left. Astrid took the baby to a cot where she began to cuddle him. For the next couple of days, Olga returned to nurse the baby and gradually Astrid took over from her. It was a time of great anxiety. Would the King of Mull learn what was happening?

On the third morning Erik appeared. "We leave tomorrow at first light."

The morning was overcast, but it began to clear as Erik directed his ship out of the bay, past the other dragon boats of several Viking kings, and into the Sound of Mull.

We were making good time when Signi sighted dragon boats—five of them with the King of Mull's insignia flying from the top mast. We watched as they gained on us.

"What could this mean, Signi?"

"It means, Caroline Morton, that the King of Mull has discovered our secret."

"But how?"

"Either one of our confidants has notified the King or someone checked the exposure site and found the baby missing."

I didn't know what to feel. By rescuing the baby, I had put an entire ship full of people in danger, including a Prince and Princess of Ljodus, and my kin. "There's too many of them, Signi."

"It is true we cannot win against such odds, but we will fight until the bitter end."

I sat down, head in hands, and felt enormously sad and frightened about how this day would end.

"Caroline Morton, stand up! What is done, is done! Die like a Viking."

She was right. Better to die a Viking. I said a prayer for us all and stood up. The men on the ship donned their armour and prepared their weapons. No one looked for someone to blame or cried or lay down in despair. They knew there was almost no chance of survival, but they stood tall. That included Signi. Armed to the teeth, she watched the dragon boats inch nearer and nearer.

"It's father, it's father!" Erik shouted. We all turned to look forward.

There, coming towards us was the Ljodus fleet, about thirty dragon boats flying the raven banner. The five boats from Mull saw them too, as they turned and fled back to their harbour.

We passed through the Ljodus fleet in safety and returned to Ljodus. That night we drank mead and toasted our safe return. It was good to be home.

A month later, after our fleet had returned to Ljodus, Signi and I were out riding south along the coastline when Signi spotted what she had been expecting. Viking long boats were coming towards Ljodus. Without a word, Signi and I turned and headed back towards the castle. We arrived and learned the visitors were envoys from the High King of Mann and the Suderays. I looked at Signi and she looked at me. We knew this was trouble.

Later that afternoon, King Tormod met with the envoys in the great room. "Welcome! Welcome!" said Tormod. "Please be seated and state your purpose."

"We have come to retrieve the child, which was stolen by the princess, Signi, and brought here in secret. This is by order of the High King."

"I am aware that a child and his mother returned with the princess, but he is in the care of his mother who came here willingly."

"Be that as it may, but it was against the will of the King of Mull, and he has taken his complaint to the High King. We hope to have your hospitality overnight and the return of the child before we leave shortly after first light tomorrow."

Signi stood and stepped forward. "I am the child's guardian and have given my word to his parents that I will protect him with my life. I cannot, with honour, hand him over to the High King. Indeed, I suspect the boy would simply be thrown into the sea before you ever return to your home port."

"Princess, we respect your honourable intentions, but we are duty-bound to fulfill King Olaf's command. We hope we can all agree that King Olaf's commands are the priority for all of us."

What a conundrum! Would Signi relent? No good could come of this for Toramagh.

A few hours later, a couple of boendrs and their thralls set out on horse-back heading for Bostadh on the island of Great Bernara in Loch Roag, a distance of about twenty-five miles by land. They were transporting several pairs of hunting falcons for the market of that trading town, surrounded by farms. It was also a great stopping place for boats travelling along the seacoast of Ljodus with goods to be exchanged for farm produce.

Signi and I then followed them, and we all met up at the ferry. No one spoke. All had capes with hoods raised. Once on the island, we rode quickly towards Bostadh, across the flat and grassy but rock-strewn landscape. Upon reaching the farms on the outskirts of the town, we slowed and followed the boendrs who were leading the way. The houses were of dry-stone construction with thatched roofs, surrounding the long sandy beach where boats could easily be pulled up and launched.

Soon we were at a well-kept home, where we all dismounted and entered. As we pulled back our hoods, I saw first two of the King's house guard, then two of the castle servants—not slaves—and, lastly, Astrid. Before anyone said a word, one of the big burly house guards pulled aside his cloak and there was baby Toramagh.

Astrid reached for him and wrapped him in her arms.

A servant spoke. "We're going to take the falcons down to a friend's home where we'll spend the night. We'll send back a serving girl with food and drink."

"Very good," said the bodyguard.

"Caroline Morton and I will return to the castle and leave Astrid and Toramagh in your excellent care. Keep them safe until we can return. If anyone asks, Astrid is here awaiting the return of her husband from a sea voyage to Trondheim to trade slaves for weapons on behalf of the King of Ljodus," Signi said.

We put up our hoods and mounted our horses. It would be dark around eleven-thirty this evening. Best to be home by then.

The next morning, a commotion outside woke me. Rushing to the window, I could see Signi clasping a wriggling baby to her chest and running toward the sea cliffs. Behind her were the bodyguards of the envoys of King Olaf.

With stunning speed and strength, Signi leapt from the cliff to a rock formation separated by time and tide from the cliff face, landing and turning to face her opponents.

"Princess," shouted one envoy, "you are going against the orders of the High King, and he will not accept your rebelliousness."

What was Signi up to? Toramagh was safe in Bostadh, wasn't he?

I raced from my room through the castle and outside. I reached the cliff edge just as the order was given by the envoys to have a bodyguard leap over to the rock pinnacle. The bodyguards looked dismayed at the danger of such a leap.

Finally, one bodyguard agreed to make the leap. After backing away from the cliff and then running forward at full speed, he managed to land on the pinnacle—on his stomach, which knocked the wind out of him. Before he could recover, Signi turned, grasping the baby even tighter. To the astonishment and horror of her people and the envoys, she leapt into the sea, which crashed and foamed at the base of the rock formation, and disappeared. We rushed to the edge of the cliffs to see if she survived the fall and still had the baby.

After waiting with bated breath for a long time, someone shouted, "Look!"

We looked and saw the empty baby blanket rise to the surface and be drawn toward the cliffs by the incoming tide. And still no sign of Signi. After about half an hour of searching the waves, people started to drift away from the scene, eyes down, faces drawn, shoulders hunched.

Signi's father approached the envoys from the High King. "It's time for you to return to the High King and give him the news that will make him pleased, I am sure."

"King Tormod, we had no idea that your daughter would take her guardianship to this extent. We are indeed sorry for your loss. We will leave momentarily. Thank you for your generous hospitality, and, again, our condolences on your loss."

"My daughter is a warrior, and she will have a warrior's funeral."

The envoys sailed away later that morning, leaving one of their own to attend the funeral.

I was in my room, too upset to think. A hooded and downcast slave brought me some food, but I couldn't stomach the thought of eating. When she just stood there, I said hoarsely, "You can leave now, thank you."

"Only you would say 'Thank you' to a slave!"

"Signi!"

She raised her index finger to her lips. "I brought enough for two. Let's eat. I'm starving."

Was I dreaming? Was this a ghost? "Signi," I asked tentatively as she ate ravenously—which I guess excluded the possibility she was a ghost. "Signi, where is Toramagh?"

"You know very well he's in Bostadh with his mother." She gulped down a bowl of milk.

"But," I said.

"The 'baby' was a seal."

"Well," I said, still confused.

"I often made the jump to the rock and dived into the sea when I was growing up. Eric and Harold found it too risky. That's how I figured out I was as capable as they were."

"Do you think they know you are alive?"

"Certainly. And Father, too. But we needed to give Olaf's men a reason to leave empty-handed."

"You know they left an envoy behind to attend your funeral?"

"That's why I'm going to dress as your thrall for a while."

"But what about your funeral?"

"You can't have a Viking funeral—a funeral pyre—without a body, so the envoy will be well entertained and then sent home the next time my father or brothers have to attend an event on the Isle of Mann."

Sure enough, within a month the envoy left with Erik as he was going to a meeting about the plans for the war with the Gaels. Upon his return, King Tormod called a meeting of his warriors.

"Men, we will be leaving in two weeks to meet up with the High King and try to re-claim the coastline from the Gaels. I have decided to make my daughter, Princess Signi, the protector of Ljodus and chief of the home guard while we are gone." He called Signi forward and rested his hand on her shoulder.

"The princess has proved herself brave in battle, and a strategic planner in difficult circumstances, as well as loyal and true to her word and commitments. I hope you will commit to her leadership." There was a unanimous cheer from the home guard.

Signi stepped forward, dressed in chainmail and a helmet, raised her sword, and shouted, "For Ljodus! For Ljodus!"

The men returned the shout.

We were walking in the castle garden soon after the installation of Signi as the protector of Ljodus.

"Caroline Morton, I want to take you to a place you will really appreciate, before father and my brothers head off to the next battle.

"Where is that, Signi?"

"Back to where we first met."

"Loch Snizort Beag on Skye?"

"Aye. The reason is a surprise."

The next day we set off in her personal long boat, the one we had come to Ljodus in. Sailing up the loch on that gorgeous summer day, I wondered what surprise was in store for me. Instead of beaching the boat where we had met, the men rowed up the river that flowed into the loch. We beached on a little island in the middle of the river, climbed up onto the low, flat, grassy meadow and followed a path through the trees until we came to an opening. I saw what Signi thought would please me: The Cathedral of the Isles.

"The King of Mann had it built to serve the people of the Isles, the Suderays. The King of Norway has become a Christian and so his viceroy has also become a Christian."

The cathedral wasn't big by mainland standards, but still imposing. It was built of stone with tiny windows, cruciform in shape, and with a tower at one end. We walked through the main door and into a dark, quiet space with the light from one window above the altar shining down on the gold and silver candlesticks, chalice, and paten. There was a large, illuminated Bible on a lectern and a carved oak pulpit opposite. Of course, this being a cathedral, the bishop's seat was just under the window. Benches filled the rest of the space. We sat down just as the monks began their afternoon office singing psalms in plainchant. It was lovely.

"Thank you, Signi, I really appreciate that you brought me here.

"There's another place I want you to see. Come with me."

After about a five-minute walk, we came to what looked like a mortuary chapel. Signi led me over to a row of effigies lying flat on the ground. "This place is called Nakylsson Aisle and is the burying place for the Nakylsson kings. Other ruling families also have dedicated areas for the burial of their kings."

I stood there for a while, taking it all in. Surrounded by my ancestors, I felt a great sense of peace and even, perhaps, communion. Warriors all, they were portrayed in chain mail and helmets with hands grasping their swords. I wondered how I could reconcile these feelings with my distaste of Viking culture. Maybe I don't have to reconcile with everything, I finally thought. Maybe just accept this is your bloodline, for better or for worse. I needed to think about that some more.

"Come on, Caroline Morton, we must get back to Ljodus. I hope you're pleased to see this?"

"More than pleased, Signi. I think it means the Vikings may finally overcome their pleasure in rape, pillage, and plunder and bring peace and prosperity to the Hebrides."

"It will not be overnight."

"But, still, there's hope."

We returned to Ljodus. On the way, I asked Signi if she thought she would ever get married.

"I cannot rule it out, Caroline Nakylsdottir." She waited for my reaction.

"Caroline Nakylsdottir?"

"That is your real name, is it not?"

I considered her question. "I'm afraid so, Signi. I've been trying to avoid that conclusion. Yes, I am Caroline Nakylsson—or more properly Nakylsdottir, originally from the Isle of Lewis and the Isle of Skye and the direct descendant of the Norse Vikings."

Signi looked quite pleased, despite my discomfort.

Back at the castle, we ate a meal with King Thormod, Eric, and Harold. I offered a toast, "To the Nakylssons. Long may we live in peace and prosperity."

I went to bed, more accepting of my identity.

When I awoke, I was not in the castle or my own bed but in a cot in a crowded cottage. Everyone was speaking Gaelic. Where was I?

"Ah, she's awake. Now give her some room to get up, boys," a man said.

"Would you like some oatmeal porridge?" a woman asked.

"Who is she and how did she get here, Father?" asked a boy, as I sat up and tried to arrange my clothing. The only familiar item was my valise, just beside my cot.

"Caroline Morton, my name is Malcolm Nicolson, and this is my wife, Margaret McPhie, and our five boys, Donald, Alexander, Archibald, Angus, and Murdoch. Margaret and I have invited you to our home in Skye."

"Oh, I know your names from the 1841 Census of Skye. How exciting! I'm pleased to meet you all."

"But who are you?" Donald asked.

"We are kinfolk. My name is Caroline Nicolson. I'm visiting from Nova Scotia."

"Nova Scotia! Why that's near Prince Edward Island, is it not?"

"It is, indeed, Donald." Donald seemed the oldest of the boys and his dark blond hair was tousled as if he had been out in a high wind. His clothes were of the poorest material and his feet were bare.

"Now, children, mind your manners. Caroline is our guest so let's not pepper her with all our questions at once," Margaret said as she handed me a bowl of oatmeal porridge with milk and butter.

"Caroline, I thought you should visit us while we are still on Skye," Malcolm said.

"While you're still on Skye?" I stopped eating my porridge.

"We'll be leaving in a week to go to Prince Edward Island."

"Malcolm, Margaret, I'm so sad to hear that."

"The lairds cannot afford to keep their estates without raising Cheviots—English sheep—and so we have been forced onto smaller and smaller areas where we cannot grow enough to feed ourselves. Many families are close to starvation and those whose land has been taken away are now living on the same land with other relatives, so the crowding is terrible. It is impossible to survive."

I had heard this story before from the McDonalds and the McKenzies in the Black Isle on the east coast of Scotland. They had voyaged to Nova Scotia in 1801.

"As soon as you're finished your breakfast, we'll go for a walk about Loch Snizort Beag," Malcolm suggested.

It was late spring, and the clouds threatened rain. The wind was from the west and gusty. The entire area of Loch Snizort Beag was a crowded, chaotic mess. The people were packed into small cottages with scarcely an acre of land for their cows and sheep to graze. Many of the children had no overcoats or shoes or even a change of clothes. Blankets were in scarce supply. The few animals looked like they were starving as well. People looked at me with sunken eyes and blank stares. I recognized well the signs of starvation after my ill-fated experience on St. John's Island with the Stewarts. Once again, I experienced the overwhelming anger that people were being treated in this manner.

"Malcolm, is this what has become of our people over the last one hundred years since the Battle of Culloden Moor?"

"It is. The landlords tried to become English aristocrats and spent money they did not have. Then they taxed the people more and more and when the people could pay no more, they brought in the Cheviot sheep and cleared the people off the land they had held for a thousand years. Even the Chief of our clan, Clan MacNeacail, has lost his estate and has moved to Australia. We live in a place of deepest poverty and despair. Our only hope is to emigrate to Prince Edward Island where many of our people have already gone."

"At one time, all this island, all the Hebrides used to belong to the Vikings from Norway," I said.

"Oh, we, the Vikings, are still here. In 1266 when the Scottish King won over King Hakon of Norway, Hakon returned the Hebrides to Scotland. Some of the Vikings returned to Norway and some, like us, stayed. Here on Skye, the MacNeacails, or Nicolsons, MacLeods, the MacAulays, and others are descendants of the Vikings. There are also Nicolsons on the Isle of Lewis."

"So, there will soon be Vikings in Prince Edward Island." I laughed.

"Aye, I hope they're ready for us."

Donald and Alexander had been walking along with us listening to their father's story. "Father," said Donald, "can we go and see St. Columba's Isle?"

"Of course, son, we shall soon enough never see our ancestors' graves again or care for the isle where the Vikings established the Cathedral of the Isles."

St. Columba's Isle is where the River Snizort runs into Loch Snizort Beag. We waded across the knee-deep water and climbed up the banks of the isle. The grass was high and little flowers bloomed here and there. Besides a few small trees, there was nothing to hide the ruins of the cathedral, built, I remembered, around 1114, while Skye was under Viking rule.

I didn't tell Malcolm that I had been on St. Columba's Isle when the cathedral was new and lovely or that I had seen the actual graves of some chiefs. It was still vivid in my mind, and I was saddened at the present state of the cathedral and cemetery. Moss and lichen covered the low stone walls. Nearby were the ruins of a stone building called Nicolson's Aisle where, Malcolm explained, twenty-eight chiefs of the clan were buried, according to tradition. After the Hebrides were returned to Scotland by the Norse, the Cathedral of the Isles was moved to the Isle of Mann and this site was forgotten, except by the Nicolsons, who guarded it for hundreds of years.

Prince Edward Island would be so different from the Isle of Skye with its mountains and strange geological formations, its fairy hills and glens and pools—even a fairy bridge and a fairy flag kept in Dunvegan Castle, the seat of the MacLeods, another clan descended from the Vikings.

Gone were the Vikings who travelled the seas in their dragon boats with raven flags flying, fighting battles, raiding, and trading. Gone were the fierce Gaels and their leader the brilliant Somerled, progenitor of Clan Donald, the Lords of the Isles, with their bards and seanachaidh singing their praises on harps in castles, the halls blazing with torches and fires, while the warriors ate and drank toasts to their chiefs and kings.

Soon there would be no one left to remember all that had been. The descendants of the Vikings and the Gaels now living in strange places throughout the world would sometimes ask their parents, "Who are we and where did we come from?" And there would be no answer.

"Malcolm," I asked, "when are you leaving for Prince Edward Island?"

"In three days, Caroline. We don't have much to pack. A few clothes and some bedding. Margaret wants to take her cooking pot and some bowls."

"What do your boys think about this plan?"

"Oh, we've explained why we are going. They understand we will have some land to rent. I think up to fifty or even perhaps one hundred acres. Prince Edward Island has been settled by previous settlers from Skye, and some say there are more Skye people in Prince Edward Island now than in Skye."

We returned to the cottage and Margaret made us some tea. She handed me a cup with the handle broken off and no saucer, a visible sign of their sad circumstances.

The door swung open and a young woman with dark hair, blue eyes, and drab, worn clothing, ran into the room. She threw her arms around Donald, the oldest son. They spoke together in Gaelic, their voices high and rushed. I understood most of what they said.

"Fanny, how did you get here from Kilmuir?"

"My cousin brought me in his fishing boat. I can only stay an hour."

"Come, come, sit down. Mother, can you give Fanny some buttermilk?"

"Donald, we've heard you're leaving in a few days. Is it true?"

He knelt beside her chair. "True, true. I sent word by a MacLeod boy who was going to Kilmuir with his grandfather."

"Will we ever see each other again, darling Donald? We have made promises to each other, and my heart belongs to you." She had handed the buttermilk to a child, too distraught to finish it.

"Fanny, there will be one more ship leaving Skye for Prince Edward Island this year. You and your family must be on it! What does your father say?" he implored.

"I don't think he will go, Donald. Some of my brothers may go, John, Murdo, and Neil. But mother isn't well, and father has bad rheumatism, so neither is fit to start over in a new land." She stood up, too edgy to sit. Donald rose with her, and they embraced.

"Then you must get your brother, John, to agree to come. He's thirty now and a tailor, so could get land and find a good wife." I could tell he was desperate.

"I'll try to come to you, Donald, and you must promise to wait for me." Her desperation was palpable and their despair over being separated was painful.

"I will have no other but you, Fanny Bruce. I give you my word—and my cousin Caroline will be my witness." He turned and seemed to implore me with his eyes.

"What!" I thought. "I'm a witness to a betrothal?" But having been chosen, I nodded my assent.

The two lovers left to sit on the beach and wait for the time Fanny must board the boat that would separate them—maybe forever. As they waited, Fanny and Donald had their arms around each other, and she had her head on Donald's shoulder. Would they ever see each other again? Even if Fanny got to Prince Edward Island, there's no telling what part of the island they might come to and then, would she find Donald?

Once the young lovers had left, I asked Malcolm, "Will you have to clear land and build a log cabin?"

"Clear land, yes, but perhaps build a frame house as there are sawmills. Much of the land has been already cleared by others and there are sawmills and gristmills and even Presbyterian churches where we are going. And Highlanders help each other get settled, so we will be well situated after a few years."

I awoke on the last day and watched as the people from Loch Snizort Beag handed smaller bundles to their children and hoisted the larger, heavy bundles on their backs. Mothers and older girls took the hands of the little children. Boys helped their fathers and grandparents. Then the exile began.

I climbed up the nearby hill to watch the long line of families slowly make their way onto the pier and travel its length until they were helped into waiting rowboats to row them out to the ship that waited in the loch. It took hours, but I waited until the ship raised its anchors and my family and their neighbours left Scotland, left Skye, after a thousand years.

I was not expecting to see the Nicolson family again.

It would be one hundred and seventy-five years until a member of the Nicolson family returned to Skye—as a tourist and a stranger.

I was surprised to find myself on Prince Edward Island in a neat little board house. Perhaps the dream senders, the ones who had invited me to come with them, had mercy on me as I don't think I could have taken another sea voyage. But I was excited to see what had happened to the family on Prince Edward Island. None of them seemed the least surprised to see me in these new surroundings so I did not mention the break in our visit. Of course, I knew everyone, the whole Nicolson family, and they welcomed me with open arms. But where was Fanny?

After getting settled and becoming tenants of Robert Montgomery, son of the original owner of Lot 59 and the Lord Advocate of Scotland, Malcolm and Donald each received one hundred acres of land on a 999-year lease, Malcolm told me. They built a house on Malcolm's lot at Brown's Creek just south of Montague. The land was excellent for farming, and a far better situation than what they had on Skye. And they were surrounded by other newcomers as well as those who had come years earlier.

Of course, adjusting to a new life in a new country is challenging, but they had lots of help from their neighbours and in a short time they were settled in and running their very own—well, it was a tenancy—farm. I was glad to spend time with them and, of course, find out what happened with Donald and Fanny.

Summer turned into fall and still no sign of Fanny. Finally, Donald told his father he was going to go to Charlottetown to see if anyone knew about a second ship from Skye. Two of us, Alexander and I, went with him for company. On the waterfront it was easy to find the agent representing the immigration company.

"Aye, it's arrived. Probably ten days ago." He was a big, burly man with red hair and whiskers, his sleeves rolled up showing the red hair below his blue shirt.

"Do you know if there is a passenger list?"

"Nay, the passenger list is tossed out by now."

"Then, did you hear of a brother and sister named Bruce, John and Fanny?" There was desperation in his voice as he leaned on the desk with both hands.

The agent shook his head. "I wish you well young man. There is no guarantee that your friends arrived here, and, well, the passengers have scattered by now. There are sixty-seven lots to which they could have gone. I wish you good luck in your search." He went back to reviewing his schedules.

With no place to turn and with a heavy heart, Donald, Alexander, and I returned to Brown's Creek and his parents and four brothers.

Over the following weeks, wherever the family went, they asked if anyone had seen Fanny and her brother, but to no avail.

One fine, bright day in October 1841, Donald's brother Alexander returned to say he had heard of a young couple, but perhaps they were brother and sister, in a house at Lot 57. Donald left on the run. If he had to knock at every door in Lot 57 that is what he would do. His determination soon began to wane as everyone he met suggested a different direction for him to look, and he followed every lead but never found the young couple.

As the weeks sped by, he and his father finished a small barn and bought a cow. The rest of the family were pleased with their situation so far, but Donald felt his sadness and disappointment growing each day he missed Fanny.

It was almost November, and the family were sitting in front of the fire sharing some oatcakes and cheese when there was a knock on the door. There stood Fanny and John, as well as her other brothers, Murdo and Neil. There wasn't a dry eye in the house for hours.

"How did you find us?" Donald finally asked, almost unwilling to let go of her in case it was all a dream.

"We just kept asking everyone we met until we met a passenger from your ship who thought you were going to the far east of the island, Lot 59, he remembered. We searched and asked and searched and asked, until we came to your door."

"We're settled in Valleyfield," Murdo said, "with fifty acres each. What a difference from our situation in Kilmuir where we were cottars. No land of our own and relying on the good will of relatives to let us stay on their land. But it is sad that our parents and brother, Lachlan, are still back on Skye."

Everyone nodded.

"It will be a few years before I can build a house and barn on my acreage, but then we can marry and move in," Donald said, holding Fanny tightly around the waist. She put her head on his shoulder and smiled in relief that she had found her Donald.

It wasn't until March 28, 1848, that Donald and Fanny were married. Although seven years had passed, it seemed to me to be but a few days. Her brother, John Bruce, and Annie Finlayson were married the same day in a shared ceremony. I had the honour of being present as a witness. We all went back to the house Donald had built on his fifty acres, and the couple showed us the table and chairs Donald bought by selling some produce.

Family members had gifted them with fireplace equipment: a poker, tongs, shovel, and hearth brush. Fanny had been preparing linen bedding, towels, and night clothes. One neighbour made them a fine pair of potholders and another had donated candles. The couple were supremely happy—a real happy ending for the whole family.

I embroidered a little poem, a house blessing, which Fanny said she would treasure. It was in Gaelic, of course, but in English it said 'Bless this house, O Lord, we pray. Keep it safe by night and day. Amen.' I made a little frame of birch bark and glued it together with pine resin. They hung it over the mantel.

I wondered where this adventure would take me next.

Donald and Fanny brushed the tears away as they remembered their wedding day.

"Couldn't be a better ending to your story, Donald and Fanny," Martha said, patting her eyes dry.

The others nodded.

"Do you think we've done everything we can to help Caroline?" Samson asked.

The others nodded again.

"It's up to her now. We've given her our stories, so she needs to have the will and the courage to take her life back after all the sorrow she's been through," Malcolm said.

"Aye, losing her husband so young, then her mother, brother, and best friend in one year is a lot to handle," Margaret, his wife, agreed.

All of them remembered losing homes, family, hopes, and dreams.

"Hardiness in the face of adversity. That's what's needed," McDonald said, and the rest chimed in, "Aye!"

CHAPTER TEN

DO OR DIE

PRESENT DAY: HALIFAX, NOVA SCOTIA

Caroline woke up at seven o'clock in the morning, had breakfast, and turned on her computer. She didn't dare look at her emails, which had been piling up for months. Instead, she opened Microsoft Word and clicked on her book. Pangur Ban came in after his breakfast, washed his face, and lay down across all her reference material and fell asleep in a splash of sunshine.

She decided to call the last chapter in her book "Die Like a Viking." It seemed fitting. Her book might never get published, but it wouldn't be for lack of effort. Her last dream had left a significant impression on her. So had all her dreams. She came from a long line of courageous people. People who had suffered greatly, but who had not succumbed to despair, and had risked everything for a better life for themselves and their descendants—and she was one of those descendants. No more lolling around in bed or sitting curled up in despondency. It was do or die time!

She read and re-read the stories she had typed and added the two that she had failed to type, then she pondered and reflected on what these stories meant, not just to her but to the people of today. Surely, no one could be but inspired by their courage and endurance. People who overcame every hardship and discouragement; people who valued family, community, and heritage. She had even learned a grudging appreciation of the Vikings, grudging being the operative word.

But, of one thing, she had no doubt, she loved them all. That was going to be difficult to put into words. How can one love people who lived hundreds of years ago? They were ordinary people. No aristocrats, except for Princess Signi Nakylsson, but when their own descendants had forgotten them, how could she convey her love for them? Then she thought, perhaps writing the book was an act of love. Not love for people long-ago, but for people she had studied and researched and dreamed about for many years, and so were a real and present inspiration.

In a way, she thought, the book is a love story, but of a very different kind—but not a romance, though there was plenty of that. She imagined her own or her sisters' children reading the stories of their courageous ancestors. But why limit the stories to her own family? Mightn't there be relatives she didn't know about right now, but who would enjoy these stories? Hopefully, the stories could be an inspiration for anyone. That would be very satisfying indeed!

That thought spurred her on even more. Lifting Pangur Ban bodily to a new location, so she could see her notes, Caroline set herself a rigorous timeframe and dedicated herself to getting the book finished.

Caroline and her sisters met in their usual coffee shop a month later.

"I have a surprise for you," Caroline said.

"A good surprise, I hope, Caroline. We've had enough bad surprises to last a lifetime," Joan said.

"A good surprise, I think. I'm back to writing my book."

"That is a good surprise. What happened? Why did you decide to go back to writing after all this time?"

"Oh, I guess you can only sit around in a state of despair for so long before you have to ask yourself, is this how I want to spend the rest of my life? What if I just got up and started to write again? And it worked."

"What is the subject of your book? Is it the same one you were working on what seems ages ago?"

"Yes, The same book. Only now I'm working on the last chapter. I didn't want to say anything until I could be sure I wasn't going to give up again."

"How are your migraines these days?" Joan asked.

"Manageable. You know, being careful not to get too tired, too hungry, too thirsty, too hot, too stressed. But there's not much I can do about changes in barometric pressure."

"Well, I'm glad they're manageable. Any news of a cure? What did your doctor say was the underlying condition?"

"Cortical spreading depression. It's like an electrical wave that spreads over your brain, causing all the strange symptoms. She really didn't have any new resources to treat the condition, so I just get to live with it." Caroline reached for a napkin.

"Caroline," Janice said, "put out your arm again."

"What's that on your arm? Caroline! Is that a tattoo?" Janice grabbed her arm to take a closer look.

"Yes, a tattoo."

"What the heck! You, getting a tattoo. Show me," Joan said.

Caroline stretched out her arm so all could see.

Elizabeth looked at it more closely. "It looks a lot like the etching on that stone you found on William McDonald's gravestone. Caroline, did you take that stone?"

"Yup. Same design. I found it on a Norse Viking website. A Viking design for sure."

"I thought you hated Vikings. You were vehemently against the Vikings. So, what is this?" Joan was still staring at the tattoo.

"Oh, don't worry. I know that Vikings were blood-thirsty killers. I'm not into Viking rehabilitation. You know, the Vikings themselves wrote about their own enjoyment of killing, so I take them at their word."

"So," Janice said, "you want to identify with them? Why in the world?"

"It's a long story. You'll have to read the book," Caroline laughed. "I think we should plan some kind of adventure together. What about a week in Pictou County? That would be a lot of fun."

"Well, you're just full of surprises, aren't you? But hey, I'm up for adventure. What about the rest of you?"

They left the restaurant feeling lighter than they had for quite a while.

"It seems that our book is going to be finished, after all," Samson said to the firsts.

"Who is this Signi person, Samson? Did we know about her before we began?" Martha asked.

"I might have guessed about her," Malcolm Nicolson said, rather sheepishly. "Although we Nicolsons changed our name from the Norse, Nakylsson to the Gaelic, MacNeacail, and then to the anglicized Nicolson, we heard stories that our family was originally Norse. But we stayed on in Skye, rather than return to Norway in 1260 or thereabouts when Norway returned the Hebrides to Scotland."

"I rather think your Signi Nakylsson isn't Presbyterian," Joseph Begg said.

"Probably the best we can say is that she never killed a Presbyterian," Malcolm said with a faint smile.

"Never mind," William McDonald said. "She got Caroline back to writing. We've got to be thankful for that."

"Aye, if she gets the book published, I guess we'll have to invite this Signi to our celebration."

The others looked skeptical.

Caroline finished the book and began to submit it to publishers interested in historical fiction. At their usual meetings, the sisters waited to hear if a publisher was interested. It would be wonderful if this effort had a happy ending.

"I think we should find another coffee shop," Caroline said. "These muffins have fewer and fewer chocolate chips every time we come here."

"We sound a little testy today," Joan said as she sipped her usual green tea.

"Testy! I'm not testy. I'm cranky. And why shouldn't I be?"

"Okay," Elizabeth said, "why shouldn't you be?" She seemed satisfied with her giant brownie.

"Because I've submitted my book to at least six publishers in the last year and no one is interested."

"I hope that doesn't mean you're going to give up?" Janice said, blowing on her hot black coffee.

"No, I've learned my lesson about giving up. I wrote this darned book and somehow it is going to get published, so I'm just going to try until I'm successful."

"That's the spirit," Joan said, then she asked for a bite of Elizabeth's brownie.

"Wish there was some way we could help," Elizabeth said as she broke off a chunk.

"Don't think there is, unless you know a publisher."

The sisters shook their heads.

"Here's another unexpected item. I've started another book."

"You have?" Janice said.

"Probably going to be about Highlanders and Vikings and be set on the Isle of Lewis and in Skye. A perfect reason to take a trip to the Hebrides. Want to come along?"

"Tell us when you're going, and we'll try to get time off work. Sounds like fun."

More months passed. Caroline was happily working on her second book and had returned to work at the bookstore when she got a letter in the mail. Finally, a publisher was interested in her book! At the next luncheon, she handed the letter to Janice, who passed it to Joan, who passed it to Elizabeth. There were big smiles all around.

"You did it! You're going to be a published author!" Elizabeth said. They all got up and hugged her.

"I know," Janice said, "let's buy her a whole box of banana chocolate-chip muffins and a bag of her favourite coffee to celebrate."

"No," Joan said, "let's take her out to supper in a fancy restaurant and ply her with wine and rich deserts."

"Why not do both?" Elizabeth said.

"We'll help you plan the book launch," Joan said, and the rest nodded.

That night, Caroline went to bed tired but happy. It was impossible to say how rewarding it was to finally be an author. Lots of work editing and learning how to promote her book lay ahead, but at least she could sell her book in her workplace. Portia would be glad to support her, she knew. What a wonderful day!

"How are we going to celebrate our book getting published, Samson?" Martha asked.

The rest of the firsts looked at Samson in anticipation. "Well, whatever we do, Caroline has to be included—and Signi, too."

"Aye, Signi was instrumental. As instrumental as the rest of us, in motivating Caroline to write this book. She will have to be invited," William McDonald said.

"I guess you would know whether we can trust her or not, Malcolm Nicolson, you being related and all."

"She's nay more dangerous than us Highlanders," McDonald said, looking at William McKenzie, who nodded agreement.

"What about the Puritans, Elkanah and Rebeccah Morton? I hope you've given them a formal invitation," Martha urged.

"Aye. We've had a good chat, and they understand it was just for the Scottish ancestors at first, but now ...," he trailed off, since everyone understood.

So, the plans began to finalize. They would all meet in Caroline's room that night for one last bout of encouragement, and to express their thankfulness that their lives would no longer be forgotten. It was a good feeling. Each tried to imagine a reader meeting them in the stories in Caroline's book and admiring—and even feeling inspired—by their lives.

"What we did, we did for our descendants, but now, with the book published, our lives might also be of value to people in each generation that reads about us," Janet Begg said with perhaps a little more emotion than she planned.

Everyone nodded. They were going to be famous!

That night, Caroline woke up to some commotion in her bedroom. She wasn't sure if she was really awake or still dreaming, but something was happening, so she sat up on the edge of her bed and peered into the darkness. Slowly, the figures of a group of people came into focus. She recognized them all from her dreams.

Samson and Martha Moore were wearing their Sunday best, she in a pale green dress and a white bonnet with buckled shoes, he in knee breeches and a knee-length coat with silver buttons over a green silk vest.

Their daughter, Martha, dressed in a lovely dress like her mother, was standing with her husband, Robert Stewart, slightly in front of his parents, David Stewart and Mary Wilson.

Squeezed into the corner near her dresser were Joseph and Janet Begg, and their daughter, Janet, and her husband, James Stewart, son of Robert and Martha (Moore) Stewart.

The Mortons were there sitting on top of the cedar chest, dressed in perhaps the finest of all, with the latest styles and materials from New England.

Caroline really liked Rebeccah's rose-coloured satin dress with lace petticoats. Elkanah's vest was ice blue silk with silver buttons. Caroline thought the men and the women were trying to out-do each other in the stylishness of their clothes.

The Highlanders, William and Ann McDonald, and William and Flora (McMillan) McKenzie were there in tartan splendour, the men wearing kilts and plaids pinned over their shoulders with enormous silver brooches with cairngorm stones inset. Their wives, on the other hand, we more modestly dressed in long blue skirts and tartan plaids that were fastened at the waist with a belt and were held over one shoulder with a less spectacular brooch.

The McDonald's son Finlay and his wife, Barbara McKenzie, were there as well, sitting on the five-drawer chest, their feet dangling two feet above the floor.

Malcolm Nicolson and his wife, Margaret McPhie, were dressed a little less splendidly than McDonald and McKenzie, but very finely, nevertheless. They were standing a little to the back of the crowd, but Caroline could see some other forms behind them.

It became clear as those from the back pushed forward that it was Signi, but who was with her?

"Caroline," Signi said, taking on a little more of a leadership role than the rest of the group might have found appropriate, "I would like to introduce my husband, Arne, and our son, Thorvald." Before Caroline could speak, Signi continued, "I know that you will want to know that Prince Arne's first wife, Astrid, died several years ago in childbirth. Prince Arne and I married and Thorvald is our own son, but I have someone with me you may not recognize as yet."

Another Viking stepped forward. Tall, with pale blond hair tightly braided in Viking style and with pale blue eyes, he wore a deep red tunic over leggings and leather shoes.

"You'll remember Toramagh," Signi said with a smile, and Signi hardly ever smiled.

"Oh, Toramagh, I have often wondered what happened to you. I'm so glad to see that you survived."

"My mother and my father told me often how you were unwilling to let me die of exposure, and so I have come to thank you."

"Well, no one I know would leave a baby to die in the forest," Caroline said, looking at Signi with raised eyebrows.

Signi didn't flinch. "Not in your world, Caroline." She held Caroline's stern gaze.

"Now then," Prince Arne said, "that's in the past. Both of you, Caroline, and Princess Signi, risked your own lives to save my son, and I am grateful to both of you."

"Caroline," Signi said, "Your ideas got us into a lot of trouble, almost got us killed, but I don't regret the risks we took. We surely had a memorable time!"

Caroline laughed. "I'll never forget it, that's for sure. And here we have Toramagh, a fine young man. It was worth it."

Caroline paused for a moment. "I want to thank each of you first families for all your help and all you have taught me. Samson and Martha Moore, you taught me that no matter how dedicated you may be to an idea, like the American Revolution, you must be willing to reconsider what effect violence and bloodshed will have on your children and their descendants. You made the right decision to stay out of the fighting and raise your family in peace."

"David and Mary Stewart, you taught me endurance in the face of overwhelming difficulty and in the face of death on Prince Edward Island. Whenever I have a problem, I think of you. Then I say to myself, you really don't have a problem at all."

"Joseph and Janet Begg, you taught me to take risks and stand up against bullies. Janet, you took a risk and married Joseph, and Joseph, you stood up to all the difficulties of establishing yourself in the New World with a fighting spirit."

"Highlanders, you took a chance to get out of the horrible situation you had in Scotland and tried to save the culture you loved by living together on the East River of Pictou County. Your cheerfulness in the face of great adversity and your determination to live freely are a great inspiration to me."

"And Nakelssons or MacNeacail or Nicolsons, we—you and I—carry those Viking genes into the future. You lived for a thousand years in the Hebrides, and I always knew, even as a child, that I was not from Nova Scotia, but from the Misty Isle. Having found you, I found home. That beach on Loch Snizort Beag where I met Signi was the last place Malcolm, Margaret, and their five sons saw before they left Skye forever. It took your descendants one hundred and seventy-five years to return and find home. But now the circle is complete, and I am more at peace. I just want to say to, you, my ancestors that I love you all. And I hope this book will inspire others by reading about your courage and endurance."

The firsts smiled and seemed to stand even taller and look more distinct.

"Oh, and by the way, who left the black stone on William McDonald's grave?" She was even more certain now that the stone had been meant for her.

"It was I," Toramagh said. "It was a gift. I had hoped to meet you and to thank you for my life."

Caroline picked up the little black stone. "What do the 'scratches' on the back mean?"

"That's my name in runes."

"I will treasure it forever. What a pleasure for me to see you again, all grown up and so handsome." Then Caroline looked around the room as an uncomfortable thought arose in her mind. "Will I ever see any of you again?" she asked.

"Don't worry. We'll be at your book launch." They all smiled. Caroline smiled.

"And," Samson said, "you can always return to us in a dream. Just call our names."

"Now," William McDonald said with his usual grin, "we all want to thank you for caring enough to write our stories and make us famous."

"I don't know about famous, William McDonald, but you never know. Stranger things have happened to me."

"Just like this meeting right now," Malcolm Nicolson said.

"Just like this meeting right now," Caroline laughed.

One summer evening in the Town of Pictou, there was a well-advertised book launch, which, because the weather was fine and all the stars had aligned, was well attended.

Caroline, wearing the McDonald plaid with the large silver brooch on her left shoulder, was sitting behind a big table with some posters of her book cover and her biography as an author, along with a splay of business cards and piles of her newly published book. She had brought some of the items in her well-travelled valise, which sat beside her chair.

Her sisters were chatting with the guests and helping with taking payments for the books that were sold. Ruth's daughter, Pauline, was there as well. That was a great comfort to Caroline, who still missed her good friend. The publisher and editors were there and had provided drinks and snacks.

Only Caroline was aware of the figures barely noticeable against the dark curtains—the firsts there to celebrate becoming 'famous'.

During an interlude in the book signing, Caroline leaned back to consider all that had happened since she decided to write a book about her ancestors and realized that even if the book had never been published, the writing had all been worthwhile for she had learned courage in the face of adversity. That would surely stand her in good stead for whatever the future held.

EPILOGUE

The sisters' trip to the Isle of Lewis and the Isle of Skye was very satisfying and Caroline got a lot of material with which to write her second book. It seemed to help in the healing of all four from the loss of Malcolm, their mother, and brother. Even though their father had died many years before, the trip brought up those memories as well. No one really gets over the loss of family, Caroline thought. They just learn to adjust to the new reality. She often thought about Ruth but thought her own family had enough to deal with, so she tried to mourn that loss herself.

Their guide on Lewis toured them around in the mostly rainy weather, common to the Hebrides. Lewis, like Skye, was settled first by Gaels—Gaelic speakers—and then by Norse Vikings starting in the nineth century. Most of the place names are Norse. Lewis has no trees. They were cut down long-ago and replaced by peat bogs.

Still on Lewis, they went to see the Callanish Standing Stones: five-thousand-year-old enormous standing stones in the shape of a Celtic cross and raised atop a hill looking over the Atlantic Ocean. The capital of Lewis is Stornoway, where the Norse Nakylssons, now MacNeacails or Nicolsons, once had a castle. It is now a ruin under the ferry terminal. Most of the Nicolsons left Lewis in the 1800s bound for Canada, but they did manage to meet one very friendly older woman who took them out for coffee and told them what she knew about her direct ancestors from Lewis and their descendants, now in Canada.

The tour of Skye was inspirational. Trips to Dunvegan Castle—home of the Fairy Flag—and to the Fairy Glen and Fairy Pools along with the trip up the Trotternish Peninsula to see the strange rock formations and Flora McDonald's grave in Kilmuir Parish, to the reconstruction of a Highland village, and most special of all a visit to St. Columba's Isle to see Nicolson's Aisle where it is said twenty-eight Nicolson clan chiefs are buried was a highlight. So much colourful history, but there was one question she kept pondering.

What would it be like to have been born and raised in the Hebrides, Caroline wondered? I will never know, she thought. But here, in Skye, she felt strangely at home. The little trip from Portree to Loch Snizort Beag to stand at the place where her ancestors had left Scotland to settle on Prince Edward Island was a special event. It felt like a circle had been closed and that she had reclaimed much of her heritage that had been lost in the Highland migration to North America. She took a deep breath and sighed with satisfaction. She had found home after all the years of searching.

Caroline wondered if she would get any more help from the 'firsts' with writing her second book. Probably not, as she intended to write about what life was like in the Hebrides now. No one believed in dreams, fairies, and other supernatural beings anymore, according to the local people. Some of them were from the Lowlands and from England, having retired to the Hebrides as it was cheaper to live there. No, she was probably on her own and that would have to do. She looked out over the loch and breathed in the sea air and felt the gusty Atlantic wind blow her curly hair in all directions.

She noticed a lively black horse on the heathered hill nearer the loch. It trotted closer until she could see its merry black eyes ... Blackie?... the fairy horse?

SOURCES

L inks may change or become out-dated. Author and publisher are not responsible for content of links.

Bumsted, J. M. (1982). *The People's Clearance 1770–1815: Highland Emigration to North America*. Winnipeg: The University of Manitoba Press. Particularly useful for the information about customs procedures in chapter seven.

Campbell, Carol, and James F. Smith. (2011) "Chapter Eighteen: Treachery" in *Necessaries and Sufficiencies: Planter Society in Londonderry, Onslow, and Truro Townships, 1761–1780*. Sydney, Nova Scotia: Cape Breton University Press. The original source for some of this is records from the Provincial Archives of Nova Scotia. Used by permission.

Campey, L. H. (2007). "A Very Fine Class of Immigrants": *Prince Edward Island's Scottish Pioneers 1770–1850*. Toronto: Natural Heritage Books.

Campey, L. H. (2007). *After the Hector: The Scottish Pioneers of Nova Scotia and Cape Breton 1773–1852*. Toronto, Ontario: Natural Heritage Books.

Campey, L. H. (2007). *With Axe and Bible: The Scottish Pioneers of New Brunswick, 1784–1874*. Toronto: Natural Heritage Books. Information regarding William Davidson and James Fraser, noted in chapter five, is from pages 58 and 59.

Cyr, Jean-Roch, "Hannington, William, in *Dictionary of Canadian Biography*, vol. 7, University of Toronto/Universite Laval, 2003, accessed June 11, 2020. Source for information regarding William Hannington in chapter five.

Grant, I. F. (1995). *Highland Folk Ways.* Edinburgh: Birlinn Ltd.

Haliburton, T. C. (1829). *History of Nova Scotia.* Halifax, NS: Joseph Howe, Halifax, Nova Scotia. Information provided included the French attack on Newfoundland noted in chapter two.

Haywood, J. (2015). *The Viking Saga AD 793–1241.* New York: St. Martin's Press.

Hon. Ezra S. Stearns, A. (1887, October). The Moore Families of New Hampshire. *New England Genealogical and Historical Society Register, Vol. 51.*

I. F. Grant, L. (1993). *The Clan Donald: MacDonalds, MacDonells, MacAlisters and Their Septs.* Edinburgh: Johnston and Bacon Publishers.

Kirkcudbright County Website. "The South of Scotland People in Pictou County, Nova Scotia" (includes link to passenger lists for Lovely Nelly 1774 and 1775 departures). http://www.kirkcudbright.co/ Accessed: April 4, 2024

Logan, G. M. (1976). *Scottish Highlanders and the American Revolution.* Halifax, Nova Scotia: McCurdy Printing Co. Ltd.

Longley, R. S. (1988). "The Coming of the New England Planters to the Annapolis Valley" in *They Planted Well: New England Planters in Maritime Canada* (pp. 14-35). Fredericton, New Brunswick: Acadiensis Press.

MacEacharna, D. (1976). *The Lands of the Lordship.* Port Charlotte, Isle of Islay: Argyll Reproductions Ltd.

MacGillivray, C. W. (2014). *Gaelic Proverbs and Proverbial Sayinngs.* St. Andrews, Nova Scotia: Siol Cultural Enterprises.

MacDonald, Archibald (1894). Editor. *The Uist Collection: the poems and songs of John MacCodrum, Archibald Macdonald, and some of the minor Uist bards. Glasgow: Sinclair.* Sources for "Beautiful Mary," by Alexander Stewart, and "The Mavis of Clan Donald," by John MacCodrum aka Iain Mac Fhearchair, in chapter seven.

MacKay, D. (2001). *Scotland Farewell: The People of the Hector.* Toronto, Ontario: Natural Heritage/Natural History Inc.

MacKenzie, W. (2002). *Old Skye Tales: Traditions, Reflections and Memories*. Edinburgh: Berlinn Limited.

Maclean, W. D. (1999). *The Highland Clan MacNeacail (MacNichol): A History of the Nicolsons of Scorrybreac*. Lochbay, Waternish, Isle of Skye, Scotland: Maclean Press.

MacPhie, Rev. J. P. (1914) *Pictonians at Home and Abroad: Sketches of Professional Men and Women of Pictou County - Its History and Institutions*. Boston, MA: Pinkham Press. Source for material in chapter four.

Marsh, J. H. (2015). "Acadian Expulsion (the Great Upheaval)." The Canadian Encyclopedia. Retrieved 1/27/2024 from https://www.thecanadianencyclopedia.ca/en/article/the-deportation-of-the-acadians-feature

Newton, M. (2019). *Warriors of the Word: The World of the Scottish Highlanders*. Edinburgh: Birlinn Origin.

Newton, M. (2020). *The Everyday Life of the Clans of the Scottish Highlands*. Saorsa Media.

Newton, Michael. Editor and Translator. (2015) *Seanchaidh na Coille: Memory-Keeper of the Forest: Anthology of Scottish Gaelic Literature of Canada*. Cape Breton University Press, Sydney, Nova Scotia. Selected translated verses from the Gaelic poem, "The Lament of the North," used by permission of the translator and publisher.

Nicolson, A. (1930). *History of Skye*. 60 Aird Bhearnasdail by Portree, Isle of Skye, Scotland: Maclean Press.

Parker, R. E. (1851). *The History of Londonderry, comprising the towns of Derry and Londonderry*. Boston: Perkins and Whipple.

Patterson, R. G. (1877). *A History of the County of Pictou*. Pictou, Nova Scotia: James McLean and Co.

Proctor, C. (1985). *Ceannas Nan Gaidheal: Ni h-eibhneas gan Chlainn Domhnaill (The Headship of the Gael: it is no joy without Clan Donald)*. Clan Donald Lands Trust. Source for "Clan Donald Incitement to Battle," in chapter seven.

Sherwood, R. H. (1973). *Pictou Pioneers*. Hantsport, Nova Scotia: Lancelot Press. Particularly useful for chapters four and five.

Smith, C. C. (2011). *Necessaries and Sufficiencies: Planter Society in Londonderry Onslow and Truro Townships 1761 - 1780*. Sydney, Nova Scotia: Cape Breton University Press.

Stratton, E. A. (1986). *Plymouth Colony: Its History & People 1620-1691*. Provo, Utah: Ancestry Publishing.

Venning, T. (2015). *Lord of the Isles: From Vikings Warlords to Clan Chiefs*. The Hill, Stroud, Gloucestershire, UK: Amberley Publishing.

Watson, William J. (Editor). (1918). *Bardachd Ghaidhlig : Specimens of Gaelic poetry, 1550-1900*. Glasgow: Northern Counties Printing and Publishing Company. Source for "I dearly Love the Highlands," by Donald MacDonald, in chapter seven.

Wilson, A. (2015). *Highland Shepherd: James MacGregor, Father of the Scottish Enlightenment in Nova Scotia*. Toronto: University of Toronto Press 2015.

Wright, E. C. (1978, 1982). *Planters and Pioneers: Nova Scotia, 1749 to 1775*, revised edition. Hantsport, NS: Lancelot Press, Ltd.

ACKNOWLEDGEMENTS

After my first book, *William Forsyth: Land of Hopes and Dreams,* a story from early Nova Scotia, was published in November 2021, I turned to all the research my mother, my sisters, and I had collected about other ancestors, especially those who had first come to Nova Scotia. I knew I wanted to tell some of their stories but didn't have enough facts about any one of them to create another book.

In the meantime, I had my DNA tested and discovered, much to my real dismay, that I am descended from Norse Vikings who lived in the Hebrides for over four hundred years, subjugating my Celtic ancestors who were also from the Hebrides. Several visits to the Isle of Skye and the Isle of Lewis allowed me to find where my Nicolson ancestors had lived just prior to coming to Prince Edward Island in 1841.

It was particularly interesting to discover the extent to which both the Highlanders and the Vikings believed in fairies, witches, omens, and portents, like the second sight. In Skye there were fairy hills, fairy glens, fairy bridges, fairy pools, fairy flags, that were part of the little tours we took from Marine House Bed and Breakfast in Portree, Isle of Skye. Gradually, the idea formed that I might tell the stories in the form of dreams, and so I began to write this book, *Traitors, Cannibals, Highlanders, and Vikings,* with the Puritans thrown in for good measure, as they were the first of my ancestors to come to Nova Scotia.

I had a lot of fun imagining and writing the book, and so I hope that readers will enjoy getting to know some more people from early Nova Scotia, and some from Prince Edward Island as well.

This book is historical fiction. The history part is about the factual information I was able to glean about my own ancestors in their particular circumstances and from their point of view. The fiction part is to form the factual aspects into an interesting story. In doing so, I had no intention to comment from a modern perspective on their lives and circumstances. I just wanted to get to know them better myself and for others to enjoy what I hope is a good story.

There are so many people to thank. The Kings County Museum was always there to help with the New England Planters who came to Cornwallis Township, Kings County, Nova Scotia, and the website, AmericanAncestors.org, had an overwhelming amount of material about the Pilgrims and Puritans who first came to New England starting in 1620. Now those were people who kept records.

In Pictou County, the McCulloch Centre in the Town of Pictou and the New Glasgow Library Genealogy Section were great places to do research. And, of course, my cousin, Evangeline 'Vangie' Way, the unofficial genealogist for the East River, was a most excellent source of material, as well as tea and oatcakes.

The Prince Edward Island Archives in Charlottetown and the genealogy folk in Montague, Prince Edward Island were also very helpful, as were descendants of the Nicolsons who still live just outside Montague on the land they were granted back in 1841.

The Genealogy Centre in Portree, Isle of Skye, and the Clan MacNeacail Society were also very helpful in discovering what there is to be known of the Nicolsons of the Isle of Skye. And these are only some of the resources used in researching the book.

A special thank you to the publishers of *Necessaries and Sufficiencies: Planter Society in Londonderry, Onslow, and Truro Townships 1761–1780*, by Carol Campbell and James F. Smith, for giving me permission to use Chapter Eighteen: Treachery, as background information for my chapter "Traitors." As well, thank you to the editor and publisher of *Seanchaidh na Coille: Memory-Keepers of the Forest, Anthology of Scottish Gaelic Literature of Canada*, edited by Michael Newton, with a Foreword by Diana Gabaldon, for letting me quote a poem in Gaelic and translated into English.

My sisters, Elizabeth, Joan, and Janice are always with me on my research trips to genealogy centres, libraries, cemeteries in Nova Scotia and Prince Edward Island, as well as many trips to the Isle of Skye, the Isle of Lewis, and other places in Scotland. They get to hear my ideas and read my manuscripts and their contribution is valuable and appreciated.

Special thanks to Tim Covell of Somewhat Grumpy Press for his skills and ability to bring this book to readers.

It is my dearest wish that these stories will inspire all who read them with courage in the face of adversity.

Carolyn Jean Nicholson

Halifax, Nova Scotia

February 2022-April 2024

ABOUT THE AUTHOR

Photo by Nicola Davison, Snickerdoodle Photography.

Carolyn Jean Nicholson was born in Nova Scotia and has lived in the Maritimes all her life. She worked in the health information management field and taught in post-secondary education before becoming a minister in The United Church of Canada. She is now retired and follows in her mother's footsteps, researching her ancestors and writing novels.

Her first novel was *William Forsyth: Land of Hopes and Dreams*, published by Moose House Press in 2021. In 2022 she co-authored the COVID lockdown novel: *Less Than Innocent*, published by Moose House Press, and contributed a story to *Blink and You'll Miss It: Moose House*

Stories, Volume 2. She also wrote *The Last Witch on Skye*, for younger readers, published by OC Publishing in 2024.

She lives in Halifax, and she often travels back to the Isle of Skye, Scotland, the origin of her Nicolson ancestors. In 2022, the story of her search for her ancestors, "Finding Home," was published in the newsletter of *The Clan MacNeacail Society of Scotland* (www.scorrybreac.org)part of the worldwide Highland Clan MacNeacail Federation.

You can contact the author through our website:
www.SomewhatGrumpyPress.com.
Help support independent authors and small presses.
If you enjoyed this book, please leave a rating or review at your favourite
retailer or review site.

Milton Keynes UK
Ingram Content Group UK Ltd.
UKHW040641131024
449481UK00001B/126